The Needle House
Robin Roughley 2013
Published by Robin Roughley at Amazon

The Needle House- Rob Roughley

Faulty Wiring

In the end he ran, simply because it was the only sane thing left to do.

When Kyle had suggested they pile into his beaten up Fiat and drive to the woods, Billy had groaned. Half an hour sandwiched on the back seat, littered with old burger wrappers and empty beer cans was a grim prospect, especially on a branding-iron hot day like this.

He thought back to the last time he'd been in the death trap on wheels. Shaun Miller had rummaged down the back of the seat looking for a fiver he swore he lost the week before. Instead of money he'd found a used condom and had spent the next ten minutes dangling the shrivelled rubber in front of Billy's face, laughing hysterically as he tried to twist away. In the end, Kyle had draped it over the rear view mirror displaying it proudly like some grotesque air freshener.

Now as the sun dipped toward the horizon, he found himself collecting wood for the fire, foraging beneath the towering beech trees, kicking his way through drifts of burnished leaves, searching for timber that was dry enough to burn.

While he trudged back and forth, his arms laden with fuel for the fire, the others occupied themselves with the serious business of getting off their faces on cheap lager.

Billy dropped the last of the kindling onto the ground, doused the timber with lighter fluid, and tossed the empty can into a patch of nettles. Striking a match, he studied the flame for a moment before flicking it toward the small pyre. Instantly, the vapour ignited and the searing blast sent him staggering back; the eruption of flame threw tall shadows careering against the trees.

Above the roar, he could hear the others laughing hysterically at his near incineration, eyes streaming, he coughed and spat out the acrid taste of smoke from his lungs. When he was sure the fire had taken hold, Billy flopped down onto the leaf-littered ground, listening as the others talked about the two topics that ruled their lives, fucking and fighting.

Yawning, he rubbed the sting of smoke from his eyes, and let his mind wander. He had heard the stories countless times before and with each new telling, the embellishments bloomed as mushrooms fed on bullshit.

As the night wore on and the fire died down to a crackle, he rose to his haunches, alert for a discarded joint or any half-full can of lager tossed carelessly to one side.

Things changed when Tommy dished out the small white pills. This was nothing new; simply another part of the ritual, whether it was smoked, sniffed, or swallowed was irrelevant, as long as they got the 'buzz'.

When two of the gang became aggressive Billy felt a familiar twist of unease.

Starting with the obligatory pushing, shoving, it quickly escalated into outright warfare. The eruption of violence ended when Shaun Miller slipped and clattered to the floor. Tommy burst out laughing and Kyle choked, spraying a mouthful of lager onto the hot coals, the liquid hissing like a stamped on cat. Despite his unease, Billy nervously joined in with the laughter until Miller whipped his head around, fixing him with a glare that promised violence.

'Come here, you little prick!' he snarled.

Billy licked his lips. 'Sorry, Shaun.'

'You fucking will be.'

In desperation, he threw a glance toward the others to see if anyone was willing to come to his aid. What he saw etched onto their faces elevated his fear to a new level. All three glared at him across the glowing embers, it was as if someone had pulled an imaginary plug from behind their eyes and replaced it with faulty wiring.

Billy Jones couldn't tell the time properly, yet he knew it was time to get out of there. His feet slithered on the grass as he tried to gain traction. Billy made a break for it.

Minutes felt like sweat-drenched hours. Twice he tripped over hidden roots as he dashed between the gnarled trunks of the old trees, slamming hard to the ground as the brambles snagged at his legs trying to ensnare him until his tormentors arrived. At last, he staggered out into open ground. On the darkened horizon, he could see the lights of the town centre shimmering behind a drizzle mist.

Billy peered into the gloom, the derelict farmhouse sat hunched in the middle of the undulating field, a black slab against the shifting shadows.

Swiping a hand over his bristle hair, he flicked the droplets of moisture away and began to run, looking fearfully over his shoulder, watching as the trees diminished until they were no more than a dark smudge on the hillside.

Reaching the door, he rested an arm against the rotten woodwork, trying desperately to drag air into his punished lungs.

The sky above appeared heavy with bloated rain clouds, the edges slashed with slivers of silver. A few seconds later, pale moonlight broke through bathing the surrounding countryside in a strange half-light. Then he spotted them, a dark mass staggering down the hillside toward the ramshackle house.

Pushing frantically on the door, he forced a gap big enough to squeeze through and backed off into a blackened room that stank of stale cat piss.

Billy scuttled forward until his grasping fingers encountered the nearest wall and then he began to inch his way to the left. Beneath his hands, chunks of rotten plaster crumbled to the floor. His fingers brushed across a patch of something yielding and slippery that clung to the pitted surface and he snatched them away in revulsion.

Eyes screwed shut he took a shuddering breath and placed his fingertips back against the wall, then shuffled sideways until he came across the wooden panelling of a door. Billy's hands skittered around the surface until he located the handle. Whispering a silent prayer, he pulled the door open and grimaced as a blast of fetid air rushed out to meet him. He paused to listen, ears straining to pick up the slightest noise. He didn't want to go forward into the yawning darkness, though turning back was no longer an option. Swallowing his fear, he slipped into the room, sweeping his arms back and forth like a terrified child playing blind man's bluff at some nightmarish birthday party.

When the drop came his mouth snapped open in terror, a scream locked in his throat. In that split second before he could vent his fear, his right foot came into jarring contact with the floor.

Billy staggered forward arms windmilling for balance. A part of his mind that seemed miraculously unaffected by the trauma, casually informed him that it was a step, nothing more than a *'stupid fucking step.'*

When the arms slid out of the darkness and took hold of him, he didn't know whether to scream or to say 'Thank you.'

As it turned out, he never got the chance to do either.

INBRED.

DS Lasser doubted whether the living room would ever feature in 'Beautiful Homes' magazine. The woodchip paper was peeling and yellowed with nicotine, the pattern on the carpet consisted of old beer and food stains, coated with a generous sprinkling of dog hair.

He looked around for somewhere to sit but the only available chair was littered with gossip magazines and empty pizza boxes.

'So, Sarah, when was the last time you saw Billy?' he asked.

Sarah Jones was in her late thirties, yet she had the harsh stamp of someone ten years older, her dark hair piled on top of her head with the grey roots shining through like the tail of a skunk.

'Yesterday.'

'What time exactly?'

'It is no use asking about the time, I'm dyslexic.'

Lasser sighed. 'Well, can you remember if it was in the morning or…?'

'It can't have been the morning,' she paused. 'I had a lie-in.'

'So, you're saying it was in the afternoon?'

'Come to think of it, it could have been the day before.'

He looked at her in disbelief; this was a complete waste of time. Billy was probably staying with one of his mates, stoned out of his brains on the cheapest drug he could get his grubby little hands on.

'What about his friends, have you tried ringing any of them?'

'Phone's been cut off,' she said before turning her attention back to the television, where Jeremy Kyle was berating a couple of teenagers about the dire consequences of having unprotected sex.

Lasser watched as the audience bayed and booed. 'Is your Michael at home?' he eventually asked.

She shrugged, her eyes still glued to the screen.

'Right, I'll leave you then.'

Sarah snapped her head around. 'Hang on, what about my son?'

Lasser stared at her, his temper beginning to rise. 'Does he still hang around with Kyle Connelly?'

'Why are you asking me?' she snapped. 'You know what kids are like nowadays, no respect. If I'd treated my mother the way he treats me ...'

'I'll tell you what, I'll call round there you never know he might have got carried away doing his homework.' He turned and headed for the door, desperate to be rid of the woman who sat in the chair with her fat legs shrink-wrapped into a pair of Lycra leggings and a T-shirt covered in old food stains.

'Well, when you find him, tell him I know he was the little sod who took the thirty quid from my purse!'

So, that's what it was all about, Billy had stolen cash from his mother and why bother tracking him down yourself when you could get the *'filth'* to do it.

He glanced over his shoulder but she had already turned her attention back to the television. Not trusting himself to speak, he headed along the hallway stepping over the assorted junk that littered the narrow space.

Standing on the doorstep he glanced at the lawn and dragged up a smile, chances are the Joneses would be missing the garden of the year competition again. The grass was patchy and brown; ancient dog turds littered the small space like some weird ornamental garden feature. In one corner an old wreck of a car was lodged against the privet hedge with patches of weeds growing out of the space were the engine used to sit.

As he headed down the pavement, a football arched overhead landing on the bonnet of the pool car with a thud, the alarm began its dull bleating. A kid of about ten ran past and grabbed the ball before booting it down the street to his mates, his shoe flying off in the process following the same trajectory as the ball.

The boy hobbled after his wayward footwear, while his friends laughed and pointed. *'Shut up, you tossers!'* he bellowed in response.

An elderly woman pulling a tartan trolley smiled at Lasser as she tottered past.

'Little buggers,' she said fondly.

Silencing the alarm, he climbed into the car. The old girl wouldn't be so blasé when the kids discovered it was easier to mug old age pensioners rather than work for a living. He slid the window down to release some of the blistering heat and started the engine, before heading off to pay Kyle Connelly a surprise visit.

Slowing to a crawl, he eased over speed bumps on Lancaster Road, the edges of the rubber curling like picked scabs. Turning right at the roundabout, Lasser did a quick double take. Maybe there was a god after all, Kyle Connelly was slouched outside the Spar mini market, head tilted as he chugged on a can.

Lasser drove past the parade of boarded-up shops; the only one still doing any business was Frank's chippy. When the council had tried to force him to move, Frank had dug his heels in, determined to make a stand against the 'bastards' at the Town Hall. Lasser remembered a couple of years earlier when Jamie Oliver had been ranting on about how bad school dinners were. Surprisingly, the local school had taken up his cause, led by a progressive hippy of a headmaster. Out went the pizzas and mechanically reclaimed chicken, replaced by healthier options, plenty of veg and pasta, fresh fruit by the bucket load. The local families hadn't been interested until the price of school dinners rocketed, then the mothers on the Lancaster Road estate had blown a fuse. One irate mother interviewed by the local rag had complained that, *'we don't pay our taxes to be dictated to by a fucking cockney barrow boy.'*

Frank had never had it so good, disgruntled mothers bought bags of chips by the dozen, passing them through the school railings to their starving kids as if they were inmates at some evil concentration camp. Shortly after, the progressive headmaster had moved on with his ponytail tucked between his legs.

Cutting left, he parked on the small car park at the rear of the buildings, climbed out and headed around the corner while Connelly was still busy draining the can.

'Good afternoon, Kyle.'

Connelly glanced over his shoulder and then spat on the floor, before turning away.

'It's funny seeing you here; I was just on my way to your place.'

'Oh yeah and why's that?' Connelly asked with a sneer.

'I'm looking for Billy Jones.'

'I haven't seen him.'

Lasser pulled out his cigarettes and lit up, a tatty looking Fiesta drove by, the driver gave a blast on the horn, and Kyle raised a hand before popping the middle finger.

'So, you haven't seen him then?'

'Are you deaf, I've already told you?'

'That's true, but you see the thing is, Kyle, you have a nasty habit of telling lies.'

'Why don't you just piss off, eh?'

Lasser watched as an ancient dog attempted to lick dry gravy from a discarded chip tray. 'Got any drugs on you, Kyle?'

'Why, do you want some?' Connelly sneered.

'Thanks for the offer, but I prefer my cocaine when it isn't mixed with Cillit Bang. Now empty your pockets.'

'What for I haven't done anything?'

'Now you see most people would look at that response with suspicion. They'd think this boy has something to hide. But I know you're keen to help, so I'll give you a minute to reconsider your answer, you can even phone a friend if you want?'

Connelly pulled back his shoulders and threw out his chest, hands bunched into fists.

Lasser held his poison gaze. 'Right then, I think a trip to the station is in order, don't you?'

Connelly frowned and then his shoulders slumped as he fell back into the default stance of every eighteen-year-old thug in the country.

'OK, I saw him last night, are you satisfied?'

'Far from it, now I want the time and place, Mr Connelly, and no more pork pies.'

'I don't know.'

'Well, was the little finger pointing to…?'

'It was about half ten.' Connelly spat.

'That's better and where was this?'

A long pause, the sun blasted down as the old dog cocked its leg against the litterbin.

'We went up to Horwich.'

Lasser raised an eyebrow in surprise. 'I bet you were surprised when you found they had grass there that you couldn't smoke.'

'Fuck off taking the piss.'

Lasser ignored him. 'So, come on, what where you doing in the great outdoors?'

Connelly shrugged, 'Just having a laugh.'

'And what time did you drop Billy off?'

Emptying the can Connelly tossed it toward the bin, it hit the side before clattering to the flags. The scruffy dog eyed the container and then hobbled over for a sniff.

'We didn't drop him off,' he paused, 'we lost him.'

'What do mean you lost him?'

'He did a runner.'

'And why would he do that when he was miles from home?'

Kyle turned, his face a parody of innocence. 'No idea.'

Lasser flicked ash onto the floor. 'So, who else was on this little outing?'

'Just a couple of mates, that's all.'

'You do surprise me; I didn't think you had any.'

'Twat!'

'Names, Kyle?'

Connelly looked at the floor for a few seconds and then mumbled three names.

'The usual suspects then?'

A frown creased the boy's forehead. 'What're you on about?'

'Never mind.'

Connelly glanced over Lasser's shoulder and just for a second his eyes widened in surprise, or was it fear?

Donald Fletcher was striding out of Spar. Some of Lasser's uniformed colleagues had nicknamed him the human pit bull. Fletcher was a fully-fledged meathead, who liked to paint the town blood red. If his Saturday night didn't end with a mass brawl then he considered the night a dismal failure.

'Right, thanks for the information, Kyle, you've been very helpful!' he saw panic bloom in Connelly's eyes.

Lasser turned away almost colliding with Fletcher. 'Bloody hell, Donald, this is a coincidence, we were just talking about you.'

The crease on Fletcher's slab of a forehead turned into a deep furrow.

'Catch up with you later, Kyle, and thanks again for the heads-up.'

He headed for the car but couldn't resist a quick peek over his shoulder. Fletcher was heading for Connelly like a faulty Exocet Missile. Kyle backed off with his hands raised, a couple of seconds later the young hoodie turned and made a break for it. At nearly eighteen stone running was never going to be Donald's forte, besides he didn't need to bother, he knew where Connelly lived.

Lasser began to whistle as he headed for the car; maybe today wasn't going to be so bad after all.

DON'T MESS WITH THE LOOK.

Jenna sighed as the bus juddered to a halt; a woman struggled on board, a buggy in one hand a screaming baby in the other. The journey home from college was taking forever, to make matters worse the man squashed at her side smelled like the inside of a charity shop. Every time the bus went around a corner, he pressed his leg against hers and grunted. As they reached the town centre, he lumbered to his feet and headed for the doors. Jenna breathed a sigh of relief and placed her rucksack on the empty seat.

She looked at her fellow passengers; the bus seemed full of people with sour expressions. Somewhere near the front, the baby began to cry again, a girl on the opposite side was listening to her iPod tapping her feet to the tinny rhythm and punching a text message into her phone. A toddler munched on a packet of sour fruits; every time he popped one into his mouth his face would screw up in shock.

By the time the bus left the town centre, Jenna was the only passenger left. She relaxed as the houses vanished and open fields took over, the cloying despair of the run down streets slowly evaporating like a filthy mirage. Fifteen minutes later she saw her stop approaching, pressing the bell she made her way down the narrow walkway. The doors hissed open and she leapt to the pavement, breathing in deeply the familiar scent of rapeseed blossom sweetening the stifling air.

Coughing a cloud of diesel fumes into her face the bus rumbled away up the hill until the only sound was the chirp of grasshoppers and the drone of bees as they busied themselves in the hedgerow.

Having to attend college was unavoidable and most of the time it was just about bearable.

An image of Tina Sheldon flashed into her mind, seventeen and four months pregnant, swaggering around the campus with her bump on display, a real woman surrounded by immature kids, yeah right.

Climbing the wooden stile, she paused for a moment to adjust the backpack and then leapt down into the field before making her way along the well-worn path.

Girls like Sheldon drove her mad but the boys were worse. Morons, who spent their time making comments about the size of your tits or the shape of your arse, or which lucky girl they'd shagged the night before. Popping a stick of gum into her mouth, she chewed furiously.

If she'd had her way she wouldn't have gone in today, though her parents had made it clear that skiving off wasn't an option.

She quickened her pace; the last few weeks had been spent in a state of nervous tension that had little to do with exams. With any luck, Patrick Fossey had spent the day on her parents' farm, whilst she'd been stuck in a classroom that reeked of cheap perfume and testosterone, trying to concentrate on an English exam.

In the distance, she could see the familiar site of the tractor ploughing the top field. Seagulls shone white against a bank of threatening clouds the colour of weathered gravestones.

As she rounded a curve in the field the house came into view, Jenna broke into an awkward run, the rucksack heavy with books slammed back and forth on her slim shoulders.

At least the exam had been a breeze. She'd done the revision, spending endless nights cocooned in her bedroom just like a teenage hermit.

Yet during the two-hour test, she'd found herself distracted by Fossey's visit, playing various scenarios over in her head, lost in the tantalising possibilities.

That was until the tutor had informed the class that the first hour had passed.

Her eyes had refocused on the page like a junkie coming out of a bad trip and for a few seconds she'd panicked at the lack of words that lay before her. For the last hour, she'd written in a kind of blind frenzy, desperate to get all her points down onto paper.

All that stress, all that strain, who needed it?

Although she would never admit it, in many ways her parents were cool. Though missing an exam just for the sake of meeting some *'weirdo writer'* as her father had so infuriatingly insisted on calling Fossey, was a definite no, no.

'But who's going to show him around, who's going to fill him in on all the important background stuff?' she had been standing at the kitchen table, her hands locked together in mounting frustration.

Her dad had smiled in that annoying way that fathers seemed to specialise in. 'What about your grandad, why can't he…?'

'You're joking, right?'

'Well, Poppet, it's either him or I'm afraid we'll have to cancel. I mean, I can't spare the time and before you ask, neither can your mother.'

Her face had flushed in anger at the use of her pet childhood name.

It made her sound like one of those spoiled brats who always seemed to be popping up on some naff cable channel showing the sixteen-year-old girls who got a Ferrari for their birthday.

'But, Dad, he can't…'

'Just stop and think about it, your grandad knows more about this place than anyone else and if you prime him with the questions you want answering,' he treated Jenna to a big grin, then everyone's happy.'

Yeah right. She loved her grandad no question about that, but over the last couple of years he had been getting forgetful, a fact she pointed out as tactfully as she could.

The smile had vanished in an instant. 'Take it or leave it, it's up to you. But it's the best offer you're going to get.'

Jenna knew from bitter experience that it would be fruitless to push for more concessions. Her father had that look in his eyes and you did not mess with ‘the look’.

15

CHIPS AND SYMPATHY

Lasser waited until the queue died down before nipping into the chippy.

Frank smiled as he entered, his comb over appeared to be held in place by chip fat, his moustache thick and wiry like some seventies porno star, the apron stained white with batter only adding to the illusion.

'Now, Mr Lasser, how are you keeping?'

'I'm getting tired of this heat, Frank.'

'You should try working behind here when the fryers on full blast,' he started to shovel chips into a polystyrene tray. 'Takes bloody years off you, it does.'

'Much like the food you serve.'

Frank grinned, showing an uneven set of yellowing dentures. 'I saw you giving Connelly a grilling.'

'I was just having a quiet word.'

'He's a little bastard that one.' Frank reached in and pulled a battered fish from the oven before slapping it down on top of the chips. 'Salt and vinegar?'

'Plenty of vinegar, easy on the salt.'

'I don't know why he can't get a job and do summat with his life. I mean, that bugger's been hanging about out there for over ten years.'

It sounded preposterous, but Frank was probably right.

'He never went to school, he spent all day kicking a ball against the wall. I used to chase the little sod off.' Frank shook his head sadly as he wrapped the greasy bundle. 'Course you can't do it now, not unless you want your windows put in.'

'I don't know why you don't call it a day, Frank. I mean, you must have a few quid tucked away by now?'

Frank looked affronted at the mere suggestion. 'I wouldn't know what do to with my time. I mean, you remember old George who had the newsagents?'

'The guy with the wooden leg?'

'Aye well, they found him dead last week, sat at the breakfast table with his face in a bowl of Sugar Puffs.'

Frank picked up a chip and popped it into his mouth. 'That's what retirement does for you.'

'I'm sorry to hear that, he was a nice bloke.'

'He said he was going to take up golf, now look at him.'

Lasser slid a tenner across the counter. 'So, what does Connelly do all day?'

The note vanished whippet quick, Frank rang the ancient till, rummaging around inside for change.

'Probably does the same as his old man, deals drugs.'

Lasser sighed; it was hardly earth shattering news.

'I tell you, I used to get on the blower to you lot, but I don't bother no more,' he sniffed.

'Why's that?'

Frank plonked the change into Lasser's cupped hand.

'Because bugger all gets done, I mean, Connelly stands there for hours on end. When the kids come out of school they're round him like flies round shit. I tell you; it used to be the ice cream man they ran to, now it's that hooligan, dishing out his little bags of God knows what.'

'Don't worry, Frank; I've got my eye on Mr Connelly.'

Frank looked unimpressed and in truth, Lasser didn't blame him, a slap-on-the-wrist and then back on the streets the same day. A perpetual cycle of Kyle Connelly's. It was as if they were cloned in some secret science facility. Churned out like some sort of retribution to a society that got what it deserved.

'You don't know a Billy Jones, do you?' Lasser asked.

Frank wiped his hands on a paper towel before tossing it into the bin. 'Aye, I know him, little runt of a lad.'

'He hangs around the shops then?'

'Yeah, he knocks about with Connelly and his mates.'

'Doing what exactly?'

Frank shrugged. 'He's their errand boy, you know if they want owt from the shop he has to go and get it. I caught him a few weeks ago trying to get to my till.'

'He was trying to steal from you?'

'Oh aye, at one time it happened on a regular basis, but not so much since I got Mandy.'

Frank whistled a single tuneless note and the biggest Rottweiler Lasser had ever seen popped up from behind the counter, all mangled ears and old battle scars.

'This bloke I know was getting shut of her, so I said I'd take her off his hands.'

'Bonny dog, Frank.'

'I tell you it's a good job he didn't get all the way over the counter. Mandy would have eaten him alive,' he smiled fondly, as if it was a cherished memory. 'Of course the others found it hilarious, sick buggers.'

The dog eyed Lasser and licked its lips before sinking slowly back below the counter.

'So, I take it the older boys knew about the dog?'

'Oh aye, they did it for a laugh. I mean, the kid was white as a sheet when he ran off, but like I said they don't give a toss.'

Lasser picked up the bundle of fish and chips the grease already seeping through like blotting paper.

'Right well, I'll see you soon, Frank.'

'Aye, you take care son and watch your back.'

Lasser smiled over his shoulder. 'I always do.'

He wandered around the corner and slid behind the wheel, before dropping the chips onto the passenger seat.

Five minutes later, he pulled onto the Three Sister's car park; a local beauty spot consisting of a small lake littered with empty plastic bottles and used condoms. A pair of swans glided through the debris. Pulling under the shade of an overhanging willow, he pushed the door open.

A council worker fired up a leaf blower and began to blow the leaves around the car park.

What Frank had said about Billy was hardly surprising; a young kid hanging around with older teenagers was guaranteed to get all the crappy jobs. His life would consist of doing whatever the others demanded, like some rite of passage leading to a life of petty crime and drug abuse. It seemed strange though, normally Billy went everywhere with his older brother Michael and he didn't seem like the kind of lad who'd let them get away with picking on his kid brother. Lasser picked up a chip and popped it into his mouth.

When Connelly had given him the three names, he had never mentioned Michael; perhaps it would be worth calling back at the Joneses' house, maybe the brother could fill him in on the details.

His stomach rumbled as he ate, he watched as a magpie flew past the front of the car and crapped on the windscreen, typical.

19

TALL TALES

Jenna let herself into the house, hurriedly kicking off her shoes in the hallway before shouldering her way into the lounge.

The smell of baking bread, as familiar to her as cut grass and damp straw, drifted in from the kitchen. Tossing her bag onto the sofa, she sprinted across the room, banging open the door and arriving in the kitchen as if jet-propelled.

Her mother stood at the sink peeling veg.

Jenna had often thought it would be nice to nip into town for the occasional McDonalds like any normal family. Though the last time she'd broached the subject her mum had like totally overreacted, backing away from her as if she were the antichrist and making the sign of the cross with a couple of home grown carrots.

Susan turned from the sink blowing a strand of ash blonde hair out of her eyes. 'Hi, sweetheart, how did the exam go?'

'It went OK, did he come?'

Her mother tilted her head slightly, her face serious. 'Did who come?'

Jenna treated her to a look of cool contempt, refusing to respond to such infantile behaviour.

Susan smiled. 'OK, yes he did.'

Jenna did a little jig on the spot, aware that she probably looked like a ten-year-old kid at a Morris dancing parade. 'Oh, wow! I can't believe he actually turned up, what was he like?'

'To be honest, Jenna, I was pleasantly surprised.'

'What do you mean?'

'Well, he seemed like a nice guy.'

'And why should that be a surprise?' Jenna felt the old frustrations beginning to build. Why did parents always have to play their little mind games?

'He was a lot younger than I was expecting,' Susan paused for maximum affect. 'In fact he was quite dishy.'

'Quite dishy!'

Susan turned back to the sink hiding a smile. 'If you want to know all the details then you'll find your grandad out back feeding the hens.'

Jenna headed to the door sliding her mother a withering glance as she passed. For a couple of seconds she contemplated slamming the back door behind her, but decided it would make her appear petulant and childish. Closing it quietly she pulled on her ever-present wellies and headed outside.

Ronnie flipped the bucket over and placed it on the ground before scratching his chin as if in deep thought. 'Well, Jenna, he was a funny kind of fella.'

She'd found him in the chicken pen, shaking grain into one of the low metal troughs, the sound reminiscent of hailstone on a barn roof. 'But you told him about the old house didn't you?'

'Oh aye, in fact we even had a ride up there.'

'So, he was definitely interested then?'

He pulled the mangled stump of a cigarette from his top pocket and began rolling it between his fingers.

'He seemed to be; in fact he said he was going to give you a ring later to go over a few things.'

Jenna thrust her hands into her pockets and kept her feet rooted to the ground, one show of childish behaviour was enough for one day. 'This is seriously cool.'

'Is it?' Ronnie grunted.

She gazed at her grandad with a look of benign pity. 'Honestly, Grandad, you have no idea. Patrick Fossey is an expert.'

'He went in tha' knows.'

Jenna's eyes widened in surprise. 'He actually went into the house!'

'Aye.'

'Did you go with him?'

Ronnie lowered himself onto the upturned bucket, a chicken approached and pecked at the dust around his feet. 'No, love, I didn't. I would have done, but he said he preferred to go in alone. Just him and this little terrier he had with him.'

'So, come on, Grandad, what did he say when he came out?'

'To be honest he didn't say much.'

'But he must have said something?'

The old man cleared his throat. 'Well, by the time he came out, it was getting late and I had to get back here to feed these buggers.'

She could imagine how the day had unfolded. Patrick Fossey asking loads of important questions and her grandad grunting one-word answers. This was exactly the kind of thing she had been worried about.

'But you told him about the needle house didn't you?'

Ronnie fiddled with the old wedding ring on his finger. 'Sorry, love, I forgot.'

'But I offered to write out a list of questions and you told me not to be stupid. You promised me you'd remember!'

Ronnie looked at his granddaughter; there was no mistaking the disappointment on her face. Bloody useless he was. 'Oh, hang on,' he fumbled in the pocket of his old jacket and pulled out a card. 'He asked me to give you this.'

She nearly removed two of his fingers as she snatched for the card. It had Fossey's name, home number, and email address on the front. She flicked it over and there was his mobile number scrawled on the back; this was just so unreal, so perfect.

She slipped the card into the back pocket of her jeans as if it were a winning lottery ticket. 'I wonder what he thought of the house.'

'You know, Jenna; I've been thinking, maybe this isn't such a good idea.'

'What!'

Ronnie winced at the shock and outrage in her voice. 'I mean, what if he wants to put us in his next book?'

Jenna squatted in the dust. 'Well, that would be fantastic.'

Ronnie pursed his lips. 'I'm not so sure.'

'Of course it would. I mean, do you have any idea how many places he visits?'

'Not a clue.'

'Like dozens,' she spoke as if talking to a small child or worse still an idiot. 'In his last book he talks about how many of these places are simply a con. You know some of these people would kill to get into print.'

'But why the hell would they do that?'

'Think about it, a lot of them are manor houses or stately homes. Places that would really benefit from having Patrick Fossey write about them, it's like a glowing endorsement.'

'And it brings the punters in?'

'I suppose so.'

'I see, so it's a money-making scam?' Ronnie sniffed.

She glared at him, unsure if he was being deliberately stupid or perhaps he'd been out in the sun too long. 'Patrick Fossey isn't interested in that kind of thing.'

'Made his money, has he?'

Jenna could feel herself becoming exasperated. 'Look, he doesn't even rely on writing to make a living'.

'What do you mean?'

'I know Dad thinks he's just some weird 'new age' writer, but what none of you realise is the fact that Mr Fossey is a psychologist,' she paused, 'an expert.'

'Really,' having met the man, this piece of news didn't really come as a surprise to Ronnie.

'He's helped the police on more than one occasion,' her voice was slowly rising in anger.

Ronnie held up his hands in an effort to placate his granddaughter.

'All I'm saying is that if he is interested and decides to write about this place then it could open the floodgates.'

'What floodgates are we talking about exactly?'

'Well, think about it, we could end up with all sorts of nutters turning up, thinking they've got the right to go where they please.'

She couldn't believe her ears. 'You're worried about people trespassing?'

'You've already said these places get overrun with folk. It's alright for them in their big bloody houses; they're probably making a fortune out of the whole thing. All we'll get is owd hippies tramping through the wheat leaving their crap everywhere,' he paused, 'or God knows what else.'

Jenna was gobsmacked, when she'd first considered contacting Fossey, her grandad had been behind her one hundred percent. The old man had even defended her against her dad when he was raising his 'over-the-top Dad concerns'. If it hadn't been for him, she would never have bothered with the research in the first place.

For as long as she could remember he'd told her stories about the farm and the surrounding land, he'd planted the seeds that had led her to this.

Instead of hanging around on street corners, getting pissed and building a drug habit, she had spent her time at the local library and history shop trawling through old microfiche films, digging out pictures and studying old maps. All with the aim of learning about the farm and the Radfield family who used to own great swathes of the Pennine moors including the farm they now called home. They'd spent countless afternoons together searching through the ruins of the old manor house, crawling through thick undergrowth to search out the remains of the ancient mosaic floor.

She had it all in her head, the layout of the place as familiar to her as her own home. In addition, there were still reminders of the grandeur of the place. The 'needle house' remained intact, perched on top of a nearby hill, like an ancient stone rocket primed and ready to blast off and the exotic gardens that tumbled down the hillside at different levels, a testament to one man's determination to manipulate and change nature.

Now he was getting cold feet, well sod that!

'Look, Grandad, we are not a stately home,' she tried to keep her voice level, tried to keep calm.

'I know that but the principle's still the same.'

'Don't be a bloody snob!'

The old man dropped the unlit cigarette back into his top pocket. 'Well, love, I've been called a lot of things in my time but 'snob' has never been one of them.'

With a deflated sigh, she looked toward the horizon, a buzzard drifted by on a current of warm air.

'Have you talked about any of this with Mum and Dad?'

He pushed his thumb and forefinger under his glasses and massaged the bridge of his nose. 'No, love, I've said nowt.' When he looked up again, Jenna was kneeling down in front of him and he had to lean back on the bucket in order to focus.

'Look, we're getting ahead of ourselves; chances are he won't really be interested. At the end of the day I'm a seventeen-year-old kid and perhaps he's just being kind.'

'You mean patronising?'

'God I hope not,' she paused, the thought too horrific to contemplate. 'But you never know.'

'Listen, when you get to my age you can smell 'patronising' a mile off, stinks worse than owd chicken shit it does and he weren't like that.'

Jenna's eyes narrowed. 'Are you sure?'

'Positive,' he sighed. 'Though in a way I wish he had been.'

'What do you mean?' It was as if a complete stranger, a doppelganger had been beamed down into the chicken pen while she had been at college.

'He was the exact opposite, focused like; he wanted to know everything about the place. I suppose I were expecting some sort of mad professor type, you know all wild hair and thick as two short planks.'

'Like I said, Grandad, he's a psychologist.'

'Well, the buggers definitely on the ball, I know that much.'

'But that's good isn't it? I mean, we want someone who's going to take us seriously.'

Ronnie looked unconvinced. 'Aye I suppose so.'

She paused for a moment, and then the penny dropped. 'That's why you didn't mention the needle house isn't it? '

'You and this Fossey bloke have a lot in common lass.' Ronnie replied uncomfortably.

'I'll take that as a compliment, anyway, let's just see if he gets in touch.'

Ronnie rose and stretched his back, a grimace on his weather beaten face.

'Oh I think he will. When he came out of the old house, he didn't say much. Well, to tell you the truth I didn't really give him the chance.'

'And why not?'

'I'm not really sure; he seemed quiet as if he were giving something some serious thought. Plus you know what the old Land Rover's like, it makes that much racket you can hardly hear yourself think, let alone hold a conversation.'

'But what about when you got back here?'

Ronnie rubbed a hand over his face. 'When I dropped him off he looked like he was going to start asking a load of questions.'

'And?'

Ronnie hesitated for a second. 'I made myself scarce.'

'Bloody hell, Grandad!'

Ronnie's wiry eyebrows shot up in genuine surprise. Jenna swearing was unheard of, it was testament to how annoyed she really was, and the sad thing was he didn't blame her.

Maybe for the first time Ronnie became truly aware of how much this whole business meant to her. To his granddaughter, having Patrick Fossey take an interest in her research was like having the second coming arrive on the farm complete with wellies and a scruffy little mutt.

She had relied on him to ask the questions, to be her representative, her gatherer of information and he had let her down, as she knew he would.

Yet despite this dawning bitter knowledge, Ronnie felt a deeper unease. By saying to little, maybe he had inadvertently said too much.

'Look, Jenna, let's wait and see what happens. I mean, he might ring tonight or tomorrow even,' he tried a smile of reassurance and came nowhere near to pulling it off.

'Yeah and he might not.'

'Well, like you pointed, we're no stately home; we've got nowt to gain.'

Patrick Fossey would be back all right and when he did return he'd want to look beyond the obvious. Ronnie swallowed, suddenly feeling a sense of creeping unease.

RED BIB.

He opens the imaginary draw and takes out the mental images, holding them in his non-existent hands. A trick he learned in the army, perfect if you wanted to distance yourself from the horror, but he isn't interested in suppression.

Everything is studied in intimate detail. At this early stage, the slightest oversight could prove disastrous.

The victim had been immaterial, though he prides himself on his ability to think on his feet, to adapt. When he spotted the boy scuttling down the hillside he'd decided to use this unexpected intrusion to his advantage, besides there came a point in any plan, where you had to move things from the imagined to the tangible.

He smiles as he recalls how it had nearly unravelled. When the older boy had entered the house, his quarry had already been dying in his arms. He'd clamped a hand over the victim's mouth, listening to the sound of shuffling footsteps in the other room, aware of the heat, aware of the blood as it seeped through his shirt. Seconds slid by, the body sagged, suddenly feeling heavier, as if the departing spirit had added weight to the corpse. He'd watched through a gap in one of the boarded up windows as the three teenagers climbed back up the hill toward the dark mass of trees.

Satisfied he wouldn't be disturbed he went to work, slipping the strap around his head and flicking on the powerful torch. He removed the boy's clothes and shoes tossing them into the darkened corner and then he began to cut, quick efficient strokes, pausing only twice to wipe the sweat from his forehead. If he wanted the plan to succeed, then leaving the body intact wasn't an option, he wanted to lead the police by the nose, from A to B from one grizzly clue to the next.

Fifteen minutes later, he had carried the boys internal organs encased in a plastic feed sack down to the septic tank. When the bundle hit the stagnant water, it released a fetid stench, dark bubbles rising to the surface as the gruesome bundle sank to the bottom. Grinning in the moonlight, the thought of some unfortunate having to search the murky depths gave him a warm inner glow. He'd walked back to the house taking time to flatten the grass as he went. Once inside he made a thorough sweep of the room, the beam of light like a third eye blasting away the shadows.

Thc van was parked two hundred yards from the house, hidden by a dark mass of trees; he opened the back doors and slid what remained of the body into the back. For the first time since he had spotted the boy he allowed himself to relax, he could feel the blood on his shirt, stiffening the fabric as it dried.

Not that it mattered; they would be disposed of thoroughly. He lit a cigarette, they never mentioned it in the brochure, but it was one of the benefits of having a wood-burning stove.

ALL THIS DUST.

Jenna had found it impossible to sleep, tossing, and turning, checking the digital clock on the bedside cabinet as if she were an excitable child waiting for Santa Claus to arrive. At half six, she heard the familiar sound of the tractor starting up, the heavy rumble of the diesel engine shaking the glass in the bedroom window. Five minutes later, she was in the kitchen making tea and toast, trying to keep herself occupied.

She headed back to her room and spent the next two hours on the laptop, scrolling through the images, pausing frequently to check a point of reference.

Fossey would be here in less than an hour.

It was bizarre, but she couldn't shake the ominous feeling, that buried in her research, there would be an error of such magnitude that she would never live it down.

Over the past few months, she'd shown her work to no one, not even Grandad, though now she was beginning to regret the decision; chewing a fingernail in apprehension, she rubbed at her aching eyes.

Fossey had phoned at half nine the night before, it was a moment she had fantasised about for so long, though in all that time, she had never allowed for the possibility that she would be lost for words.

There had been an awkward pause on the line as he waited for her to answer a simple question, she stood rigid gripping the phone like a sprinter grips the baton.

Her mum had hovered at her shoulder, a concerned look on her face. For God's sake, she didn't need her mother holding her hand. Miraculously she'd found her voice and began to talk and the great thing, the amazing thing was that he'd sounded like a normal person, not some 'stuffy expert.'

He listened patiently, asking open-ended questions, allowing her to explain the whole thing to him. When she did hesitate, he simply pointed her in another direction and off she went.

She looked out of the window again. The fields rolled away into the distance, levelling out at the valley bottom before rising to the shimmering horizon.

The house was empty, Dad was out on the tractor and her mum and grandad had headed off into Horwich to do the weekly shop. Grandad would have been dropped off at the 'Radfield Arms' for a pint and a game of dominos with some of his old friends, Mum would pick him up on the return journey.

It was weird but she'd wanted them all to be here when Fossey arrived; it would have been embarrassing, but still pretty cool.

Before she'd left, Mum had double-checked she would be OK.

'I know I'm being over protective, but don't forget if you need your father, he's in the top field and he's got his mobile.'

Jenna had virtually pushed her into the car, Grandad had given her his customary small wave as they drove away looking like a wizened old gnome off on his holidays.

A flash of light sparkled at the window; Jenna dashed across the room and peered out over the fields. A Range Rover appeared in the distance, weaving its way along the narrow lane. She held her breath as the vehicle approached, when it turned onto the drive, she swallowed her nerves and bolted for the door.

By the time the car pulled up at the house, Jenna was standing by the front door, trying her best to appear nonchalant.

Patrick Fossey waved through the open car window, before vanishing in a cloud of dust.

A few seconds later, he climbed from the car, wafting both hands in front of his face his eyes screwed up tight.

'Sorry about that, I should have slowed down a bit,' he smiled and coughed. 'Hi, Jenna is it?'

Mum had been right; he did look younger than the cover photo on his book.

'Hi, Mr Fossey.'

A scruffy terrier appeared at the side window, licked the glass, and disappeared from view.

'Pleased to meet you,' he thrust out a hand. Jenna shook it, feeling the colour rise in her cheeks. 'Is it OK if I let the dog out?' he asked.

'Yeah, yeah that's fine.'

'I promise he won't chase anything,' he pulled open the door; the animal looked at them both from the back seat. 'I'm afraid he's a bit on the lazy side. Come on, T, out you get.'

The dog remained rooted to the spot, as if pondering whether it was worth the effort. Then he shook himself and leapt down, cocking his leg against the tyre of the Range Rover.

'Would you like to come in and have a drink or something?' as soon as the words left her mouth Jenna cringed, what was the matter with her! All the nerves of the night before came flooding back like long lost friends. *'A drink or something,'* she could not believe she'd actually said that.

Fossey smiled. 'A cold drink would be great, help me get rid of all this dust.'

'I think there might be a couple of cans of beer in the fridge.'

'Fruit juice would be better if you have it.'

'What, oh yeah, you're driving.'

'Well, yes, but it's a little early to be cracking open the beers.'

Jenna blushed bright red, he'd only been here a couple of minutes and she'd managed to convey the image that she was a young tart who was trying to pry him with drinks. Way to go girl.

Ten minutes later, ensconced in the kitchen, she was beginning to relax.

He told her to drop the 'Mr Fossey' it was Patrick to his friends. Jenna beamed and poured them both a cold glass of homemade ginger beer.

'And you say your grandad makes this?' Fossey held up the glass, studying the dark brown drink.

'Mm, apparently it's a very old recipe.'

Fossey took a long swallow. 'It's delicious.'

The dog wandered around the kitchen sniffing at everything before curling up at Fossey's feet and feigning sleep.

'I still can't believe you're here.'

'Why's that?'

'I just never thought you'd be interested in my …' she paused, suddenly using the word research felt wrong. Research was done by professional's not seventeen-year-old girls who were still at college.

'Let me tell you, Jenna, it's been a long time since I've read anything that interested me more than your correspondence.'

She looked at him in suspicion. 'Really, you're not just saying that?'

Fossey held up his hands. 'Believe me, if I wasn't intrigued then I wouldn't be here.'

Lifting a CD disk from the kitchen table, she held it out.

'What's this?'

'I didn't know if you'd be in a rush, so I transferred all the files from the computer and burnt them to disk for you.'

'That's great, but I've left today free.'

'Really?' she tried to keep the silly grin off her face and failed.

'Well, yeah, I was hoping you could show me around?'

'That would be brilliant.'

'I checked with your mother to make sure it would be OK.'

Jenna frowned, she'd kill her, all that fussing and yet she'd gone behind her back, checking up on Fossey.

'I was concerned you might be doing revision, your mother mentioned you had exams coming up.' Fossey explained.

' I don't have another for a couple of weeks and anyway I have revised enough. I can afford to take time off.'

'And how are they going so far?'

'OK, I think.'

'Well it's a while since I did any exams but I remember the nerves well enough.'

She smiled, the thought of him sweating over an exam seemed bizarre, but the admission made her warm to him even more.

'So, where would you like to go first?' she asked.

'Well, if it's OK with you I'd like to take another look at the old house.'

'Gamekeepers Cottage?'

'Is that what they were? I did wonder.'

'My great-grandfather lived in one of the houses.'

Fossey placed the glass into the sink. 'Right well, if you're ready we can get off.'

'Oh right, just hang on a sec,' crossing the room she opened the fridge and pulled out a small basket. 'I've put up a few sandwiches and a couple of cold drinks.'

'More ginger beer?'

She smiled in embarrassment. 'He always makes too much, we've got about four crates of the stuff left from last year, but he says the longer you leave it the better it tastes.'

'A wise man, your grandad'.

MISCONCEPTION.

Ashley studied the painting of his father with barely concealed loathing. It had been commissioned when he'd been in his early fifties and even then his jowls had started to sag, the hair receding, the shoulders stooped. Hardly a flattering image, not that his father would see it as such.

At forty-three Ashley had long ago given up any form of pretence, his father might have a title, but he was still a fool and an arse. He looked around the oak-panelled room, he'd never liked this house, and every time he was forced to come back here, he despised it even more. Too many bad memories of growing up in a home that felt more like a boarding school. He noted that the room hadn't changed in over forty years; the grandfather clock still ticked away in the corner the large open fireplace contained a pile of dust-covered logs stacked in the grate. Yet Ashley knew the tray of decanters would be filled with the finest malt whiskies, the grate littered with the stumps of expensive cigars, no expense spared by his father especially when it came to life's little luxuries.

The drive down from Scotland had been tiring and uneventful, giving him the perfect opportunity to finalize things in his mind. He had no doubt his father would be outraged when he learned the truth; he would see it as a betrayal. Not that Ashley cared, he heard the front door slam, a few seconds later the man himself entered with his usual bluster, unaware of his son standing in the corner he headed straight for the decanter. Ashley watched as he filled his glass to the brim with single malt.

'Good afternoon, Father.'

Malcolm turned his head in surprise. 'Didn't see you there, my boy.' he replied before tossing his head back and swallowing the contents of the glass.

It had been eight months since he had seen his father and he could feel the instant animosity coming from the old man in waves. When he'd been younger it had bothered him enormously, this strange reticence that titled families seemed to possess. However, now he was glad of the fact that they hardly ever communicated, it made it easier to twist the knife.

Malcolm poured himself another glass. 'And where the hell is Roberts? When I went out I distinctly told him to mow the front lawn.'

'I've had a word, dispensed with his services.'

Malcolm slammed the empty glass down on the table. *'You've done what!'*

'I've let him go.'

'Sacked him?'

'Not as such.' Ashley pulled out a cigarette. 'I explained the situation and he was very understanding.'

Malcolm narrowed his eyes, for the first time his only son was beginning to make him feel nervous. 'Situation, and what situation are we talking about, Ashley?'

Ashley raised an eyebrow in surprise, he couldn't remember the last time his father had used Christian name, as a child, he had always referred to him as 'boy' or if he was feeling particularly paternal 'son.'

'Look, Father, you seem to be labouring under a misconception.'

'What are you waffling on about?'

Ashley was beginning to enjoy himself; his father was a weak, pathetic specimen of a man. In any other circumstance, he would have been a failure, probably drinking his life away in some godforsaken inner city slum.

'Lord 'Malcolm Radfield' sounds impressive doesn't it and looks good on the letterheads.'

The vein in Malcolm's temple began to throb, his mouth dry, the need for another drink growing.

'Though being a Lord becomes laughable when you have no money in the bank.'

Malcolm refilled his glass, the decanter tinkling on the crystal and then he wandered over to the ox blood Chesterfield, sitting down with a grunt.

'You were always one for over-egging the pudding.'

'You think so?' Ashley watched as the old man fumbled in the cigar box.

'Look, there's been a Radfield in this house for over a hundred and fifty years; we've had the odd blip before...'

'Talking of houses, I have a buyer.'

Malcolm snapped his head around his jowls flapping. *'I thought I told you this house is not for sale, not now, not ever!'*

'Oh I agree,' Ashley smiled when he saw the look of befuddlement plastered on the old man's ruddy face. 'I'm talking about the house in Fife.'

'Certainly not, that house has been…'

'Spare me the history lesson, we have no money, do you understand the consequences of that fact, Father? You,' he pointed a finger at his father, 'have squandered almost all of it.'

'I...'

'Look,' he pointed at a portrait on the wall, there were some similarities to Malcolm, the same bulk and stooped shoulders, but the eyes spoke volumes as to the determination of the man. 'It took that man a lifetime to build up this families name and when I look at you I find it impossible to comprehend you are of the same stock. Now I'm here to inform you that the house in Scotland will be sold whether you approve or not.'

'You can't do that!' Malcolm blustered.

'Do you honestly think I would have come all the way down here just to discuss this with you, the deals done and while we're on the subject of 'done deals' I've taken over the directorship of the company.'

Malcolm's hands shook, the cigar crumbling between his grasping fingers.

'The other members of the board are in agreement,' Ashley smiled. 'So, how does it feel, Father, to be officially known as a liability?'

It took a massive effort on his part but Malcolm brushed the tobacco flakes from his trousers, picked up the whisky, swirling the amber liquid around before draining it.

As the spirit burned down his throat, his rage blossomed into outright hatred for his son, the damn audacity of the bastard. Yet despite this, he managed to drag up a smile. 'So, my boy, what are your intentions, what will you do with all this new found power?' he spread his arms wide, his voice dripping contempt.

'You have no idea, no concept of the position you've left us in, do you? You talk about 'Power' but what you fail to understand is that there is no 'power'. We have tenant farmers who have more money in the bank than we do!'

Malcolm shrugged his shoulders. 'And how is the great Ashley Radfield going to stop the rot?'

'You forget, Father, I've already dispensed with the services of one luxury we can't afford and getting rid of another shouldn't prove too problematic.

NOT RIGHT.

Fossey shook his head. 'It's hard to believe it used to be three houses.'

They were standing twenty yards from the property, directly above, the sun raged in a sky of perfect blue.

'If you look closely you can see were the other front doors used to be.' Jenna pointed towards the house.

To Fossey, the house resembled a huge slab of black butter left out in the sun making the roof sag; even the stone walls appeared bowed, as if straining under some huge invisible weight.

'Did your great-grandfather have a family?'

'According to the records he had two girls and four boys, though two of the boys died when they were children.'

He tried to imagine what it would have been like raising a large family and having to share the small space with two others.

Somewhere up high, a skylark began to sing.

'My dad keeps talking about knocking it down.'

'So, it isn't used anymore?'

'Not really, when I was a kid they used to store sacks of grain and stuff up here, but that was when we kept cattle.'

'Do you have any idea when the place was last occupied?

'Nineteen fifty-six,' she replied instantly.

Fossey looked at her and smiled. 'That's very precise.'

'It's all on the disk,' she explained. 'My grandad remembers it back then, he said the place always gave him the creeps.'

'Did he say why?'

'Not really, he can be kind of vague at times but he did say the house was always cold even in the middle of summer.' Jenna bent down and ruffled the dog's ears.

'And what do you think?'

'Sorry?' she looked up and frowned.

'Well, you're the expert here.'

Jenna chewed at her bottom lip, all the things she knew about the area where specifics, hard concrete facts dug up over a two-year period. Now he was asking for her opinion and opinions and facts where very different animals.

'Well I've been up here a few times on my own and I know what he means about the place being cold. The last time I couldn't even go in,' she paused, 'I remember standing at the door telling myself I was an idiot but it didn't make any difference, I still couldn't force myself to do it.'

'I noticed the chill yesterday.'

'Really!' she looked up her excitement mounting.

'Mm, I mean, it's not uncommon in empty houses, they're open to the elements, there's no heating and half the slates are missing off the roof.'

'I guess,' the excitement evaporated.

'The thing is to keep an open mind; I mean, none of this is an exact science.'

Jenna nodded. 'Of course.'

'Right I'm going to take another look around, do you want to come?'

'Is that OK, I mean, I don't want to get in the way or anything?'

'Look, if it wasn't for you then I wouldn't even be here.'

She felt a rush of pride. 'If you're sure?'

'I'm positive.'

They moved towards the house along a path of flattened grass. The dog ran ahead sniffing at an old gorse bush, flush with yellow blossom. Fossey could tell that at one time the garden had been looked after, 'forget-me-nots mingled in with the tall grass, there was even an ancient piece of trellis with a rose wrapped tight around the structure fighting a battle of supremacy with the dreaded ragweed.

Reaching into his pocket, he pulled out a small Maglite. 'I should have brought this with me yesterday it would have made things a lot easier.' Flicking on the torch, he pushed the door open and stepped into the room.

Jenna followed close behind. 'God it smells worse than ever in here.'

Seemingly oblivious to the stench, Fossey shone the torch around the room. In one corner, an old chair, bristling with mildew, had been tipped onto its side revealing the rusting springs beneath. The floor was littered with fallen plaster and yellow sacks with *'Warburton's quality feed'* stencilled onto the plastic. He flicked the beam towards the ceiling revealing places where the wooden latticework had become visible after the plaster had become dislodged and dropped to the floor. Moving the beam to the right he picked out a door, the black paint peeling off in long curling strips.

He could hear Jenna following as he crunched across the room. The dog had its nose to the crack at the bottom of the door, its sides puffing in and out as he gave a brisk yap and backed away, hackles rising.

For the first time Fossey began to have doubts about having Jenna with him. This place didn't feel right, the night before when he'd committed his experience to the computer he'd read it back a few times and an uncertainty had set in. Perhaps he had embellished the experience, yet now he was back, those doubts were beginning to diminish.

He looked over his shoulder; Jenna looked wide-eyed and nervous in the gloom.

'You OK?'

She nodded in response and tried to smile.

Turning back to the door, he made a decision, twisting the end of the torch the light began to fade and he heard Jenna draw a sharp breath.

'It looks like the batteries are on their way out,' he turned, 'Come on, I've got a spare set in the car,' he watched the look of relief sweep across her face as they retraced their steps.

'I'll leave the door open; it might let some of the stink out,' she said as they crossed the threshold.

Once outside, he shielded his eyes against the glare of the sun and looked toward the hills. He could see dense woodland, a dark green mass contrasting with the purple of the heather. Deep in amongst the trees he spotted the top of a conical tower the slate roof shining gunmetal grey in the sun.

'Is that the needle house?'

Jenna followed his gaze. 'Yeah that's it.'

'If we have the time I'd like to take a closer look at it.'

'No problem.'

He sighed. 'It seems a long way to go back to the car just for some batteries.'

'I can go if you like.'

'No it's OK, I'll nip back inside and have a quick look around, are you OK out here for a few minutes? It's just that if the torch does give up the ghost then I think it's best if we're not both in there at the same time.'

'You mean you want me to like stand guard or something?'

'Would you mind?'

'No that's fine,' she replied a little too quickly and then blushed.

'Right, I'll be as quick as I can.'

'Don't worry there's no rush.'

Fossey smiled. 'Come on, T.'

She watched as they disappeared back into the gloom.

This time he didn't bother with the preliminaries, heading straight to the door he pushed it open.

Cool air swept out to meet him and he reminded himself not to get carried away, the front door was open and the air was being drawn through like smoke up a chimney, a simple explanation. He moved into the kitchen as the light picked out various objects. A large table stood in the centre of the room and on its surface stood an old cracked mug that was almost unrecognisable, cocooned beneath a thick spider's web. A handful of discarded six-inch nails had been scattered across the dusty surface and an ancient transistor radio stood upright, its innards trailing behind on the table top like some small dismembered animal. Shining the beam to the left, he could see the black bulk of an ancient Aga. Yesterday Ronnie's trousers had been held in place with a length of bailer twine and yet here, rusting away in the dark, was an appliance which was probably worth a couple of grand of anyone's money.

'T, where are you boy?'

Silence, then a scratching sound coming from the far corner of the room, he strode forward and found the dog hidden behind the bulk of an old welsh dresser the wood swollen with damp.

'What have you got there?'

The dog whined and backed off, Fossey crouched on his haunches, the clothes had been screwed up into a bundle, he could see the pale blue of the jeans and a washed out red T-shirt. He looked at the dog, its ears were plastered close to the head, panting, wide-eyed as if he had just spent an hour chasing the neighbour's cat. Fossey reached out and the animal scuttled backwards, a low whine building in its throat, tongue lolling. Fossey shifted his feet and the sole of his shoe came up with a tacky stretching sound. He trained the light onto the floor; he was standing in the middle of a pool of dark liquid, his fingers hovered over the stain, his eyes drawn back to the clothing. T barked once, a sound full of urgent panic, his claws scrabbled on the stone flags as he tried to gain a hold, then he bolted for the door.

A few seconds later, he heard Jenna; her voice muffled by the thick stone walls.

'Are you alright, Mr Foss...Patrick?'

'I'm fine, Jenna, I won't be a minute!' he shouted before turning back to the stain.

Fossey dipped his finger and brought the torch to bear on his fingertip, even in the gloom he could see the crimson-turned-almost-black.

Rising quickly he headed across the room, as he reached the door he flicked off the torch, dropped it into his pocket and pulled out his mobile.

Jenna was still standing about twenty feet from the house, a look of puzzled concern on her face, the small dog held tightly in her arms.

'Are you OK?'

Fossey swished through the tall grass, punching in the numbers as he walked towards her. 'I think we have a problem, Jenna.'

GHOST TOWN.

Ten minutes later, Lasser pulled into the station car park, a frown of confusion creasing his brow. Usually at this time of day, you would have to drive around a few times until you found somewhere to park, yet today the large square of tarmac was deserted. He parked in a bay, climbed out and headed towards the main entrance, half expecting to see a tumbleweed blow past. The building itself was relatively new, built on the edge of town, but in Lasser's opinion it looked more like an industrial unit than a police headquarters.

Pushing through the door, he stopped to enjoy the air-conditioned atmosphere before walking across to reception. Colin Meadows sat behind the front desk, his nose buried in The Enquirer.

'Glad to see you're keeping abreast of current affairs, Colin.'

Meadows had the decency to blush; the magazine vanished into an open drawer.

'Sorry, boss.'

'Don't apologise, it makes a refreshing change to see someone reading a quality piece of investigative journalism. When Barry's on duty it's the Times or the Daily Mail,' he looked around at the empty room, normally you'd expect to find at least one thug slouched in one of the lemon coloured plastic chairs.

'How come it's so quiet around here?'

'Haven't you heard?'

Lasser felt the frown resurface. 'Heard what?'

'Everyone's up at Rivington; apparently there's been a murder,' he whispered like some gossipmonger who doesn't really like to spread rumours. 'Some bloke rang in stating he'd found a pile of blood-stained clothing in an old farmhouse. WPC Harper went to check it out and since then it's been bedlam.'

'Who took the initial call?'

Colin looked bemused. 'I did.'

45

‘So, did this ‘bloke’ leave his name?’

‘Er yes, yes he did.’

Lasser began to tap his fingers on the desk in mounting frustration. With idiots like Meadows and those plastic plods who rode around town on mountain bikes topping up their tans it was a wonder the police force still existed in any meaningful fashion.

Meadows rummaged around among a small pile of paperwork, paused for a moment, stuck on a pair of glasses, and began to go through the stack a second time.

‘Ah here we are, the man’s name was Fossey.’

Lasser leant across the desk and plucked the paper from Meadows’ hand.

‘Fossey!’

‘Yeah, first name….’

‘Patrick.’

Meadows frowned. ‘Do you know him?’

Lasser ignored the question and studied the logging details.

‘This call came in over four hours ago!’

Meadows began to look uncomfortable. ‘That’s right.’

‘So, why didn’t you let me know about it?’

‘Well you were already out on a job and I thought…’

‘Look, I am not a frigging community bobby, I have no interest whatsoever in forging meaningful links with thieving little scrotes, do you follow me?’

Meadows blanched. ‘Yes, but...’

‘When you get a call like this, as a senior officer I expect to be informed immediately, not in a few hours or when it suits you.’

He threw the paper across the desk, Meadows made a grab for it and missed, swallowing he bent to retrieve it. When he looked up Lasser had vanished, the door hissing quietly shut on its hydraulic hinges.

Lasser stormed across the car park, his mind full of conspiracy theories. Perhaps Meadows had been acting on orders from Hopkins to keep him in the dark; he wouldn't put it past the bastard.

He slid behind the wheel, the heat inside the car matching his mood. Maybe he should just head for home, but the name Patrick Fossey had stirred his curiosity.

Twelve months earlier he'd been forced to go on one of those personal development seminars he despised so much, Fossey had been the guest speaker.

Lasser had attended the seminar with the intention of hating every minute of it, he only hoped there'd be a chance to do some heckling and maybe get pissed in the free bar.

He'd expected all the usual tosh, 'people commit crime because they come from underprivileged backgrounds, broken homes, they're not responsible for their actions. Blah, blah, blah '

However, to his surprise, Fossey had been different; Oh, some of the rhetoric included the usual banal bullshit. Yet he'd also spoken about choices, he had been forceful in his defence of the victims and scathing about some of Lasser's superiors, which he had to admit made a refreshing change from all the arse licking that usually went on at these events. Despite his best intentions, he had begun to warm to the man. By the wonders of modern technology, he had discovered that Fossey had helped a couple of forces in the past in tracking down one or two 'colourful characters.'

So, what was a top shrink doing in an old farmhouse out in the middle of nowhere?

Starting the car, he headed off the car park and paused at the junction; turning left, meant heading for home for another night of cheap beer and crap television. Lasser lit another cigarette and turned right. Why should Hopkins be the one to have all the fun?

47

SOMETHING'S UP

Ronnie loitered on the car park of the Radfield Arms, watching as another police car thundered past, lights flashing, and sirens wailing. That was the third in less than five minutes, he checked his battered old Timex; Susan should be here any minute now.

A plain white transit rounded the corner and shot past.

Pulling the stump of a cigarette from his pocket he lit up, ruing a government who made old men stand outside in all weathers just to have a bloody fag.

At the sound of tyres on gravel he looked up, Susan waved through the Land Rover window; dropping the cigarette, he trudged over and climbed in.

'Sorry I'm a bit late, Dad, the traffic's been horrendous,' she pushed a strand of hair behind her ear.

'It's alright, love.'

'How are Bert and Sam?'

'Same as always,' he replied. 'Ere, Sue, you haven't noticed a load of cop cars knocking about have you?'

Flicking on the indicator, she pulled back onto the road. 'No. Why?'

'Well, four have gone past in the last five minutes and it looked like they were in a hell of a rush.'

'Maybe there's been an accident; you know what folk are like on this road, especially on a Saturday afternoon.'

'Aye I thought of that,' Ronnie paused and scratched his chin. 'But there were no fire engines or ambulance, just police cars.'

Susan slowed for a bad bend and then accelerated as the road straightened. They both heard the siren at the same time. Susan glanced in the mirror, her eyes widening in alarm, she yanked the wheel sharply to the left as the police car overtook at high speed. The hedge side brambles scraped down the side of the Land Rover as the car disappeared along the winding road.

'Daft bastard!' Ronnie straightened his glasses, yanked a hankie from his pocket, and mopped his sweating brow.

'Are you alright, Dad?'

'Aye, love, no thanks to that idiot.'

Susan swallowed down the panic. 'You were right about them being in a rush.'

'Driving like that it wouldn't surprise me if we found the daft bugger arse up in a ditch.'

Susan checked the mirror, before carefully pulling back onto the road, a moment later her phone began to twitter.

'Can you get that, Dad?'

Ronnie fumbled in the foot well, retrieved Susan's bag and rummaged through the contents before pulling out the phone.

'It's the green button.'

'I know that, lass.' he slapped the phone to his ear. 'Now then, Jenna love, did he turn up?'

Susan indicated and turned right onto a narrow lane.

'You bloody what!' Ronnie's voice was cracked with disbelief.

Susan hit the brakes, a bag of shopping fell off the back seat and clattered to the floor.

'What's the matter?'

Ronnie held up a hand as he listened to his granddaughter, Susan watched nervously as his eyes grew wide in shock.

'Dad?'

'Shush! Go on, Jenna love, I'm listening.'

Susan snatched on the handbrake.

'Listen, Dad, I don't know what's going on but you….'

'Right, love, we're on our way.'

Ronnie stabbed a gnarled finger at the off button and turned to his daughter.

'You had best get up to the old house, love.'

'Why, what's happened?'

'I'm not really sure but that's where all the police are heading.'

'Is Jenna OK?' Susan could feel the panic flare in her chest.

'Aye, love, she's fine, but she thinks some bugger's been murdered up there.'

'Murdered?'

'Aye, come on, love, get your foot down.' Ronnie urged, a flush of colour rising in his grizzled cheeks.

Susan released the handbrake and did as he asked.

SURPRISED.

He stood on the edge of the woods and watched as the police car pulled up behind the Range Rover, the blue lights turning lazily in the heat haze. A frown of confusion flitted across his face. He had been prepared to be patient; prepared for the long game, the last thing he had expected to see was this. Lifting the field glasses he trained them at the house, the image blurred for a moment and then the house sprang into view. Sweeping slowly to the right he spotted the man as he made his way toward the septic tank. A moment later, a dark-haired WPC came into view and followed him along the path. Reaching down he stroked the dog's ears, the German Shepherd licked the back of his hand, warm and wet.

The girl looked to be about sixteen, long blonde hair framing a face that in a couple of years' time would be stunning.

It was tempting to stay and watch the proceedings, though caution told him to distance himself from the area, nothing would be gained by staying longer. Although the police would not find a body, they'd obviously found enough to get them interested.

He turned and immediately spotted the old man in the yellow jacket, a small sheltie on a wandering lead standing by his side; both man and dog looked directly at him.

'Afternoon,' he raised a friendly hand and began slowly to make his way toward them, his own dog tight against his right leg. 'Lovely day, isn't it?'

The man was in his sixties dressed as if he were expecting some kind of heavy thunderstorm. His waterproof jacket and stout walking boots at odds with the old flat cap perched on top of his head.

Sunlight dappled down between the huge trees, casting light and shadows. As he approached, the old walker visibly tightened his hand on the lead, a worried frown crinkling his forehead.

'Er yes, yes it's grand,' he licked his lips.

The killer smiled warmly.

'Hello, boy,' he bent and offered the back of his hand to the small dog.

'It's a 'she' actually.'

'Oh right, sorry about that, old girl,' his eyes raked the surrounding area.

'Is something going on at the old house?'

'What makes you think that?'

'It's just that I thought I heard a police siren,' he smiled, his white dentures looking at odds against the grey pallor of his skin.

'Well, I suppose you could say that. I was just watching through my glasses but then again you knew that already didn't you?'

The old man blinked, looking perplexed at the admission. 'I must admit I did wonder what you were doing'

'Of course you did,' his eyes made another sweep of the trees. 'And I could say I was bird watching but you wouldn't quite believe me would you?'

The dog walker swallowed. 'Right well I'd better be going, it's getting late,' he gave the lead a tug and the sheltie stood and shook itself.

'If you must know they're looking for a body.'

The old man stopped and turned. 'Excuse me?'

'Give it another ten minutes and this place will be crawling with the law.'

'Look, this really is none of my business.'

'So, if we go our separate ways, I can rely on you to keep your mouth, shut can I?'

'I...,' the old man paused as if he were giving the question some serious consideration. Then he turned and began to run, dragging the hapless dog with him, his new boots swishing through last years' fallen leaves.

The man made one last careful sweep of the area then moved forward.

A couple of seconds later the old rambler felt an enormous weight hit him from behind. He slammed to the ground, the dog lead slipping from his fingers, dazed and winded, his asthma kicked in immediately.

'I promise I won't say anything,' he managed to utter, though his throat seemed to have shrunk to the size of a drinking straw.

The killer flipped him over and knelt by his side, pulling a plastic carrier bag from his pocket. 'I know you won't, old cock,' he slipped the bag over the man's head, pulling it down with a sharp tug. Then he placed his hands loosely around the scrawny throat, applying gentle pressure.

Thomas Kitts had always thought himself a fit man, he would often sneer at Martha, his wife, as she sat eating her chocolates, pointing out a heart attack was on its way if she carried on gorging herself. He, on the other hand could walk for miles, he could still ride his bike he was active!

As the hands closed around his throat and the bag cut off his air, he realised that it was all a lie, his virility was an illusion. His struggles were ineffectual; he tried to lash out with his fists, though his body knew the truth that his mind had kept hidden.

He took a huge shuddering breath and the plastic moulded itself to his screaming mouth.

Twenty seconds later, it was over.

The man waited a full minute, his eyes scanning the trees as he counted down the seconds. His own dog eyed the sheltie as it ran between the trees, the long lead trailing in its wake.

When he pulled the bag free, he had to laugh at the stencilled motto, *'every little helps'* how true he thought as he slipped the carrier bag back into his pocket.

I DON'T KNOW

'What's happening?' Jenna was standing by the Range Rover as another white transit van bounced across the field heading toward the house. The police were everywhere.

'Forensics are going in now.' Fossey nodded towards a group of men struggling their way into white paper boiler suits.

Jenna chewed at a fingernail. 'I managed to get in touch with Mum, she's on her way.'

'Good,' he paused, 'look maybe we should make our way to the bottom of the field and wait for her there.'

'OK, what shall I do about T?'

'Leave him in the car; he'll go to sleep.'

Jenna frowned. 'Can't we drive down?'

'I'm afraid not, the police don't want anything moved.'

Jenna looked puzzled. 'But why, I mean, your car's not in the way or anything?'

'No, but they want to check it over.'

'But why would they want to do something like that?'

He could hear the confusion in her voice.

'Well, it appears it's because I was up here yesterday.'

She couldn't believe what she was hearing. *'They think you're a suspect?'*

Fossey smiled. 'The police are paid to be suspicious, Jenna.'

'But didn't you tell them that my grandad was with you?'

'Yes, but he didn't actually come into the house with me, he stayed outside.'

'But if you were guilty of anything,' she said. 'Why would you call the police to report it? I mean, it's ridiculous.'

'Look it'll all get cleared up quickly enough, let's go and wait for your mum OK.'

Jenna nodded reluctantly, her mind befuddled. 'OK'.

They moved away from the car and headed down the path. The police officer who had responded to the initial call was standing by her car in conversation with a male colleague.

Jenna glared at the woman as they walked past, throwing her daggers.

'What did your mother have to say when you told her what was going on?'

'I didn't get to speak to her; it was my grandad I told.'

'And what did he say?'

'Not much, I think he was in shock.'

'I'm not surprised.'

As they made their way across the field, Jenna spotted the familiar dark green Land Rover approaching along the lane. 'They're here,' she set off running toward the approaching car.

By the time Fossey arrived, Ronnie and Susan were out of the vehicle and Jenna was in full hyperactive mode trying to explain everything at once.

'Calm down, Jenna, love.' Ronnie's cap was askew, his eyes wide.

'Calm down! Look, Grandad, there might be a dead body in the house,' she pointed toward the dilapidated structure. *'There might be a murderer watching us right now.'*

Ronnie looked uneasily toward the mass of trees on the hillside. 'Bloody hell, Jenna, you've got a vivid imagination.'

'Well, we don't know, the killer could be anywhere.'

'Afternoon, Susan,' Fossey said as he approached.

'Good afternoon, Patrick, this is awful.'

Jenna eyed her mother, since when did she get to call him Patrick?

'What the bloody hell's happened? Our Jenna said summat about some blood-stained clothes?' Ronnie asked.

'Patrick found them in the kitchen.' Jenna said, trying her best to appear in control of her emotions.

'Under normal circumstances I wouldn't have bothered ringing the police. After all, you get people squatting in old empty properties all the time and they leave all sorts of rubbish behind.'

Ronnie grunted. 'Tell me about it, there was a load of them traveller types parked on a bit of waste land in Horwich last year, never seen such a bloody mess.'

Susan suddenly looked hopeful. 'Perhaps that's what it is. I mean, we hardly ever come up here anymore, anyone could have been living in there, and we'd never have known.'

Fossey pursed his lips. 'I don't think so.'

She placed a protective arm around her daughter. 'So, what are the police doing now?'

'The forensic team have gone in,' Jenna said.

'Dear God.'

'Aye it's a bugger.' Ronnie pushed the cap back onto his head.

'Right, well there's nothing we can do here and I refuse to just stand around like some morbid rubber-necker.'

Jenna looked at her mum in alarm. 'But we can't just go home and pretend this isn't happening.'

'Listen, Jenna, the last thing the police need are spectators cluttering up the place. Besides, we need to get back and tell your dad what's happened.'

'You go, we'll wait here.'

Susan shook her head. 'I don't think so, young lady; you're coming home with us.'

'Mr Fossey, a word, now.' Detective Hopkins, was standing twenty feet away, he crooked a finger beckoning him over.

'Fascist.' Jenna hissed, as Susan looked at her daughter in shocked surprise.

'I'm on my way.' Fossey turned his back on the officer. 'Look, Susan, when they've finished with me would it be OK if I called in on my way home, just to let you know what's going on.'

'Of course that would be fine.'
'But, Mum…'
'Come on, Jenna, home.'
She cringed, her mother was treating her like a child, it was excruciating.
'Fossey!' This time there was no mistaking the anger in the voice; Hopkins was rapidly losing his patience.
Fossey raised an eyebrow and smiled. 'Hopefully I won't be long, but if it gets too late I'll ring in the morning.'
Jenna felt a strange panic rising in her chest. 'I won't be going to bed early, not after this.'
Susan looked out toward the old house and shivered. 'I agree, just call, it doesn't matter about the time.'
'OK, I'll see you all later,' he turned and headed toward Hopkins.
'How come they want to talk to him?' Ronnie whispered.
'Because they're idiots, Grandad,' she sighed in frustration. 'Apparently, they want to know what he was doing up here yesterday.'
'But I was with him, he weren't on his own.'
'He was when he went into the house.'
'So he was,' Ronnie sounded surprised as if he had just born witness to some miraculous insight.
'Oh for God's sake don't you start as well!' For some unfathomable reason she felt close to tears.
Susan squeezed her shoulder. 'Come on, sweetheart, let's get you home.'
Jenna sat on the cramped back seat of the van surrounded by spilled shopping; as they drove away, she could see Patrick, his figure distorted through a shimmering mass of unshed tears.

'So, you're telling me you were up here alone with a seventeen-year-old girl researching for some *'book'* you're writing?' Hopkins voice was laden with innuendo.

'That's correct.'

'Nice work if you can get it, Mr Fossey.'

He didn't bother with a reply he didn't see the point.

'And WPC Harper informs me that you were also up here yesterday.'

'Yes.'

Hopkins scowled and then tried to smile, though it was obvious he had the kind of face that found smiling difficult. 'You're a writer?'

'Amongst other things,' he replied.

'I take it it's not a full time occupation?'

Fossey shrugged. 'It's getting to be that way.'

'So, what is it you do exactly Mr Fossey?'

'I'm a Criminal Psychologist.'

For a fraction of a second, Hopkins eyes widened in surprise. 'I see, so this research you're doing is of an academic nature.'

'Of a fashion.'

Hopkins looked flustered, a look of confusion flashed across his face. As a representative of the law he was duty bound to be in charge, he asked the questions, he applied the pressure. However, Fossey could see the other facet of the man's character, the one that said here is a fellow professional, a 'Criminal Psychologist' no less, and all of a sudden the man was out of his comfort zone.

Hopkins cleared his throat. 'Right then, Mr Fossey, I don't think we need keep you any longer.'

'If you don't mind I'd like to hang on for a while.'

Hopkins gave a curt nod. 'Of course, though I must ask you to keep clear of the crime scene.'

A car horn bleated in the distance and Hopkins turned as a dark blue Audi bounced its way along the rutted path, dust flying in its wake.

Hopkins grunted, a sound thick with derision.

Fossey wandered over to the Range Rover to check on the dog, as expected T was curled up on the front seat, dead to the world.

When he looked back, Hopkins was having a heated conversation with the new arrival, both men stabbing fingers at one another. The newcomer laughed with more than a hint of sarcasm and then headed over toward Fossey shaking his head as he approached.

'Patrick Fossey, well I never,' he smiled and thrust out a hand. 'You don't know me but I attended one of your seminars last year.'

'Oh right.'

'So, what's gone on here then?' he hooked a thumb over his shoulder.

'I take it Detective Hopkins hasn't briefed you?' Fossey asked.

Lasser grinned. 'Not as such.'

Hopkins went stomping past, his face flushed with anger. *'Harper, with me now!'* he bellowed.

WPC Harper leapt from her car and hurried past.

'Take no notice, Cathy, he's hormonal.' Lasser said with a smile.

She grinned nervously as she jogged toward the house.

Lasser looked around and drew in a deep breath as if enjoying the country air. 'So, you found some blood-stained clothing?'

'I think so.'

'You mean you're not sure?'

Fossey shrugged. 'Ninety percent sure but then again I could be wrong.'

'Oh I doubt that. I wouldn't imagine you're the kind of bloke who'd drag us out if you weren't certain of your facts,' he fiddled with the cigarettes in his pocket. 'I saw a few of our boys around the back of the house, you have any idea what they are looking for?'

Fossey explained about walking around the house with WPC Harper, and finding the septic tank, the surface covered with green algae apart from a small circle where black water shone through like dark beer.

'So, you think something's been dumped in the tank?'

'I never said that.'

'Then why mention it?'

Fossey didn't reply.

Lasser grinned. 'Right, well I'm going to take a look around, you care to join me?'

'I've already been warned about keeping clear of the house.'

'Hopkins can hardly refuse the help of a fellow officer and an eminent shrink, now can he?'

They made their way to the house, as they crossed the threshold Lasser waved a hand under his nose. 'I'm not too keen on the air freshener,' he mumbled.

The kitchen was a hive of activity, the boards had been removed from the window, an electric cable threaded its way over the windowsill, a moment later they heard the rumble of a small generator, and the gloomy space was suddenly flooded with stark white light.

One of the paper suited forensic team headed toward them carrying a large plastic evidence bag.

'Hello, Carl mate, what have you got there?'

Carl stopped and opened the bag. Lasser peered inside.

'T-shirt, jeans and a pair of trainers' Carl said.

'What size?' Fossey asked.

The man looked at him quizzically over the top of his paper mask.

Lasser nodded. 'It's alright, Carl, he's almost one of us.'

'Well, according to the label in the shirt it's a size ten and the jeans are a twenty-eight inch waist.'

'Male or female.' Lasser asked.

'Hard to tell, I mean, you know what kids are like today, half the time you don't know who's who.'

Lasser nodded in understanding. 'Where's Hopkins?'

'He's outside checking out the septic tank.'

'I can't think of anyone more suited for the job.'

Above the mask, Carl's eyes crinkled in amusement. Lasser crossed the room swerving to avoid the huge table, when he saw the stain on the floor he stopped.

'That is a lot of blood.'

'Now you see why I made the call.'

'I certainly do,' he looked around the room. 'It doesn't look like anyone's been using this place to squat.'

'Not unless they're a very tidy individual.' Fossey replied.

Lasser grunted in response. 'Right, let's go and see how my esteemed colleague's shaping up.'

Outside, the heat of the day was slowly leaking away, the sun wavered low in the sky bathing the surrounding fields in peach infused light.

Hopkins had managed to remain downwind of the stink. Harper was leaning over the wall attempting to dredge the tank with a long length of rope that presumably had some form of hook attached to the end.

Lasser sighed. 'They should have a vacuum pump up here. I mean, this is like something out of the bloody dark ages,' he turned to look at Fossey. 'Do you think there's anything in there?'

'You mean a body?'

'Yeah.'

Fossey thought for a moment. 'It just seems strange.'

'What does?'

'Well, if someone has been killed up here, then why leave the clothes behind. I mean, theres no evidence of a body, so we have to presume it's been removed somewhere...'

'The tank?'

'Possibly, but why leave the clothes behind in the first place. I mean, if you're going to commit a murder then you dump the clothes with the body or simply leave the body in the house'

'That makes sense.'

'I think I have something, sir!' Harper was pulling hard on the rope, leaning back slightly to take the strain.

'Spenner, don't just stand there give her a lift.' Hopkins bellowed.

PC Spenner looked appalled at the prospect. 'But I've no gloves, sir.'

Lasser headed back into the kitchen, grabbed a couple of the plastic sacks from the floor, and strode down the path folding the sacks as he went.

Hopkins scowled as Lasser grabbed the rope and started to pull. Gradually the cable began to appear over the wall, long strands of thick green slime dragged up by the nylon cord plopped onto the grass.

After a few seconds the bag appeared, it teetered on the top of the wall then slid onto the floor spilling the contents onto the grass.

'Fuck me.' Lasser hissed, stepping back quickly as the blue grey mass slithered free of the sack. Harper began to retch, letting go of the rope she lifted a hand to cover her mouth, when she realised she was still wearing the glove she heaved even more.

'Not on the bloody crime scene!' Hopkins screamed.

Harper scuttled away to a patch of nettles and brought up the spaghetti bolognaise she'd had the night before.

Dropping the rope, Lasser moved forward, it was eerie, but the mass looked like a living thing, as if they'd dredged up some alien creature from the bottom of some primordial swamp. He knew it was an optical illusion but to Lasser it appeared to pulse and squirm in the late afternoon sun.

'Well, Charlie, I don't know about you but it'll be a while before I order the sea food platter again.'

Hopkins glared at his colleague.

Fossey crouched and studied the grotesque mess. The intestines coiled together as if still encased in the stomach cavity, the greyish colour mottled by the filthy water that had seeped into the sack. Fossey frowned as he peered closer, a small circular disk glinted up at him, and he reached out a hand.

'Here, what do you think you're doing?'

Ignoring Hopkins, he gingerly plucked it free.

'What've you got?' Lasser asked.

Fossey held it out, the disk lying flat in the palm of his hand.

'Looks like a button to me.' Fossey replied.

Lasser grinned and pulled a small evidence bag from his pocket, he held it out and Fossey dropped it into the plastic sleeve.

Lasser stood up and gave it a shake. 'Look, Charlie, do you think it could be a clue?'

WHO KNOWS?

By the time Fossey pulled up in front of the farmhouse, it was almost dark.

He'd left the crime scene just as reinforcements had begun to arrive. The small generator working overtime as a dozen halogen lights were rigged up.

Hopkins had been busy marshalling the troops, whilst Lasser took a back seat, standing with Fossey by the side of the Range Rover smoking a cigarette.

'He's a marvel to behold isn't he?' he said with a smirk, watching as Hopkins bollocked Paul Collins, the dog handler, because the animal had decided to take a dump right under his nose. It was almost as if the dog was passing judgment on the proceedings.

'Are you sticking around?' Fossey asked.

'By rights I should have been home,' he checked his watch, 'two hours ago. Though it's not often we get something as exciting as this turning up. Besides, I might get a few brownie points for acting 'above and beyond.'

'You mean you're waiting to see if Hopkins implodes?'

'That obvious is it?'

'Only to the trained eye.'

Lasser laughed aloud. 'Anyway it's been nice meeting you, Patrick.'

'Likewise,' Fossey had started the engine and then handed a card to Lasser. 'Just in case you need me for anything.'

'I might take you up on that.'

The sun was wobbling to earth as Fossey parked by the side of the tractor its dull bulk casting a long shadow.

For a moment, he stood there enjoying the silence, and the smell of cut grass and lavender on the warm evening air.

As soon as the front door opened, a security light blinked into life. Jenna headed toward him in a way that was not quite running but was too hurried to be called a brisk walk. Susan appeared in the doorway and stood watching them both.

'What's happened, have they found anything?' Jenna asked, her face etched with concern.

'Come inside, the kettles just boiled.'

Jenna spun around in annoyance but her mum had vanished back inside.

'Come on, it's better if I let you all know what's happened.'

'Oh yeah of course.'

Ronnie was sitting at the large kitchen table, drumming his gnarled fingers on its surface; the flat cap perched on the top of his head. He still wore his old suit jacket, as if he had just come in or was in the process of going out somewhere.

Jenna's father stood at the sink washing his hands.

'So, lad, what's happened?' Ronnie asked.

Jenna chewed a fingernail looking anxiously at Fossey.

'The police are still there.'

David turned from the sink drying his hands on a tea towel. 'But have they actually found anything?'

Fossey paused for a moment. 'Well….

'They have, they've found a body. I just knew it!' Jenna covered her mouth with a shaking hand.

'Be quiet, Jenna, let the man finish,' David snapped.

She glared across the room at her father and then resumed chewing her nails into extinction.

'Well, no, they haven't actually found a body.'

'So, why are they still up there?' Ronnie asked with a frown.

Fossey sighed wondering how best to break the news. Jenna was a smart girl but she was still only seventeen.

'It's alright Patrick we'd like to know.' Susan moved to Jenna's side, her hands clasped together.

'They've found some remains...'

Jenna thrust her hands into the pockets of her jeans. *'Oh God!'*

'Forensics have removed them for analysis.'

'But they might not be human remains?' David asked hopefully.

'It's a possibility.'

'But you think they are?' Susan asked.

'In all honesty, yes,' he didn't see the point in keeping the details to himself. It had happened on their land and in his opinion that gave them the right to know as much as possible.

Ronnie lit a smoke, this time a full one that he pulled from a battered looking cigarette tin. 'I knew we should have flattened that place, didn't I keep saying it, David?'

David glared at his father-in-law. 'All right, Ronnie, don't start going on about it now.'

'But I kept saying some bugger would end up having an accident. I mean, all it needs is some yobbo to break a leg in there and they could sue the bloody arse of us.'

Jenna couldn't believe what she was hearing. 'For God's sake, Grandad, listen to you, this isn't someone having an *accident*. It's not some *little kid* messing about and getting hurt. Someone's been murdered and all you can talk about is how much it *could cost us*!'

Ronnie looked flustered. 'I didn't mean it like that, love. But let's face it if we had knocked the owd place down then summat like this wouldn't have happened.'

Susan waved a dismissive hand. 'Let's not get into all that. Now would you like tea or coffee, Patrick?'

'Well, if you don't mind I'll be going. I just called round to let you know the situation,' he paused. 'Besides, it's been a long day.'

'Of course, and thanks for calling.'

'No problem,' he turned to Jenna. 'I'll take a look at the research and ring you in a couple of days if that's OK?'

Despite the events of the last few hours, Jenna found herself smiling. 'That would be good.'

'Do me a favour, Jenna, and empty the dryer will you, your dad's overalls should be dry by now.'

She looked at her mother as if she had just asked her to clean out the chicken shed. *'Me!'*

Susan raised an eyebrow. 'Honestly, Patrick, anyone would think she was a stroppy teenager.'

Jenna glared and marked it down as another insult she would have to bring to her parents attention.

Fossey smiled. 'Right, I'll see you all soon.'

He headed to the door with Susan close on his heels.

Outside the scent of heather was stronger than ever, Fossey saw the fleeting form of a bat zip through the security light.

When they reached the car, he turned. 'Look, Susan, sometime over the next couple of days I would imagine the police will be paying you a visit.'

'I don't doubt it.'

'If it's someone called Hopkins then keep your answers brief.'

She frowned. 'We've nothing to hide.'

'I realise that, it's just that he'll start with the premise that you do.'

'I see.'

He climbed into the car and she held the door open, resting her hand on handle. 'When you said they found remains what exactly did you mean?'

'Well, I didn't like to go into too much detail not with Jenna there.'

'I thought as much.'

'They found body parts in an old grain sack.'

This time she emulated her daughter by placing a hand over her mouth. 'My God and they actually found these things in the house?'

'No,' he paused, 'they were in the septic tank.'

Susan Fotheringay felt the colour drain from her face; her legs suddenly seemed fragile as if incapable of supporting her weight. She shivered, crossing her arms over her chest.

'And the blood stain you found looked fresh?'

'I'm afraid so. Look you go on in, I'll watch you from here.'

She looked out into the dark; beyond the cone of the security light everything appeared indistinct, shadows layered upon shadows. Within the space of a couple of hours everything that was familiar to her had been fundamentally altered and she didn't like it one bit.

'OK and thanks again for calling.'

'Not a problem, and if I find out anything more then I'll let you know straight away.'

She nodded before turning and retracing her steps to the front door, a journey she'd made a thousand times day and night. The dark had never bothered her before, yet now she felt an unfamiliar sense of apprehension slide into place. A feeling that made its home in her mind like a wanderer returning home after a long exile, kicking off his walking boots and settling down into the comfortable armchair. Home at last.

NO POINT

Lasser hung around until half ten, up since six the soggy egg Mcmuffin he'd consumed that morning was no more than a distant memory. He said his goodbyes, ignoring the smug look of satisfaction on Hopkins face as he headed for the car.

Now he sat at home trying to concentrate on some banal programme about teenage pregnancies.

The young girl on the television chewed gum, bemoaning the fact that the council hadn't offered to house her in some new apartment.

It was strange how these people all seemed to have the same stamp about them, a certain something that didn't really have a name nevertheless, you knew it when it was in front of you.

She whined about the price of nappies and powdered baby milk, whinging about the fact that she couldn't go out with her mates the way she used to.

She looked like a female version of Kyle Connelly, he smiled, wondering if Donald Fletcher had been round to pay him a visit.

An image slipped into his mind, Billy Jones, a skinny runt of a kid last seen somewhere near Rivington. Carl had pointed out the clothes were on the small side, though it was inconclusive as to whether they belonged to a male or female, but still...

Lasser checked his watch, half past eleven.

Ringing the lab at this hour would be pointless, since the cutbacks, forensics ran on a shoestring budget. Unless it was a dire emergency, they clocked off at five like regular office workers. The only course of action was to find out what Billy had been wearing. He groaned, the thought of paying Sarah Jones a visit at midnight and having her answer the door in a baby doll nightie wasn't exactly a thrilling prospect.

Weighing up his options, he found that he didn't really have any, if his superiors discovered he'd not followed the correct procedure then he'd be in the shit and he could guarantee Sarah Jones would like nothing better than sticking the boot into some copper.

Grabbing his car keys, he pulled on his jacket and headed out of the front door. The warmth of the day had evaporated leaving a chill in the air and for a moment, he considered nipping back in to retrieve his overcoat. Then he remembered the stench that permeated around the Joneses' living room and decided he would rather freeze.

Fifteen minutes later, he was driving down Lancaster Road, the radio on, a late night *'love fest'* where everyone was either broken hearted or head over heels in love.

Pulling up outside the Joneses' house, he dragged himself out of the car, just as a hooded figure slid around the corner and stopped. Lasser cocked his head to one side.

'Can I help you, son?'

The figure approached slowly, a hand dipped into the pocket of his tracksuit and Lasser stiffened. Michael Jones slipped into the jaundiced cone of the streetlight, smiling as he pulled a bunch of keys from his pocket.

'Had you going then didn't I?'

Lasser heaved a sigh of relief. 'You could say that,' he looked at the boy, of all the Joneses' Michael was the only one who hadn't been in constant trouble with the law. Sarah would be disappointed with the way he was turning out.

'What you doing here?' Michael asked.

'I was just passing, so I thought I might as well call to see if Billy had returned home.' It sounded implausible, what sort of copper comes knocking on your door at midnight unless armed with a battering ram.

'Well, I've just nipped the garage for some cigs and he wasn't in when I left.'

'Listen, Michael, when I called round earlier I asked your mother if she had any idea what Billy was wearing.'

'Yeah I know, she mentioned some copper had called,' he paused and stuck a cigarette between his lips. 'I don't know why you're bothering. I mean, we're not the sort of family who have to be in by ten.'

'I spoke to Kyle Connelly earlier...'

Michael spat onto the pavement.

Lasser frowned. 'I thought you and Connelly were mates?'

'Not anymore.'

'Any particular reason for that?'

Michael shrugged. 'I just got tired of standing around on street corners like a five year old.'

'So, what do you do now?'

Michael flicked him a glance. 'I'm at college.'

Lasser raised his eyebrows in surprise. 'Really, studying what?'

'Information Technology.'

'Good for you,' he tried to keep the condescending tone from his voice but failed miserably.

'Right well I'd best get in,' Michael began to move away.

'So, you don't have any idea what he was wearing do you?'

'Knowing him it was probably skanky jeans and a reddish T-shirt. I mean, the dirty little sod never gets changed.'

Lasser felt his stomach slip. 'Right, thanks for that, Michael.'

'You should go home and get some kip, you look knackered.'

'Thanks for the advice, son.'

Michael headed off up the path, letting himself in and closing the door without looking back.

Shit. Lasser climbed back into the car and pondered what to do next. Jones had been right; he did feel bone weary, though if he simply returned home without getting this checked then he really would be in the brown stuff.

The clock on the dash said twelve forty, the station was ten minutes away, he could pass the information on and be home in bed by half one. Decision made, he got his foot down.

BURNING THE CANDLE

For the second night in a row, Jenna was finding it impossible to sleep. She watched as another minute clicked into infinity, marked by the digital clock on her bedside cabinet.

Clambering off the bed, she pulled the curtain back and slid the window open. Cool air flowed into the darkened bedroom, resting her elbows on the windowsill she peered out into the gloom.

For as long as she could remember this had been a nightly ritual, enjoying the silence and looking out at the stars, although tonight she could find no solace in this simple, familiar act. Sinister shadows seemed to pool around the front of the house, massing under the trees and bushes, an ideal spot for a killer to remain undetected. Jenna shuddered and pulled the window closed before swishing the curtains shut.

'Human remains,' those two words revolved around her brain, in the same way a cheesy pop song could become lodged in your head, going around and around for days until you felt like screaming.

Jenna stood in the middle of the room staring at nothing, her mind working overtime. With a huff she headed for the door and out onto the landing. For a moment, she considered turning on the light and then dismissed the idea as childish. She made her way downstairs, avoiding the steps that creaked and crossed the lounge in darkness, her hands bunched into fists in an effort to control the feeling of creeping unease that tracked her across the room.

The sliver of light under the kitchen door halted her in mid stride; her mind, already on high alert, provided the image of the lunatic in the kitchen, picking out the longest, sharpest knife from the rack. Turning it between his fingers, testing its weight, a maniacal grin smeared across his twisted mouth, *'cutting time'!*

The idea was preposterous; the house was locked and alarmed, no one could get in not unless they broke a window and she would have heard that, wouldn't she?

Gritting her teeth she crossed the room quickly, not giving her mind the opportunity to conjure up any more frightening scenarios, she thrust the door open ready to scream.

Her grandad turned from the sink and she let out a shuddering sigh of relief.

'Hello, love, can't you sleep either?'

She smiled, suddenly feeling foolish. 'Not a chance.'

'Want a brew?'

'Please.'

He flicked the kettle on, before spooning two sugars into a cup.

Jenna slid out a chair and sat down. 'I can't stop thinking about what's happened.'

'Aye, lass, I know what you mean.'

'And what did Patrick mean by human remains?'

Ronnie shrugged; he could take a guess but had no intention of telling Jenna.

'It could mean anything, love.'

She looked up at the ceiling. 'It doesn't seem like Mum and Dad are having trouble sleeping.'

'Aye well, your dad has to be up early, he's ploughing over near the woods today.'

She grunted in response, unconvinced. 'I wonder who it is.'

'Who, what is?'

'The body, Grandad, or whatever it is they've found.'

'Oh right,' he paused, 'well I dare say we'll find out soon enough.'

Headlights suddenly swept over the kitchen window, like twin searchlights probing into the room. Jenna looked at her grandad in surprise, then leapt to her feet and dashed across the room.

Ronnie dropped the spoon into the sink. 'Who the hell can that be at this time of night?'

Opening the door, she peered outside.

'It's the police!' she hissed, her voice full of nervous urgency.

Ronnie scowled and pushed himself away from the sink, grimacing as his lower back gave a twinge. By the time he reached the door Jenna had moved outside, the security light blinked on. Ronnie watched as a tall man walked into the cone of light and strode towards them.

'Good evening, I'm Detective Sergeant Hopkins,' he pulled out a wallet and flipped it open, holding it out for Ronnie to examine.

'It's no use showing me that, I've not got me glasses on.'

The wallet disappeared; he turned away from Ronnie as if he'd already decided any further conversation with the old man was pointless. 'I take it you're Jenna Fotheringay?'

She recognised him immediately as the Nazi who had been disrespectful to Patrick, she felt her hackles rise. 'That's right.'

'I need to speak to your parents.'

'They're in bed, they have to be up...'

'Yes well, I think it's probably best if you go and wake them.'

Ronnie grunted. 'Hang on, lad, what's this all about?'

'I don't know if you're aware, but there's been a serious crime committed inside a property that you own. Now I'm sorry if the possibility of a *murder* is inconvenient but we have certain procedures that must be followed,' he smiled, though his eyes looked anything but friendly.

'I suppose you'd best come in then.' Ronnie turned on his heels and went back into the kitchen.

For a couple of seconds Jenna stayed in the doorway blocking his path. Hopkins frowned and took a step towards her forcing her back.

'Thank you,' he strode into the kitchen, looking around as if he was prepared to pull a gun from his pocket and start blasting away at the first hint of trouble.

'You nip up, Jenna, and wake your mum and dad.'

'OK,' she crossed the room heading for the lounge; the thought of leaving her grandad with the slimy Hopkins worried her. She didn't like the way he looked down his nose, as if he was in some way superior and they were a family of bumbling country folk.

As soon as the kitchen door closed she dashed across the lounge, taking the stairs two at a time and slapping on the light as she headed across the landing. She tapped lightly on the door; even under the circumstances barging in didn't seem right. After a few seconds with no response, she knocked harder the panic rising.

Her mum opened the door, bleary eyed, hair askew.

'What is it, Jenna, what's the matter?' she asked, sotto voiced.

'That copper we saw this afternoon.'

'What about him?'

'He's downstairs. Hurry up, Mum, I don't want to leave Grandad with him for too long,' her voice was full of urgency her eyes frantic.

Susan nodded as if this drastic news was no real surprise. Grabbing her housecoat, she headed out onto the landing closing the bedroom door as quietly as possible. By the time she turned, Jenna was already at the top of the stairs.

'Come on, Mum, hurry up,' she hissed.

Susan shushed her with a hand and followed her daughter down the stairs.

Hopkins was standing in exactly the same spot as if he had been unplugged from the mains. Ronnie was busy pouring hot water into three mugs.

'Are you sure you don't want a brew, lad?'

'No thank you,' he turned as Jenna and Susan bustled into the room.

'Where's your husband?' he asked with a scowl.

Susan pulled the dressing gown tight around her body. 'Asleep and if you don't mind I'd like to keep it that way, he has to up in three hours and I'm sure I can answer any questions you might have.'

Hopkins tilted his head slightly before pulling a pen and pad from his pocket.

'I understand and besides I can always catch up with him later should the need arise.'

Susan slid around the table and took the cup Ronnie offered her.

'Would you like to sit down?' she asked.

'I'm fine thank you.'

'So, how can we help?'

'It's a matter of clarification. Now as I'm sure you're aware we have a police presence at a property owned by yourselves.'

'Have they found any more remains?' Jenna blurted out the question before it had formed in her mind and then cringed as Hopkins turned to look at her.

'Do you mind telling me how you know about what's been discovered?' his Gestapo eyes pinned her to the spot.

'I ....'

'Patrick Fossey called on his way home and explained what was happening.' Susan explained.

Hopkins slowly slid his eyes away from Jenna.

'Did he really and what else did *Mr Fossey* tell you about the proceedings?'

'Nothing, he just thought we had the right to know.'

Hopkins looked keenly at Susan as if inspecting a prime suspect. 'Unfortunately I can confirm what Mr Fossey divulged is true. We have found human remains and we are continuing to search the area,' he smiled again. 'So, now you've been fully briefed, I wonder if we could get back to the issue at hand?'

Jenna dug what few remaining nails she had left into the palm of her hand, chewing at her bottom lip in an effort to keep her growing anger under control.

'Fire away, lad.' Ronnie said before taking a gulp from the mug.

'I've already ascertained that Mr Fossey was up at the house yesterday but could you tell me the last time any one of you visited the property?'

'I think I was the last one up there.' Ronnie replied.

'I see and when was this exactly?'

Ronnie pursed his lips and whistled. 'God, it must be six months back, I nipped up to hammer a couple of boards back over the windows.'

'And while you were there did you notice anything out of the ordinary?'

'Such as what?'

'Well, for example, was there any evidence that someone had been using the place to live in?'

'You'd have to be bloody desperate to live in that draughty old place.'

'That's not what I asked.'

Ronnie frowned, pompous bugger. 'Like I said I only hammered a few nails in, I didn't actually look around the place,' he pulled out his battered tin and took out a cigarette.

'I must say, I'm surprised you haven't demolished the building before now, after all it hardly appears safe.'

For the first time Ronnie looked flustered 'Aye well, we used to keep stuff up there, it's handy for storage, besides no bugger ever goes in.'

'I think it's obvious that someone's been using the place without your knowledge don't you?'

Ronnie didn't answer, he lit his cigarette and peered at Hopkins. He didn't like this bugger, not one bit.

Hopkins smiled as if he could read his mind and then turned back to Jenna.

'And what's the relationship between yourself and Patrick Fossey?'

She squared her shoulders and glared, right she'd had enough of this.

'I…'

'There's no relationship between my daughter and Mr Fossey. In fact, they only met yesterday.' Susan interrupted.

Jenna's mouth snapped shut. She was seething; this slime ball had no right coming here in the middle of the night and grilling them as if they had something to hide. Yet the presence of Hopkins was only part of the reason for her anger. She threw her mother a look of irritation; she was old enough to answer the questions herself. Although it was obvious, her mother didn't think so.

Hopkins scribbled something in his notebook and looked up as if he hadn't heard a word Susan had said.

'But you must have had some initial contact with Fossey or did he simply turn up unannounced?'

'Well…'

Susan stood up. 'Listen, Sergeant, I don't know…'

'Please, Mrs. Fotheringay; let your daughter answer the question.'

Ronnie jabbed his cigarette out in the ashtray and sighed.

Jenna composed herself. 'I wrote to him.'

'How many times?'

'About four I think and then we spoke on the phone to arrange when he was coming to the farm.'

'And do you have copies of these letters you sent to him, Jenna?'

'Well, no, I mean, I sent emails not actual letters.'

Hopkins looked toward the ceiling as if absorbing some important fact.

'When I spoke to Fossey earlier he said he was involved in research for a book.'

'That's right.'

'And you were helping him with his research in what capacity?'

Susan began tapping her foot on the floor in mounting irritation. Hopkins ignored her.

Jenna felt unsure how to reply, she wasn't actually helping him with the research, she'd merely provided him with information that he'd found interesting. However, as she tried to explain this to Hopkins she got the impression he didn't believe a word of it and she had to admit it sounded implausible, a teenage girl with a keen interest in local history. God, at best it made her sound like some saddo who had no friends or worse still a stalker who had a crazed infatuation with Patrick Fossey.

When she'd finished, a brittle silence descended on the room as if she'd just told a tall tale that had fooled no one.

Hopkins slid the notebook into his pocket and sighed loudly.

'Right, I think that's all for the time being. And I'm sorry for calling at this late hour but I'm sure you can appreciate in circumstances like these we have to cover every angle.'

Susan placed her cup on the table. 'That's quite all right we understand; I just wish we could be more helpful.'

Hopkins nodded. 'Just one more thing, until we have a clearer understanding of the events, my advice would be to keep your doors and windows locked at all times.'

'You mean the bugger might still be knocking around!' Ronnie asked in surprise.

'It's impossible to say but I can't see the point in taking any unnecessary risks.'

'We won't be taking anything for granted, Sergeant.' Susan replied.

Hopkins turned to Jenna. 'And in my opinion, that means no wandering off into the countryside with virtual strangers.'

Jenna's mouth dropped open, the condescending bastard.

'Don't worry, we'll be keeping a close eye on our daughter.' Susan replied.

Jenna thrust her hands onto her hips and looked at her mother in dismay. Susan looked back with a closed expression while Ronnie seemed to have suddenly found something of immense interest in the bottom of his cigarette tin.

Hopkins nodded and smiled in satisfaction as if his mission had been accomplished, then he spun on his heels and headed for the door. He left without looking back.

As soon as the door closed, Jenna spun to face her mother. *'I hope you're not going to take that man seriously, he's an idiot?'*

'Idiot or not, he does have a point, we can't simply let you go wandering all over the place until they catch whoever's responsible for this.'

'But...'

Ronnie snapped the lid shut on his tin. 'Your mum's right, sweetheart, it ain't safe.'

'But Patrick wants me to show him the needle house and the gardens!'

'I'm sorry, Jenna, but that's not going to happen, at least not yet.'

'You can't do that, I mean, I'm not a child, not that you'd guess it with the way you lot carry on.'

'That's beside the point; anyway, I think Patrick will agree with us and even if he doesn't, there's no way I'll allow my daughter to go wandering around the countryside when there's a maniac on the loose.

Jenna opened her mouth, convinced she was going to say something she would later regret, but in that moment, she couldn't have cared less.

Her father suddenly appeared in the doorway, hair mussed from sleep, he yawned.

'I thought I heard a noise.'

Great, Jenna thought, just sodding great.

HANGING

The beam of torchlight wavered as he climbed the steps, the light picking up ancient cobwebs littered with the tiny corpses of mummified insects.

As he reached the top, the narrow passage opened into a broad wooden platform. Re-arranging the weight on his shoulder he heaved the body through the trapdoor before climbing in after it.

Dead birds littered the floor; he could hear the flapping of agitated wings above in the rafters.

Narrow slots had been built into the tower for ventilation and under normal circumstances; he would have switched the torch off as on a clear night such as this the tower could be seen from miles around. Any light seeping from the windows would turn have turned the building into a land-locked lighthouse.

However, over the past couple of weeks, the man had cut lengths of plywood to cover the apertures; this stopped any light leaking into the night whilst he was working. Moving into a corner he retrieved the thick rope and tossed it over the beam above, his fingers moving with practiced ease as he made the noose. When satisfied, he placed it around the boy's neck and heaved the body upwards securing the end of the rope into a metal spike driven deep into the mortar.

He stood back and shone the light on the cadaver as it twisted and settled, the rope making a satisfying creaking sound.

Lighting a cigarette he switched off the light, the darkness settled around him like a filthy shroud. Every time he took a pull on the smoke, the tiny light illuminated the dangling legs.

He thought back to the old man in the woods and tried to figure out if it would have any bearing on his plans. Putting the plastic bag over the ramblers head had been inspired thinking no one would question an elderly man whose heart had given out under the strain of walking up the steep hill, whether it would fool the authorities was another matter. In an ideal world, he would have disposed of the body in a more satisfying manner. Although in many ways he had been fortunate as the walker had been alone and the woods deserted. By the time he'd finished the cigarette and placed the butt into his pocket he decided he'd made the right decision. Trying to hide the body would have been a mistake; the police would have been out in force looking for an elderly man lost on the moors. Now, with luck, they would dismiss the whole episode as a tragic accident.

He flicked on the torch and looked at the body, pleased with his handy work.

BAD DAY

When the clock started to bleep incessantly, Lasser reached across the bed, picked it up and skimmed it across the room in anger before going back to sleep. Now the ring tone on his mobile droned its way into his brain.

'Hello,' he yawned into the mouthpiece.

'Morning, boss.'

Lasser reached for his cigarettes already convinced it was going to be a bad day.

'What can I do for you, Colin?'

'You asked me to ring immediately if anything serious came up.'

Lasser swung his legs out of bed and checked his watch, almost nine o'clock, Jesus. 'Fire away, Colin my man, I'm all ears.'

'When I came on duty this morning I obviously went through the calls logged during the night.'

Lasser began to lose interest; that was the trouble with the desk sergeant, you got no information at all out of the bugger, or you got the complete unabridged version.

'For Christ sake, Colin, get to the point.'

Meadows cleared his throat. *'Sorry. You see the thing is they've found the body of an elderly gent at about six o'clock this morning.'*

'Anything suspicious?'

'Not as such, apparently one of our lads responded to a call last night. A Mrs Kitts reported her husband missing after going out for a walk and someone called Crombey discovered a body this morning that seems to fit the description.'

Lasser stood up and crossed the room, pushing into the bathroom he started to take a leak. 'Look, I know I said I wanted to be informed when something serious came up but some old guy croaking is hardly front page news?'

'I realise that, but the body was discovered in Rivington.'

Lasser heard the smug tone floating down the phone. 'I see.'

'Apparently, he was lying in woodland about three hundred yards from where they found the clothes and the er...'

'I think the word you're searching for is entrails.'

'Thanks for that boss that's just what I need as I tuck into my sausage butty.'

'No, Colin, thank you, I appreciate the call. I don't suppose you have any idea were Hopkins is?'

'He left for home at four this morning, so I would imagine he'll be at home getting some sleep.'

Lasser grinned, a bit of good news at last. 'And what about the body?'

'Still up there.'

'Right, I'm on my way.'

'Very good, I'll log the information into the system.'

Lasser grunted and ended the call.

Twenty minutes later, showered, shaved and with a slice of burnt toast clenched between his teeth, he climbed into the car. The heat was already building, the traffic through the town centre clogged with parents dashing their kids off to school.

Lasser sat in a queue of stationary cars waiting for the lights to change.

After his late night conversation with Michael Jones, he'd called back at the station to log the information about the missing Billy Jones.

The lights changed and he got his foot down.

Chances are this Kitts fellow would be a straightforward heart attack; that was the problem with the elderly they never knew their limitations. If he ever made old bones, then he intended doing nothing that would cause him to perspire. Forget taking up jogging and skydiving. Only last week the local paper had done an article on one of these elderly daredevils. The headline proclaiming that *'Perky pensioner George, ninety six years young takes up snowboarding,'* it was all bollocks.

Free of the town centre, the traffic thinned out and Lasser made good time as he headed out into open countryside.

He knew he would have to tread carefully with the forensic team but part of him was itching to know what they had discovered about the remains they had pulled from the septic tank, and even though he thought Hopkins an idiot, he was still in charge of the case. Lasser thought about his conversation with Connelly. If he hadn't pressurised the little scrote then he wouldn't have the ace he now held up his sleeve. If it did turn out to be Billy then he would receive a pat on the back from his superiors and that would get right up the nose of Hopkins, which was always an added bonus.

As the body had been found so close to the old house, it would give him the perfect excuse to have a proper look around without Dick Dastardly throwing him black looks.

Lasser clicked on the radio, singing along to Pulps *'Common People'* as he lit his second cigarette of the day.

PLEASE

Jenna spent the morning locked in her room stoking the burning anger. Every few minutes she would think of another injustice her parents had inflicted upon her, and the anger would reach a new peak.

It was all a lie, a farcical act, they pretended to treat you as an adult, they nodded and smiled in all the right places, as if they actually gave a shit about what you had to say. When all along they were just mugging you off like some imbecile unable to make any decision without their express permission.

She peered out of her bedroom window, the fears of the night before were already fading. It was going to be another scorcher and she'd have to spend it cooped up in her room, because as things stood she didn't trust herself to speak to any of her family, the bastards.

When a knock came at the door, she ignored it.

A few seconds later and the tap came again.

'Who is it?' she shouted.

'It's me, love, is it all right to come in?'

OK, Grandad, if you want to try and worm your way out of this, let's see you try.

'Come in.'

Ronnie opened the door just enough to poke his head into the room. As if he expected Jenna to be waiting on the other side, ready to throw some hard object at him. He visibly relaxed when he saw her standing there empty-handed.

'I was wondering if you fancied coming to help me feed the hens.'

Typical, she could imagine her family discussing what they could do to *'cheer up their little poppet,'* and the best they could come up with was feeding the sodding chickens.

'Look, Grandad, I don't mean to be rude but I stopped helping you with the hens when I was about ten years old.'

'Aye, lass, I know,' he ventured into the room still looking uncertain. 'I just thought it might help cheer you up a bit.'

'And why would I need cheering up?'

He began to twist the flat cap between his hands, as if wringing out an old dishcloth.

'I thought you might be upset about what went on last night.'

'Why, Grandad, what went on last night?'

Ronnie sighed. 'You're not going to make this easy, are you, lass?'

'No, I'm bloody well not!'

'Listen, we're just concerned, that's all.'

'I understand that but what you lot fail to realise is that I am not little 'poppet' anymore!'

He held up his hands as if Jenna had just pulled out a gun and told him to 'stick 'em up'

'I know, love, and you're right, we shouldn't have been so….' he hesitated at a loss for the right word.

'Dictatorial?'

'Aye, I suppose that word will do as good as any.'

Jenna sat on her bed and gave her grandad a cool look of reproach. 'It's just not on. I mean, I'm as shocked as anybody about the murder, it's horrible and vile and if you want the truth then wild horses wouldn't drag me anywhere near the old house. But I don't want to be told where I can go and who I can see.'

Ronnie plopped the cap back onto his head. 'I know you're a sensible girl, love….'

'But that's just it. I'm not a 'girl.' I don't need people making decisions for me anymore. You know how hard I've worked. I did well in my GCSEs, I'm doing fine at college and then there's all the research....'

'I know, lass.'

'Will you stop saying. *'I know, lass'* it doesn't help.'

'I'm sorry, I …' Ronnie snapped his mouth closed so fast Jenna heard his dentures click together.

Despite her annoyance, she couldn't help but smile, her grandad looked at her hopefully and Jenna wiped the grin from her face and replaced it with a stoic expression of determination.

'Listen, love, I didn't come up here to argue.'

'Then why did you come?'

'I thought maybe we could try and sort this out.'

Jenna sighed. 'What's the point, you heard what they said. I have to stay close to the farm until college starts next week. If they don't find the person responsible by then either Mummy or Daddy will run me into town, so I don't have to stand around waiting on my own for the bus. I mean, have you any idea how patronising that is?'

'Aye, I can see your point, but...'

'And what about Patrick, he asked me to take him to the gardens and the needle house. But how can I do that when you lot want to keep me locked up in here?'

'Hang on love you're hardly being locked up.'

'Oh, so it's all just my imagination is that what you're telling me?'

'No, of course not.'

Jenna turned, opened up her laptop, and clicked it on.

'Look, I've got nothing else to say and I'd like to check my emails,' her fingers moved quickly over the keys. Ronnie remained standing in the middle of the room like a spare part.

She checked her inbox and her heart skipped. A message from Patrick, she clicked on the envelope and began to read.

'I suppose I'd best go then.' Ronnie turned for the door.

'He wants to know if I'm free this afternoon to take him up to the woods. He says he's had a look at the disc I gave him and he's very impressed with my research.'

'And so he should be, lass, I know how hard you worked putting it all together.'

'But don't you see it means nothing if I'm stuck here.'

Ronnie could see she had a point. This had all been part of her dream and now she was being stopped from following it through and it just didn't seem right. 'Listen I'll tell you what, I'll have a word with your mum and dad explain things properly to them.'

'Thanks for the offer but it won't make any difference.'

'Ah but it might, especially if I come with you.'

Jenna's eyes widened as the penny dropped.

'Do you really think so?'

'I'm not making any promises but I can try. Besides you're right, it's not up to us to say what you can and can't do. You're a young woman and that has to count for summat.'

Jenna felt a glimmer of hope.

'Besides, I can always bring the owd shotgun with me,' he smiled.

Jenna nodded. 'Go for it, Grandad.'

OPTIONS

As he drove away from the centre of Manchester, the intense dislike that Ashley felt for his father had solidified into outright hatred. He'd spent the morning with the family solicitor, a poisonous old vampire, who in Ashley's opinion had bled the family dry for more years than he could count.

Walters had sat in his walnut lined office like some stick insect dressed in a thousand pound suit, watching Ashley with a half-smile on his lips.

Of course, he spouted all the old platitudes, claiming he was sorry that the Radfields would no longer be requiring his services, especially after so many years, but the smile told a different story. As the family solicitor Walters was well aware of the financial situation that the Radfields now found themselves in, after all he'd caused a lot of them himself.

By the time he left the office, Ashley had been convinced that if he'd had one of the shotguns in the boot of the Jaguar then he would have gladly gone back inside and given the old bastard both barrels.

He forced his fingers to ease their vice like grip on the steering wheel and thought about what to do next. The sale of the estate in Scotland was going ahead though the price had been greatly reduced, the agent, another bloodsucker, had said that it was due to the present economic climate.

Ashley ground his teeth together in anger. Despite its condition, the Scottish estate was still a beautiful place to live. It was where he had spent the best years of his life, probably the only place he had ever been truly happy. From the age of sixteen he'd been shipped up there to attend boarding school it was a family tradition and then onto university. Once he had his degree, he'd taken on the task of looking after the estate.

He had made a good job of it as well, opening the doors to the paying public and cutting back on staff had brought money in, and for a while, everything had looked economically sound. Then they had suffered three terrible winters in succession, the weather a mixture of relentless driving rain mixed with heavy snow showers that had kept away even the hardiest of punters. Soon the slippery slope had suddenly become steeper than a ski jump.

All the effort, all the sacrifices had, in the end, counted for nothing.

In an ideal world, he would have sold the Pennine land and the house and stayed in Scotland. Nothing would have given him greater pleasure than selling the place his father called home. He could have stuck the bastard in an old people's home and forgotten about him. Though that was not going to happen, the estate in Fife was not self-sufficient, the house down here was.

The answer was the quarry; William Radfield had used it to make the family fortune and Ashley intended doing the same. Any farmland that still belonged to the estate was virtually worthless, only good for grazing sheep. His grandfather, another wastrel had sold all the profitable land to fund his gambling addiction. A succession of worthless men who had added nothing to the family coffers, grabbing all they could whilst dragging the family name through the dirt.

He pulled the car onto the gravel driveway, parked in the front of the house and sat for a moment looking at the sandstone building that loomed before him, its bulk casting huge shadows onto the unkempt lawn. He eyed the paint peeling from the mullioned windows and the weeds growing in the wrought iron gutters. It was a disgrace a complete and utter disgrace.

The one crumb of comfort was the fact that his father would not be around for much longer. On his arrival from Scotland, Ashley had been pleasantly surprised to see the old man looking so frail, the shake in his liver-spotted hands, the purple veins that spread out from his nose and onto his cheeks and the shortness of breath. Slowly but surely whisky and old age was taking its toll.

As far as he was concerned, the day when his father finally keeled over could not come soon enough. He just hoped that he was there when it happened; he wanted to be able to look down into that bloated face and smile.

With this image in mind, Ashley walked to the house with a new spring in his step.

JUST LIKE OLD TIMES

Michael bounced Kyle Connelly's head off the metal shutters.

'What the fuck do you mean he did a runner?'

Connelly tried in vain to pull away but Michael had his hand twisted in the collar of Kyle's jacket, Connelly was going nowhere.

'Look, Mickey, I've already told you it was nowt to do with me.'

Michael gave him a shake and spat onto the back of Connelly's shaven head. *'Lying cunt!'*

'I'm not, mate, why would I do something like that?'

Michael dragged Connelly around and pushed his face in close. 'Did you give him anything?'

'What do you mean?' Connelly looked baffled, as if the thought of actually giving anything to anybody was an alien concept.

Michael drew his fist back and Connelly cringed back in anticipation.

'Did you give our Billy any fucking smack?'

Connelly looked shocked as if he would never do a nasty thing like taking drugs.

'Honestly, Mickey, we gave him nothing,' he pleaded.

'So, why the fuck did he run off?' Michael jabbed a finger into Kyle's chest. 'And why didn't you go and find him?'

'We looked, mate, honest but it was pitch-black. I mean, we could see fuck all.'

'OK, so you looked for him.' Connelly nodded his head rapidly. 'Though that still doesn't explain why he was running in the first place does it?' Michael cocked his fist back, Connelly panicked, he had seen Michael Jones hit people before and when it was someone else who was taking a hammering Kyle had always found the process highly amusing, but now the fist was aiming his way he suddenly lost his sense of humour. *'It was Shaun!'* Connelly virtually screamed.

Michael relaxed his grip a fraction. *'Miller?'*

'Yeah, Billy laughed at him when he fell on his arse, so he set off after him.'

When Michael stepped back, Kyle felt the tension drain away. Blowing out through pursed lips, he heaved a sigh of relief. Miller was a mate but he didn't intend taking a beating on his behalf.

Kyle didn't see the fist coming though he felt his nose explode well enough. As he slid to the floor the metal shutters at his back rattled in the frame. He felt Michael lash out again catching him a fleeting blow on the top of his head. The blood sliding from his nose coated his lips and teeth, Kyle tried to spit it out, but the blood merely frothed from his mouth like a baby blowing bubbles.

Michael turned and walked away, two small boys who had been playing football against the wall looked wide-eyed at him as he strode past.

He crossed the road, thrusting his hands into his pockets, he'd told Billy he shouldn't hang around with the likes of Connelly and Miller, in Michael's opinion they were all twats. Although Billy had a stubborn streak and refused to listen.

Michael sighed, when he was Billy's age he'd been the same, always running with the gangs trying to impress. Gradually he'd realised they were using him to do all the things that they couldn't be bothered with.

Since starting college all that had changed, his tutor had told him he had a natural flair for computers and with this newfound knowledge, he was starting to turn his life around. For the first time he could see a future that didn't entail signing on the dole and getting into trouble with the *'filth.'*

Five minutes later, he pushed open the front door of his home and walked into the living room. It felt strange but he had never realised until now how much the place stank, the odour of stale cigarette smoke and fried food laced the air. It smelt more like the inside of a burger van, rather than someone's home.

As usual, his mother was sprawled on the sofa with a cigarette clamped between her lips, the television flickering in the corner.

Sarah shifted her bulk and peered at her son with bleary disinterested eyes.

'You got that money off our Billy yet?'

Michael looked at her, the shirt stretched over her lumpy chest, full of old food stains, her hair looked as if she hadn't been brushed in days.

'No I haven't. In fact, nobody knows where he is. '

'Little sod, just wait till I get my hands on him,' she took a huge pull on the cigarette. 'While you're there stick the kettle on and make me a brew.'

The audience on the television were clapping and cheering as a scrawny man stormed from the stage. Michael watched, convinced that the disappearing figure reminded him of someone. Then he realized that it could have been anyone from the estate. The streets were full of men who looked exactly like him. Men who didn't give a toss about their kids, who only concerned themselves with where the next drink or drug was coming from.

The camera cut back to the stage, where an overweight woman sat lodged into a chair that was too small for her. She had a damp tissue clutched to her cheek her hair hung lank and unwashed across a hard looking face.

'Poor cow.' Sarah Jones stubbed out the cigarette before immediately lighting another.

Michael felt a sudden urge to be out of the house, away from these streets where no one gave a fuck about anyone apart from themselves. His mother turned her head and looked at Michael with a quizzical expression on her sour face.

'Have you put that kettle on yet?

Without uttering a word, Michael turned and walked from the house.

PUZZLED

According to Harper forensics were on their way, but due to an accident on the ring road involving, of all things, an ice-cream van, they had been held up.

Lasser could smell the wild flowers that grew in abundance in the shade of the trees. Maybe he should come here more often, clear his head, get a bit of exercise, instead of sitting on his arse in a house that no longer felt like any kind of home. ‘And you say you found him at around six o’clock, Mr Crombey, is that about right?’ Lasser asked.

Norman Crombey nodded, he felt a little calmer now that the police had arrived, a little more in control. When he first came across the body, he hadn’t known what to do; the slumped figure had seemed so out of place amongst the wild flowers.

‘That’s right, officer, I thought while it was such a nice morning I’d get some fresh air. Although, I never expected to come across something like this,’ he risked a glance toward the body and Lasser saw the man shudder and then quickly turn away.

‘I can believe that,’ he replied. ‘And you’re sure you haven’t touched anything?’

‘Good God, I couldn’t, I mean, I wouldn’t.’ Norman looked mortified at the mere suggestion.

Harper was standing guard over the corpse, he waved her over. When she arrived he told her to take a statement off Mr Crombey before heading over to the body.

Crouching onto his haunches Lasser heaved the corpse onto his back. The face looked grey and mottled as though badly bruised apart from the nose, which seemed vivid by comparison. It looked as if the old guy had been suffering from a heavy cold, though Lasser knew it was simply were the blood had pooled overnight.

Poor sod, there were obviously worse ways to die but there was something desolate about being alone when you snuffed it. Still, it looked like it had been quick. One minute you're out enjoying a nice stroll and then 'bam', you're sprawled in the damp grass twitching out your last few minutes of life.

He stood and looked around; the old house was visible through a gap in the trees, a couple of police cars and a white van were still in evidence, parked in the field at the front of the property.

Turning his attention back to the body he patted his way around the coat then unzipped one of the pockets of the jacket before pulling out a small wallet, one hundred percent genuine leather stamped onto the front. Thomas Kitts bus pass, complete with a passport size photo showing the deceased frowning at the camera. At least they had identification; he studied the image then looked down at the dead man. It was surprising how quickly death altered a person. There was no mistaking the man's identity but spending a night face down in the wet grass had left Kitts looking like someone who'd fallen asleep in the bath, his hands and face grey and wrinkled.

Lasser frowned and looked back to where Harper and Crombey were standing. The WPC was busy taking notes in her little black book. His eyes followed the trail that led from where they were standing back to the body. Then from where the corpse lay, another trampled path headed down the hillside toward the edge of the trees. Lasser headed down the trail. It appeared Kitts had been standing at the edge of the trees, probably looking down the hillside to see what was going on at the old house. He had stopped at the end of the flattened grass, from here, Kitts would have had a grandstand view of the proceedings.

He could almost see him, a vaporous image watching the comings and goings as the place began to fill with coppers. The old man would have stood here storing it all away for future use; it would be something to tell the missus or his mates in the pub.

'Oh I was there when they found those body parts.'

Then the sudden pains in the chest, Kitts managing to stagger back up the hillside but then the nagging pain had blossomed consuming everything else. Lasser pulled out a cigarette and frowned, if Kitts had been standing in this spot when he began to feel unwell then why try to climb back up the hill, surely it would have made more sense to head toward the house, towards help....

'Excuse me, sir.'

Lasser turned, while he'd been deep in thought, Harper had somehow managed to sneak up behind him. 'What is it, Harper?'

'Well, sir, apparently Mr and Mrs Kitts have been staying the weekend in a small caravan not far from here.'

'And?'

'According to dispatch his wife is still there.'

Lasser sighed. 'You're saying that the woman hasn't been informed about finding the body of her husband?'

'That's right, sir.'

He could smell the scent Harper was wearing, sweet, and heavy. She'd probably gone overboard with the perfume bottle trying to get rid of the stench from the septic tank.

'Well, someone's going to have to tell the unfortunate woman, aren't they?'

She looked at the ground. 'Yes, sir.'

He let her stew for a moment as he looked up the hill toward were Kitts lay staring up at the trees with milky, unseeing eyes.

Crombey was talking urgently on his mobile, now the man was over the initial shock he was probably telling his wife about the discovery he had made. Harper shuffled her feet in the grass and Lasser made a decision.

'It's OK, Cathy; I'll get someone else to do it'

'Thank you, sir.'

‘But you’ll have to stay here, at least until the forensic team arrive.’

‘No problem,’ she answered, suddenly efficient again.

‘I’ve got somewhere I need to be, so I’ll catch up with you later.’

AMAZING

Something didn't feel right, her parents had agreed she could go with Patrick, as long as Grandad tagged along. At first, she'd been amazed that they had folded so easily. Now she was beginning to have her suspicions. It was the sort of trick they would pull, seemingly making concessions but there would be a clause attached somewhere. Despite her misgivings, Jenna couldn't quell the feeling of excitement as she waited for Patrick to arrive.

She'd made a few sandwiches and popped three bottles of ginger beer into her rucksack. She was busy raiding the cupboard where they kept the chocolate biscuits when her mum came in, carrying a basket laden with eggs.

'Is he here yet?' she asked.

Jenna thrust a handful of Kit Kats into the bag. 'Not yet.'

'When he gets here, I'd like a word before you disappear.'

'What about?'

Susan began to transfer the eggs from the basket into the large earthenware dish on the kitchen table. 'I just want to make sure he understands the situation that's all.'

'For God's sake, Mum, I think he's already aware of the situation don't you?'

'That's as may be but personally I don't want you wandering around these fields until they catch whoever's responsible for all this,' she sighed. 'Though as both your father and grandad have pointed out we can't keep you locked up forever.'

'Dad said that?' Jenna asked in surprise.

'Yes he did.'

'Wow, cool.'

'Listen, your dad might be a farmer but that doesn't mean he lives in the dark ages.'

Jenna fastened the straps on the rucksack and hoisted it onto her shoulder. 'I didn't mean it like that. I just thought he'd be the one who objected the most.'

Susan frowned. 'So did I, but apparently your father thinks you'll be perfectly fine.'

'And I will be Mum,' a bee flew in through the open window the drone of its wings surprisingly loud, it bounced off the glass a couple of times before finding its way back outside.

'Just be careful and no wandering off on your own.'

'I might be young Mother but I'm not stupid.'

Susan sighed. 'Do I really sound that bad?'

Jenna smiled and nodded. 'I just don't want to be treated like a ten-year-old that's all.'

Susan held up her hands. 'OK, you're right; I won't give Patrick the third degree.'

'Thank you.'

'Just keep your mobile on and expect regular calls from your overbearing mother.'

Both of them heard the sound of the car pulling up on the driveway and Jenna was out of the door without replying, swinging the rucksack onto her back as she went.

Susan resisted the urge to follow and instead took out her frustration on a bunch of carrots, lopping off the leaves with the big cutting knife.

Fossey was already out of the car. 'Good morning, Jenna, how are you?'

'I'm fine,' she beamed.

'Did you manage to get any sleep?'

'Eventually, after Hopkins had delivered his midnight tutorial on how we're all doomed unless we stay locked up in our bedrooms.'

'I had my suspicions he might pay you a visit, though to tell you the truth I thought he would have left it till this morning,' he paused, 'and your parents are OK about you coming with me?'

She looked up shielding her eyes from the sun. 'Well, yeah, though I did have to make one small concession.'

'I take it your grandad's coming with us?'

'How did you know that, has my mother spoken to you? Because if she has then I am going to have serious words with ...'

'You can relax; it was just a lucky guess on my part.'

'A lucky guess, I…

'Morning, Ronnie.'

Jenna looked over her shoulder; her grandad was stomping toward them with the familiar cigarette stump on the go, blue, black smoke trailing over his shoulder.

'Morning, lad, looks like it's going to be another grand day.'

'Have you sorted the chickens Grandad?' Jenna asked.

'Course I have. I'm ready for the off.'

'So, what's the best way to tackle this, take the car or on foot?' Fossey asked.

Ronnie grunted. 'If you want to see the needle house then we can drive up to the gardens and walk from there unless you fancy a six mile hike across country'.

'Bit hot for that, we can take my car if that's alright?'

'Aye, lad, it's fine by me. The top road's a bit rough nowadays and the suspension on the Land Rover ain't what it us to be.'

Jenna looked at Fossey and raised a knowing eyebrow.

A minute later, they were driving away from the farm; Ronnie perched in the back stroking the small dog, Jenna in the front with the rucksack at her feet. The fields swept by as Fossey navigated the narrow lanes.

Ronnie cleared his throat sounding like an old tractor on a very cold morning. 'So, have you heard owt else, lad?'

Fossey glanced in the rear view mirror. 'I'm afraid not.'

Jenna slid down the window. 'I was telling Patrick what a pain Hopkins was.'

'Aye I suppose he was a bit full of himself.'

'Grandad, he was obnoxious.'

Ronnie nodded his head in agreement. 'Fair enough, lass.'

Fossey slowed as they entered Rivington village, driving past a row of small cottages, roses growing in the tiny front gardens, picture perfect. Opposite was a large imposing public house, a multitude of mullioned windows absorbing the sunlight like a black hole, a pair of stocks positioned on a small patch of lawn in front of the pub. The sign, bearing the name the Radfield Arms, hung from a wooden structure that looked like a set of gallows.

'I take it it's the same Radfields that are on the disc.'

'Did you get to look at it?' Jenna asked.

'Only briefly, it was getting late and I wanted to be up early so I thought I'd save it till tonight.'

'They used to be minted at one time, owned practically everything around these parts.' Ronnie said with a sniff. 'Take the next left, son.'

Fossey indicated and turned onto a narrow lane, the trees on the verge crowding in tall and gnarly, until eventually it felt as if they were driving through a tunnel of shifting green and browns.

'I hope we don't meet anyone coming the opposite way.' Fossey said, they'd travelled half a mile and he hadn't seen one passing place.

Ronnie lifted the flat cap from his head and gave his scalp a quick scratch before plonking it back on. 'Nah, you should be alright, mind you, it's different at weekends you get all sorts of mad buggers coming up here. Blokes on motorbikes flying around as if they have a death wish.'

'My grandad's not keen on motorbikes.'

'I've nowt against bikes I've had a few myself over the years. It's just that nowadays you get these middle-aged men thinking they're Barry Sheen.'

As far as Fossey was concerned Ronnie had a point, after all, the only people who could afford a top of the range bike were people who had disposable income, which equated to the middle-aged men that Ronnie disliked.

'And the bloody mountain bikers are as bad, I tell you I was driving up here last year and one daft sod came flying out of the trees, nearly flattened him all over the road.'

'He'd prefer it if everyone was on foot wouldn't you, Grandad?' Jenna said with a smile.

Ronnie stuck his head between the front seats. 'No need to be sarky, love. I just think that folk should have a bit more respect. I mean, this fella actually stopped and gave me a mouthful as if it were my bloody fault.'

Jenna frowned. 'You never told me that.'

'Don't worry, I gave as good as I got. I told him he was a bloody idiot who should have stabilisers on his bike if he couldn't control it.'

Fossey smiled, he could imagine the scenario, Ronnie with the cigarette clamped between his teeth pointing an arthritic finger at the biker, the rumble of the Land Rover belching diesel fumes into a perfect summer's day.

Thirty seconds later, the tarmac suddenly ended and the car began to bounce along the unmade road. After hitting one particularly deep pothole, the front of the CD player popped off and disappeared into the foot well. Fossey slowed down, he was relieved they had come in the Range Rover he didn't think his stomach would have survived the trip in Ronnie's old wreck.

'Comfy motor this.' Ronnie said as if he had read Fossey's mind. 'Normally when I come up here in my old heap, I've lost my false teeth by now.'

'Oh, Grandad, don't be gross!' Jenna pointed to a small passing place on the left. 'You can park here it's not far and the car won't get much further.'

'No problem,' he manoeuvred into the space and turned off the engine.

The West Pennine moors lay before them, endless miles of windswept fields and woodlands. The backbone of England.

'That's Winter Hill.' Ronnie pointed to the highest peak, a hulking mass that swept up toward the horizon.

Fossey could see a jumble of buildings on its summit, at the centre a huge white mast thrust skyward. 'I wouldn't like to spend a night up there when the weathers bad.'

'I camped up there a few times when I was a young lad, nice enough in summer but a bitch of a place in the winter.'

'I can imagine,' Fossey paused, 'what are the buildings for?'

'The TV mast's been up there since the late sixties. All the other dishes have been added over the years, it's all to do with this digital stuff.'

'The mast's over six hundred feet tall.' Jenna added.

Fossey looked at her and raised an eyebrow.

She blushed, fully aware that she sounded like some techno geek. 'We went up there with the school once, a sort of day trip.'

'I can't see the point in it myself.' Ronnie shook his head as if puzzled by the modern world.

'It was interesting, Grandad, well, as interesting as stuff like that can be to a twelve-year-old.'

The three of them climbed over a wooden stile and headed off into a thicket of Scots pine trees. It was cooler in the shade, shafts of sunlight lancing through the latticework of overhead branches bathing the ground in pools of honey-coloured light. The stillness under the trees felt stifling even the sound of their feet deadened by the blanket of needles that smothered the ground.

'So, do the Radfields own this land?' Fossey asked.

Jenna looked toward her grandad, who nodded for her to answer.

'They used to, but now the woodlands belong to the local water authority.'

'So, have they sold off a lot of the land?'

'Well, yeah, but they still own a lot. Though it's mainly moorland now, Oh, and the quarries still belong to them.'

Fossey adjusted the rucksack. 'And do any of the family still live in the area?'

'Oh, aye, Lord Malcolm still lives over yonder.' Ronnie waved his hand in a northerly direction.

'So, how do they make their money, now?'

'Who knows how these buggers ever make their money, they call themselves *'gentlemen farmers'* but I can't ever remember seeing Malcolm with his arm shoved up the arse end of a cow.'

Fossey smiled at the image.

Five minutes later and he began to see a change in the surrounding fauna, the fir trees gradually thinned out, replaced by beech and oak, interspersed with rhododendron bushes, all in full bloom, reds and mauves in abundance. The temperature cooled slightly, though Fossey's shirt was rapidly becoming damp with perspiration. He adjusted the backpack and wiped the back of his hand across his forehead. The unexpected site of the lake stopped him in his tracks, it was oval shaped the banks covered with yellow gorse bushes with the occasional weeping willow trailing in the water, the surface was mirror still and black. Standing in the centre was a small island with a man-size bronze statue on a sandstone plinth. Two small waterfalls were positioned at either end of the lake. At this time of year only a trickle of water fell from each though Fossey could imagine that in the winter or after a heavy summer downpour, they would look impressive as the water swept down from the hills to cascade into the lake.

'Do you like it?' Jenna asked, a bright smile on her face

Fossey adjusted the pack again. 'It's unexpected.'

'More bloody money than sense.' Ronnie added cryptically.

The statue in the water was of a naked man standing with his legs apart both his arms stretching skyward as if he were reaching for some unobtainable goal.

'William Radfield was the one who had all the gardens built and the needle house.' Jenna said, as she pulled a rubber band from her pocket and tied her hair back in a tight ponytail.

'And he was?'

Ronnie grunted. 'First of the Radfields to make any cash.'

'I see and when was this?'

Jenna took over. 'He was born in 1810 and died in 1904.'

'And how much land did they own back then?' Fossey asked. He was sure that Jenna had probably put all this information on the computer but he wanted to know anyway.

'By the time William died he owned over seventy thousand acres.'

Fossey was surprised, he had no real concept of how much land that amounted to but he was sure it was more than he would ever own.

'And what about now?'

Jenna frowned as if he had asked the one question for which she had no definite answer. 'It's hard to say really,' she blushed as if ashamed by her own inadequacies.

'One thing's for sure it's a damn site less than they used to own and if I had to take a guess I'd say it were less than ten thousand.'

Jenna glared; this was about facts not guesswork. 'Oh come on, Grandad, you don't know that for sure.'

'Think about it, the water board own a great bloody chunk of it and then there's all the farms like ours that they use to own.'

'So, your farm belonged to the Radfields? I hadn't realised.'

Ronnie folded his arms. 'My father bought it off them in the sixties.'

Fossey slung the bag from his shoulder and pulled out the drinks, Jenna took one but Ronnie shook his head.

'I can't stand the stuff.'

Fossey looked at the old man in surprise. 'But I thought you made it?'

Ronnie began to fumble in his pocket. 'When I was a young 'un, it's all we ever got to drink. I tell you when all you've supped for fifteen year is ginger beer, then you never want to taste the stuff again,' his hand emerged clutching a dark brown bottle. 'Cider's my tipple of choice,' he unscrewed the top and took a big gulp.

Fossey watched as his Adam's apple bobbed up and down.

Jenna looked at Fossey, smiled, and shrugged as if to say. 'What can you do?'

SNEAK

With all the doors and windows open, the foul smell had all but vanished from the ramshackle house.

Lasser stood in the doorway, the sun hot on his back. 'Alright, lads, have you found anything?'

'Nothing so far, sir,' both men were on their knees searching the small parlour.

'Well, keep up the good work,' the cliché slipped from Lasser's lips with practised ease.

The men nodded glumly before returning to the task. Lasser remembered how much he had hated doing fingertip searches. At first, you'd be convinced you would be the one to find that vital bit of evidence that would help nail some bastard. As time wore on you'd start to lose interest, the excitement would dissolve and time would drag.

He moved through to the kitchen, being a detective sergeant wasn't the best job on the planet but it sure beat crawling around on your hands and knees for a living.

It was the same story in here, Lasser counted five people all doing the same thing, searching for something that probably didn't exist.

He spotted Carl from forensics coming in through the back door and headed over.

'Morning, Carl'

The man from forensics looked at him in surprise. 'I didn't expect to find you here today, boss.'

'I know, I'm a sucker for a good murder, where's Hopkins?'

'Apparently he's on his way, and I don't think he'll be chuffed if he knows you've been here.'

'I happened to be passing, so as a courtesy to a fellow officer I thought I might call in to offer assistance.'

Carl grimaced. 'I can't see Hopkins falling for that one.'

'Believe it or not it's the truth; I've just been up in the woods, some old bloke out strolling when his ticker packed in, open and shut job. So, while I was close I thought it my professional duty to just nip down here to keep up with developments.'

'Well, I'm afraid it's been a wasted journey.'

'Still drawing blanks?'

'Afraid so.'

Lasser pulled a crumpled pack of cigarettes from his pocket and headed through the back door. Carl took a quick look around the room before following him outside.

'What about the stuff we found yesterday, surely Doctor Death has found something?' Lasser lit a cigarette and offered the pack to Carl.

'He was just starting when I left, but that button you found in the bag?'

'What about it?'

'It came from a Barbour jacket.'

'Forgive me, Carl, but I buy all my clothes from Primark so I'm not really a fashion expert.'

'I'd never have guessed.'

Lasser grinned through the smoke. 'Just get on with it.'

'The Barbour is an expensive piece of kit.'

'How expensive?'

'Put it this way you won't find your average teenage yobbo wearing one.'

'So, we could be looking at someone who isn't short of a few bob?'

Carl shrugged. 'No comment.'

'Still, there's no guarantee it came from the murderer,' Lasser pondered. 'It could have been on the floor for years and it just got pushed into the bag with the remains.'

'Could be, boss.'

In the distance, they saw Hopkins car pull up at the bottom of the field, a moment later the man himself emerged and headed over toward a small group of reporters.

'Tonight Matthew, I'm going to be Inspector Morse.'

Carl grinned and dropped the cigarette onto the trampled path. 'Right, I'd better look busy before he gets here.'

'Right and thanks for the info, as soon as you get the results about the other stuff?'

'Don't worry; I'll give you a bell.'

'Good man.'

Carl disappeared into the house while Lasser wandered down toward the septic tank, enjoying the cigarette. A large plastic sheet lay pinned to the ground. Lasser surveyed the mess; a man dressed in something that resembled a chemical warfare suit was slowly picking his way through the pile of detritus.

Maybe his counterpart would get lucky and the button would prove to be vital, still, knowing Hopkins he wouldn't recognise a clue if it came with a tag attached saying *'This is a clue.'*

Heading to the car he climbed in and slowly bumped across the field, as he drove past the waiting reporters he gave a blast on the horn. Heads turned and Hopkins looked over his shoulder to see who had disturbed his fifteen minutes of fame. Lasser held up a hand, keeping his face serious, a man on a mission. Hopkins looked enraged, hatred burning in his eyes.

What a tosser, Lasser thought as he drove away.

He found Connelly in his usual spot, standing on the precinct, sipping tentatively on a can of special brew.

'What the fuck do you want?' Connelly winced, both eyes blackened, he had a large strip of plaster covering the bridge of his dismantled nose.

'You should be at home in bed, Kyle, not out here frightening all the little children.'

'Look, I'm busy.'

'Billy Jones, have you heard from him yet?'

'No I fucking well haven't.'

'Would you tell me if you had?'

Connelly cocked his head and sneered. 'What do you think?'

'I need to know exactly where you last saw him.'

Connelly's eyes shifted in their narrow sockets.

'You thick or what, I already told you that yesterday.'

'Yes well, today I need you to be more specific.'

'Look I can't remember, I was pissed OK, I mean, I've already told Michael...' Connelly's mouth snapped shut.

Lasser smiled. 'So, it was Michael who rearranged your face?'

Kyle glared. 'I'm saying nowt.'

'It looks like our friend can pack a punch.'

'Fucker sneaked up on me didn't he,' Connelly snarled.

It was always the same with pond life like Connelly, if you gave them enough rope or riled them enough then they'd always hang themselves or throw their toys out of the pram.

'So, I can gather by the state of your face that you upset Michael in some way?'

'He just got a lucky punch in that's all.'

Lasser looked up and down the deserted road; it was turning into one of those oppressive days were everything seemed to take an effort. The only sign of life apart from Connelly, and he didn't really count as a life form, was a ginger cat cleaning itself on the garden wall opposite. 'Look, Kyle, I know you were drunk and probably high as a kite but I need you to think. Now, presumably when you got up there you were sober, am I right?'

'You know me, officer; I'd never drink and drive.'

'Yeah right, so where did you park the car?'

The boy frowned as if it were some sort of trick question. 'George's Lane, then we went through the Chinese Gardens and into the woods.'

Lasser didn't like the way this was going. 'And when Billy did his disappearing act, which way did he run?'

'He ran off through the trees and down the hill.'

'Away from where the car was parked?'

'Yeah.'

'The last time we spoke you told me you'd followed him?'

Connelly pulled out his cigarettes and lit one, though it looked like an effort to place the cigarette between his swollen lips.

'We tried to but that little fucker can run you know and then he just kind of vanished.'

'What do you mean?'

Connelly was looking more uncomfortable by the second. 'Well, there was this old knackered house in the middle of nowhere and we thought that maybe he'd gone in there, but it was too bloody dark to see owt so we came away.'

Lasser looked skyward then back at Kyle.

'And you didn't see anyone else hanging around the place?'

'Are you kidding, like I said it was dark, plus we was all pissed out of our heads.'

'I see, so you just left him?'

'Hey hang on, we thought he'd just given us the slip, I mean, what were we supposed to do spend all night looking for him?'

'So, let me just clarify what happened.' Lasser smiled and Connelly swallowed. 'You and your group of *'mates'* chased a fourteen-year-old boy with the sole intention of beating the crap out of him and then you simply left him in the middle of nowhere?'

Connelly's hand trembled as he took another pull on the cigarette.

'I never said anything about beating anyone up.'

'Yesterday you told me Miller was angry with Billy'

He could almost smell Connelly's tiny mind as it started to overheat.

'I'm saying nothing else.'

Lasser poked his head forward and Connelly swayed backwards as if he expected Lasser to head butt him.

'You don't need to say anymore, Kyle, I've got the picture.'

He left Connelly on the wall sucking on the cigarette like a comforter.

Back in the car, he thought about what Connelly had told him, if it was the truth then the remains from the septic tank belonged to Billy Jones.

He considered going round to the Joneses' palatial home to have a word with Michael but in the end, he couldn't see the point, the family would know soon enough.

He would pay Doctor Death a visit then, hopefully, he could provide a definitive answer. Then he would head back to the station to inform his superiors. Putting a name to the remains would put a big tick in his book but it still didn't solve the mystery of where the rest of the body had vanished to and it put them no nearer to catching the killer.

With a heavy sigh, Lasser pulled away from the small car park and headed out toward the hospital.

GETTING WARMER.

Jenna led them along a series of interlocking paths heading deeper into the dense woodland. Fossey could feel the ache in his legs, the sweat oozing from his open pores.

After about twenty minutes of climbing, they emerged into a large open field, wild flowers grew in abundance, butterflies skittered through the still summer air. Out of the cover of the trees, the heat intensified and Fossey took another long drink from the nearly empty bottle of ginger beer.

'Believe it or not this used to be a cricket pitch,' Jenna said.

Fossey looked to his left where two low sandstone buildings stood, the fronts had been left open, the flat roofs edged by a small carved wall.

Jenna pushed a stray strand of hair out of her eyes. 'If it was a hot day then the people would sit on the roof and watch the match and if it started to rain they'd simply move below into the shelter.'

He could picture the scene; young men in flannels dotted around the field, the sound of leather on willow and the older members of the family clapping politely as they watched their team from the terraced roof, while sipping cold champagne.

He had to admit; the more he saw of this place the more it intrigued him.

'You know, Jenna, from what you've shown me so far this place is too big to fit into a section of the next book.'

He saw her face suddenly crumple with disappointment. 'Oh, right.'

'What's up, lad, all this not interesting enough for you?' Ronnie snapped, pushing the cap back on his head.

'No wait, what I mean, is that I may have to reconsider how I normally do these things.'

Jenna looked at him uncertainly. 'I don't follow.'

'What I meant to say is that this area deserves more than just a few short passages.'

'You mean you want to do a full chapter?' Jenna could feel the excitement building, it felt like when she had been a child and she was ripping the paper from a present under the Christmas tree. It was thrilling but there was always the chance you'd be disappointed once the present was revealed.

'To be honest, I think this place could fill a small standalone book.'

'You're kidding.' Jenna squealed.

'Absolutely not,' he paused watching in amusement as Jenna threw her arms around Ronnie and hugged him, the ever-present cap slid down over his eyes as she nearly bowled him off his feet.

'Oh, Grandad, this is fantastic!'

'Careful, Jenna love, you'll have me on my arse.'

'Oh sorry,' she pulled away and turned to Fossey her eyes shining. She couldn't believe it; this was just so unreal and then before she could think about it or stop herself she was hugging the writer. She spun away her face flushed with embarrassment; Ronnie looked on with a broad smile across his weather-beaten face.

'Right then, next stop the needle house.' Fossey said.

She threw him a quick look over her shoulder and then hurried away across the field.

'Thanks for that, son, you've made her day.'

'No need to thank me, Ronnie. She's the one who's done all the hard work; it's her belief that's sold this place to me.'

'Aye well she knows her stuff that's for sure.'

Jenna strode through the tall grass, the butterflies fluttering away in delicate panic. Her cheeks burned with embarrassment; it was unbelievable, he wanted to do a whole book not just a few chapters but a full sodding book!

She risked one more glance just to make sure it wasn't some dream. As she turned she slammed into something hard, the air flew from her lungs in a loud gasp. Jenna felt herself falling and then large hands were gripping her shoulders, steadying her.

'Sorry, love, are you OK?'

DOCTOR IN THE HOUSE

Molder peered at him over the top of the file, his half-moon glasses perched on the end of an aquiline nose. Lasser had often thought that the Chief Pathologist wouldn't have looked out of place in some Nazi death camp.

'Do you want a mint?' Molder asked holding out the pack.

'No thanks.'

'Are you sure now?' he shook the bag as if Lasser was a shy child who couldn't make up his mind.

'Course I'm bloody sure,' Lasser snapped. 'Just get on with it.'

Molder frowned and pushed the mints into his pocket.

'Firstly you have to understand that without an actual cadaver then I'm limited to what I can tell you.'

Here we go 'Mr Evasive' is in town. Lasser thought peevishly.

'But what I can say is that the body tissue you found had only been in the water for a short time.'

'Could you be more precise?'

'It's difficult, though decomposition wasn't evident so I'd say less than forty-eight hours.'

Lasser pinched the bridge of his nose between thumb and finger, yesterday's headache resurfacing.

'And what about the sex?'

Molder raised an eyebrow. 'There has to be a better way of phrasing that question, officer?'

Lasser shrugged, if there was then he couldn't think of it.

'Well, once again it's hard to be certain but the general rule of thumb is that the male internal organs are slightly larger and heavier than the female. Therefore, if you were to push then I would have to say that the organs in question belonged to a young male. But don't quote me on that.' Molder warned.

So, that was it, the body of Billy Jones was out there somewhere minus his vital organs.

'Any idea what was used to remove them?'

Molder dropped the file back onto his desk and stood up. 'Do you fancy a cup of sludge from the machine of death, my treat?'

'Yeah, go on then.'

The drinks machine stood in the corridor just outside the path labs.

Molder began to feed loose change into the slot. 'You know of all the machines in the hospital this one takes the least amount of money.'

'Are you really surprised about that?'

Molder looked bemused. 'Well, the one on the maternity ward is always running dry.'

'Must be all those nervous fathers pacing up and down wondering if their life will ever be the same again.'

'Coffee?'

'Hot chocolate if they have it?'

The little plastic cup dropped into its holder and started to fill.

'Now, with regards to what the killer used...'

'Don't tell me without a body you can't be precise?'

'Correct.' Molder handed the cup over and punched a couple of buttons.

'So, what's your educated guess?'

The pathologist didn't answer until his cup had been filled then he pulled it from the machine and looked up and down the deserted corridor as if checking for spies.

'What you have to understand is that the clean precise removal of certain organs is no easy task. But I'm quite sure the heart was removed by a blade, approximately four to five inches in length, straight edged and probably tapering to a very thin point.'

'What about the rest?'

Molder took a sip of his drink. 'Pulled.'

Lasser frowned. 'What do you mean pulled?'

'Exactly, what I said. The lungs are rather tricky things to remove with a knife, the ones that you brought had been twisted and then yanked from the body cavity, it's the same with the intestine although obviously, they would be easier to extract.'

Lasser swallowed, finding the things had been bad enough but to hear Molder describe their removal was making him feel sick.

'And I'm afraid until the rest of the body turns up, I can't really tell you anything else.'

Lasser dropped his drink into the wastebasket, he thought about shaking Molder's hand but changed his mind when an image popped into his head of the pathologist holding Billy Jones's heart in his hand like some demented Dr Frankenstein.

Lasser slipped his hands into his pockets. 'Well, thanks for your help, doc.'

'Not a problem and good luck with finding the body,' he spun on his heels and vanished back into his lair.

MISSING OR WHAT?

Ashley was considering killing his father.

Perhaps he could push him down the stairs, after it was probably how he would go in the end. He could see it as though it had already happened, his father emerging from his bedroom en route to the drinks cabinet, shuffling along in his carpet slippers. He played through the delicious image in his mind, his father's head slamming against each step, the crack of fragile bones snapping on the way down. He would lie at the foot of the stairs with dark blood leaking slowly from his ears. Maybe it was just what the place needed, a haunting, the tour guides pointing down at the floor saying, *'and this is the exact spot were the late Lord Radfield met his end.'*

Although it was hard to plan someone's demise when you couldn't find them.

He stalked through the old house entering rooms that he hadn't been in for years.

Rooms mothballed like museum pieces, pale grey dust covers thrown over antique furniture as if they belonged on the set of some period drama. Each room was a testament to the failings of his father, like another bit of land sold off to fund his squandering ways.

He lingered in the doorway of the library and looked around at all the leather bound books. Occasionally his father would come down here, not to brush up on his Latin but simply to get drunk and fall asleep on the huge sofa. He crossed the room and peering out, he could see his father's car parked in its usual spot onto the driveway

Ashley considered shouting out his name but instantly dismissed the idea. Shouting could be misconstrued as concern, so he sat on the Chesterfield and waited, his anger building to volcanic proportions.

HEARD NOWT

'Good God, Ronnie, what's the world coming to?'

Jim Woodman shook his head in disbelief before taking an appreciative bite from one of Jenna's cheese and pickle sandwiches.

The four of them were sitting in the shade of a large elm tree, somewhere close by a jackdaw squawked.

'Aye, Jim, it's a rum 'un.'

'So, what have the police said?' Woodman asked.

'Bugger all really.'

Jenna fumbled in the rucksack, pulled out a bottle of ginger beer and handed it over to Jim.

'Thanks, Jenna.'

'You think this Kitts fella might have headed this way?' Fossey asked.

Woodman shrugged. 'There's no way of knowing but it seemed as good a place to start as any. I mean, a lot of walkers head into the gardens.'

'Don't sound good if he went missing yesterday afternoon.' Ronnie said before lighting a cigarette.

'Claire brought his wife over to our place; they'd been staying in one of the caravans. Apparently she had the police out late last night and they said he'd probably ended up in some boozer and lost track of time.'

'Bloody useless they are.' Ronnie grumbled.

Jim took a small sip from the bottle as if he expected to be marooned in the middle of the desert with no idea where the next drink was coming from.

'I've never even met the bloke.' Jim said. 'But apparently he's clocking on a bit and doesn't carry a mobile with him. I mean, can you credit it in this day and age?'

Ronnie fumbled in his pocket and pulled out a phone that was slightly smaller than the average house brick.

'I always carry mine; you never know when you might need it.'

Fossey tried to think back to when he had last seen a phone like the one Ronnie was brandishing, probably twenty years ago and back then it would have been a yuppies latest toy.

He dropped it back into his jacket and patted the pocket as if it contained a loaded gun.

'Anyway what are you doing up here?' Jim asked.

By the time Ronnie finished explaining things, Fossey had finished his drink and Jenna was red-faced with a mixture of pride and embarrassment.

'So, you're thinking of doing a book about the Radfields? Jim asked, raising an eyebrow at Fossey.

'That's the general idea but I want to concentrate on the area not just the family.'

Jim stood up and brushed dry grass from the seat of his trousers. 'Well, just be careful, I don't know about Ashley Radfield but his father was always trying to sue some bugger or other, weren't he, Ronnie?'

Ronnie looked embarrassed. 'That were a long time ago, Jim.'

'Aye I know but people like the Radfields never change. I mean, they didn't end up with all that money through being right with folk that's for sure.'

'Well, Malcolm's getting on a bit now so he might have mellowed.'

'Aye, you could be right, besides according to Bill Roberts, his Lordship spends most of his time sitting in the garden with an empty whisky bottle by his side, reckons his gout gives him gyp. '

'What's gout?' Jenna asked.

'It's what you gets when you eat too much rich food and sup all them fancy wines.' Ronnie explained.

A mobile started to ring, a plain old beep, beep.

Jim fished it from his pocket. 'Hello, Claire love, what's up?'

Jenna started to pack away the sandwiches, rolling up the empty tin foil and putting it into the rucksack.

'When was this?' Woodman's face crinkled with concern. 'Right, I'm on my way,' he pushed a button to end the call and sighed. 'The police have turned up at our place; apparently they found him this morning down at the bottom end of the woods it looks like a heart attack.'

'He's dead!' Jenna said rising to her feet.

'Afraid so, according to Claire someone from the village was out walking this morning when they came across him.'

'That's terrible,' she said, chewing a fingernail.

'Right well, I'd best get a move on. Claire says his wife's in hysterics.'

Ronnie brushed some crumbs from his jacket. 'Aye, say hello to Claire for us will you?'

'No worries, I'll see you all again,' he turned and strode off down the path, a big man in a checked shirt and jeans, tan rigger boots swishing through the tall dry grass.

Fossey picked up the rucksack and hoisted it over his shoulder. 'Do you still want to go to the needle house, Jenna?'

'Oh sure,' she replied distractedly.

'If you prefer we can always leave it for another day?'

'No honestly I'm fine. I was just thinking about that poor man.'

'Just out of curiosity how big are these woods?'

Ronnie paused for a moment to calculate. 'Well, from the needle house, which stands at the top end, down to the cottages is just short of two miles.'

'So, when Jim Woodman said that Mr Kitts had been found at the bottom end that would be down near where your own land starts?'

'That's right but the woods stretch for over three miles along the bottom end.' Ronnie eyed Fossey from under his thick eyebrows. 'Why, what are you getting at?'

'Nothing, I'm just trying to get a sense of scale.'

Jenna had been standing quietly listening to the conversation, then her eyes widened as if she suddenly understood some hidden agenda. 'You don't think Mr Kitts had anything to do with what's going on at the old house do you?'

'Don't be bloody daft, Jenna, you heard what Jim said this bloke were an old man.'

'I'm not saying he actually killed anybody.'

'Well, what are you saying?' Ronnie sounded flustered.

'It just seems strange that a man should die so close to where we know someone's been murdered.'

'Don't even go there, Jenna, I mean, he could have snuffed it right at the other side of the woods. And besides the police told Claire it looked like a heart attack.'

Jenna sighed although the air around her remained agitated.

Fossey adjusted the backpack. 'Anyway, we'd better get going otherwise we'll never get there.'

They set off, after a few minutes Fossey started to sweat again and Ronnie continued to stroll along as though the heat was only an illusion.

Fossey tried to keep track of where they were going but after a series of right and left turns he gave up and concentrated on trying to breath, the air felt heavy as if it wasn't really air at all but rather the rarefied atmosphere of some alien planet.

Insects buzzed around his ears as if attracted to the sweat that was seeping from his open pores. Jenna came to a stop at the bottom of a long flight of stone steps.

Fossey looked up, the steps were in sets of twenty, then they levelled off and began again.

'Don't tell me we have to climb this lot?' he asked.

'Afraid so,' she set off with Ronnie close on her heels.

Fossey took a deep breath and followed. By the time he'd climbed four sets the muscles in his legs were beginning to throb. A minute later and he knew he was going to have to ask the others to stop, however, just as he opened his mouth to admit defeat Ronnie piped up.

'Hang on, Jenna; I'm going to have to stop for a couple of minutes.'

'Oh OK,' she looked at Ronnie in surprise and then skipped back down.

Fossey stood with his hands on his hips breathing deeply. 'I need to do more exercise.'

'You know when I was a kid I used to be able to run up and down these bloody things all day.' Ronnie said.

Fossey could believe it, putting an exact age on the farmer was difficult but he had to be into his seventies. 'I'll tell you, Ronnie, if you hadn't stopped then I would have been on my knees in the next thirty seconds.'

Jenna rocked back and forth on the heel of her trainers, her cheeks were a little flushed, but apart from that, she appeared unaffected by the tortuous climb.

Ronnie puffed on a roll up, as if it contained pure oxygen, a minute later he dropped it onto the floor. 'Right I'm sorted.'

Fossey felt like crying.

UNENVIABLE TASK.

The grilling from DCI Simms had gone better than expected. After explaining about the missing Billy Jones and the link to the old house, Simms had given him the job of breaking the bad news to Sarah Jones.

Once clear of the office, Lasser had arranged to meet WPC Harper at the house.

Turning onto Lancaster Road, he spotted the blue and white car parked by the curb.

When he tapped on her window she turned, a cautious look on her face; around here kids would often take the piss. His own car had been spat at on more than one occasion. He didn't blame her for staying in the car, a WPC standing alone on a street like this one was asking for trouble.

She smiled in recognition and opened the door.

'Right come on, let's get this over with,' he said.

Climbing out, she adjusted her belt giving the baton a sharp tug. 'I'm ready, sir.'

He walked up the grubby path, knocked on the door and waited; he could hear Harper behind him shuffling her feet nervously.

When the door opened, Michael Jones stood in the hallway looking at them with suspicion.

'What do you want?'

'Is it alright if we come in, Michael? '

He shrugged and walked back into the house, Lasser followed, Harper crossed the threshold and closed the door quietly behind her.

Some things never change, Sarah was as permanent as the moon, she probably only ever moved from the sofa when she had to go to the toilet or answer the door to the take-away man on his little moped. *'I've no money, darling, but I'm sure we can come to some agreement.'* Lasser shuddered at the image.

She was watching one of the never-ending reruns of Jerry Springer, the volume turned up loud as if she were hard of hearing.

Michael strode across the room and turned the set off.

'Hey, what the hell do you think you're doing? I was watching that!'

Michael didn't reply, he simply nodded his head toward Lasser; Sarah turned and glared at them both.

'What do you want?'

'Sarah, we have some news about your missing son.'

'What's the little sod done now?'

'I think you should prepare yourself for a shock.'

'Little bastard will end up tagged before he's done,' she continued as if Lasser hadn't spoken.

'Shut up, Mother, and listen!' Michael snapped.

She shifted her bulk, like some obscene beached whale. *'Don't you tell me to shut up, who the fuck do you think you're talking to?'*

'Sarah, we have reason to believe that Billy's dead' Lasser said trying to imagine he was breaking the news to a mother who actually gave a toss.

Sarah blinked; Michael looked at them in disbelief.

'Dead, what the hell do you mean he's dead?' she reached for her cigarettes, her fat fingers caught the packet as it slid across the small coffee table, teetering on the edge before falling to the floor.

Lasser sighed, under normal circumstances WPC Harper should take over from here, comforting the distressed mother but Harper remained rooted to the spot and to be honest he didn't blame her, how could you comfort a monster like Sarah Jones?

The woman in question was trying to get to the packet but her bulk was making it an impossible task.

'Michael, you can see I'm struggling,' she gasped.

Her son watched her with cold eyes.

'This is your fault.'

'Pass me my cigs!' she shrieked.

Michael ignored her and turned to Lasser.

'How do you know he's dead?'

'We found some clothing, Michael, and we believe it belonged to Billy, now...'

'What, that's it, just some bloody clothes?'

Lasser could hear the attempted sneer in Michael's voice but for all his bravado, he was fooling no one.

'Unfortunately no, we also found some other evidence that leads us to that conclusion.'

'Pass me the fucking cigs.' Sarah was rocking back and forth on the sofa trying to build up momentum.

Lasser opened his mouth and Michael turned and launched himself at his mother, by the time Lasser scrambled across the room Sarah Jones's mouth was spewing blood from where her son had planted his fist.

Grabbing him from behind Lasser pulled the boy away, his arms and legs thrashing, from the corner of his eye he saw Harper yank the baton from its sheath.

'Leave it!' he shouted as he manhandled the struggling boy across the room, the last thing he wanted was Harper wading in with the bloody stick. Over Michael's shoulder, he could see Sarah with both hands clasped to her face the blood seeping out between her entwined fingers. That must have hurt, Lasser thought but you would never guess it looking into her eyes. They appeared detached as if they were working their way through some complex puzzle. Lasser saw the exact moment when the penny dropped, when everything slotted into place with a satisfying click. Sarah's eyes sprang wide.

'I want to press charges; you two saw how he went for me.'

Michael tried to pull himself free and it took all Lasser's strength to keep him heading toward the door.

'I want to sue the little shit!' her voice rang around the room with a kind of maniacal glee.

Harper stood in the doorway of the living room the baton still in her hand.

Lasser saw her take a couple of steps toward Sarah, the stick beginning to rise.

'Harper, get out here now!'

She turned and looked at Lasser with a bemused expression and then she shook herself and headed quickly out of the room.

By the time they got to the front door Michael had ceased to struggle, just like Pinocchio with his strings cut. Lasser steered him through the front door and into the derelict garden.

Harper came out behind him, slamming the door hard in her wake.

'Fucking bitch.' Michael sobbed.

'Come on, son, let's go for a drive.'

He kept hold of Michael's sleeve as they headed toward the car.

'He can't be dead?' The boy sounded shell-shocked, tears slipping from his eyes.

'I'm sorry, Michael.'

'Was it Miller or Connelly?'

Lasser didn't know how to respond, it was bizarre but the thought had never occurred to him that one of Billy's own *'friends'* could be responsible for all this.

'Come on let's just get in the car.'

Michael snatched his arm free. *'Because if it was one of them then I'll fucking kill them.'*

Lasser opened the passenger door and Michael slumped into the seat, rubbing his eyes with the sleeve of his jacket.

Harper looked at Lasser across the roof of the car, a heat haze shimmering between them.

'Jesus, I can't believe what just happened in there. Do you think she meant what she said about pressing charges?'

Lasser thought for a microsecond before answering. 'Oh you can bet on it, if she thinks she can make money then she'll go for it.' He could see the front page, a close up of Sarah Jones holding up a photo of her youngest son in his school uniform, big fat crocodile tears leaking from her sly eyes, her features crumpled in a parody of agony.

Harper shook her head as if she couldn't comprehend that women like Sarah Jones actually existed.

'Do you think I should go back in there?'

'You want to give her the chance to add police brutality to her list?'

She nodded in understanding.

'Just get an ambulance down here, let them see to her.'

'I understand, sir.'

Lasser climbed into the car and Harper watched as he drove away, before sliding the baton back into its socket.

SKINT

The tower reared upward arrow straight a perfect example of Victorian architecture. Fossey knew it was an illusion but the building appeared to sway toward him as if ready to uproot itself from the earth and crash down burying them under tons of weathered sandstone.

At the base, ferns grew in abundance, vivid green against the darkened stone.

'So, do the Radfields still own the tower?' he asked.

Jenna shook her head. 'The water board took it over in nineteen seventy-one, along with the woods and gardens.'

'Any idea why they sold it?'

'Same reason people always sell summat, because they needed the money,' Ronnie replied and then added. 'Besides, when the water board bought the place it was on the understanding that the buildings and gardens had to remain intact.'

'I see, so the Radfields didn't have to fork out the money for the upkeep of the place any longer.'

'That's about the size of it.'

It made sense, if you found yourself on the skids then the last thing you would want is to spend money on the upkeep of a building that you never used anymore.

'Have you any idea why they actually needed money?' Fossey asked as he rolled up the sleeves of his shirt.

Ronnie's lips were a thin line, he looked like a man who thought he'd already said too much. He glanced at Fossey then spun away and wandered off around the corner of the building.

Jenna, who didn't seem to have any problem dishing the dirt, took over. 'To be honest it was William Radfield who made the families fortune.'

'By doing what exactly?'

'Quarrying local stone.'

Fossey slid the rucksack from his shoulders and slipped his jacket on. In the shade of the tower the temperature had plummeted.

'So, are the Radfields still involved in village life?'

'Not really, like Grandad said Lord Radfield is an old man now and his son lives in Scotland most of the time.'

'So, what was the purpose of this place?' he asked slapping his hand against the stone structure.

'That depends on who you believe, some say it was built for the female members of the family somewhere they could come and relax.'

Fossey frowned, the views from the top would no doubt be spectacular but from where he was standing, he couldn't see any windows to enjoy it from, just narrow openings like arrow slots in a castle keep.

'And what do the others say?'

Jenna shoved her hands into her pockets and chose her words carefully. 'Well, according to some the Radfields were into practical magic,' she shrugged. 'They used it to help make their fortune, and this is where they used to come to hold their,' she paused, as if she couldn't find the right word, 'meetings.'

Fossey watched as Jenna blushed.

He knew how she felt, whenever he talked about this kind of stuff he always felt slightly ridiculous as if he should know better, a man of his age.

'Right, so that's another angle we'll have to look into.'

'Do you believe it?'

'We can't discount the possibility. I mean, we have to look at this from the mind-set of how people thought back then. Talk of witchcraft and dark magic was a common occurrence. For example, if you were living a life that consisted of abject poverty, having hardly any money for food let alone anything else yet here was a family who seemed to have an endless supply of wealth, then people would become suspicious of how that wealth was being obtained and rumours would spread.'

Jenna looked disappointed. 'So, you think it's just rumours?'

'Not necessarily but in situations like this we have to be one hundred percent certain before we commit anything to print.'

Jenna nodded gravely. 'I understand.'

Ronnie reappeared from his trip around the building, a cigarette clasped between his lips.

'It looks as if someone's been inside.'

'Inside?' Jenna headed over as Fossey hoisted the rucksack over his shoulder and followed.

The door to the tower was housed in the north-facing wall, a stout metal slab painted dark green. He could make out names that had been scratched into the surface, the earliest one from nineteen seventy-three. The door itself was secured by a large padlock.

'Maybe the water board have been doing some maintenance work.' Jenna said.

'I've had a look around and I can't see owt.'

'Well, they might have been doing something inside.'

'Aye, love, I suppose so.'

Fossey rapped his knuckles on the door as if he expected someone to open it from the inside.

Ronnie pulled off his cap and scratched at his head. 'The last time they did any work on this place was over twenty years ago, a winter storm blew a few slates off the roof and they had the scaffolding up to replace them.'

Jenna nodded as if she remembered the incident even though it happened three years before she was born.

Ronnie began to back away from the structure making his way up the hill, the ground was steep, though he was sure footed, like an old mountain goat in a flat cap.

'Grandad, what are you doing?'

'Well, some buggers definitely been in, the windows have been boarded up.'

Jenna shot up the hill, Fossey clambering up after her.

'See.' Ronnie pointed a bony finger at the apertures.

'Oh, yeah.' Jenna shielded her eyes against the glaring sun.

'It was most likely done to keep the birds out.' Ronnie said.

'Have you ever been inside, Ronnie?' Fossey asked.

'Only once when I was a nipper.'

Jenna turned to her grandad. 'I never knew that.'

Ronnie cleared his throat as if he'd just let slip some great secret. 'Oh, I was only a kid, to tell you the truth I'd forgotten all about it.'

'So, come on what was it like inside?' Jenna asked.

'I can't really remember, love, it must be sixty odd years back.'

Jenna frowned as if the answer was unacceptable. 'But you must remember something?'

'To tell you the truth I shouldn't have really gone in, Sid Williams was the gamekeeper back then and he used to keep all sorts of bits and bobs inside.'

'Go on.' Jenna prompted.

'Aye well, I was out nesting one day and I sees him come out with a gin trap in his hand...'

'What's a gin trap?'

'Believe me, love, you don't want to know. Anyway, I sees him leave and he didn't lock the door, so, being a nosey little sod I waited until he'd gone and then I sneaked in.'

Jenna sighed as if she were used to her grandad dragging out his tales. 'Come on, Grandad?'

'You have to understand it was dark in there but I remember the stone steps leading up and bloody cobwebs everywhere.'

'Did you go to the top?' she asked a hint of excitement in her voice.

'Did I buggery.'

'Oh, Grandad,' it was like listening to a long-winded joke with a feeble ending.

'Aye well things were different back then, I mean, nowadays if you get caught somewhere you shouldn't be then nobody bats an eyelid but back then you'd cop it if you were caught.'

'I suppose so,' she replied, unable to hide her disappointment.

'I mean, Sid had hands like bloody shovels and if he'd caught me he'd have used them to tan my arse.'

Fossey checked his watch. 'Right, if you two are ready we should be making our way back.'

Just then Jenna's mobile twittered, she pulled it from her pocket and frowned.

'Mum checking up,' she moved away before answering it.

Fossey finished the last of his drink.

The heat of the day was beginning to subside, the shadows beneath the trees lengthening and pooling together.

'She was just seeing if we'd set off home.' Jenna said with a frown as she headed back towards them.

Ronnie looked up at the sky, 'Aye, we'd best get a move on.'

Jenna huffed, 'Or she'll have the search parties out looking for us.'

BONDING TIME.

'How did he die?' Michael's voice was no more than a whisper.

Lasser rubbed a hand across his face the whole thing was ridiculous. What had he been thinking bringing the lad out in the car, acting as if he was some kind of do-gooder social worker? Yet in all honesty he hadn't known what to do, if he simply let Michael go he would have gone straight round to pay Miller or Connelly a visit.

'We're not sure.'

They were parked outside the local B&Q store, Lasser was waiting for his phone to ring.

'What do you mean; you must know how he died?'

'Look, Michael, I'm not going to say I can understand how you feel but I can't go into detail, at least not at this stage.'

'You're all the fucking same aren't you?' he spat.

Lasser shrugged, it was a fair comment but the last thing he was going to do was tell Michael that they'd found his brothers internal organs dumped in a septic tank. Oh, and by the way we'll get round to finding the rest of him as soon as we can. 'I'm sorry, Michael, but I have to stick to the rules.'

'Stick to the rules, yeah right,' there was no mistaking the anger in his voice.

A moment later Lasser felt his phone vibrate in his pocket.

'I won't be a second,' he climbed out and wandered a few feet from the car. 'Thanks for ringing back.'

'No problem what can I do for you?' Fossey asked.

Lasser suddenly felt ridiculous, he'd already dropped a bollock, he should have locked Michael in the car and then gone back into the house to check on his mother. He was the attending officer and he'd literally fled the scene leaving an inexperienced WPC in charge of a volatile situation. The more he thought about it the more he broke out into a cold sweat and now he was going to top it all off by disclosing information to someone he hardly knew.

'Lasser, are you still there?'

'What... Oh yeah, sorry, I was miles away,' he gnawed at his bottom lip trying to come to a decision.

'Is everything OK?'

Lasser drew a deep breath. 'Listen, you know the B&Q in town?'

'Yeah.'

'Well...' Lasser sighed, the seconds ticked by, somebody pushing a trolley full of paint clattered past.

'Look.' Fossey said. *'I can be there in about twenty minutes.'*

In the end everything came down to trust, Lasser pushed a hand through his hair. 'OK. I'll be waiting on the car park,' he said as he ended the call.

He turned; Michael had climbed from the Audi and was watching Lasser with narrowed eyes.

'What are we waiting for?'

'A friend of mine, he might be able to help.'

'I don't need any help.'

If Michael wanted to leave then he'd be in no position to prevent him. The kid couldn't be more than eighteen and Lasser ate too many curries, washed down with too many cans of booze to be able to keep up with him. In addition, he didn't fancy the embarrassment of chasing the boy across the busy car park. Lasser took a step toward him and then stopped; for one, he had no right to hold him and two, he would look totally fucking stupid trying to stop him. It would end with Michael leaping over the chain link fence that bordered the car park without breaking sweat while he pitched a fit. He could just imagine Fossey turning up as they wheeled him into the store on a trolley, parking him by the returns desk while they waited for an ambulance to arrive.

'Who said anything about you needing help?' Lasser said.

'What the fuck are you talking about?'

'Look, Michael, I know you probably think all coppers are tossers and...'

'I never said that, I just want to know why we're sat here like a couple of dumb bastards.'

For that particular question, Lasser had no answer.

BALLOONS

Molder dropped the scalpel into the metal receptacle, his domed forehead creased in puzzlement. The newly deceased Thomas Rodney Kitts lay on the slab, his hiking days well and truly over. Molder looked at his notes, aged sixty-four, height five feet seven inches and a little over ten stone in weight.

In the past five years, Kitts had been to see his doctor twice, on both occasions it was with asthma related problems. The GP had followed the standard procedure by prescribing an inhaler.

Nothing remarkable, nothing out of the ordinary and therein lay the problem.

Pulling off his surgical gloves, he dropped them into the flip-top bin.

Sixty-four was by no means old; however, it was still old enough to have accumulated a heap of medical problems.

The heart that lay in the metal dish was a relatively healthy one; Molder had examined it thoroughly and could find no real reason why it should have failed. In many respects people were like cars, one minute they were running along just fine and then bang the engine would blow. However, once you stripped down the component parts the signs were there, pipes got clogged and moving parts seized through wear and tear.

He reached into his pocket and snapped on another pair of gloves, if there was one thing he hated it was writing the term *'cause of death unknown'* on the certificate.

As far as he was concerned, it pointed to an inadequacy in the individual who was carrying out the post mortem, in this particular case, him.

He leaned in close, his nose inches from the grey face, his eyes scanning the dead man's features. When he came to the neck he stopped, the marks were very faint, a pale blue bruising. He turned the head to the left and pushed his glasses up from the end of his nose, more marks.

Molder heaved the body over, the bruises on the back of the neck appeared more pronounced a slightly darker shade of blue.

Snapping off his gloves he headed to the phone in his office, time to inform the authorities that Mr Thomas Kitts aged sixty-four had been murdered.

SUSPICION

He watched as they made their way toward the tower, tracking them with the field glasses. Being the height of summer, the trees and banks of bushes offered plenty of cover. The man who came into view was the same one who had been at the old house, the one who had raised the alarm. Although he was sure he had never laid eyes on the old man in the flat cap before. He smiled as he watched them climbing the stone steps, the girl trotting ahead her breasts bouncing as she ran. And, old father time tramping on like some badly-dressed scarecrow brought to life. The Marlborough man looked fucked, his face flushed with the exertion of climbing a few steps, it was pathetic.

He was lying in a thicket of laurel bushes perfectly concealed, the black dog at his side panting quietly. This was bizarre, he never considered fate had a hand in anything, after all, if you planned well enough then chance didn't enter the equation did it? Yet he had to admit to being more than a little surprised when he spotted the trio walking through the forest.

The old man took off his flat cap and scratched at his scalp, a moment later he began to make his way up the hill brushing his way through the tall ferns. Just for a second the man felt his pulse quicken then old father time stopped and turned pointing towards the boarded up windows. A couple of minutes later the three of them began to move away back down the hillside. He watched as they vanished into the rapidly fading light, waiting a full two minutes before rising to his feet. Firstly, they had turned up at the old house and now here at the tower. He lit a cigarette, of course there was no way they could know what was hanging from the rafters, yet he couldn't shake a feeling of unease. He blew a smoke ring and allowed himself a tight smile. Perhaps he was looking at this the wrong way. Maybe it would have been better if he'd left the door open; the sight would have given the girl nightmares for the rest of her life, much better than any hardnosed copper finding the boy. In a way, he had been surprised that the woods had been so quiet; he thought the police would have been out in force by now searching the area but of course being seen wouldn't have been a problem, after all what was more natural than a man walking his dog. This theory worked well when the sun was up, people would nod and say hello as they passed and then you were forgotten. Anonymity could be found in the ordinary everyday things. However, as the last of the light bled away and the shadows deepened you had to be careful. The dark changed people's perceptions, it made them look at things more closely; your average dog walker could suddenly morph into someone dark and sinister.

Closing his eyes as he felt in his pocket, he rubbing the tiny square metal plate between his fingers, feeling the edges, the flat surface where the letters were inscribed.

When the truth came out the Radfields would be ruined, the family name would be connected to murder and mutilation for eternity. Gone would be the days when people spoke about them in reverential tones. All their lies and filth would be dragged out into the light, stripped bare for all to see. Maybe fate was playing a part after all. Perhaps it was time for another victim; he smiled in the gloom as the dream unfolded before him.

IMPRESSED

I must be in the wrong job Lasser thought. The house was impressive, a barn conversion with a low thatched roof and a window that stretched the full length of the building.

He just hoped Fossey knew what he was doing.

After explaining about Michael attacking his mother, Fossey had suggested the boy come home with him for a while.

'Are you sure that's wise?' Lasser had asked.

Fossey shrugged. 'Like you say arresting him isn't an option and if you simply let him go then, he'll go looking for those other kids.'

'Well, you're welcome to ask him but I don't fancy your chances.'

Fossey had wandered over to the car; Lasser lit another smoke, so much for cutting down.

A seagull landed on the car park and began pecking at an ice-cream wrapper squashed flat into the tarmac. By the time he'd smoked the cigarette, the seagull had departed with the wrapper clasped in its beak. Lasser heard the sound of a car door closing.

'Right, do you want to follow us?' Fossey asked.

Lasser turned; Michael was back in the car, face stern, eyes front as if set on some distant horizon.

'Er yeah, yeah no problem.'

Now Lasser looked around at the garden, an undulating lawn swept around the front of the house with mature bushes and trees dotted here and there. Landscaped, Lasser thought as he headed over to the Range Rover.

Michael was standing at the front of the car looking at the house with a bemused look on his face.

'This is some house you've got here.' Lasser said.

'It's too big for someone living alone,' Fossey said. 'But I like the countryside,' he explained.

'You won the lottery or something?' Michael asked.

Fossey smiled. 'Come on let's get a drink.'
Inside, the house was a strange mixture of old, new, oak beams, and rough stone walls contrasting with the bachelor furniture, all black leather and gleaming chrome. Under normal circumstances, Lasser would have thought *'drug dealer,'* you couldn't afford a place like this unless you were up to something dodgy.
Fossey led them through to the kitchen, the small terrier heading straight for the water bowl.
'I'm afraid it'll have to be Coke, is that OK?' Fossey asked pulling open the fridge.
Michael nodded, his eyes flitting everywhere, probably taking an inventory so he could come back and nick it all, Lasser thought.
Then his phone began to ring, checking the number he grimaced and headed for the door.
'Won't be a minute,' he went outside, the phone clasped to his ear. 'What do you want, Meadows, I'm busy?'
'DCI Simms would like a word with you, Sergeant.'
Inwardly Lasser groaned. 'I'm on my way back to the station, I...'
'I'll put you through now.' Meadows voice sounded curt as if he knew Lasser was in for a roasting and was relishing the prospect.
'What do you mean...?'
The phone clicked and for a moment Lasser thought the line had gone dead and then Simms voice filled his ear, light and friendly. Lasser cringed; in his experience when a senior officer was *'light and friendly,'* it normally meant they were getting ready to stick the knife in.
'Now then, Sergeant Lasser, where are you?'
'I was just on my way back to the station, sir,' he lied.
'And what have you done with Michael Jones?'
Shit!
'You see WPC Harper informed me that you took the boy into custody for attacking his own mother.'

Lasser scrubbed a hand through his short hair. 'Well, that's not exactly true, sir.'

'So, you didn't arrest the boy?' The voice was still pleasant, but Lasser wasn't fooled.

'No, sir, I thought under the circumstances it would be better not to inflame the situation.'

A pause on the line, Lasser looked out into the garden, keeping his lips locked together....

'You were concerned he might go and pay Kyle Connelly and his cronies a visit, is that it?'

'Yes, sir.'

'Well, you can forget about that for the time being, we've got the three of them in custody.'

'Right.'

'Look, I can understand why you wanted to get the boy away from there, after what Harper told me the mother seems a bit unstable.'

'You could say that, sir.'

'But leaving an inexperienced WPC behind to clean up the mess wasn't exactly your finest hour was it?' The DCIs voice had altered slightly, a small inflection of disapproval had crept in.

'No, sir, I realise that.'

Lasser heard a scrunching noise down the phone as if Simms was in the process of screwing up his contract and dropping it into the bin.

'Forget about that for the moment. I've just had Molder on from the path lab.'

Lasser frowned, what did Doctor Death want with Simms? 'I see....'

'Thomas Kitts, suspected heart attack victim.'

'Yes.'

'Well, apparently it wasn't a heart attack; the unfortunate Mr Kitts was suffocated.'

'What!' Lasser watched as a magpie flew past, a dark omen if you believed in that sort of thing.

'I want you to get back up to the woods and liaise with Hopkins; we need to know if there is any connection between the Jones boy and Thomas Kitts.'

'I'm on my way.'

'Right, I'll send some more uniforms up to help with the search and keep the press at bay. It's bad enough now, but if they get wind that there's a double murderer on the loose then the buggers will have a field day.'

'Understood, sir.'

'And one more thing, Sergeant, keep me informed, I don't expect to hear information second-hand, is that understood?

'Loud and clear.'

The line went dead; Lasser heaved a sigh of relief and then thought about Kitts. Well, at least he wasn't to blame for that; it had taken the pathologist the best part of a day to find out that the old guy had been snuffed out. Slipping the phone back into his pocket he quickly made his way into the house. Michael was sitting at the kitchen table sipping his drink, Fossey was emptying a can of dog food into a metal bowl.

'I've got to go,' he said. 'Will you be OK, Michael?'

He received the briefest of nods in response.

'Don't worry, he's going to help me fix my laptop aren't you, Michael?'

'I'll have a look at it but I've told you I'm no expert.'

Fossey dropped the spoon into the sink and crossed the room following Lasser outside.

'It was my boss on the blower; they've taken three kids into custody,' he kept his voice low his eyes fixed on the back door. The last thing he wanted was for Michael to get wind of the news.

'Do you know who they are?' Fossey asked.

'Oh yes, until a few months ago they were all friends of Michael.'

'I see.'

'Listen if I don't go I'm going to get my arse chewed,' he smiled apologetically.

‘No problem.’

‘I’ll ring later,’ he climbed into the car, a couple of seconds later he was heading down the drive, wheels spinning on gravel.

SIEGE

Twelve months ago, she would have found the whole thing thrilling, not the murder of course, only seriously weird people got a thrill from that kind of thing. Nevertheless, the TV and radio reporters parked on the lane in their high tech vans would have had her dashing for her grandad's binoculars.

However, twelve months ago she had been just a kid with posters of the Stereophonics plastered on her bedroom wall. Between leaving school and starting college she'd grown up a lot, all the schoolgirl crushes had been deconstructed and filed away as immature nonsense.

Jenna pulled open the bedroom curtain a fraction and looked down to where the vans were parked, she could see big cameras on tripods pointing toward the house and people milling around as if they were waiting for something to happen.

Just like a siege, she thought as she yanked the curtains closed, the realisation she was a prisoner in her own home landed like a heavy stone dropped down a very deep well.

She looked around the room; it was as if she could feel the walls closing in, her world shrinking by the minute. Leaving the bedroom in a huff, she made her way across the landing; halfway down the stairs she stopped, her mother was sitting on the sofa a worried frown on her face, her dad was pacing up and down his big hands scrunched into fists.

'It's not bloody on, Susan, I mean, the sods came running across the field, they didn't give a toss about the wheat they were trampling down. I mean, why the hell didn't you ring me and let me know what was going on?'

Susan glared up at him. 'I tried ringing, but as usual you would have had the music on too loud.'

'I tell you, if I'd had the shotgun.'

'Oh that would have really helped wouldn't it? You're as bad as my father that was his first response; I tell you they'd love you to do something like that. I mean, what could be better than having some lunatic farmer waving his gun around?'

Jenna stood on the stairs her stomach curdling as she watched the scene unfold.

'So, what do you suggest?' he asked.

'We just have to sit tight until...' she stopped as if suddenly at a loss for words.

'Until what, I mean, come on, Susan, this is a working farm. I need to be out there,' he jabbed a finger at the window.

'You think I don't know that?'

'What about the police, will they be able to shift them?'

'I don't see how, it's not like they're trespassing.'

He slumped into his favourite chair, feet splayed, elbows on his knees.

'Look, Dave, we have to just let things run their course. Someone has been murdered on land that we own, I mean, the media are bound to be interested.'

'But the combine is due to turn up the day after tomorrow. If they can't get onto the fields then they'll simply turn around and go and what happens then? They'll still want paying and we've hired the bloody thing for two weeks, so we have to fork out a fortune and the crops will still be out there rotting in the fields.'

The more Jenna listened the angrier she became; she could feel the tension wafting up the stairs like the scent from a bubbling casserole. Didn't these people, these *'reporters'* realise the damage they were causing. Of course they did, they just didn't give a toss, what did they care about a field of rotting crops, what did they care about the money that would be wasted?

'Maybe I should go down to the gate and have a word with them.'

'No way.'

‘Why not, I mean, I could just explain that we know as much as they do?’

Her mother shook her head. ‘It doesn’t work that way, Dave.’

‘Look, nobody could be sorrier than me about what’s happened, like your dad said, we should have knocked the place down years ago. But we can’t turn the clock back,’ he stood up. ‘But I refuse to simply sit here like some common criminal. I’ll be up at five as normal and in that tractor and if one of those idiots wants to get themselves flattened then that’s up to them.’

Jenna watched as her dad stormed across the room slamming the kitchen door behind him. Her mum stared into space and then wiped her eyes before standing up and going to the window.

Jenna hesitated for a moment, unsure of what she should do; a few seconds later she retraced her steps heading silently back to her room.

PANIC ATTACK

Michael grabbed his coat and headed across the room.

'You're going then?' Fossey was standing in the kitchen doorway.

'Yeah, yeah I gotta go,' he swiped a hand across his nose like a junkie desperate for his next fix.

'I don't know where you live, Michael, but it's got to be a good way from here?'

'I'll be alright,' he replied, zipping up the jacket and thrusting his hands into the pockets.

'You didn't manage to fix it then?' Fossey asked nodding towards the computer.

'No sorry, mate, I don't know what's up with it.'

'Never mind I hardly ever use it anyway'

Michael frowned. 'So, why did you ask me to have a look at it?'

'Oh come on, Michael, you're not an idiot. I asked you here to give you a chance to calm down. I asked you to fix the computer to give you something to do.' Fossey sighed. 'But obviously it hasn't worked because now all you want to do is get back home and pay your old friends a visit.'

'What do you know about them?' Michael snarled.

'Next to nothing but I know it'll be a wasted journey.'

'What the fuck you on about?'

'Lasser told me your friends have been taken into custody.'

'I fucking knew it!' Michael exploded, he'd had hold of Connelly had the murdering bastard pinned against the wall and he'd let him go with just a bloody nose.

'That doesn't mean they're responsible.' Fossey crossed the room and sat down on the sofa. T scrabbled across on his stomach and flopped into his lap.

'Well, they must have done something otherwise the coppers wouldn't have taken them in would they?'

'So, the police don't make mistakes is that what you're telling me?'

Michael glared across the room, the last of the sunlight streamed in through the massive window throwing oblique shadows onto the polished oak floor.

'Look, I don't know if these people are responsible or not. What I do know is that if you go back there then you'll just get more frustrated, more angry and after what Lasser told me I can't imagine your mother welcoming you back with open arms....'

Michael took two steps toward Fossey his hands bunched into fists. *'What the fuck do you know about my mother?'*

'Only what Lasser told me.'

Michael pointed a shaking finger. 'Yeah, well he knows sod all then, doesn't he?'

'He was there when you attacked her.'

Michael rubbed at his eyes, all the frustration, all the guilt gnawing at his brain. What did this bastard know, sitting in his massive house with his big fuck-off car.

'Why don't you sit down, if you still want to go home later I'll give you a lift?'

Michael shook his head violently. 'I gotta go now.'

'Why? The police won't let you see these boys and your mother doesn't want you. So, where will you go?'

'Fuck off saying that!'

'I'm only being honest; if you'd prefer I could always lie to you. I could tell you that she's going spare wondering where you are, I could say she's combing the streets looking for you. Would that make you feel better?'

'Fuck off!' Michael screamed the veins in his neck rigid, his throat raw as if someone had set about it with a Brillo pad.

'It's not your fault you know.'

'What do you know, eh, come on, Mr Smart Arse, fucking tell me?'

'I know you feel responsible for what's happened.'

Michael glared for a moment, his breathing ragged and then his shoulders sagged. ‘I just forgot about him, how the fuck could I do something like that?’

‘You were close?’

‘Yeah, but then I started college and...’ he dropped his head.

Fossey ruffled the dog's ears. ‘You just grew up, Michael, it isn’t a crime.’

‘I knew what he was doing; I used to be mates with that lot. They do smack and coke and fuck about, Billy was only fourteen, and I should have stopped him.’

‘And how would you have managed that?’

‘I don’t know!’ Fossey could hear the anguish, the sense of loss. ‘But I never even tried; I was too busy trying to get some stupid sodding diploma.’

‘Listen, I don’t know about you or your family but I do know that time is swallowed up. You want to change your circumstances but doing it means you have to be prepared to give up certain things. Believe me I’ve got qualifications up to here.’ Fossey tapped a hand to his forehead. ‘But I never had the time to go anywhere, the few friends I had stopped asking me because I always said no, because there was always more studying to be done.’

‘But...’

‘Did he look up to you?’

Michael frowned, thrown by the question.

‘I suppose so,’ he eventually mumbled.

‘That's what younger brothers do, you smoked dope, and he followed suit?’

‘Yeah, but...’

‘So, sooner or later he would have started to take an interest in what you were doing at college.’

‘Well, now he’ll never get that chance will he?’ Michael replied bitterly.

‘That’s not really the point.’

‘What are you talking about, I let him down, I should have been there for him.’

'You were doing the right thing, that's what really matters. The fact that your brother won't be around to follow you is tragic but it isn't your fault.' Fossey stood up and crossed the room, Michael watched as he sat down at the computer and tapped at a few keys.

Fossey turned. 'You know I think it's a software problem, I keep trying to access the updates, but something's stopping me from downloading them.'

Michael crossed the room slowly until he was standing at Fossey's shoulder.

'You're OS is probably corrupted,' he mumbled.

'OS?' Fossey asked.

'Yeah, it means operating system.'

'So, it's broken?'

Michael sighed heavily, suddenly all the anger, all the frustration seemed to bleed out of him. 'Not necessarily,' he paused and tapped at a couple of keys. 'Give me an hour or so and I should be able to sort it.'

Fossey stood and offered Michael the chair.

'I'll get us another drink.' Fossey said.

LITTLE YELLOW LIGHT

Ashley sat in the huge gloomy kitchen picking at the burnt omelette without relish.

He'd never liked this room; it always reminded him of an operating theatre twinned with an abattoir. The sink and work surfaces were heavy stainless steel, pale moonlight splashed through the window reflecting a myriad of scratches on the surface of the metal. The steel interspaced with large wooden slabs used for the cutting of meat, the walls were painted a militaristic grey colour, like the base coat of a chieftain tank. As far as he was concerned, it was just another morbid room in a depressing house. He had a vague memory of sitting here as a child while the cooks prepared food for a dinner party.

Letting the knife and fork rattle onto the plate, Ashley laughed, a bitter bark. Dinner parties, by God, the way things were going he would be eating microwave meals for one, living in a single room while the house fell down around him, a male equivalent of Miss Haversham.

Picking up the plate, he scraped the food into the bin before dropping the plate into the huge earthenware sink.

His eyes flitted to the window, a frown forming on his high forehead, in the distance, a sickly yellow light flickered like the haze from an autumn bonfire.

The greenhouse, someone had lit the paraffin heater used to keep the winter seedlings warm and dry.

Pulling open a drawer, he lifted out a flashlight and flicked it on and off a couple of times before heading out into the garden. Outside the air was sultry as if the world were somehow holding its breath in expectation of some momentous event, the gravel beneath his feet crunched like seashells on a beach. Ducking under the low branches of a huge elm tree, the yellow light continued to flicker in the darkness.

William Radfield had erected the greenhouses, but like everything else his father touched they were falling into disrepair, panes of glass shattered or missing altogether, paint peeled from the wrought iron frames the metal slowly rusting away beneath.

Standing at the door, he shone the torch inside; the light picking up grape vines withered and twisted that had broken free of their restraints and now lay on the floor like a nest of long dead snakes. Vegetable boxes full of weeds lay scattered on the ground; the slick smell of paraffin laced the air.

Ashley made his way inside, heading down the narrow central aisle, stepping over plant pots and bits of wood. Leaves that had drifted in through the broken windows rustled as he walked, a pane of glass cracked beneath his feet. Despite the missing windows it felt intolerably hot, he could feel beads of sweat seeping from his pores. At the far end of the structure, the paraffin heater flickered casting small moving shadows against the grimy glass.

As he approached, the fumes became thicker; he coughed clearing his throat in an effort to dispel the stench. Light from the torch flickered and began to fade. Cursing, he gave the casing a shake; the light bloomed shortly before fading back to a sickly glow.

Reaching the heater, Ashley swivelled the switch on top, the flame popped then died, the elements pinging as they instantly began to cool.

As he turned to leave, the light swept into the corner and then moved on. Ashley stopped, an acid breath locked in his throat, his hand jittered the beam careered around the narrow space. Taking a backward step, he collided with a tower of interlinked plant pots, the small terracotta construction crashed down; he spun around, a scream on his lips, his heart slamming like an old bilge pump.

The exit seemed to stretch away from him, an optical illusion a trick of the mind.

Get out of here, get to the house and ring the police, his rational voice screamed. Yet he remained rooted to the spot, unable to comprehend, unable to move, his legs unresponsive. Get a grip man; you have to be sure, the thought of having the police turn up only to discover it was an old bundle of rags was too embarrassing to contemplate. Oh, he was sure that while they were here the police would be sympathetic.

'Quite understandable, sir, anyone can make a mistake.'

Yet when they left, the rumours would start. His mind conjured up a group of faceless uniformed men, discussing their days work.

'I tell you the man's losing his marbles, must be all that interbreeding.'

Shaking his head to dispel the distressing image, he stood erect and straightened his shoulders military style. Then slowly he began to move the feeble light back into the corner.

His father was sitting on the floor his legs splayed out in front, the torch light reflected off the patent leather brogues. His tan trousers stained dark at the crotch, the wax jacket thrown open as though someone had been rifling through the pockets. Head thrown back, the barrel of the shotgun clamped between his dentures, his face had been twisted out of shape by the blast that had removed the top of his head.

Ashley swallowed and forced himself to look again. The stock of the gun had been jammed into the soft earth; the twin barrels slick with blood.

Ashley grimaced, was this not what he wanted is this not what he'd prayed for? With the old man dead, he could concentrate on moving ahead with his plans. It all made a kind of perfect sense, a twisted logic.

The torch light wavered and died, the dark swarmed in, creating a black hole that suddenly filled Ashley's mind.

In the cloying darkness, he sensed movement. He imagined his father twitching, flexing his legs and rising, one liver spotted hand on the windowsill, jagged glass slicing into dead flesh as he pushed himself erect. The head swaying with a wet slurping sound, like a child sucking the last of a milkshake through a narrow straw. *'Come here, boy, I'll teach you a lesson you won't forget.'*

Ashley heard, or thought he heard the first shuffling footsteps of his dead father, as he moved toward his only son. *'I told you, Ashley, you don't get rid of me that easily.'*

Ashley turned and ran.

TOO DARK

As far as Lasser was concerned it was a waste of time, there were a dozen uniformed officers wandering around aimlessly amongst the trees, the beams from their flashlights crossing one another like some cheap light show at an illegal rave.

At the bottom of the hill, the derelict house remained lit like some evil fairy grotto. Perhaps stumbling around in the dark was his penance for leaving Cathy Harper, Simms way of slapping him on the wrist. Lasser yawned and lit a cigarette, if that were the case then he'd count himself lucky to have escaped so lightly.

'Oh Christ!'

He turned. 'What are you moaning at, Parker?'

'I just stood in a pile of dog mess, sir.'

Lasser sighed. 'You can call it *'shit',* Parker, I won't be offended.'

He heard sniggering in the dark and smiled to himself. God he felt knackered, checking his watch he groaned. He had put in a request for a generator to be sent up but he wasn't holding his breath, in fact it wouldn't surprise him if the bloody thing turned up with the sun.

Police tape had been stretched out between the trees, though he couldn't be certain that it was in the right place, there could be a dozen dead bodies littering the area and they wouldn't know.

'Sir, what are we looking for exactly?'

'Obviously you're looking for bugger all, Parker, aren't you?'

'Sorry, sir,' the light swept away from his face.

'To tell you the truth, I haven't got a clue.'

'But...'

Lasser's phone began to chime, holding up a hand to silence Parker; he slapped it to his ear.

'Hello.'

'Where are you, Lasser?'

Simms again, maybe this wasn't his penance after all.

‘I’m up in the woods, sir, we’re making a thorough search of the area and...’

‘Right, you’re the nearest.’

‘The nearest for what?’

‘Do you know where Radfield Manor is?’

‘Well...’

‘I need you to get over there.’

‘But what about the search?’

‘Listen, you know as well as I do that you’ll find nothing wandering around out there in the pitch dark.’

‘Yes, sir,’ Lasser gripped the phone tight his anger bubbling away nicely.

‘I’ll get Hopkins to coordinate with the men you have up there, you get your backside over to the Manor House.’

‘Can I ask why?’

A small chuckle floated from the handset. *‘See, when you put your mind to it you can pretend you're a police officer.’*

For once Lasser was glad it was dark; at least Parker couldn't see his face burning with embarrassment. The line went quiet as if the old sod was waiting for a reply to the insult. Lasser didn’t intend to give him the pleasure.

‘Lord Malcolm Radfield was found dead about an hour ago.’

Bloody hell they're dropping like flies. ‘Right, sir.’

‘Harper is at the scene, she says it looks like suicide but with the way things are going lately I don’t want anything taken for granted.’

‘I understand.’

‘So, that means doing everything by the book, no wandering off to take some hoodie joyriding, no nicking the family silver, do you understand?’

‘Yes.’ Lasser didn’t bother with the ‘sir’ he felt too annoyed.

‘So off you go, lad,’ the connection ended.

Lasser pushed the phone into his pocket. ‘Parker!’

'Yes, sir.'

'Something's come up, I've got to go.'

'Right, sir, what do you want us to do?'

'Well, I could say I want you to carry on with the search but I know for a fact that as soon as I'm gone you'll all be playing hide and seek, so I've a special job for you.'

'Very good, sir.' Parker replied without relish.

'I want you to go down to the farmhouse and find Hopkins, from now on he's in charge of the search and you'll receive your orders from him.'

'Hopkins.' Lasser could hear the dread in Parker's voice.

He looked at the young constable, he probably joined the force thinking it was all going to be high-speed chases and drug busts and here he was standing in the middle of a wood at half past eleven at night with dog shit on his shoes.

Sod it. 'Listen, you just play your hide and seek, let Hopkins find you if he wants to.'

He could see Parkers teeth gleaming in the dark.

'Thanks, sir.'

He grunted and began to climb his way up the hill, by the time he reached the top his calves were throbbing his breath ragged. Climbing into the car he rested his forehead against the steering wheel and waited until his breathing returned to something like normal.

Lord Malcolm Radfield, he seemed to remember seeing a picture of him opening a local fete last summer. From what he could recall, he looked like your typical aristocrat all tweed and no chin.

He started the car and headed off down the lane.

It took him twenty minutes to find the house, twice he took a wrong turn, the second time he found himself driving into a sheep pen. Pulling into the narrow turning that led to Radfield Manor, he made his way along the gravel drive that snaked its way under large Scots pines.

The headlights picked up Harper's car parked in front of the house, switching off the engine he climbed out.

The house was in darkness, either there was no one in or the knobs had forgotten to pay the electricity bill. He headed around the side of the house and almost collided with Harper as she rounded the corner, Cathy gasped and snatched at her baton.

'At ease, Rambo,' Lasser said with a grin.

'Oh it's you, sir,' her hand slipped off the polished wood.

'Who were you expecting Jack the Ripper?'

'Sorry, it's just this place gives me the creeps.'

He looked up, the house loomed over them as if eyeing up a tasty morsel. 'Bet it looks lovely in the daytime.'

'I don't know about that,' she replied, unconvinced.

'Right, where's the body?'

Harper pointed toward the trees. 'Over there, sir, in the greenhouse.'

'Who found him?'

'His son, Ashley Radfield, he's waiting in the study, sir.'

'Not clutching a piece of lead pipe I hope.'

She smiled as they made their way along the path.

'I hear Simms had you in earlier for one of his little informal chats.' Lasser asked as he held back a branch.

Cathy Harper ducked underneath. 'I'm sorry, sir, I shouldn't ...'

'You have nothing to apologise for, I shouldn't have left you on your own.'

'To be honest after you'd gone a couple of reporters turned up, so they saved me the trouble of trying to hold her hand.'

'So, she actually rang the papers then?'

'It looks that way, sir.'

They reached the door of the greenhouse, Harper pulled out her flashlight.

'The body's at the far end.'

'And how did he do the dirty deed.' Lasser asked as he made his way inside.

'Shotgun.'

'No doubt about his intentions then.'

'None at all.'

Lasser concentrated on making his way along the narrow aisle.

He could here Harper clattering about behind him, so much for women being light on their feet.

When he reached the far end, he took a deep breath before shining his torch down onto the body.

'Doesn't look much like a Lord now does he?'

No reply, he looked over his shoulder, Cathy was standing about ten yards away, a sickly smile on her face.

Shining the beam around the small area Lasser crouched onto his haunches. 'Are SOCO on their way?'

'They should be here any minute, sir.'

It was difficult to tell how old Radfield had been; the pressure of the blast had distorted the features, the cheekbones had been forced upwards, one eye was open and glaring from a ragged socket the other screwed shut, hidden behind a mass of black and purple. He could see the hole in the glass directly behind the head; they'd probably find what remained of Lord Radfield's brains in the rhododendron bushes.

'Yeah, that'll do it every time,' he muttered. 'Do we have any idea how the son came across the body?'

'Apparently the paraffin heater was on and he saw the light from the kitchen window, when he came to investigate this is what he found.'

Lasser riffled through the pockets of the wax jacket. 'Must have been a shock finding his old man like this?'

'It was a shock for me, I know that much'

'Well, no obvious suicide note,' he paused as the light picked out a label stitched to the inside pocket, the name Barbour woven into the fabric in blue italics.

'I think forensics are here, sir.'

Apparently, the button they had found at the house came off a Barbour jacket, according to Carl it was, *'an expensive piece of kit.'*

Closing the coat, Lasser counted the buttons, lining them up with their corresponding holes, the bottom one was missing.

'Sir, forensics.'

Lasser turned, he could see two white suited figures moving beneath the trees, like a couple of stark white aliens looking for someone to abduct.

'Right, you said Radfield was in the study?'

'That's right, sir.'

'I'll go and have a word but don't let anyone remove this body without my say so, is that understood?'

She snapped to attention. 'Yes, sir.'

He clattered his way back to the entrance, images of dead kids and buttons floating around his brain.

RESTLESS

Jenna paced back and forth like a death row inmate hoping for a last minute reprieve. An image popped into her mind, her mum and dad lying in bed with their backs to one another, the slab of an argument separating them. Her father waiting for the morning to come then he could get on the tractor and kill himself some reporters, and her mother dreading the first sign of light at the bedroom window.

It was all so unfair.

She sat in front of the computer her fingers hovering over the keys, the small sensible part of her mind told her to wait. Patrick wasn't some personal crusader working on behalf of the Fotheringays but perhaps he could help, perhaps he knew how to handle the media.

She began to type, it wasn't as if she was expecting him to come dashing straight over. Though of course that would be great. She read the email twice, replacing any words and phrases that made her sound desperate or needy, then she sent it on its way and stood up to peek through the curtain.

It was dark outside but she could still see a couple of vans parked on the lane, tiny interior lights sparkling in the night. Letting the curtain swing shut she pulled an exercise book from her bedside cabinet and tried to do some revision. Two minutes later, she closed the book, learning about the reproductive lifecycle of the Sea Horse seemed somehow unimportant when your liberty was at stake.

Crossing the room, she went onto the landing and made her way downstairs. As she entered the kitchen, she half expected to see her grandad sat at the table smoking a cigarette but the room was in darkness. Shimmying around the table, she pulled open the fridge door, the small interior light pooled around her feet like a miniature spot light. Jenna grabbed a carton of orange juice, pushing the door closed with her hip.

This had become something of a ritual, when she needed to think or a piece of revision had refused to sink in she would come down to the kitchen and either stand at the sink looking out of the darkened window or sit at the table to sort through the problem. She knew her mum worried about her not having enough friends but then again her mother had never met the idiots who went to college. She filled a glass and took a sip, it was all so unbelievable, she thought back to the time when she'd gone up to the old house but had been unable to go in. Had she had some sort of premonition, had she picked up some weird vibes that had stopped her from entering the house? She shivered, watching her own reflexion in the darkened glass, her eyes wide and alien to her. Jenna turned away from the image, annoyed at the fear she had seen in the reflexion. Crossing the kitchen, she made her way back to her room, closing the door quietly behind her.

Sitting in front of the computer, she took small sips of the drink, all the time her fevered brain itching to check her mail to see if Patrick had responded.

Get a grip, it was half twelve at night, he'd probably be in bed. The fact that she now thought of him as Patrick was unbelievable, it was as if she had stopped being just a teenager and morphed into a woman overnight. Well, almost, the fact that her mum and dad still treated her as if she was a little kid sort of blighted the fantasy. Maybe Patrick was at his computer going over the research that she'd provided. She felt a rush of pride, he hadn't picked holes in it, in fact, he'd told her how good it was and how much he appreciated the effort she had put in.

Then a thought floated into her head like a discarded Coke bottle washed up onto some pristine beach, maybe sending him the email had been a mistake. Here she was trying to convey the image of someone who was young but in control, someone he could rely upon not to become carried away with fanciful notions, a balanced individual. With a groan, she went to the sent box and reread it. Oh she had done away with all the really cloying *'Please help me'* shit. Yet the text still read like some seventeen-year-old bimbo had written it, as if she was being held captive by some shady character who was threatening to sell her into the sex trade if he didn't come to her rescue, like this instant.

She slammed the lid down, bastard emails. Why did they never read the way you wrote them? Snatching back the curtains she glared out into the night, her eyes shining with frustrated tears, then she flopped back onto her bed gazing up at the sliver of a moon. Cringing inside as she imagined him opening the email and wondering what she was wittering on about. Thinking he could have a bunny boiler on his hands, he would probably send her a polite message, saying he had decided not to run with the idea and he was going to some far off Scottish island for the foreseeable future.

She pulled the duvet over her head in mortification, it was always the same, in the end she always screwed things up.

NOT THE SHARPEST KNIFE IN THE BOX

Lasser couldn't remember the last time he'd woken with a sense of purpose. Instead of disappearing under the covers cursing his shitty job and his own stupidity, he headed straight for the shower with a spring in his step. Twenty minutes later, he was sitting at the kitchen table sipping coffee and munching on a piece of toast smothered in Marmite.

Six forty-five, too early to ring forensics, the lazy sods only seemed to start work after they'd munched down a couple of Danish Pastries and drank a gallon of Caffè Latte. Drumming his fingers on the table top, he yawned. It had been half past one when he finally got home to a house that was stifling, he'd moved from one room to another opening windows before heading into the back garden to escape the heat.

Cracking open a can of something cheap and nasty he'd gone over the details of his conversation with the grieving son.

Radfield junior had turned out to be a cool customer, a million miles away from the Kyle Connelly's of this world. Though Lasser was convinced they shared one thing in common, both of them were liars, the trouble was proving it.

He'd found Radfield sitting at the kitchen table, a tumbler of whisky clasped in his hand.

'Ashley Radfield?'

'And you are?'

'Detective Sergeant Lasser.'

'Please, take a seat.' Radfield had gestured to one of the empty chairs.

'WPC Harper informs me that you were the one who found your father?'

'That's correct.'

'I'm sorry for your loss; it must have been quite a shock finding him like that?'

'You could say that.'

'Can you tell me, when did you last see your father?'
Radfield had pinched the bridge of his nose between thumb and finger as if trying to stop a nosebleed. 'That would have been about two o'clock yesterday afternoon.'
'And how did he seem to you?'
'In what context are we talking, Sergeant?'
Here we go Lasser thought, another man who can't answer a simple question; it wouldn't surprise him if this man turned out to be a barrister. 'Well, did he seem preoccupied or different in any way?'
Radfield had leaned back in his chair, arms folded across his chest. 'It was difficult to tell with my father. You see I've only recently moved down from Scotland and to be truthful we didn't really keep in touch.'
'So, your move down here is permanent?'
'It is now.' Radfield replied, his face impassive, his eyes had closed down like shutters over a jewellers shop.
'So, would you say your relationship with your father was a difficult one?'
'I would say it was almost non-existent rather than difficult.'
Under the sink, a pipe grumbled as if taking exception to the answer. 'So, why did you move from Scotland, if you were estranged from your father surely it would have been better to remain up there?'
Radfield had cocked his head slightly to one side, looking hard at Lasser.
'I fail to see the relevance of that question, where I choose to live is nobody's business but my own.'
'Under normal circumstances that would be perfectly true but in situations like this we have to try and understand why someone would decide to end their life in such a fashion.'
Radfield had lit a cigarette, the smoke trailing from his nostrils.

'I would have thought that *'fashion'* had very little to do with it, my father was always a practical man, to him it would have been the method most guaranteed to achieve his aims.'

'You told WPC Harper that you noticed a light coming from the greenhouse?'

'That's correct it was an old paraffin heater.'

'Lit by your father?'

'I presume so.'

'You saw it from the kitchen window and went to investigate?'

Radfield didn't bother with a reply he merely nodded, looking bored as if he couldn't wait to get back to his game of billiards or hunt down a fox.

'And have you been out of the house today, Mr Radfield?'

'I was in Manchester until about eleven-thirty, when I arrived home there was no sign of my father.'

'I see.' Lasser paused, looking around the gloomy room. Christ if this was living the life of an aristocrat then you could keep it. 'The car parked around the back, does it belong to you?'

'No, it's my father's.'

'So, I take it the car hasn't been moved today?'

'I couldn't be certain about that, you see I fell asleep around five o'clock, so my father could have returned, and I wouldn't have necessarily known about it.'

How convenient. 'Never mind we can always check up on that later, if we need to,' he added darkly.

'So, what happens now?'

'Well, we try and ascertain why someone like your father, someone with power and influence would want to remove the top of their head with a twelve bore shotgun.'

Radfield had narrowed his eyes. 'I sincerely hope you're not suggesting anything untoward about my father's death?'

'Absolutely not, I'm just doing my job.'

Radfield regarded Lasser, as if he were some kind recidivist masquerading as a police officer, a hundred years ago, he would have probably had him horsewhipped and thrown off the property.

'Right, Sergeant, I'm sure you can appreciate this is a very stressful time for me and I have people who need to be informed of this tragedy. So, unless you have any further questions?'

Lasser had stood up. 'Not at the moment.'

He had left the mausoleum-like kitchen, smoking a cigarette by the side of the dark blue jag before making his way back to the greenhouse. By the time he arrived, they were in the process of loading the body into the back of a transit with blacked out windows.

'Harper, where the bloody hell are you?'

'I'm in here, sir.'

He heard the sound of a plant pot breaking as she clattered her way out of the greenhouse.

'I thought I told you that the body wasn't to be removed without my say-so?'

She pushed a stray strand of hair back under her cap, her face flustered.

'I know, sir, I'm sorry but forensics were told to remove the body as soon as possible.'

He heard the sound of the late Lord Malcolm Radfield sliding into the back of the van on a metal gurney. 'Who told them that?'

'According to them it was Chief Inspector Simms, sir.'

The van started to pull away.

'Here, what the hell do you think...?'

His voice was drowned out by the sound of the wheels spinning in the gravel as the van shot off along the drive.

'For fucks sake, why didn't you come and get me?'

She backed up as Lasser loomed over her. 'I'm sorry; they just picked the body up and headed for the door. I tried to tell them that they couldn't without your permission but they said they didn't need it.'

Simms sends him on a wild goose chase looking for clues in woodland at night and then admits he did it just to take the piss. Then the old sod drags him over here telling him to be *'professional'*, all that *'leave no stone unturned'* bollocks and then he has the body pulled out from under his nose.

Yes well, two could play that game.

He flicked the cigarette stump into the garden and decided he had waited long enough.

It was only half past seven but the sun was already slamming down with a ferocity that had him sweating before he climbed into the car. Turning on the radio he caught the last couple of minutes of the local news.

'And finally, the police have revealed that they are not looking for anyone else in connection with the death of Lord Malcolm Radfield. The seventy-eight-year-old peer, who died from gun shot wounds, was found by his son late last night.... ' He snapped the radio off, it was always the same, he had only been asleep for a few hours, and yet the media had managed to get their hooks in. That was probably the reason Simms had told forensics to get their skates on and move the body. By the time the reporters got a whiff of the story the body would be tucked up in the morgue, thereby saving Ashley Radfield from having unsavoury types with telephoto lenses climbing up his ivy-covered walls to get a look at the body. As if the death of someone with a title should somehow be handled differently. Lasser could almost feel the enamel on his teeth cracking with rage. It wouldn't surprise him if Simms had told the grieving son to keep Lasser talking while they sneaked away with the body, like Burke and Hare.

A conversation unfolded in his head like a scene from a bad cop movie, Simms on the phone talking to Radfield.

'Now look your grace, you just sit tight, I'm sending over one of my men. He isn't the sharpest knife in the

box, so just keep him busy for a few minutes and we'll see to the rest.'

Lasser pulled out his cigarettes, the anger beginning to build.

STEREOTYPE

Simms looked across the desk at Hopkins, the Sergeant was sitting ramrod stiff as if he had an invisible plank of wood shoved down the back of his light blue shirt.

'Right, what do we know so far?'

Hopkins produced a note pad, inwardly, Simms sighed; Hopkins was the perfect model of a modern day police officer. He was efficient and could be relied upon to follow directions to the letter. The only drawback was that he didn't have any real flair for the job; any instincts he possessed were buried beneath layers of officiousness.

Simms watched as he flicked through the pages, as if they had all the time in the world.

'What about Connelly and his cronies, do you think they had anything to do with the killing?' he asked.

'Well, sir, we've established that they were all there the night Jones died.'

'I realise that but were they responsible, is there any evidence that any of these boys actually went into the house?'

Hopkins studied his notebook for a few seconds. 'No hard evidence, sir.'

'And all the clothing these boys own has been checked by forensics?'

'Yes, sir, and they've all come back negative, though of course they could have destroyed the evidence.'

'Hardly likely though is it, three petty criminals, a bit of drug dealing, the odd court appearance for affray. I can't really see them disembowelling a fourteen-year-old boy can you?'

Hopkins pursed his lips. 'Difficult to say, sir, if they were high on a banned substance then it's always a possibility.'

Simms looked out of the window, wishing he were on the golf course. 'Let's look at that, shall we? Say, for instance, Connelly did the killing, he comes staggering out of the house in the pitch black covered head to toe in blood. Now, let's say they've been partaking of a *'banned substance'* and they're all off their tiny little heads. Can you really see them pulling together, showing some team spirit? One of them loading the entrails of this poor boy into a sack and throwing it into the septic tank while the others dispose of the body so well that we can't seem to find it. Then they all make their way home and agree to keep quiet about what they've done. Honour amongst thieves, is that what you are suggesting, Sergeant?' Simms could feel his patience begin to unravel.

Hopkins might not have been in touch with his intuition but he could still tell when his boss was getting ready to explode. 'I'll admit it does seem a little unlikely, sir....'

'What about Kitts?'

'We're still searching the area, sir.'

'Right well, I won't keep you any longer but I want you to widen the search area, Jones's body has to be somewhere and I want it found before some reporter stumbles across it, is that understood?'

'Yes, sir.' Hopkins rose to his feet, sliding the notebook into his pocket he headed for the door. Simms watched him go, thinking he was glad that retirement was only a couple of years away. He imagined the police force of the future, manned by an army of people like Hopkins, all with PhDs and not an instinct between them. The mere thought of it made him shudder.

DONE ONE

Lasser wasn't surprised when Fossey told him that Michael had left sometime during the night.

'I thought he might do a runner,' he said.

'So, what do you think he'll do?' Fossey was on his way to see Jenna, considering it was a Friday morning the traffic was moving well.

'I'll get some of the mountain bike plods to keep an eye out for him, besides even if he goes looking for trouble he won't find any. We're keeping his 'friends' in custody for a while yet.'

'So, you're working on the assumption that either one or all of them are guilty?'

'No comment.'

'Come on, Lasser.'

'If you want my opinion as much as I dislike the scrotes, I don't think they lost the plot and killed the kid.'

'So, you're still looking?'

'Not me personally, Hopkins is in charge of the murders.'

'Murders?'

Fossey heard the sigh floating from the in-car speaker.

'You heard about the old guy they found in the woods?'

'Thomas Kitts?'

'How do you know his name?'

Fossey explained about meeting Jim Woodman in the woods.

'I see. Well, it turns out he didn't die of natural causes, someone strangled him.' Fossey heard the blare from a car horn. *'Get out of the way, you daft bastard!'*

It sounded as if Lasser was sitting in the passenger seat.

'I should let you go before you have an accident.'

'No problem and if I hear anything about Michael I'll let you know.'

'I'd appreciate that.'

He clicked off the handset and swept down the slip road.

When he arrived at the farm, there was one TV van parked on the lane, and as Fossey pulled up onto the long drive and switched off the engine Jenna appeared at the front door and sprinted toward the car, her hair flowing out behind her.

'Morning.'

'Wow, I wasn't expecting you,' she replied, a broad smile fixed onto her face.

Fossey nodded toward the van. 'I see you're down to one van?'

'Oh yeah, I'm sorry about the email, I don't know what I was thinking,' her hand went to her face covering the blush.

Fossey smiled. 'Don't worry about it.'

Ronnie appeared at the door peering out into the yard. 'You two coming in, or what?' he asked before disappearing back inside.

The inside of the house was a cool oasis against the persistent heat.

'Are you on your own, Ronnie?' Fossey asked.

'Our Susan should be home any minute,' then they heard the sound of a car on gravel, crunching to a stop. 'That sounds like her now.'

A moment later, she came into the kitchen with a carrier bag in hand.

'Hello, Patrick, I thought it was your car on the drive'

'Hello, Susan.'

'I've just been listening to the news on the radio; they're saying that Lord Radfield was found dead last night.'

'You bloody what!' Ronnie looked flustered; he snatched the cap from his head and headed for the living room, a couple of seconds later he vanished.

Susan shook her head, a wry smile on her face. 'He'll be ringing his friends, nobody can gossip like an old farmer. Anyway what can we do for you, Patrick?'

'I'd like to say I was just passing but I've got a couple of things I need to discuss with you.'

She placed the bag on the table. 'That sounds ominous,' she smiled.

He didn't smile back.

WAITING GAME

When he'd gone in to see Simms it had been grudgingly, Lasser was half expecting to be shot down in flames but the big boss had surprised him.

'So, you think there could be a link between Jones and Radfield?'

He had to be careful with his response; too keen and there was a chance that Simms would hand the whole thing over to Hopkins, just to spite him.

'Well, nothing's definite, sir, but according to forensics the button came off a Barbour jacket and it seems a bit of a coincidence that Radfield was found wearing an identical jacket with a missing button.'

Simms nodded his grey head. 'Right, get back up there and see what the son has to say on the subject.'

Lasser didn't need telling twice, he virtually ran from the office before Simms could change his mind.

The traffic began to move through the town centre, ten minutes later and the shitty houses and vandalised shops had vanished like a filthy mirage. It always amazed him how quickly the shabby streets gave way to fields of golden corn and yellow rapeseed. After a couple of miles large houses began to appear dotted along the side of the road. Properties with long drives and double garages, manicured lawns and landscaped gardens. It may as well have been a million miles from Hindley, where the kids roamed around in packs and the houses resembled squats.

He slowed and turned right at the cenotaph, the country lanes began to narrow the trees became older, larger. The heavy scent of vegetation wafted in through the open window, like the lettuce he often bought and then forgot about until it rotted away at the bottom of the fridge. He passed the house where they'd found the entrails of Billy Jones, he could see a couple of uniforms at the gate standing guard in case any reporters tried to storm the place.

Five minutes later, he was pulling up the drive of Radfield Manor. In daylight the house appeared less foreboding, the yellowing sandstone made the place look like a giant slab of Madeira cake. Lasser pulled up at the front door and climbed out, placing his fists into the small of his back and stretching before heading around the side of the house. He stopped and looked toward the greenhouse; the sensible thing would be to take another look, just to be on the safe side, you never knew what could be missed when searching by torchlight. Eyeing the lawn, he took great pleasure in cutting across the grass instead of sticking to the path, he ducked under the large elm and strode toward the dilapidated glasshouse.

Last night with all the commotion, he'd not really taken notice of the state of the place, now with the sunlight shafting down through the trees he could see the wear and tear; it looked as if a strong wind could send the lot crashing to the ground. The thin slats of wrought iron that made the frame, were rotting and missing panes of glass gave the greenhouse a patchwork appearance. Hardly the sort of thing you would expect to find on a country estate. He frowned, thinking back to the conversation he had with Radfield in the large shabby kitchen, shabby being the key word. Knackered greenhouse, tatty kitchen, maybe the whole wealth thing was a lie. However, was that reason enough for Malcolm to chew on the barrel of his own shotgun?

'Can I help you, Sergeant?' Ashley Radfield stood about ten feet away, one hand thrust into his coat pocket as if concealing a gun.

'Ah, Mr Radfield, good morning, I just thought I'd take another look around while the sun was shining.'

'Are you looking for anything in particular?'

'As a matter of fact I am.'

'And what might that be?' Ashley asked, slipping his hands into the pockets of his tweed jacket.

'Ah now, that would be telling,' he saw the angry expression flit across Radfield's face as he turned and walked into the greenhouse.

There was nothing remarkable about the space where Malcolm Radfield had ended his life, just a small stretch of dirt littered with weeds.

Ashley followed, but halfway along the aisle he stopped as if reluctant to go any further.

'Look, I don't know what all this is about but if you tell me what you're looking for I might be able to help.'

Lasser ignored him, reaching out he moved a few plant pots to one side, holding his breath as he scanned the ground, if the button turned up then he was knackered it would be back to watching Hopkins strutting around while he sunk back into the shit.

'Sergeant?'

Lasser held up a hand and smiled to himself, he could hear the annoyance in Radfield's voice. He would be used to people jumping to his beck and call, yes sir, no sir, three bags full sir. Ignoring the question, he began to scrabble around amongst the weeds; of course the button could be anywhere, lost in a million places. Lasser just hoped that Radfield had lost his while he was butchering poor Billy Jones.

'Sergeant Lasser!' Annoyance had slipped out of the window and fury had sneaked in to take its place, it was all there in the voice.

Lasser turned, surprised when he saw the look on his Lordship's face. Going solely off the voice, he had expected to see anger, fury even, but Ashley Radfield returned his smile, white teeth flashing.

'If you must know, I'm looking for a button,' Lasser said.

'A button?'

'That's right, when you called us in last night I happened to notice that your father had one missing from his jacket.'

'And you've come all the way out here to look for it.'

'Tell me something, Mr Radfield, do you have any idea where your father might have been two nights ago?'

'I seem to remember telling you that my father was normally at home by seven o'clock.'

'So, he was here then?'

'I also recall informing you that my father and I didn't really get along. But I know he was a man of routine, so although I can't swear to the fact it's more than likely he was tucked up in his room emptying another bottle of scotch.'

'So, you're saying he had a problem with alcohol?'

Radfield sighed. 'My father was well into his seventies, he'd been a drinker all his life. Now if I get to that age and my only vice is having a little too much scotch then I wouldn't consider it a *'problem'* would you?'

Smarmy tosser, Lasser thought. 'But he could have been out of the house and you wouldn't necessarily have been aware?'

'It's possible I suppose, though...'

'It's just that I don't know if you're aware but two nights ago a young boy was murdered not far from here.'

'Of course I'm aware, though I fail to see what that has to do with my father.'

Lasser pulled out his cigarettes and lit one before sliding the packet back into his pocket; he blew smoke towards one of the missing panes of glass, watching as it trailed through the open space. 'You see, the thing is when we were searching the murder scene, we came across a button that had originally been attached to a Barbour jacket and when I arrived here last night I happened to notice that your father was wearing the same sort of coat and that it was shy one button.'

It was like watching one of those cartoons on the television where some characters face turns puce as the anvil is dropped onto their big toe.

'I certainly hope you're not suggesting my father had anything to do with that?'

Lasser gave a slight shrug of his shoulders. 'It's a possible clue and I'm sure that if the boot was on the other foot then you'd want us to look into it?'

'This is preposterous.'

'Well, you've already stated that you can't account for his movements on the night of the murder.'

Radfield spun on his heels and began to walk towards the exit.

'Where are you going, sir?'

'To ring my solicitor.'

Lasser frowned. 'Is that really necessary?'

'Oh I rather think so. I mean, I may not have seen eye to eye with my father but I knew him well enough to know that he wasn't capable of murdering anyone.'

'You'll forgive me but that isn't the first time I've heard that particular nugget.'

Radfield stopped and turned. 'Oh I am quite sure that's true but you see the thing is my father was a coward, a weak ineffectual man.'

Lasser raised an eyebrow, so was Adolf Hitler, he thought.

'All he was interested in was shirking his responsibilities and drinking the finest single malt he could get his hands on.'

'People can do the strangest things when they've had too much to drink.'

Radfield laughed out loud, a mocking bitter bark.

'Sergeant, my father was an old drunk. Tell me, if this had happened in some inner city slum, would you be shaking up the derelicts that sleep in the shop doorways,' Radfield pointed into the corner of the greenhouse and Lasser resisted the urge to look just in case his Lordship had a spare wino just for such an occasion. 'Would they be your prime suspects, because that's what my father was. Oh, he might have lived in a large house and driven around in a Jag, but that was only an accident of birth.'

'You don't tend to find many inner city winos that'd have access to shotguns though do you, sir.' Lasser added petulantly, this bastard was starting to enjoy himself, starting to take the piss.

Radfield shook his head as if he suddenly had the measure of the man standing in front of him. 'I'm afraid I'll have to take your word for that. Now if you'll excuse me I have a telephone call to make,' he spun on his heels and marched out of the greenhouse.

Lasser rubbed both hands across his face, as much as he hated the idea, the more he thought about it the more ridiculous it seemed. Before coming up to the house, he'd spoken with Carl from forensics who'd told him that the old man was basically on his last legs and even if he hadn't topped himself then he would have been dead within the next few months. Bad heart, high cholesterol, Christ he'd even had bloody gout. An image reeled through his head. Malcolm Radfield hobbling over rough moorland in pitch darkness. His dickey heart hammering, the blood trying to make its way through veins that resembled the waste pipe attached to a kitchen sink. Tackling a scrote like Billy Jones, the kind of kid who never left the house unless he had a kitchen knife in his pocket. In addition, there was Thomas Kitts to consider, he tried to picture two elderly men fighting to the death beneath the trees.

Snarling, he hurried out of the greenhouse as if trying to escape his own stupidity.

FIFTEEN MINUTES OF FAME

It took Michael the best part of two hours to walk back to town. Two hours with the early morning sun stoking his anger. Once he got back to Hindley, he made his way to the local Tesco and drew out the forty quid that amounted to his life savings from the cash dispenser. Walking into the store, he ignored the guard who eyed him from behind the monitor, buying twenty cigarettes from the kiosk before headed for the drinks section, his head throbbing, his mouth bone dry.

When he saw his mother on the TV screens, he thought he had finally cracked, the last few hours of stress and anger tipping him into a strange world of unreality. Yet no matter where he looked her image glared back at him, she was on every television screen in the electronics department. Her fat lips set in a grimace, her eyes leaking tears, the image of a woman in anguish. He moved closer and then simply stopped and stared, the camera panned around the room then back to her. She was sitting on the sofa in their living room, a handkerchief clasped in her nicotine stained fingers, yet the place looked unfamiliar, the stack of magazines that usually littered the room were nowhere to be seen, the cushions were straight, the curtains open. Even the television in the corner of the room was off. Michael shook his head, a bizarre thought came into his head, he was eighteen and he couldn't remember a time in his life when the television had been silent. It was a constant, like the earth orbiting the sun - and now it was blank. This one simple fact made his hatred reach a new level, it was a game for her, an act, and he knew the only reason she ever did anything was to make money. Billy was dead and she didn't care. The image on the screen vanished and was replaced by a farmhouse that looked derelict, the camera swept in over the field revealing a close up of half a dozen coppers in white paper suits milling around. Michael moved forward until he was standing in front of the screens.

'Can I help you?' The woman smiled at him, she was small and frumpy with a sprinkling of dandruff on the shoulders of her uniform, a smiley badge, stating that she was happy to help, pinned to her chest.

'No,' he turned away, the television showed a reporter talking directly to the camera, the house now a backdrop in the corner of the screen, a police car swept past the driver slowing as he bumped across the field.

'It's terrible isn't it?'

Michael frowned at the woman. 'What is?'

'This business on the television, I mean, I go walking up there with my husband, it's a lovely spot. You just never imagine something like this will happen. I mean, not locally.'

Michael thrust his hands into the pocket of his jacket.

'What that poor woman must be going through, I can't even begin to imagine,' she shook her head. 'Apparently she shops in here,' she spoke in a whisper as if passing on classified information. Michael almost laughed aloud in disbelief, the thought of his mother doing anything as arduous as pushing a trolley was laughable.

'Is everything OK?'

The security guard had appeared from nowhere, he stood at the side of the woman with hands on hips, his hair shaved short a line of tattooed stars ran from behind his left ear before disappearing below the collar of his pale blue shirt.

'Oh everything's fine, Tommy, we were just talking about this poor woman.'

The guard glanced at the shop assistant and shook his head. 'Are you after buying a television, son?'

Michael threw him a sour look, 'No.'

'I see.'

'But there's no law against looking, is there?'

'That depends on if you actually intend to purchase anything.'

‘I’ve already bought some cigs.’
‘Got proof of that have you?’
Michael frowned. ‘What are you talking about?’
‘Listen, Tommy, he’s not doing any harm,’ the woman looked at the security guard and tried to smile.
Tommy held out his hand. *‘Receipt?’*
Michael looked at the man in disbelief. ‘I don’t see you giving any other fucker grief!’
‘Watch your language.’ Tommy glanced around, people were beginning to stop and stare, a woman with an empty buggy hurried past as if she was looking for a child to fill it.
‘I think you'd better come with me.’
Michael shook his head. ‘No chance, I’ve done nothing.’
The shop assistant shook her head as if she could"t believe what was happening. ‘But, Tommy, he was just watching the television.’
‘Look, Laura, I’ve been watching him on the monitors.’
‘Fucking weirdo.’ Michael felt his hands bunch into fists.
Tommy took a step forward the colour flushing up from his shirt collar, anger flaring in his eyes.
‘Hang on, pal, I followed this lad into the store, I was behind him when he bought the cigarettes.’
Tommy spun around, a thickset man in a check shirt and paint-splattered jeans was looking directly at him.
For the first time the guard looked unsure of himself, a kid in a baseball cap muttered the word *‘wanker,’* as he strolled past.
‘So, unless you got proof that he’s actually nicked anything, I think you owe him an apology,’ check shirt said.
‘Don’t bother, pal, I’m used to tossers like him.’ Michael spat.
The guard glared but stayed rooted to the spot, Michael headed for the doors.

Once outside, he ripped the wrapper off the cigarettes and lit up, pulling the smoke deep into his lungs, before blowing it out into the hot summer air. First stop was Connelly's house; he just hoped he would find him at home. Michael set off walking, images of his dead brother rolling around his head like a washing machine on slow spin.

TAKING STOCK

Lasser pulled into the small lay-by, cut the engine off and climbed out, his mood as dark as the tarmac beneath his feet. Maybe this constant heat was scrambling his brain. He looked out over the open countryside in the distance he could see the traffic on the M61 a seemingly never-ending stream of commuters travelling in and out of Manchester. A kestrel hovered nearby, after a few seconds it plummeted to earth disappearing in thc grass before rising back into the clear sky. Trouble was, Hopkins was now in charge of a double murder and all he was left with was figuring why some overweight snob had decided to top himself. It was probably the same reason other people did the dirty deed, money worries or maybe he'd just had enough of life. Christ, he could sympathise with that.

He kicked a stone, watching as it bounced across the narrow lane and into the ditch. Right, it was time to stop fucking about and look at the facts. Billy Jones murdered late Wednesday night in a house in the middle of nowhere. At the time, he had been running from his so-called friends who probably wanted to beat the shit out of him. If they were not responsible for Billy's death then it meant that either the killer had followed Billy into the house or he had already been waiting inside. Lasser took a drag on the smoke, the thought that Billy had been unlucky enough to try to hide in a house that contained a vicious killer seemed far-fetched at best. So, that meant that the person responsible had watched as the kid headed for the house, after all, the field was huge, it would have taken Billy at least a minute to cover the open ground, time enough for the killer to see which way he was running and conceal himself in the house. After all, the cottage backed onto a narrow lane with plenty of tree cover and it made sense that the killer must have had a car, or more likely a van, to carry the body away in. Lasser pictured the scene, moonlight on the field, Billy staggering down the hillside, according to Connelly they had started the night at the top end of the Chinese Gardens and that had to be well over a mile from the house. He was a kid who could probably move fast when he needed to, though the panic of being chased would have tired him quickly. Besides knowing the type of people he was dealing with Billy might have even popped a couple of pills or smoked a fat joint, so he could have been wrecked. The house would have been a last resort, a place to hide because he was incapable of running any further. The man had watched and made his way to the house, entered and waited. Lasser dropped the cigarette onto the floor, it sounded reasonable enough. People murdered for all sorts of pathetic reasons, he had been in the job long enough to know how these things worked. Trouble was this was completely different. He thought back to the murder enquiries he had been involved in and every one without exception had been a domestic that had gone too far or drug related. The sad thing was that the four domestic murders had all been avoidable; each of the women had called the police on numerous occasions to complain about their partner's behaviour. Lasser recalled the escalating violence against Colleen Shaw, the bruises on her arms, the screaming of abuse at the man who had thrown her across the room, a woman with plenty of fire in her eyes. Six months later, he had gone out to see her again and the spark had vanished. He had spent over three hours trying to get her to see sense, one of her eyes had been swollen shut, and he had seen the finger marks around her neck where her boyfriend had tried to throttle her. By this time she was broken, unable to take on board what he was saying. Lasser had made sure she had a place at the women's refuge, he had made it his business to keep in touch, and for a few months, it seemed as if she were turning a corner. The last time he'd seen her she'd been talking about going to college and maybe getting a place of her own. Three weeks later, she had been having a night on the town, the first time she been out in almost two years, trouble was she had bumped into her ex. He had been off his face on cheap cocaine and cider. By the time her girlfriend got help Colleen had been dragged behind a parade of shops, raped and murdered, her body dumped amongst the bins, a place littered with empty beer cans and used condoms. He had been the first on scene at the boyfriend's house and found him slumped at the kitchen table. Grabbing the gobshite by the hair, Lasser had lifted his head from the table, the eyes had fluttered open but there was no recognition, though there had been blood around the mouth from where Colleen had bitten him. Lasser had let go and the head had slammed into the table top, the man's nose exploding in a shower of blood.

When the case had gone to trial the boyfriend had denied any knowledge of what had happened, the sad thing was Lasser believed him. He had sat in the dock hollow-eyed looking like a hunger strike victim, he didn't have a clue where he was, let alone what he was being accused of. A horrific crime, nevertheless it was murder. You could see how it had happened, bad drugs fuelling the brain of a man who cared for nothing. The last he'd heard, the killer had found God and was repentant for his sins, typical bullshit.

Yet this business with Billy Jones was different. Whoever had killed the boy had shown a level of control and according to Molder, a certain degree of skill had been required to remove the internal organs. Lasser sighed, then there was Kitts, it was impossible to know if the same man had killed him but the chances of two killers, murdering their victims within three hundred yards of one another seemed unlikely. He believed in coincidence but not to that extent. Which could only mean that the killer of Billy Jones had been up in the woods when Kitts had come wandering along. Lasser scratched his chin and thought back to the path of flattened grass that had led to the edge of the trees. Maybe Kitts hadn't been the one standing looking out across the open field. Suddenly it made sense, the killer had been watching the house, keeping his eye on the place. When he'd turned, there was the unfortunate Thomas pretending he was an elderly Ray Mears, but why kill the man?

He rested his arms on the roof of the car, then pulled them away with a hiss, the metal red hot. Cursing he rolled down his sleeves and tried again. Unless the killer was doing something suspicious, something that Kitts would have remembered and maybe reported to the police. Lasser smiled, that was more like it. Research had proven that murderers would often return to the crime scene, it gave them a buzz to watch the police bungling around while they jerked off. Lasser rubbed his hands together suddenly feeling on a roll. They were looking for a man who had no qualms about disembowelling a fourteen-year-old boy and who had enough control to kill an old man and try and make it look like natural causes.

He glanced at his watch, by rights he should be trying to find out more about Malcolm Radfield's past, though maybe that could wait for a while.

DISCOVERY

The dog strained at the leash, back legs scrabbling at the soft earth, nose to the ground. *'He's onto something, sir.'*

Hopkins tried to keep up but both man and animal were surging ahead up the steep hillside.

'Collins, slow down!' he bellowed.

The dog handler skidded to a halt. 'Sorry, sir, it's just that he's dead keen.'

'I can see that but we go at my pace, do you understand?'

'Yes, sir.'

'We do not go blundering, we do not trample, we go lightly.'

'Understood, sir.' Collins reined the dog in, pulling the German Shepherd tight to his side.

Hopkins turned; he could see the line of men moving slowly up the hillside, fluorescent jackets shining in the afternoon sunshine. Each had been supplied with a baton for searching through the undergrowth; all of them had their heads trained on the woodland floor looking for clues.

'Come on, you lot, keep up!'

The men raised their heads, though no one quickened their pace.

'Am I talking to myself here?'

A chorus of apologies drifted up the hillside, Hopkins grunted in approval as he saw the men begin to jog toward him.

'Right, Collins, get a move on.'

The dog handler extended the lead again and the animal dashed forward. Hopkins set off in pursuit; shafts of sunlight blasted down between the canopies of leaves, the air heavy with summer scents. He could hear the sound of his men closing behind so he quickened his pace. In his book, it was important to lead from the front, to lead by example. Collins had extended his lead, the dog dragging him along.

'Collins, I bloody well told you to slow down!'

Once again, the dog handler stopped in his tracks and waited for his boss to catch up.

'You're meant to be in control of that animal at all times, not the other way around.'

'Yes, sir.'

PC Spenner fell in by their side. 'It looks like he's onto something, sir.'

Hopkins turned, Spenner smiled at him, hands on hips.

'Well spotted, constable.' Hopkins injected just the right amount of disdain into his voice, a trait he had perfected over time and loved to use at every available opportunity.

Spenner blushed. 'I...

'Right, you lot, get up here.' Hopkins bellowed.

Spenner looked nervously over her shoulder. Twenty seconds later the men had gathered around in a rough semicircle. 'As Spenner here so kindly pointed out it appears the dog has picked up a scent.' Hopkins noted the look of disgust that some of the older officers directed toward Spenner. 'Now, from here on it's eyes and ears open, that doesn't mean treating this like a Sunday stroll in the park and it doesn't mean discussing how United will fair on Saturday, am I clear?' He didn't wait for a response but turned and gave Collins a nod before setting off again. Hopkins redoubled his effort, surging ahead, leaving lesser mortals to puff and pant in his wake.

'Do you think the dog's going to find the body, sir?'

Hopkins stared at Spenner in disbelief.

'What do you think you're doing?'

The young PC looked bemused. 'I don't understand, sir?'

Hopkins could feel the heat rising from his shirt collar his face darkened in anger.

'You should be down there with that lot.'

'But I thought...'

'Listen to me, Spenner, if you intend making a career for yourself then you'd do well to remember that you're here to do my bidding and nothing more, is that clear?'

Spenner snapped to attention. *'Yes, sir.'*

'That doesn't include trying to second guess me or putting your own personal spin on a situation, it simply means doing exactly what I say to the letter without question.'

'Understood, sir.'

'Right, get back into line and do your job.'

Spenner turned and trudged back down the hillside, a few seconds later Hopkins heard scathing laughter drifting up the hill.

Collins was reining in the big dog to avoid another roasting, pulling back on the leash as the animal strained forward. When they reached the first flight of stone steps the dog hesitated for a few moments, sniffing the ground in concentration, a few seconds later and it was off again.

Hopkins smiled to himself, if he could get a result on the case it would help to catapult him further up the ladder. At thirty-two things had gone well, his grand career plan on schedule and this could be the crowning glory, this could get his name onto the front pages of the newspapers.

The heat of the day was becoming unbearable, although he never considered loosening his tie, or removing his jacket. He allowed himself a tight smile, if Lasser had been here he would probably have been stripped to the waist by now. As far as he was concerned, that man represented everything that was wrong with the force. A man who went through his working day with a disdain for everyone he met. Moreover, he was lazy and arrogant and angry because he knew he would never get any further in the job, he had reached his limit. In fact, it was a miracle he had achieved the rank of detective sergeant. Hopkins jogged up the steps picturing a scenario where he had surpassed Lasser in rank, the day would come he was convinced of it. Lasser would be apoplectic with suppressed rage, having to address him as sir, having to kowtow to his every whim. Hopkins surmised that Lasser would last six months before he cracked, which could result in him asking for a transfer. As far as he was concerned, this outcome would be unacceptable. He wanted the man gone, preferably working nights as a security guard on some run-down industrial estate.

Stopping, Hopkins looked up; the flight of stone steps appeared to stretch into oblivion. Collins had let the lead out to its full length, the dog sweeping left to right, after a few seconds it gave a loud bark and shot off to the left.

'This way, sir.'

'I'm not blind, Collins.'

He skipped up the steps then veered left following Collins into bushes, by the time he made his way through the thicket, dog and handler were jogging ahead. It looked as if they were closing in on something; Hopkins just prayed it would lead to a fruitful result.

Glancing over his shoulder, he wasn't surprised to see Spenner emerging from the foliage, like a lapdog trying to impress, keen to make himself known to his master. Yes well, people like Spenner could be used; they were always prepared to go the extra mile to ingratiate themselves with an authority figure.

'Here, sir!'

Hopkins turned but Collins had disappeared around a large block of rhododendron bushes, the dog barking wildly now, a high-pitched yap that sounded strange coming from such a large powerful animal. When Hopkins rounded the wall of greenery he stopped in surprise. The tower soared toward the sky, looking oddly out of place amongst the huge beech trees. Collins was standing at the metal door; the dog on its hind legs, front paws paddling at the door.

'Collins, control that animal!' he bellowed. *'And stop it barking, I thought you were meant to be an expert handler?'*

Collins didn't reply, he merely turned and moved away, the dog now reined in and trotting by his side.

Hopkins eyed the padlocked door. *'Collins!'*

The handler turned; if looks could kill then Hopkins would have been writhing on the leaf-littered floor gasping out his last. Hopkins ignored it, he wasn't being paid to pamper to a glorified dog walker.

'Sir?'

'Are you sure about this?' he pointed at the door.

'Max doesn't make mistakes.'

Hopkins nodded in response and then gave the padlock a shake.

'Should we break it off, sir?'

Hopkins swiped a bead of sweat from his forehead and turned. 'And what do you suggest we use, Spenner?'

The young officer glanced around as if he expected to find a pair of bolt cutters in the long grass.

'Well...'

'Besides if you took the time to look then you'd see that this plaque attached to the door tells us that this building belongs to United Utilities. In addition, if you look closely you'll see that it also provides us with a phone number. So, if it's alright with you, I'll give them a ring before we start attacking the door with sticks.'

A few of the men had caught them up; a couple sniggered at Spenner as he withered under Hopkins disdain.

'Right, you lot, spread out, I want this place cordoned off and the area searched, is that clear?'

Nods and *'yes, sirs'* followed, he pulled out his mobile and punched in the number, keeping his fingers crossed.

NOT A PROBLEM

'So, where is he now?' Michael stood on the doorstep of Connelly's house, a carbon copy of his own home, same weeds in the garden, same paint peeling from the front door. He could even smell fried food wafting out through the open door.

Kyle's mother twisted the ring in her nose, wincing at the sting. 'I'm telling you they took him away yesterday and I haven't seen him since. I haven't a clue what he's meant to have done but you know what the coppers are like, any excuse.'

Michael bit his lip in frustration.

'And how are you coping?' she asked.

'I'm alright.'

'I couldn't believe it when I heard about your brother.'

'His name was Billy,' he said through gritted teeth.

She flicked the cigarette stump into the garden. 'I saw your mum on the news earlier, she must be going spare?'

'So, he's not in then?'

For a moment, she looked confused and then the penny dropped. 'No, I've already told you he got carted off yesterday.' Michael turned to go. 'I'll tell him you called when I see him.'

He didn't bother with a reply, he couldn't see the point.

On the street, an ice-cream van trundled past, blasting black smoke from the exhaust. Pulling out another cigarette he lit up, his eyes glued to the gum-littered pavement. He could go round to Miller's house but he knew it would be a waste of time, the filth had them banged up, but eventually he would get his chance.

'Hello, Michael.'

He looked up; Tina Sheldon smiled at him nervously, a crop top showing the slight swell of her stomach, the make-up thick on her face.

'Alright, Tina.'

'How are you?'

Michael looked up at the sky. 'Why does everybody keep asking me that?'

The ice-cream van had stopped, kids were migrating towards it, running with money clasped in their grubby hands. Some nursery rhyme warbling in the still summer air like the Pied Piper attracting a town full of rats.

'I'm sorry, I didn't mean to…'

'When's the baby due?'

She looked at him in surprise. 'Four months to go yet but I just wish it'd hurry up, I'm sick of walking around like this,' she held her arms out, the shirt slid up revealing the bottom of a black bra. 'How did your mum take it, you know about Billy?'

Michael dropped the cigarette onto the floor and stamped on it. 'I don't wanna talk about that bitch.'

Tina raised an eyebrow and sighed. 'Why, what's she done now?'

'Just leave it, Tina.'

'OK, sorry,' she paused, before looking skyward, 'so where are you off to?'

He shrugged, suddenly feeling tired, as if the long walk from Fossey's house, coupled with the dragging weight of Billy's death had left him washed out. He looked at her; they had known each other from junior school, sat in the same classes. He remembered when they had gone onto high school, Tina was placed in the higher sets and had shown a real flair for art.

'If you don't want to go to your mums, you could come home with me?' she smiled sadly as if she already knew he was going to refuse her offer.

Michael hesitated and then shrugged. 'Why not, the way things are at the moment she's the last person I want to see.'

She looked at him aghast. 'Are you sure?'

'Yeah, why not.'

They set off, as they walked past the ice-cream van Michael watched the owner hand over a pouch of tobacco to a kid who looked about ten.

'I hate this frigging town.'

She looked at him, a crooked smile on her face. 'I know what you mean.'

'Do you still do art and stuff?' he asked.

'I was going to college...'

'I know, I've seen you there a few times.'

'Yeah well, the baby's due at the end of the holidays so I don't know whether I'll be able to keep going.'

'What about your mum, won't she watch the kid when it's born?'

'You're joking, right? She didn't even want me to keep it in the first place.'

'What about your old man?'

Tina snorted. 'He's even worse; he told me he wants nothing else to do with me. I wouldn't mind but he's got kids everywhere.'

Michael grimaced. 'Do you know if it's a boy or a girl?'

'They couldn't tell but I'm hoping for a girl.'

'Why's that?'

She paused for a moment. 'Then I can dress her up, you know buy her nice things'

Michael found himself smiling. 'Have you thought of a name yet?'

'If it is a girl I wanted to call her Becky.'

'What if it's a boy?'

'Christ, don't say that I don't want a boy. I mean, you know what it's like around here, all the lads are a pain in the arse,' she spoke without a hint of irony.

'Hey, Jones, how's your Billy doing!'

Michael stopped in his tracks and looked across the road, Brett Halliwell was leaning against the bus stop, a sneer on his face, another lad by his side that Michael didn't recognise.

'What did you say?'

Halliwell grinned. ‘Didn’t say anything, pal.’
Michael checked the road and began to cross, halfway over he felt a tug on his sleeve.
‘Don’t, Mickey.’ Tina looked at him warily. *‘He’s just a scumbag druggie.’*
‘Tina making it all better is she, helping you forget? Yeah well, she’s good at that aren’t you, Tina?’
At the look of fury in Michael’s eyes, she released the sleeve and took a backward step.
He stormed across the road; Halliwell pushed himself away from the bus stop and began to bounce up and down on the balls of his feet. ‘Come on then, big man, Kyle reckons you’re a hard fucker so let’s...'
Michael suddenly lunged forward, Halliwell raised his fists and Michael lashed out, his trainer sinking deep into Halliwell’s crotch. As he doubled over, Michael snapped his knee up, smashing it into the boy’s mouth. Halliwell crashed to the pavement, the other boy backed away with his hands half raised.
‘It’s fuck all to do with me, mate,’ he said nervously.
Brett Halliwell lay sprawled on his side, his eyes flickered but refused to open, he coughed, and two teeth slipped from the wreckage of his mouth.
‘Jesus.’ Tina looked down, her eyes wide in shock.
‘Come on, let’s go.’ This time Michael was the one pulling her away. The ice-cream van drove past, the sound of ‘Popeye, the sailor man’ blasting from the speaker on the roof. When she glanced over her shoulder, the unknown boy had vanished but Halliwell remained rooted to the pavement.
‘Christ, did you see the state of his mouth?’
Michael could feel the adrenaline surging through his body; he quickened his pace with Tina struggling to keep up.
‘Slow down, Michael,’ she gasped, he stopped and turned, her cheeks were flushed, she saw his eyes shining, and then the tears broke free. Tina looked on in

shock, she couldn't remember the last time she had seen anyone cry, least of all someone like Michael Jones.

She opened her arms, a reflex action and he took a hesitant step forward into her embrace.

KILLNG TIME

Jenna stood at the kitchen sink, lopping the leaves from a cauliflower, her mind in turmoil. When Patrick had told them about the missing boy and Thomas Kitts, she'd felt her world unravel, her grip on normality slipped and now she was hanging on by her fingertips.

To try to keep herself sane she'd fed and cleaned the chickens, she'd even run the Dyson through every room in the house. What she really needed was to bc outside; under normal circumstances she would have taken herself off for a long walk and thought things through in a rational manner. As things stood, that was an impossibility, the media were still parked on the lane and there was no way her parents would let her out of their sight.

For the first time she considered the possibility that the murders would taint the whole area for her, the places she loved would forever be linked with the slaughter of William Jones and Thomas Kitts. She tried to imagine walking through the familiar countryside without having to look over her shoulder, without feeling like there was a killer hiding behind every tree.

A figure walked past the kitchen window, her breath caught in her throat, a sense of panic fluttered her senses, her hand tightened on the handle of the knife. A few seconds later, and her grandad strolled in through the back door.

He stopped and looked at her in surprise. 'Bloody hell, Jen, things must be bad if you're peeling veg.'

She dragged up a smile. 'I'm just trying to keep busy.'

'Where's your mother?'

'Upstairs, she's on the phone to Claire Woodman.'

As if on cue, Susan came through the door, her face flushed with anxiety, ignoring them both she went straight to the kitchen window.

'Mum, what's the matter?'

'I've just come off the phone to Claire; she said four police cars have just gone flying past her place with lights and sirens flashing.'

'Any idea where they were going?' Ronnie asked.

'She said they were heading toward the Chinese Gardens.'

Jenna looked nervous. 'I wonder if they've found something.'

'You mean like a body?' Ronnie said.

Susan frowned at her father. 'Honestly, Dad.'

'It's OK, Mum, I'm sure we were all thinking the same thing.'

She let the net curtain swing back into place. 'She also said the police were being followed by a line of vans with satellite dishes on the roof.'

'Reporters! That's why you went to the window to see if they'd left?'

'Yes, but unfortunately they're still there.'

Jenna peeled back the curtain. 'Why can't they just leave us alone?'

'Claire said she'll see if Jim knows anything and get back to me.'

'Does Dad know what's happened?'

'Hang on, Jenna; I've only just come off the phone.'

'Do you want me to give him a ring?'

'No, thanks, love, I'll do it.'

'Perhaps I should give Patrick a call.'

Susan turned. 'Jenna, he only left an hour ago, give the man some peace.'

Jenna felt the tension flood through her system. 'What do you mean by that?'

'Look I am pleased about the book, we're all proud of you, sweetheart, but the man does have other things to do.'

Jenna felt her face burn, score another point for mother. 'I was only going to tell him about the police and the reporters. I mean, it's no different than you ringing the Woodmans.'

'Jenna, it's completely different, Jim and Claire are friends of ours, they're our closest neighbours, and what's happened here can affect them as well as us.'

'But...'

'I'm not saying Patrick isn't a nice guy but at the end of the day he doesn't have to carry on living here when this is all over.'

'What has that got to do with anything?' she took a step forward, all the anger and frustration welling up inside. From nowhere a sudden tension had been injected into the air like some odourless nerve agent.

Susan sighed. 'Look, I'm not trying to be awkward....'

'Well, it sounds like it to me.'

Jenna felt a hand on her shoulder. 'All right, Jenna, calm down love.'

Susan saw the look of anger flash across her daughter's face as she spun away to face her grandad. *'What do you mean calm down? I'm sick of you lot treating me like some kind of infant.'*

'Oh for God's sake, Jenna, stop over-reacting.' As soon as the words left her mouth, Susan cringed.

When Jenna turned, it was with slow deliberation. 'So, you think I'm over-reacting?'

'Look, I didn't mean it to come out like that.'

'If you didn't mean it, why did you say it?'

Susan tried to backpedal. 'We're just concerned, Jenna, this is a stressful time for us all.'

'I know that, but this has nothing to do with what's going on here.'

The kettle began to boil; Ronnie eyed it, watching the water bubble away in the little see-through plastic slot.

Susan looked baffled. 'I don't understand.'

Jenna knew what she wanted to say but her brain suddenly felt heavy and sluggish. 'I'm seventeen and I feel like a prisoner,' it was a weak response, her chance to tell her mother what she really thought. Yet that was the best she could come up with?

'Oh, so you mean we should just let you go wandering off, is that what you are saying? I mean, there's a maniac out there who's already killed two people but we shouldn't bother taking precautions.' Susan was aware that her voice had taken on a mocking quality, horrified at how much she sounded like her own mother.

'I'm not saying that at all but I need to be given some responsibility. I need to feel that you trust me to do the right thing and I'm not talking about wandering off on my own.'

'Of course we trust you.' Ronnie flicked off the kettle.

'Then prove it.'

Susan frowned. 'And how do you propose we do that?'

'I don't know how; just don't make me feel like you're watching me all the time.'

'But we don't; up until all this started you could do what you wanted,' she paused, 'within reason.'

'Oh come on...'

'Look, I know it's not always easy living out here and you've missed out on certain things...'

'But that's just it; I haven't missed out on anything. I mean, do you think I want to hang around in town getting a drug habit and losing my virginity to one of the morons who hang around on the street corners.'

Ronnie couldn't remember the last time he had blushed; it might have been on his wedding night over fifty years ago when he saw his new wife naked for the first time.

'I love living here, I just want,' she paused, 'things to get back to normal.' It sounded lame, pathetic.

'Right, who wants a cup of tea?' Ronnie asked.

Jenna glared at her grandad, when she saw the upset etched onto his face; she suddenly felt a wave of guilt wash over her. She was pathetic, moaning because she felt smothered when the reality was her family loved and cared about her and all she could do was throw it back in their faces. Jenna sighed, 'Why not.'

Ronnie smiled tentatively and turned to the sink glad to be doing something with his hands. It took him a moment to realise that something had changed with the view. *'The vans have gone!'*

Daughter and granddaughter peered over his shoulder; Jenna rested her hand on his arm.

Susan sighed. 'Thank God for that, maybe now your dad can relax a little.'

Jenna blew out between pursed lips; her dad wasn't the only one.

EXTRACTING THE URINE

Lasser was furious when he found out Hopkins had stumbled onto something. Meadows had sounded smug on the two-way, claiming he didn't really know what was happening but whatever it was it was big.

He was steaming toward the Chinese Gardens, his mind fizzing with anger. He slowed as the lane began to narrow, trees crowded in on either side, as if deliberately trying to slow him down; the surface of the road growing patchy forcing him to dodge numerous potholes. Fumbling in the pocket of his jacket, he pulled out his cigarettes and pressed the lighter into the small socket. A moment later, the front wheels dropped down a long gash in the road, the suspension grinding as the wheels struggled free.

'Fuck!' The cigarette dropped from his fingers and rolled into the foot well.

If Hopkins solved this thing he'd be unbearable, he could picture his smug face on the news, the hero of the hour, lording it over everyone at the station. Lasser's teeth took a battering as he ground them together in frustration, the urge to get his foot down tempered by the state of the road. As he rounded the corner, he saw a white transit van dipping and leaning as it moved along in front. He could see the logo splashed across the back doors, the words Orbital Television curling around an image of the earth.

This just got better; it seemed everyone knew what was going on apart from him. They pulled up on the left, two men climbed out, one of them holding a camera on his shoulder. By the time he reached the van the men had vanished into the trees. An assortment of police vehicles and white transit vans stretched along the narrow lane.

Lasser slammed the car door before scrambling over the wall and heading off into the woods. He could see the reporters thirty yards ahead, weaving their way through the trees, it seemed they had no trouble knowing which way to go.

The ground beneath his feet began to grow steeper, the leaf-littered floor causing him to slither and slide his way down, in the distance he saw the unmistakable flash of a yellow high viz jacket.

The tower seemed to materialise out of the browns and greens of the forest, a group of reporters were talking amongst themselves, a couple of photographers snapped off images of the uniforms as they beat their way through the undergrowth.

He spotted Carl dressed in a white paper boiler suit, which probably meant they'd found something grim.

'Afternoon, Carl,' he said as he approached.

Carl pulled down the paper mask that covered his nose and mouth. 'All right, boss, I didn't expect to see you here.'

'Why do you always say that, I mean, why should it be such a bloody surprise?'

'Well, I just thought with DS Hopkins being in…'

'Fuck him, now what have you got for me?'

Carl looked surprised by the outburst then he hooked a thumb over his shoulder. 'The dog picked up the scent.'

Lasser sucked his teeth. 'Bad?'

'The body is at the top of the tower; what's left of him is hanging from a crossbeam.'

'Is Hopkins inside?'

'He was but he came out pretty sharpish.'

Lasser smiled grimly. 'Not got the stomach for it, eh?'

'It's not that, it's just as soon as the cameras turned up he went out to be interviewed. In fact he's over there now.'

Lasser looked toward where Carl was pointing and sure enough he could see Hopkins standing amongst a patch of ferns, surrounded by reporters, tiny lights lancing out from the cameras all trained on the immaculately dressed Hopkins.

'He should be doing his job, not preening for the media,' Lasser snapped.

'You know what he's like; he's only interested in number one.'

'Yeah well, I might as well take a look around while he's having his fifteen minutes.'

'I've seen nothing.'

'Good man.' Inside the tower the air was musty with age, sunlight pooled in through the open door flooding the narrow space with light; apart from a couple of tea-chests stacked against one wall the small space was empty. To his right, stone steps spiralled upward; he could hear the muffled sound of footsteps from above, so he began to climb. He caught the scent when he was halfway up, the unmistakable stench of decomposing flesh. By the time he reached the trapdoor entrance his stomach was twitching and rolling at the fetid onslaught. As he poked his head through the gap, a camera flash lit up the gruesome scene. Billy Jones hung from the end of a thick rope, his face a swirling kaleidoscope of black and blue flesh, the eyes swollen shut. Lasser closed his eyes but the image remained seared into his brain.

'Hello, Lasser, you have one twisted individual to catch.'

Monty Marsh held the camera loosely in his large hands; his huge frame seemed to fill the tiny space.

'Not me, Monty, that's Hopkins job.'

'Does he know you're here?'

'What do you think?'

Marsh smiled. 'I take it he's still auditioning for Crimewatch?'

Lasser nodded before hauling himself up onto the platform. 'How did you guess?' he asked before turning his attention to the hanging slab of meat.

'Welcome to the world of the sick mind.' Monty said.

'That's mild for you.'

Monty shrugged. 'I'm trying to get out of the habit of using expletives; the grandkids were starting to pick up some of my more colourful phrases.'

Lasser smiled and then looked at the boarded up slots in the walls, reaching out he gave one a tug but the timber held fast.

'We either need to get these boards off the windows or get some lighting up here.'

'That's up to Hopkins isn't it?'

'Come here, Monty, see if you can get one of these boards loose.'

The crime scene photographer reached out and gave the sheet of plywood a pull. 'You do realise he'll go mad when he finds out?'

'Not interested, now come on, pull,' both men yanked and slowly the board began to come loose, sunlight spilled into the small space, Monty gave one final tug, grunting with the effort then the wood came free the nails sounding like a small animal caught in a trap. Lasser took the board and placed it carefully against the wall. Dust motes spiralled in the air, the sight of the corpse swinging was both pitiful and grotesque. Billy's bare legs were lathered with the dried blood, the incision started at the neck and ended an inch above the pelvic bone. The body cavity was a red maw of ragged flesh, the skin mottled with mauves and blues.

'Poor little sod.' Monty snapped off another picture.

Lasser looked at the floorboard beneath the corpse, the dust had turned ochre where it had soaked up the blood. He frowned, then crouched on his haunches, the tiny metal square glittered in the half-light.

Pulling an evidence bag from his pocket, he slipped it inside.

'What have you got there?' Monty asked.

'Something you wouldn't expect to find in a place like this.'

Monty took the bag and held it up close to his face. 'It's a bloody cufflink.'

'Mind your language, Monty.'

The cameraman smiled ruefully and handed it back. Lasser opened the bag and jiggled the cufflink around, then peered closely at the small gold plate. The crossed guns inscribed onto the metal were tiny, Lasser grinned. When he'd gone up to the Radfield's home, he had noticed the same emblem carved into the stone lintel that spanned the huge front door.

'Right, Monty, I'll leave you to it.'

'Leaving so soon?'

'Unlike some, I prefer to follow up on a lead rather than practising flashing my pearly whites at the camera.'

'What about the evidence, are you going to pass it onto Hopkins?'

Lasser grimaced, that was the big question, if he decided to keep hold of it then he ran the risk of Hopkins finding out and then he would go straight to Simms, bleating about how a fellow officer had held back vital evidence in a double murder case. As much as he despised the man, he didn't want to give him any bullets to fire.

'No, I'm not going to give it to him.'

'Are you sure that's wise?' Monty asked with a frown.

'I only said I wasn't going to personally hand it over, that doesn't mean I can't leave the bag in your capable hands.'

'You want me to do it?'

Lasser held the bag out, after a few seconds Monty shrugged and plucked it from his fingers.

'By the way you know what Hopkins is like when he's in the starring role, he hates to be interrupted.'

'So, I shouldn't disturb him, is that what you're saying?'

'That's up to you but I wouldn't want to be the one who stops him in mid flow.'

'I'll wait until he pops up here then.'

Lasser began to disappear back down the steps. 'I'll catch you later, Monty.'

Back outside, he glanced down the hillside, Hopkins was still busy making a name for himself, pointing at individual reporters, turning this way and that to offer the camera a profile shot. Shaking his head in disgust Lasser began to clamber back up the steep incline.

Once back in the car, he slapped on the air con. His shirt clung to his back as he swiped the sweat from his face with the back of ahand. In order to turn around he had to travel further up the rutted lane until he found a spot where he could attempt a three-point turn. Facing the right way he set off, his head buzzing with the need to get a move on, though the derelict road had other ideas.

As the car banged down another pothole, he thought of Sarah Jones trying to sell her story to the local rags.

He hoped she was the one to identify the body, perhaps she'd look upon the wreckage of her son and realise that she bore some responsibility. The kid had been fourteen yet he'd lived the life of someone older. Cheap booze and even cheaper drugs, coupled with a mother who didn't care where her son was or what he was up to. A father who was in and out of jail, both willing to turn a blind eye when their offspring turned up with stolen goods, giving them a pat on the back, instilling in them that only mugs worked for a living.

At last the road began to widen and Lasser got his foot down, Billy might have been a thief and a tearaway but he hadn't deserved to die, especially not like that.

He grimaced; when he'd made the link between the button from the Barbour jacket and the murder, he had been elated though the feeling had been short lived. Even now after finding the cufflink, he still couldn't see the late Malcolm Radfield as the killer. At the junction he turned left, a cow peered at him over a five bar gate its jaw moving lazily as it chewed on a clump of clover.

So, where did that leave him? Well, a button was one thing, but a cufflink with the family coat of arms inscribed on the surface, went way beyond mere coincidence.

He slowed as a tractor and trailer rumbled past, a few seconds later the rich smell of liquid cow shit drifted into the car. He grimaced at the onslaught, slid the windows up and lit a cigarette to help mask the stink.

If old man Radfield had been incapable of murder then that left his son with some serious explaining to do. He flicked on the radio and tuned into the oldies station, John Lennon's nasal tones singing about the 'Nowhere Man'.

SEPIA

The sun was sinking toward the wooded hills, a raspberry-coloured sunset.

Fossey headed around the back of the house, weaving his way through the small apple orchard, the fruit-hanging heavy on the gnarly branches. He stopped and picked one, rubbing it to a high sheen on the sleeve of his jacket before taking a bite. This time last year, he'd been travelling the country doing book signings and the fruit had been left to rot on the branch.

Perhaps Ronnie could take them off his hands; after all, he liked to make his own cider and besides it would give him the opportunity to pick the old farmers brains. When they'd been walking up to the tower, he had the distinct feeling that Ronnie knew more about the Radfield family than he had prepared to divulge.

On the other side of the trees, he cut through a gap in the bushes and headed out into open fields. The dog dashed about amongst the tall grass, occasionally leaping into the air to get his bearings.

The heat of the day bled away, a faint mist rising from the ground.

His phone began to vibrate, he checked the screen, Jenna's name flashed on and off in time to the beat.

'Hello, Jenna, I was just thinking about you.'

'You were?' she sounded shocked and more than a little pleased.

'Mm, how are things at your end?'

Her sigh sounded like a light breeze sifting through dry grass.

'Not too bad I suppose, it's just that with all this going on I feel like a bit of a prisoner. I mean, my mum and dad are worried and I understand that,' she paused, *'I just wish the whole thing had never happened.'*

'Well, I might be able to offer you and your grandad a bit of a respite…'

'A respite?'

'You see I have a small orchard in the garden...'

'Wow really?'

'It's only a few trees but it's been a bumper crop this year and I know Ronnie mentioned he liked to make his own cider. So, I was wondering if the two of you would be interested in coming over to help me pick the apples. I mean, Ronnie can have the lot, I just don't like to think of all the fruit going to waste.'

'That would be brilliant.'

He could hear the change in her voice, melancholy replaced by unbounded excitement.

'Right well, you clear it with your mum and ring me back with a decision.'

'When do you want us there?'

'I'm no expert but I think they are ready to pick now, in fact I've just eaten one.'

'So, we could come tomorrow?' she asked tentatively.

'I don't have a problem with that, in fact whatever suits you best.'

'I'll ring you back in ten minutes,' she paused, *'possibly less.'* The phone went dead.

He whistled and the dog leaped to its feet, in the distance he heard the boom of a shotgun, in the next field a murder of crows took to the sky.

FLUFFY TOYS

Michael squinted as he stood on the threshold of Tina's bedroom; all the walls were painted bright pink the bedding was pink even the curtains were a shocking cerise colour with red sequined hearts stitched onto the cloth. A multitude of soft toys covered the bed.

'Sorry about the mess,' she said.

'What mess?'

She smiled in embarrassment. 'I know it looks like a ten-year-olds room,' she shrugged. 'I keep meaning to change things around a bit but I don't see the point until the baby gets here.'

'I just didn't think it would be so,' he paused, 'pink.'

She handed him a can of Coke and sat down on the bed, Michael looked around for somewhere to sit but the only chair in the room had a giant teddy bear on it. Tina shuffled higher up the bed scattering the soft toys onto the floor. He perched on the edge of the mattress; sunlight filled the room, spilling across the crimson carpet, it was like sitting inside a giant boiled sweet.

'I can't believe what you did to Halliwell.'

Michael rubbed his knee, he could feel the swelling from where he had made contact with Halliwell's face. 'He's a prick.'

She took a sip from her can, looking closely at his profile. She had always fancied him though when they had been at school together he had continually ignored her. Occasionally, she would catch his eye and flash him her best smile and he would simply look through her as if she didn't exist. In fact, for a while getting Michael Jones to notice her had become something of an obsession. Her skirts had become shorter, her makeup thicker, the false tan coating her legs browner. Trouble was the less she wore the more he ignored her, of course she got plenty of attention from other boys but that wasn't what she had wanted.

Now he was in her bedroom, something she had dreamt about and although he still looked gorgeous, there was a sadness etched on his face. She thought about how he had felt in her arms, it had been heart-breaking and thrilling to feel the sobs wracking through his chest, slamming against her own heart.

'Are you OK?' she asked, her voice little more than a whisper, as if afraid that she would break some imaginary spell and he would vanish in a puff of smoke.

He dragged up a smile that was full of heartbreak. 'I just can't believe he's gone,' he rubbed at his eyes. 'I mean, he could be a little shit at times, but...'

'He was still your brother.'

His shoulders slumped, the adrenalin that had swept through his body had long since abated, leaving him feeling battered and drained.

She tried to think of something to say, something that would offer some sort of comfort. At seventeen, she was used to offering advice though it was usually to girlfriends who were having boy trouble. She ran through some of the stock phrases she had used in the past, though nothing seemed appropriate. When she did open her mouth to speak, she wished she had kept it shut.

'Do you know how he died?'

For a few seconds he continued to look at the carpet when he did turn to look at her his eyes were ignited with fury. She resisted the urge to jump from the bed and dash from the room. 'I'm sorry; I shouldn't have asked it's none of my business,' she tried to keep the panic from her voice, the words tripping over one another in her effort to defuse the situation.

'I haven't got a fucking clue; I mean, how sad is that? When the copper said he couldn't go into detail I just nodded my head like a dumb fucker.'

His voice started to rise and Tina cringed inside, any minute now, her mother would come barging in and then God knows what would happen.

'What copper?'

'His name's Lasser, he was the one who told me about Billy, he was there when I hit the fat bitch.'

'You hit your mother,' she whispered, her own mother could be a nightmare. In fact there had been plenty of times when they had stood toe to toe, screaming at one another although Tina had always known that it would never get physical.

'Believe me, she deserved it.' Michael said darkly.

She picked up a cabbage patch doll and hugged it to her chest.

'So, you can't go home?'

'I'm never going back there, besides knowing her, the place will be crawling with reporters by now.'

'What makes you say that?'

He told her about seeing his mother on the TV screens in Tesco, his voice faltering in shame.

Tina chewed a nail. 'That must have been awful?'

'She was acting like this perfect Mother who'd lost her little baby, it made me want to throw up.'

'But why would she do that?'

'Look, you don't know what she's like; the only thing she'll be interested in is how she can make money out of this.'

Tina plucked at a thread of cotton on the duvet, in a town that had more than its fair share of dysfunctional families, the Jones clan stood out more than most.

'So, what are you going to do, I mean, if you can't go home where are you going to stay?'

He stood up, suddenly agitated. He hadn't thought this through, the urge to get hold of Kyle Connelly and make him pay had turned into nothing and he had no intention of setting foot in the family home again. He knew he could call on certain people who would let him doss on their sofa for a few days, the trouble was they were the kind of people he was trying to break away from. Perhaps he should have stayed at Fossey's house; maybe the writer had been in a position to help him find out more about what had happened to Billy. He should go back; Michael checked his watch and was shocked to discover that it was almost six o'clock.

'You could always stay here if you want?' Tina was looking at the floor, her face obscured by her long blond hair.

'What about your mother?'

She shrugged. 'If she'd been bothered about lads staying over then maybe I wouldn't be in this mess in the first place.'

'Do you know who the dad is?'

'What sort of question's that? I mean, I know what people like Halliwell are saying, Tina Sheldon the slag, opens her legs to anyone.'

'Hang on; I never said that, I was just curious that's all.'

'Well, for your information I do know who the father is,' she snapped.

'OK, take a chill pill.'

She glanced up and smiled. 'So, do you want to stay?'

'Just for one night if that's OK?'

'You can stay as long as you like.'

'Tomorrow, I'm going to see a man who might be able to help me find out what really happened to Billy.'

'Is it the copper?'

'Nah, his name's Fossey,' he took a long drink from the can and swallowed down a burp.

'So, does he live around here?' she asked.

'Horwich.'

'So, how are you going to get there, I mean, have you got any money?'

'I've got a bit of cash but I can always walk it.'

'Jesus, Mickey, it's miles away, it'll take you hours.'

'Two and a half, that's where I was last night, so I know how long it takes.'

She leaned over and slid open the drawer on her bedside cabinet. 'Here, take this,' she held out four twenty pound notes.

Michael held up his hands. 'I can't take your money, Tina.'

'Of course you can, listen I don't need it. Honestly I want you to have it.'

'No way,' he backed up shaking his head.

'Please,' she pushed the money toward him. 'Whatever you don't use you can just bring back.'

'But you're having a kid you're going to need all the money you can get.'

'I'm not bothered about that.'

Michael looked at her outstretched hand. 'I don't get it, why would you want to help me?'

She didn't reply, he watched as she rolled the money into a narrow cylinder.

'Listen, what are you doing tomorrow?' he asked.

'I'm not doing anything, why?'

'Well, why don't you come with me?'

'What to see this ...?' she tried to remember the name.

'Fossey.'

'But why would you want me tagging along?'

He tried to think of another reason and found that he couldn't. So he settled for the truth. 'I just want you there.'

She looked at him perched on the edge of the bed, the hardness had gone from his face, replaced with bewilderment.

'Are you hungry?' she asked.

Michael sniffed and rubbed at his eyes. 'Starving.'

'I can make beans on toast.'

'Sound.'

She stood up, pulling the T-shirt down over her bump. 'Well, if we have a busy day tomorrow, we might as well have something to eat,' she smiled. 'I have to keep my strength up you know.'

'You don't have to come, I mean, if it's too far.'

She ignored him. 'Do you want a brew with your tea?'

'No thanks', I'm fine with this,' he shook the can at her.

'OK, I won't be long,' as she walked past he took hold of her arm and stood up, dipping his head he brushed her cheek with his lips.

'Thanks.'

Tina felt herself blush. 'It's no problem, Mickey, I want to help.'

She turned and hurried from the room, Michael kicked off his trainers and lay on the bed, two minutes later he was asleep.

JOKING

'I promise you this, when my solicitor gets here I'll make sure he puts in a formal complaint about your behaviour, Sergeant.'

Lasser looked at Ashley Radfield, his aristocratic face bone white with anger.

'We're not here to discuss my behaviour, Mr Radfield. What I'd like to know is why a cufflink bearing your family coat of arms was discovered beneath the hanging corpse of a fourteen-year-old boy?'

Ashley crossed his legs and pulled a small silver case from his pocket.

Lasser waited until he had extracted a cigarette and pulled out his lighter. 'You can't smoke in here,' he said with a smile, pointing to the *'no smoking'* sign pinned to the wall.

Radfield's lips became a thin bloodless line. 'I've already explained I'm saying nothing until I've seen my solicitor.'

'And why would that be? I mean, it doesn't look too sparkling you refusing to help the police in such a serious matter. If you genuinely have no idea about any of this then why don't you open your mouth and say so?'

'And you'd believe me would you? I tell you I have absolutely no idea what you are referring to. You'll be satisfied and apologise, is that what you are saying, Sergeant?'

'Hardly.'

'So, you can understand my reluctance?'

'Not really, I just know that if I was in your situation I'd want to get the whole thing sorted. I understand that you value your privacy, it's natural, though once the rumours start it'll impact on you more than most.'

'Meaning what exactly?'

'Well, nobody likes to have their family name splashed all over the tabloids do they? Though to be honest you've probably had dealings with them in the past...'

'Just what the hell do you mean by that?'

'You know the type of thing, opening summer fetes, judging the weirdly shaped vegetables at the agricultural shows.'

Radfield's eyes narrowed until they were no more than slits. 'I have friends who work in the media. When all this is over I'll avail myself of their services to make sure they turn their attention in your direction.'

'I've always wanted to get my picture on the front page of the Daily Sport,' Lasser replied with a grin.

'You're very droll aren't you; let's see how long your sense of humour lasts when they're going through your bins.'

'Did you hear that Harper?'

Cathy was standing in a corner of the room, her eyes flicked toward Lasser. 'Yes, sir.'

'Failing to cooperate with an ongoing murder investigation and threatening a police officer, it's turning into a busy night for you, Mr Radfield.'

Ashley sat back in his chair the beginnings of a smirk on his face, though his eyes remained hard and unflinching. 'I don't make threats, Sergeant.'

'Oh, so it's a promise, is that what you're telling me?'

'As I've already said, I will act on the advice of my solicitor. Until then I suggest you spend your time trying to catch whoever was responsible for this terrible crime.'

The door opened, Lasser glanced over his shoulder. DCI Simms poked his head into the room.

'A word, Sergeant.'

Simms stood in the corridor the buttons on his dress uniform gleamed in the artificial light, the crease in his trousers razor sharp. 'My office. Now.'

As they made their way through the station Lasser began to feel like a condemned man, Simms remained tight-lipped, fellow colleagues glanced at them and then looked away. This did not look good. Simms pushed open the door to his office and ushered Lasser inside.

Hopkins was sitting in one of the two chairs facing the desk; he didn't turn around but remained facing the wall as if there was already someone sitting in the chair opposite.

Lasser slid in beside his colleague.

Simms walked around the desk and sat down. 'Right, Lasser, what's going on here?'

'I'm sorry, sir, I don't follow.'

'Hopkins informs me that you were up at the crime scene today, according to him you were snooping around?'

'I call it doing my job, sir.'

Hopkins snorted. 'You had no right being there and you know it. I'm in charge of the Jones and the Kitts investigation.'

'I did look for you, Charlie, but someone said you were busy talking to the media.'

'That's enough, Lasser,' Simms opened a draw in his desk, placing the bagged cufflink on the table. 'Now; Sergeant Hopkins informs me that you found this at the crime scene?'

'That's correct, sir.'

Hopkins turned in his seat. 'That evidence should have been handed to me personally, Lasser.'

'It was handed to you personally.'

'By a crime scene photographer nearly two hours after you found it....'

'It isn't my fault you like spending so much time in front of the cameras.'

'Enough!' Simms bellowed. 'Lasser, you should have been nowhere near that crime scene, I gave you strict orders to follow up on the Radfield suicide, is that correct?'

Lasser nodded. 'Yes, sir.'

'And when I give a direct order I expect my men to follow it to the letter.'

From the corner of his eye, Lasser saw Hopkins nod in agreement; he was loving this, the pompous twat. 'Understood, sir, it won't happen again.'

'I hope not because this isn't the first time I have had to draw attention to your lack of discipline, is it?'

'No, sir.'

Simms nodded, 'Right, good.' The DCI looked down at his desk and Lasser risked a quick glance at Hopkins, his counterpart glared back clearly he had been expecting Lasser to get a lot more than a simple bollocking. 'Now then, Hopkins, can you explain why you were talking to the press when there was a crime scene that you clearly had not taken the time to search?'

'Sir?' Hopkins appeared baffled by this sudden turn of events.

'It's not a trick question, Sergeant.'

Hopkins cleared his throat. 'Well, sir, I was in the process of searching the tower when the reporters turned up en masse, so I decided to secure the area before things got out of hand.'

Simms nodded. 'Very commendable, so you go outside and organise your men to keep everyone well back, is that what you are saying?'

'That's correct, sir.'

'And then you went back into this tower to conduct your investigation?'

'Yes, sir.'

'So, can you explain why you received this piece of evidence a full two hours after it had been discovered?'

'Well, like I said earlier, sir, it should have been brought to my attention sooner.'

Simms sighed, to Lasser it was the sound of a man who was close to retirement and couldn't wait to be shut of the lot of them.

'Listen, Hopkins, you were right when you said that your colleague here should have been nowhere near that tower. But what you fail to grasp is that you should have been there to tell him to butt out, you should have been the one who found the evidence.'

'Excuse me, sir, but...'

'Lasser was doing his job, I agree he should have been doing it somewhere else but nonetheless he was doing what he's paid to do.'

Lasser nodded. 'Thank you, sir, I am glad you see it that way.'

'Don't push your luck, Sergeant,' Simms turned back to Hopkins. 'Now let me be specific. You don't get paid to hold impromptu press conferences. When you attend a crime scene I expect you to give it your full attention, not run to the cameras as soon as they show up just so you can get your face on the bloody television, is that understood?'

Hopkins looked as if he was on the edge of losing it completely; a vein in his temple began to throb. 'Excuse me, sir, but I was simply following procedure, I...'

'Enough!'

Lasser kept his face straight. Simms might be getting long in the tooth but there was nothing wrong with his lungs.

'Don't say another bloody word and don't ever try to quote procedure to me. You failed to do your duty, now stop trying to cover your sorry arse and get out of my sight.'

Hopkins looked around the room as if he expected some mystery abettor to materialise and fight his corner, after a few seconds he stood up spun on his shiny heals and left the room.

Simms ran a hand across his eyes, a heavy sigh slid from his lips. 'Now, do you mind telling me why you have Ashley Radfield in one of the interview rooms?'

As he explained, Simms kept nodding, all the time his fingers held the evidence bag.

'And this was found on the floor beneath the body?'

'Yes, sir.'

'And you're sure the coat of arms belongs to the Radfield family?'

'Positive, I recognised it from when I first went up to the house.'

'So, what does he have to say about all this?'

'Not much, he says he's waiting for the family solicitor to arrive.'

'Well, that's hardly surprising.' Simms stood up and wandered over to the window. 'And what do you make of it; do you think the Radfields are responsible for any of this?'

Lasser chose his words carefully. 'I'm not sure, sir, obviously it seems suspicious but its early days.'

Simms raised an eyebrow. 'That's a very diplomatic response, Sergeant.'

Lasser nodded.

'Right, it appears for the time being your case is overlapping with Hopkins. Now I want no more of this nonsense, I expect you two to work together and that means sharing information, it does not mean winding one another up. I realise that you two have different methods,' he paused, 'I also realise you think Hopkins is full of shit and to a large degree I would agree with you.'

'Yes, sir.'

'Though if he could put his ego to one side then I'm sure he'd make a half-decent copper.'

Lasser said nothing.

'From the look on your face, I see that you disagree with my assessment?'

'No comment, sir.'

This time Simms laughed aloud. 'Just try to get on because if he turns up here with another complaint I might start to believe him, is that understood?'

'Yes, sir.'

'Right, you look worn out so I suggest you head home and grab an early night.'

'I'd rather stay and have another word with Radfield.'

'I bet you would but if he's waiting for representation to arrive then I can't see the point in you hanging around.'

'But...'

'Go home, Lasser, you'll have your chance tomorrow.'

MAKING TRACKS

Michael opened his eyes to a world of pink, he blinked in confusion, Tina emerged from beneath the duvet and smiled, and suddenly everything came crashing down.

'What time is?' he asked, stifling a yawn.

'Half past seven.'

'Jesus, how long have I been asleep?'

'Hours. When I came back up with your beans on toast you were well gone.'

'I can't remember the last time I slept that long,' he ran a hand across his short dark hair.

'I did try to wake you but you just kept snoring.'

Michael looked at her. 'I know it used to drive Billy mad, a few nights he slept in the bath, he said it was either that or he was going to smother me with his pillow.'

Tina smiled. 'Listen, my mum's gone to the shops and then she calls around at my aunties, so if you want to get a shower there's no problem.'

He grimaced. 'Are you sure you don't mind?'

'Don't be daft, I'll make some breakfast, and then we can get going,' she paused, 'that is if you still want me to come?'

She looked good in the morning, sometime during the night, she'd removed the makeup, it made her look younger he even noticed a spray of freckles across her nose.

'Mickey, are you OK?'

'Yeah, I was just thinking you look different.'

'Oh God, don't,' her hands went up to cover her face. 'I look like a tramp in the morning.'

'No, you look good.'

She looked at him cautiously as if waiting for him to burst into mocking laughter. She couldn't remember the last time she'd let a boy see her without her makeup. Yet for some reason while he had been sleeping she had found herself taking it all off, scrubbing at her face with moist wipes. Then she had sat on the edge of the bed and watched him sleeping. As the room began to darken, Tina had changed into her Hello Kitty pyjamas and lay down by his side. Sometime during the night, he had slid his hand onto her waist pulling her close until she could feel his warm breath on her face. She had cried at the unfairness of life, for the first time she regretted being pregnant, hated the fact that the child she was carrying would make a relationship with Michael impossible. Right now he was hurting, the death of his brother a raw, open wound. However, eventually he would return to some form of normality and then he would see right through her. Eventually the tears had stopped and she had slept wrapped in his arms.

'You don't need all that makeup on; you look better without it.'

She felt her face burning with embarrassment. 'I'll put the kettle on.'

Before he could climb from the bed, she had left the room.

An hour later, they were heading out of town on the number thirty-two bus. Tina had dug out a pair of trainers from the bottom of her wardrobe and slipped on a pink hooded sweatshirt the name *'Gold digger'* emblazoned across the back.

Thankfully, the bus was empty apart from a couple of elderly woman who sat gossiping about how hot it was.

Michael tried to slide open a window but the catch was locked solid. 'Listen, this place is in the middle of nowhere, are you sure you'll be OK walking?'

'I'll be fine besides if it gets too much you can always give me a piggyback.'

'I just hope he's in.'

'Who is he anyway?'

'Just some bloke, I mean, after Lasser pulled me out of the house he didn't have a clue what to do with me. He knew if he let me go then I'd head straight to Connelly's house...'

Tina put a hand to her mouth. 'It was you who broke his nose, wasn't it?'

'Yeah and if he had anything to do with Billy's death then he'll get more than a bloody nose.'

After seeing what Mickey had done to Halliwell she could imagine what waited in store for Kyle Connelly.

'What makes you think he'll be able to help you?'

'Well, he must be mates with Lasser, so maybe I'll be able to tap him for information. Besides what else can I do? If I try to go round to my place my mother will either get me arrested or try and get me to act like the grieving brother in front of some twat of a reporter.'

Tina looked out of the window; the houses had given way to fields. She tried to imagine what it would be like to have a mother like Sarah Jones; instinctively her hand went to her stomach.

'I'm glad you decided to come,' he said.

She looked at him and smiled. 'I wanted to; I just didn't want you to think I was being pushy.'

'I can't imagine you ever being pushy,' he chided.

'Sod off,' Tina punched him lightly on the arm, a wide smile on her face.

Twenty minutes later, he stood up. 'We need to get off here.'

As the bus pulled away, Tina became aware of the silence, the only sound being the drone of bees in the wild flowers that grew at the roadside. In the distance, a heat haze shimmered, blurring the horizon, making everything indistinct.

'I think there's a lane about half a mile back that way.'

'You don't sound so sure?' she said pushing a hand through her hair.

'It was dark when I set off but I am pretty sure I came past this bus stop.'

They set off, occasionally a car or van would go thundering past, causing a cooling draft that lasted a couple of seconds before the heat began to throb again. She was glad she'd had the sense to dig out her trainers, at least it made walking a little easier, though after twenty minutes, her mouth began to feel parched, her hair, damp with sweat, began to curl.

After what felt like an age they came to the turning, Tina looked down the narrow lane, she could see the band of black tarmac weaving its way across the patchwork fields, not a house in sight. She blew her fringe away from her forehead.

'You OK, Tina?

'I'm fine,' she smiled.

'I should have brought something to drink.'

'Don't worry, Mickey, I won't faint on you.'

'I just didn't realise how far it was,' he looked annoyed at his own lack of foresight.

'I can't believe you walked it all the way back into town, especially in the dark, it would have freaked me out.'

'Yeah well, I had other things on my mind,' he replied darkly.

Tina flicked him a glance. 'So, how far away is this place?'

'About an hour's walk I think.'

Placing her hands on her hips, she grinned. 'Well, we'd better get going, coz if I stand here much longer then I'm going to start melting.'

'OK, but let me know if you need a break.'

'It looks like you might end up giving me that piggyback after all.'

SEEING THINGS

He rotates the aerial on top of the portable television, until the grainy picture crackles into focus. The police have found the body, now he wants to see what the media make of it all. Concealed in the high bank of bushes that looped around Radfield Manor he had watched as the police officer arrived. Half an hour later, Ashley had been led from the house; the shock on his lordship's face, the uncertainty, the fear, had made the man smile.

On the TV, the tower clicked into focus, it felt strange to see the familiar place on the small screen, he pressed the remote and the sound gradually increased. It was the same copper who had been on the news at the derelict house. The killer smiled, he could see right through the man. It was obvious he loved to be in front of the cameras, the way he kept turning his head, pointing at various reporters and then answering their questions with his chest thrown out and a look of mock severity on his face.

'I am afraid at the moment I can't answer that.'

'Well, can you confirm that the body is that of William Jones?' someone asked.

'I can neither confirm nor deny that supposition.'

The man cracked open a can of lager.

'Though I would like to take this opportunity to reassure the public that the police are doing everything within their power to apprehend the person responsible for this terrible crime.'

It was as if he were reading from a prepared script, the words meaningless, the sentiment behind them false. If this was the man in charge of the case then it was a miracle that the body had been discovered at all.

The camera cut back to the studio, where the presenter began to talk about the recession and its impact on the local economy.

He flicked the television off and thought of Radfield sitting in a police cell, having to explain where he had been at the time of the boy's death. He could see it with perfect clarity, Radfield trapped in some small windowless room demanding to be let out immediately, did they have no concept of the man they were dealing with!

Still it was all immaterial, eventually he would walk from the police station to a barrage of media attention, his face would be plastered over the front pages, details of his family history would be poured over. And the cracks would begin to show. People would begin to understand what the family had done to amass their wealth; the man took a sip from the can. Radfield would remain tight-lipped, make no comment and batten down the hatches until the public lost interest, and then simply carry on with life as if nothing had happened. However, just as things began to get back to some sort of normality, he would intervene. Ashley Radfield would find himself back in front of the police and this time there would be no doubt as to his guilt. No amount of money or slippery lawyers would be able to wipe the slate clean. The man tossed a salted peanut into his mouth and watched as a pair of legs encased in Wellington boots walked past the window.

FANCY SEEING YOU THERE

It was a mirage it had to be. 'Pull over, Mum.'
'What do you mean, pull over?'
Jenna swivelled in her seat, peering out of the rear window of the van.
'I'm sure that was Tina Sheldon,' she could see the couple trudging along the narrow curb; wilting in the oven heat.
Ronnie leaned forward between the front seats. 'Tina who?'
Susan pulled the van tight to the curb.
'Sheldon, she's in a couple of my groups at college.'
'I've never heard you mention her before, love, is she a friend?' Susan asked.
Jenna opened her mouth to answer; a few days ago, she would have snorted in derision at the mere idea but things had changed. She now felt uneasy seeing someone walking the country lanes with a maniac on the loose, even if that someone was Tina Sheldon.
She yanked on the door handle.
'Jenna, I told you yesterday I haven't got the time to wait while you chat to one of your college friends, I've got deliveries to make.'
'I know, Mum, I won't be a minute.'
Scrambling out of the van, she heard her mum. 'Two minutes, if you're not back you can come with me to Platts.'
As she walked along the narrow pavement she wondered what someone like Tina could possibly being doing all the way out here, after all, she had never appeared to be the type of girl who liked long country walks. Every time she had seen her at college, she had been tottering around on high heels looking like Jodie Marsh's kid sister.
Jenna suddenly wondered why she had made her mother pull over; after all, she knew hardly anything about the girl. For a moment, she considered simply

turning and walking back to the van. She could always tell her mum she'd been mistaken. Looking up she realised it was too late, Tina and the boy she was with were approaching fast.

'Hi.' Jenna smiled.

Tina looked as if she were rapidly melting, her long straight hair beginning to curl at the ends, her face flushed with perspiration. This didn't look like a nice stroll in the country; it looked as if they were on the run from something.

'Jenna.' Tina's voice was laced with surprise.

'Hello, Tina, I thought it was you,' she glanced at the boy, she was sure she'd seen him somewhere before, he was tall with short black hair framing an angular face his eyes pale blue.

'What are you doing here?' Tina asked.

Jenna suddenly felt ridiculous; she had nothing in common with this girl. 'Well, I'm just on my way to see someone.'

'So are we.'

Jenna wondered whom they could possibly be on their way to visit; it was not like there were many houses around here. Maybe it was drug related; perhaps they were here to meet some dealer.

'Do you know this area?' Tina asked.

Jenna shrugged. 'Sort of, I mean, I don't actually live around here but I sometimes deliver stuff.' She decided to leave out the fact that it was usually with one of her parents, which would have sounded decidedly lame.

'We're looking for someone called Fossey.' Tina said before swiping a hand across her brow.

Jenna blinked; maybe the sun was scrambling her brain. *'Fossey?'*

A sudden image flickered in her mind, Patrick handing over a small package wrapped in gaffer tape while they handed him a wad of dirty money.

She swallowed. 'Well, actually I have. In fact I'm on my way there now.'

Jenna was beginning to wish she had kept her mouth shut and then she looked at Tina and a wave of guilt washed over her, she looked flustered and hot. 'We could give you a lift if you like?'

'That would be great, my feet are killing me.' Tina winced, bent down, and rubbed at her calves.

The boy slid his hand onto her back, Tina looked up and smiled at him.

'Come on then, before my mum decides to drive off,' they hurried toward the van; Jenna slid the side door open. 'Mum, they're going to Patrick's, is it OK if we give them a lift?'

Susan looked puzzled and then smiled. 'Of course it is, love, climb in.'

Tina scrabbled in, Ronnie shuffled across the back seat to make room for them both.

'You two look hot and bothered,' he said.

'I can't believe this heat.' Tina wafted a hand in front of her face in an effort to cool down.

Reaching over the back of the seat Ronnie pulled two bottles from his bag.

'Here you are, love.'

'Oh thanks,' she handed one to Michael, then tried to loosen the top of her own bottle, he twisted the lid and swapped with Tina.

'Thanks,' she tilted the bottle and drained half of it in one long swallow. 'Wow, this is well cool, what is it?'

Jenna peered over her shoulder. 'Ginger beer, my grandad makes it.'

'I've never had it before; I always thought it would taste gross.'

Ronnie grunted. 'If you want another I've got another couple of bottles back here.'

'So, how do you know Patrick Fossey?' Susan asked, glancing in the rear view mirror.

Michael met her gaze. 'Well, I wouldn't say I know him, I've only met him once.'

Ronnie wound down the window and Tina closed her eyes as a cooling breeze filled the van.
'Oh, that's better,' she said.
'So, is he expecting you?' Susan asked.
Michael shrugged. 'Not really.'
Five minutes later, Susan slowed the van and turned down a narrow driveway, the trailer rattling along behind them. When the house came into view Tina's eyes widened. *'Wow, look at this place!'*
The house was nestled amongst the trees, Patrick's Range Rover parked on a circular patch of gravel.
As soon as the van stopped, Jenna leapt out. T came hurtling around the corner of the house, when he was a couple of feet away he leapt into her arms.
Patrick appeared from the cover of the trees, a pair of garden shears in his hands.
As he approached, the van door slid open and Michael climbed out followed by Tina.
'Michael, I didn't expect to see you again so soon.' Fossey smiled.
Jenna looked at Patrick in surprise.
'Patrick, where do you want the trailer?' Susan asked.
'It's OK, Susan, I can unhook it here and we can drag it around the back later,' he worked the handle to drop the leg then unhitched the trailer.
'OK, I've got a few deliveries to make and Jenna's got money to get a taxi...'
'There's no need, I'll drop them off later.'
'Are you sure?'
'Positive.'
Susan smiled in relief. 'Brilliant, well I'd best get going, see you two later.'
Jenna raised a hand and Ronnie nodded.
Michael was looking closely at Fossey; Tina couldn't stop looking at the house.
Ronnie took out the makings and began to roll a cigarette. 'So, Patrick, where are these apple trees?'
'Round the back, come on follow me.'

Tina looked at Michael who shrugged, they followed as he made his way around to the rear of the house.

Ronnie looked at the gnarly apple trees neatly set out in three rows. 'You've got a good crop there, son.'

'Well, I hate to think of them going to waste, so when you mentioned you liked to make your own cider I thought you might as well make use of them.'

'It's much appreciated,' Ronnie rubbed his hands together and then wandered off to check the fruit.

'Look at him, he's loving it.' Jenna smiled.

'So, I take it you guys all know one another?' Fossey asked.

Jenna nodded. 'Tina goes to the same college as me.'

'Pleased to meet you, Tina.' Fossey held out his hand, she looked at him baffled, then smiled and gave his hand a quick shake.

'Michael, could you give me a lift bringing the trailer around the back and then we can make a start picking the fruit.'

'If you want.'

'Jenna, I've got some cold drinks in the fridge, do you and Tina want to grab them and bring them outside?'

'No problem,' they headed toward the back door with the small dog on their heels, Fossey and Michael made their way back to the front of the house.

When they reached the trailer, he stopped. 'So, what can I do for you, Michael?'

'Look, I didn't mean to fuck off without saying anything.'

'That's not a problem; I can understand how sitting around here would have been hard.'

Michael dragged the pack of cigarettes from his pocket and lit one. 'I just needed to find out what had happened to him.'

'And did you?'

'Not really, I couldn't face going home. I just didn't know what to do.'

Fossey sighed. 'That's hardly surprising.'

'So, I was wondering if you'd heard any more about what happened?'

Fossey shoved his hands into his pockets. 'I take it you haven't seen the news or read any papers?'

'I saw my fat bitch of a mother on the television but to be honest I felt like smashing the fucking thing.'

'So, is Tina your girlfriend?'

Michael gave a slight shake of his head. 'No, she's just a friend.'

'She seems like a nice girl.'

'She is but I don't see what this has got to do with anything. I want to know if you can tell me how my brother died and if you can't or won't then I may as well piss off back to town.'

'I can tell you how he died, but as for the why, then I'm afraid you know as much as I do.'

Michael looked hard at Fossey; as if he was trying to gauge if he was telling the truth.

'So, go on.'

'As far as I know your brother died from stab wounds.'

Michael turned away, his hands clenched into fists. It had been one of the scenarios that had been running around his head. In the end he supposed it didn't really matter. He'd just needed to hear it from someone, needed to understand the basics of it.

'That bastard, Connelly!'

'You don't know for certain it was him.'

'So, you're saying it was someone else?' Michael looked at him, a cautious expression on his face.

'I don't work for the police, Michael; they're under no obligation to tell me anything.'

Michael kicked at the gravel. 'I just feel I should be doing something.'

Fossey could hear the anguish; see the latent fury in his eyes.

'I understand but you have to think rationally, the police will be doing everything they can to catch him...'

'And you expect me to believe that?'

'Look, this isn't the same as chasing someone who's been stealing car radios, Michael.'

'What's that supposed to mean?' he asked with a frown.

'Come on, you're not a fool; you know exactly what I mean.'

Michael looked at his shoes, when he looked up; his eyes were brimming with tears.

'Wow, just look at this place,' they were standing in the middle of the kitchen, Tina looking around the room like a wide-eyed child.

Jenna had to admit it was impressive, gleaming steel everywhere; it looked as if the kitchen had been installed and never used.

'So, are you two a couple?' Jenna asked as she grabbed the cans of Coke from the huge fridge.

'Well, no we're not actually together; I've just been helping him get over what happened to his brother.'

'His brother?'

Tina looked at Jenna, she had seen her a few times at college and had always had her down as a stuck up bitch. She always seemed to have her nose in the air as if she thought she was better than everyone else. Now it was as if she were seeing her for the first time, she was wearing a pair of hipster jeans and a light green shirt; her long blonde hair pulled back in a practical ponytail.

'His brother was the one who just got murdered.' Tina whispered in a fragile voice.

Jenna dropped the can; it hit the floor and exploded, spraying cola around the room like a demented Catherine wheel.

'Shit!' Tina bent quickly and picked it up, the can continued to erupt she could feel it spraying into her hair and down the front of her T-shirt. Dashing across the room, she tossed the can into the garden. When she turned, Jenna was rummaging under the sink; a couple

of seconds later she emerged with a long role of blue paper towel in her hand.

'Christ, he'll bloody flip!' Tina screeched.

Tearing of a long length of towel Jenna began to mop up the mess; Tina grabbed a handful and joined her.

'If we're quick he might not notice,' Tina scrubbed furiously at the tiles her face flushed with anxiety.

'Patrick won't mind.'

'I'd mind, I mean, this place was immaculate.'

Jenna felt sick to her stomach; Michael Jones was the older brother of William.

Tina had rummaged a bin liner from one of the drawers and was dropping the soggy paper into the sack.

'I wonder if he has a mop and bucket,' she hissed.

'Don't worry I'll get it.' They looked up; Patrick was standing at the back door with a smile on his face.

'It was an accident,' Tina blurted.

'Well, I didn't think you'd deliberately spray a can of Coke around the kitchen,' he headed across the room and pulled open a door. Tina could see a wall that seemed to consist of nothing but bottles of wine; he emerged pushing a mop bucket on wheels.

'I'll do it,' she said reaching out a hand to grab the mop.

'No you won't, Tina, I can manage. But you could do me a favour, Michael's upset would you check on him while I get this lot sorted?'

'Sure,' she dashed for the door, like a schoolchild who has suddenly escaped a session of corporal punishment.

'She just told me about Michael,' Jenna hissed.

Fossey sighed. 'I thought it might come up.'

'But what's he doing here?' Jenna whispered.

Fossey turned on the tap and slid the bucket under the flowing water. 'He came to find out if I know anything about how his brother died.'

'I can't believe this, I mean, how is he?'

'The same as anyone would be,' he turned the water off. 'He's furious and riddled with guilt, he feels responsible and helpless...'

'So, what's he going to do now?'

Fossey shrugged. 'What can he do? I mean, at the moment he doesn't feel able to go home, he stayed with Tina last night so we'll just have to wait and see what he decides to do.'

Jenna twisted her hands together in panic. 'I feel so sorry for him.'

'In situations like this it's best to act as normally as possible.'

'Oh yeah sure, I understand.'

'Right, grab the drinks and I'll get the floor mopped.'

'No problem,' she gathered up the cans and headed outside, if anything it was even hotter. Grandad was still wandering amongst the apple trees; occasionally he would reach up and cradle the fruit in his large hand. Tina and Michael were standing side by side, he was looking at the ground and she had an arm linked around his waist. Taking a deep breath, Jenna headed towards them.

A BIG DAY

'Let me assure you, my client is only too willing to assist in any way possible.'

Lasser grimaced; Radfield's solicitor looked like a human praying mantis. He appeared to be made up of sharp angles; even his head looked triangular, his eyes set wide apart as if capable of disappearing around the side of his head.

It was stifling in the interview room, the pale yellow walls scuffed and stained from past confrontations with volatile prisoners; Lasser could even see the outline of a boot print on the ceiling. Before entering, he had taken three aspirins washed down with a can of Red Bull in an effort to shake the beginnings of a headache, now he was buzzing.

'Well, yesterday your client certainly didn't appear keen to help us with our inquiries.'

DCI Simms was sitting by his side, Harper standing guard by the door.

Mantis man pulled out a pair of horn-rimmed glasses and perched them on the end of his nose, then he picked up a thin file from the desk and flicked through the pages.

'With regards to that, my client has raised certain concerns about your interviewing technique, Sergeant.'

Simms moved in his seat the chair creaked. 'Look, Mr Walters, we're here to discover if Mr Radfield can help us in any way with this inquiry. Let me also add that I have complete confidence in Sergeant Lasser's interviewing technique. What I fail to grasp is why your client appears reluctant to clear this matter up?'

Walters placed the file back on the desk. 'In order to avoid any confusion my client has prepared a statement...'

Simms held up a hand. 'Forgive me but we're not interested in prepared statements, we simply want to ask

Mr Radfield some questions that hopefully he can provide the answers to.'

Walters looked sideways; Radfield gave a slight nod. 'Very well, Chief Inspector, though I must warn you that if you try to coerce my client in any way then I will advise him to cease the interview immediately.'

Simms sat back in his chair. 'Sergeant?'

'Mr Radfield, could you tell us your whereabouts on Wednesday night?' Lasser asked.

'Could you be more specific?'

'Well, let's say from five o'clock onwards.'

Radfield folded his legs. 'I was at home.'

'Could anyone verify that?'

'My father could but as you're well aware he is no longer alive.'

'So, you spent the night at home, doing what exactly?'

Radfield shrugged. 'Not much, I'd driven down from Scotland the day before and only arrived mid-afternoon, so I was tired, in fact I fell asleep quite early.'

'And where was your father?'

Radfield paused. 'Well, we spoke earlier on in the day'

'About what, precisely?'

Lasser saw a look of anger bloom in Radfield's eyes.

'Family business.'

'Is that the reason you'd travelled down from Scotland?'

Walters lifted the file from the desk and started to make notes.

'In part.'

'Tell me, did you have a good relationship with your father?'

'I fail to see what that has got to do with anything.'

'So, you didn't get on?'

Walters looked at Lasser over the top of his ridiculous glasses. 'You are making assumptions, Sergeant; I would strongly advice against it.'

Lasser returned the solicitors poison gaze. 'It's a simple question; all I expect is a reply that makes sense.'
Simms chair creaked again.
'I believe I've already stated that my father and I didn't really see one another, Sergeant, in fact this was only the second time this year. Is that specific enough for you?'
Walters scribbled away, his fountain pen a blur.
'Forgive my ignorance but you haven't really answered the question have you?'
Radfield blanched, Lasser could see the muscles in his jaw contracting. 'Excuse me but...'
Simms tapped his pen on the desk like a miniature gavel. 'So, you came down from Scotland to discuss business with your father...'
'I have already said that. We had a conversation that bears no relevance to any of this, when he left I had a couple of drinks and fell asleep in the chair.'
'And where did your father go?' Lasser asked.
'I am not,' he paused, 'was not my father's keeper. The following day I had an appointment in Manchester with a solicitor. I got back to the house by two and looked for him but as you well know he was probably already dead by then.'
'When you said you looked for him, what do you actually mean?'
'If you are asking if I looked under all the beds and checked in the wardrobes then the answer is no.'
'I am not interested in where you didn't look,' Lasser said with a smile.
'Look, I had a walk around the house, checked the rooms but I had no reason to believe that anything was amiss, so it was not an intensive search if that is what you are implying.'
'So, you have no idea of his whereabouts from the time your conversation ended until you discovered him the following night in the greenhouse?' Lasser asked.
'That's correct.'

Lasser decided it was time to change tack. 'Now moving on to another matter, can you give any explanation as to why we should find a cufflink belonging to a member of your family at a crime scene?'

Walters suddenly sat up straight, Radfield eased back in his chair.

'My client is in no position to either confirm or deny that the cufflink belonged to a family member. As for the place it was found, I am sure that you are aware that,' he paused to check his notes, 'the needle house did at one time belong to the Radfield family. Now I am sure it is not beyond the realms of possibility that this item could have been there for a number of years.'

'Well, hopefully once we've finished searching the house we'll have some clarity on the matter.' Lasser said.

For the first, time Radfield looked rattled. *'What do you mean; you have no right to search my property?'* he tried to stand but Walters took hold of his arm.

'Calm down, Ashley, the police are within their rights.'

'But this is scandalous!'

Lasser had heard enough. 'Look, Mr Radfield, what would you have us do, do you think we should merely ignore this evidence is that what you are suggesting?'

Radfield glared across the table. 'But Walters has already explained that cufflink must have been there for years. I mean, members of my family used to use the tower all the time.'

Lasser nodded. 'We appreciate that, but surely you can understand that we would be failing in our duty if we didn't follow every avenue of investigation.'

Radfield slumped back into his chair. Simms slipped the pen back into his pocket.

'Ultimately we want to catch whoever did this as quickly as possible,' Lasser stood up. 'Because nobody deserves to die like Billy Jones, do they, Mr Radfield?'

Ashley opened his mouth to reply but Walters interjected. 'We could not agree more, Sergeant. However, I believe my client has been most forthcoming in his dealings with you. Now, I would suggest that unless you have any objections, Lord Radfield should be released immediately.'

A silence fell over the room then Simms nodded to Harper who opened the door; Radfield stood up and removed his camel hair jacket from the back of the grubby plastic chair.

Simms turned. 'I am sorry, Mr Radfield, but it'll take a couple of hours to process the relevant paperwork, though you're more than welcome to use the coffee machine if you feel the need.'

Radfield looked at his solicitor; Walters gave a slight shrug of his insect like shoulders. Lasser grabbed his coat and followed Simms out of the door.

In the corridor, Simms spun around. 'Right, get yourself up to the house I want you to make sure they don't miss anything.'

'No problem, sir.'

'I'll make sure admin take their time with the paperwork.'

Lasser hooked a thumb over his shoulder. 'What do you make of him?'

Simms removed a bit of fluff from the sleeve of his jacket. 'Well, I'd be lying if I said I liked the man, though that doesn't make him a killer.'

'True enough.'

'But you think he's guilty?'

Lasser thought for a moment. 'It's hard to tell though it seems strange that we found two pieces of evidence pointing toward the family.'

Simms made his way to the coffee machine. 'What are you having?'

'Coffee, please.'

Simms punched in the number; the plastic cup dropped into the holder and began to fill. 'When you say strange, what do you mean exactly?'

Lasser pursed his lips. 'I don't know exactly but it just feels odd.'

Simms handed him the cup then punched in another set of numbers. 'Explain?'

'Well, I can understand one piece of evidence being left behind, in the heat of the moment, anyone can get careless, but two?'

Simms took a sip of his drink and winced. 'We follow clues, Lasser, that's what we do.'

'Of course, sir, but why would a person go out with the sole intention of killing someone and yet be so careless as to leave a cufflink behind that bears the family crest?'

'You think someone planted them?'

Lasser shrugged. 'Not necessarily, the button could have come from anywhere and, like Walters said, the cufflink could have been up there for years.'

'So, let me get this straight, you're saying Radfield's innocent?'

'I'm saying I'll keep an open mind until I have more facts.'

'And what about Thomas Kitts, do you have any theories regarding his death?'

Lasser blew on his drink and took a sip. 'Well, until Molder looked at the body, we all thought Kitts had died of heart failure.'

'So, the killer was trying to make it look like natural causes?'

'It seems that way, which implies that he definitely didn't want us making any links between the two.'

Simms thought this over for a moment. 'Or perhaps he was just being careful, after all Kitts was killed out in the open.'

Lasser nodded, Simms might be spending his last couple of years behind a desk, but it was obvious he still had the instincts of a good copper.

'It's possible; even though the place is pretty remote there was still the chance that someone could have been out and about.'

'So, you think it was the same man?'

'If it wasn't then we have two killers on the loose which seems unlikely.'

Simms nodded. 'Agreed, now I suggest you use this time to get up there sharpish and keep me...'

'Informed, sir?'

Simms smiled, Lasser dropped the plastic cup into the bin.

NOT AS EASY AS YOU THINK

It was taking an age to pick the apples. Ronnie had adopted the role of slave driver, pointing out the fruit that hung from the highest branches. Fossey and Michael spent the afternoon scrambling amongst the branches of the twisted old trees picking the fruit and dropping it to the lawn beneath. Jenna and Tina were placing the apples into plastic sacks and Ronnie was dumping them into the trailer.

Tina grimaced, placed her hands in the small of her back, and stretched. Fossey had provided her with a rubber band, and her hair was now tied back in a neat ponytail.

'Are you OK, Tina?' Jenna asked.

'My back's a little stiff that's all.'

Jenna wiped a hand across her forehead, even though they were shaded beneath the trees it was still hot work. 'Right, that's enough. Grandad!'

Ronnie looked toward his granddaughter. 'What's up, Jenna love?'

'We're taking a break.'

He looked bemused as if he was in charge of a crew that had suddenly turned mutinous.

Fossey looked down from amongst the branches. 'Sounds like a good idea to me,' scrambling down, he dropped the last couple of feet and then ran a hand through his hair dislodging a couple of leaves. 'Right, let's get out of this heat for a while.'

Michael and Ronnie wandered over. Even though it had to be about eighty degrees, Ronnie was still wearing his jacket, his face serene.

When they entered the kitchen, he made the grand gesture of removing his flat cap.

Fossey pulled open the fridge door and pulled out a six-pack of lager, then handed them out.

Ronnie studied the can for a moment as if he were checking the ingredients.

'I've got wine if you'd prefer it, Ronnie?'
'Pearls before swine, lad,'
'Right good, now let's go and relax.'
'Bonny place you've got.' Ronnie said a hint of admiration as they made their way into the lounge. 'How long have you lived here?'
'Six years, though to tell you the truth the place is way too big for someone living alone.'
Tina leaned back into the sofa; it felt as if she was melting into a huge marshmallow, Michael smiled at her, he looked more relaxed. During the afternoon, while he'd been scrambling amongst the branches he hadn't said a word, now he looked somehow calmer as if he'd been sorting things out in his head as he worked.
Ronnie was perched on the arm of the sofa his old work boots planted firmly on the oak floorboards.
'I take it this place used to be a barn?'
Fossey nodded. 'Yeah, I knew the guy who owned and he was selling it off at a reasonable price, so I took the plunge.'
'It must have taken a lot of work to get it looking like this?' Jenna said.
Fossey smiled. 'I spent two years living in an old caravan on the front garden.'
'So, you did some of the work then?' Ronnie asked.
'I did what I could, though all the structural work was done professionally.'
'Aye well, they've done a good job.'
Fossey glanced at Tina, her eyes were closed a small smile on her face. He wondered if Michael was the father of her unborn child, he hadn't mentioned it. Then again why would he?
Ronnie pulled out his tobacco tin.
'Grandad!' Jenna was glaring at him; she made a quick sweeping gesture with her right hand.
'Oh right sorry, force of habit.'
'It's OK, Ronnie, I don't mind if you smoke.'
'Are you sure, lad?'

'I'm positive, it doesn't bother me.'

A few seconds later, Ronnie was puffing contentedly on the cigarette and then he nodded toward Tina. 'She's nodded off.'

Fossey drained his can. 'Why don't we let her sleep, after all it's hot out there.'

Michael nodded, 'Yeah, no problem.'

Ronnie stood up and headed for the kitchen, his old work boots sounding loud on the polished floor. 'We might as well make a start after all those apples won't pick themselves.'

Jenna tapped him on the shoulder. 'What did your last slave die of, Grandad?'

As they left the room, Fossey took a cream coloured throw and placed it over the sleeping girl; her eyes flickered but didn't open.

NEEDLE IN A HAYSTACK

Lasser stood at the upstairs window looking out through the mullioned glass at the group of reporters gathered at the bottom of the long driveway. Behind him, he could hear the sound of drawers being yanked open the contents riffled through then slammed shut.

The vista from the bedroom window was spectacular, the house stood on a natural rise commanding uninterrupted views over the valley below. No other properties were visible just wheat fields and undulating hills.

Turning from the window he sniffed, the bedroom had an earthy damp smell, the wallpaper yellowing with age, even the furniture looked careworn, in some bizarre way it reminded him of Sarah Jones's living room.

Either Malcolm Radfield had cared little for the material things in life or he'd been desperately short of cash. Ashley had stated that he'd driven down from Scotland to discuss *'family business'* and with the look of this place Lasser was sure that the family finances would have been high on the agenda. Although he had yet to hear of a case where struggling to pay the gas bill had turned someone into a psychotic killer.

'Have you checked the bedside cabinet?' Lasser asked.

Spenner nodded. 'Yes, sir, nothing out of the ordinary.'

'Right then, I think we've done in here, you can start on the next bedroom.'

Spenner spun on his heels and strode from the room, a man on a mission.

As much as he disliked Radfield, Lasser was struggling to come up with a motive, and no matter how bizarre or misguided there was always a reason for murder, the problem was finding it. Radfield had no alibi for the Jones killing and asleep in the armchair was lame by anyone's standard. However, if he had been responsible then why move the body from the old house to a place that was bound to lead to suspicion, and why leave a cufflink directly under the corpse? None of it made sense, Simms had stated that they follow the facts, though Lasser was starting to think that maybe they were not facts after all.

Spenner came striding into the room, his face triumphant. 'Look at this, sir,' the shirt was starched white, hanging from an old-fashioned wire coat hanger. Spenner held it up in front of him like a trophy killing. 'One of the cufflinks is missing, sir.'

Lasser picked up the sleeve; the small gold square was a match for the one he had found in the tower.

'We've got him, sir.'

Lasser could hear the excitement in Spenner's voice, his eyes shining with a fanaticism any suicide bomber would have been proud of and yesterday he would have felt the same. Now he felt uneasy, as if he was being led around by the nose, here is clue A, now join the obvious dots to clue B.

'Good work, Spenner,' the constable puffed out his chest, a big stupid smile on his young face. 'Bag it and tag it.'

'Straight away, sir.'

Lasser headed for the door.

Five minutes later, he was in the car with a cigarette clamped between his lips as he radioed through to dispatch asking to be patched through to Simms.

'So, that's a definite then?' The DCIs voice crackled through the handset.

'No doubt, sir, Spenner found the shirt hanging in one of the wardrobes.'

'Do we know whose bedroom?'

'Not yet but I am sure Radfield will be able to help us out.'

'Right, so what are you up to now?'

Lasser paused, it was decision time he could either try his usual bullshit approach or break a long held habit and tell the truth.

'Well, sir,' he paused, 'there is someone I'd like to have a word with if that's alright with you?'

'Is it connected to the case?'

'I'm not sure at the moment.'

The line went quiet. *'OK but remember no cutting corners and do not even think about keeping things to yourself.'*

'I understand, sir.'

'I hope so, Sergeant.'

He could hear the underlying threat, he watched as a robin hopped across the gravel drive and disappeared into the long grass that passed as a lawn. 'What about Radfield?'

'Well, let's just say I'll be looking to keep him in for a little longer, now get your skates on, I don't want you disappearing for the day.'

Lasser ended the call and blew smoke through the open window, a moment later a scabby black cat emerged from the long grass with the robin clamped between its jaws. With a shake of his head, he started the car and eased down the long driveway. As he approached the gates the reporters began to move forward, cameras flashed, four constables linked arms shepherding them back to the side of the road. Lasser swept past keeping his face stern and his eyes forward.

Perhaps going to see Fossey would turn out to be a mistake but the guy was meant to be a criminal psychologist and he needed to run a few things past him.

Once he hit the B roads, he got his foot down, the window wide open, the sweet smell of summer flooding the car. At the crossroads, he paused to get his bearings his fingers drumming an angry tattoo on the steering wheel, then he swung right and slammed his foot down on the accelerator.

Fossey had spent time in the old house, he'd been the one to raise the alarm, so he must have had a good look around, formed some sort of theory as to the type of man they were looking for. The more he thought about it the more aggravated he became. He'd managed to keep the image of Billy's butchered corpse from his mind, now it came jittering back in glorious Technicolor, the body somehow shrunken the eyes screwed shut in agony, a dark cavity that used to house a living, beating heart.

He shook his head in an effort to dispel the harrowing image and missed the narrow right hand turn. *'Fuck.'* he slammed on the brakes, the seat belt biting, black smoke poured from the tyres leaving smears of melted rubber on the road. He reversed and turned right; the lane began to narrow so he eased off, his temper abating as the car slowed. He slowed for the tight right hand bend and then snapped the wheel left onto Fossey's narrow drive.

Pulling up behind the Range Rover, he climbed from the car and flicked the cigarette into the bushes. He could hear the low murmuring of voices coming from the side of the house.

Fossey was sitting on the short-cut grass with some old bloke in a flat cap and a blond haired girl who looked to be about seventeen. The real surprise was seeing Michael Jones sitting slightly apart from the others, aimlessly picking at the blades of grass.

Fossey spotted him and raised a hand in surprise. 'Lasser!' he clambered to his feet, Michael turned, a scowl forming on his face.

'I need a word.' Lasser said.

Fossey made his way over; Michael leapt to his feet and followed.

To Lasser, Fossey looked as if he'd been under a sun bed that had just been fitted with new tubes, his face red and blotchy.

'I didn't have you down as a sun worshipper,' he said.

'Picking apples to make cider,' Fossey hooked a thumb over his shoulder. 'I'm sure Ronnie will let you have a few bottles when they're ready.'

Lasser smiled. 'I look forward to it.'

'Is this about my brother, do you lot know who killed him yet?'

'Hello, Michael, how are you?'

'How do you think I am?' It was if someone had slipped some speed into his drink, from being lethargic and distant he was now wired, a black sense of anger coming off him in waves.

Lasser held up both hands. 'Look, I just need a quiet word with...'

'Is it to do with my brother?' Michael repeated, colour flying to his cheeks.

'I'm sorry but I can't discuss ...'

'You're all the fucking same,' he spat out the words, his eyes charged with fury.

'That might well be true but I still can't discuss...'

Michael lunged, both hands bunched into fists, Fossey reached out a hand to stop him, but all he managed to do was pluck at the sleeve of his T-shirt. By the time Fossey spun around, Michael was sprawled on the grass; Lasser kneeling at his side, a firm grip on his left arm.

'Get the fuck off me!' Michael twisted his head, his eyes manic.

'What's happening?' Jenna was dashing toward them with Ronnie trailing behind.

Lasser released the arm and rose before taking a quick step back, Fossey studied the Sergeant's face, he appeared nonchalant as if the sudden outburst of violence had never happened.

Michael sprang to his feet and spun around ready to charge again.

Lasser didn't move, his arms hanging loosely at his sides, a picture of calm. 'Look, Michael, just calm down.'

'Calm fucking down, are you taking the piss or what?'

Jenna stood by Patrick's side, shocked by what had happened. 'What do you think you're doing?' she looked at the newcomer in disgust as if he were the incarnation of every schoolyard bully.

Fossey placed a hand on her arm. 'Take it easy, Jenna, Lasser was just defending himself.'

'But he knocked him down!'

Lasser slipped both hands into the pockets of his coat; Fossey had to admit the detective knew exactly what he was doing. As soon as he got Michael onto the floor he'd stood up and backed off trying to defuse the situation and now he'd put his hands into his pocket to give the impression that as far as he was concerned the whole thing was finished. However, when Fossey looked into the Sergeant's eyes he saw a different story, a hardness that spoke volumes.

Fossey stepped between them. 'Take it easy, Michael.'

The boy jabbed a shaking finger at the detective. *'But he knows what happened and he treats it like some kind of fucking game.'*

Lasser shook his head. 'Believe me, Michael; nobody's treating what happened to your brother as a game.'

'So, why won't you tell me what happened?' Michael's jaw jutted out, his eyes blazing.

Fossey moved his position slightly until he was blocking Lasser from view. 'Because that's not the way these things work, Michael.'

Michael's eyes were flitting everywhere, as if looking for something else to attack. 'But I have a right to know, how would you feel if your brother had been killed and you had someone who knew why and yet they wouldn't bloody tell you?'

Jenna wanted to turn and run, suddenly the heat of the day seemed to evaporate, the flesh on her arms rising in fear. When she looked up she could see the anguish on his face, she locked her hands together in an effort to stop them shaking.

'Come on, Michael, you know the score. I could feed you a load of bullshit; I could even give you a name.'

Michael whipped his head around. *'A name?'*

Somewhere in the distance a magpie laughed.

Lasser sighed. 'Yeah, but it wouldn't be the name of the killer, though you'd simply latch onto it and then what?'

'Tell me who it is?'

Lasser pursed his lips in disappointment. 'That's the wrong question, Michael.'

'What the fuck are you talking about?'

Fossey slid his hands into his pockets. 'He's saying you have to trust him, Michael.'

'Trust a copper!'

'It sounds as if you have to start trusting someone, lad.' Ronnie had his tin out; he stuck a cigarette paper to his bottom lip then pulled out a small pinch of tobacco.

Michael looked at the old man. 'What, you think coz he's a copper, he's going to tell me the truth?'

Lasser could feel his own anger growing, this was the same old bullshit the same old woe is me attitude. 'What is it with people like you, Michael?'

'Me?'

'I mean, come on, why don't you explain why you find it so hard to trust a copper?'

The boy's face twisted into a sneer. 'You're joking right?'

'Not really, you have a problem with the law because you spent so much time breaking it.'

Fossey watched as Michael's mouth fell open, Lasser remained unmoving his hands back in his pockets.

'Go and fuck yourself,' Jones spat.

'Oh come on, son, if you expect me to start treating you like an adult then why don't you act your bloody age.'

Fossey glanced at Jenna; she was a carbon copy of Michael, her mouth open in shocked surprise, Ronnie was putting a match to his cigarette his eyes placid and watchful.

'And what the fuck is that supposed to mean?'

'Listen, I spend my days chasing little scrotes who will lie, cheat and take the piss at every opportunity.'

'Little scrotes like me, is that what you're saying?'

'If the cap fits, wear it.'

Fossey would have thought it was impossible for Michael's mouth to open any further. It was obvious he had never been spoken to like this before; he looked at Fossey as if he expected some kind of support, his eyes bemused.

'You...'

Lasser took a step forward. 'Never mind me, Michael, we're talking about you. When I saw you that night you told me you were going to college trying to get your life sorted and I thought what a load of bollocks.'

'Hey, hang on!' Jenna was astonished, it was no wonder Michael hated the police if this was what he had to put up with, Fossey placed a hand on her arm and shook his head.

'Well, that's where you are wrong; I do go to college, I...'

'Not for much longer.'

Michael's hands bunched into fists. 'Are you threatening me?'

Lasser shook his head. 'There you go again, Michael, always thinking you're being victimised. I mean, you could probably go into that house now and put the television on and find out who we have in custody...'

'I fucking knew it!' All the anger came flooding back like a faulty firework that keeps reigniting.

Lasser ignored him. 'Then you could go on the rampage, all because you had a name. Trouble is, Michael, it would be the wrong name but you wouldn't believe that because in your eyes all coppers are liars aren't they?'

'I...'

'So, you'd go and play the big man out for revenge and then we would have to get involved and you could wave goodbye to any idea of a career in IT. You'll go to jail just like your old man,' his voice was laden with sarcasm. 'Though it'd be all right, you could play happy families. But, when you do get out no employer will touch you, they won't be interested in what you did at college, the fact that you could be the next Bill Gates will mean sod all to them. Then you'll move back to the estate, drift back to your old mates but hey, you can always start selling some crack to the little kids just like your dad used to do, probably make him proud.'

Michael stood rooted to the spot, his face rigid with disbelief.

'I,' he looked at the ground; Jenna watched horrified as tears slipped from his eyes, gravity did the rest. *'Just need to know.'*

'Come on, lad, let's go and get a drink.' Ronnie placed an arm around Michael's shoulder, for an instant he tried to pull himself free and then he seemed to sag as Ronnie led him away.

Jenna looked at Lasser, her eyes blazing. 'You disgusting man, is this how the police treat people. He's just lost his brother and you speak to him like that,' she spun away and stalked toward the kitchen door.

Fossey ran a hand across his forehead, the skin tender from where the sun had caught it.

'That was harsh.'

'Yeah well, I'm pushed for time...'

'So, that gave you the right to ridicule him, is that what you're saying?'

He looked at Fossey, maybe he was a bloody do-gooder after all. 'Jesus Christ, you're meant to be a psychologist, so, you work it out.'

Fossey looked up at the sky, for the first time in days he could see dark clouds gathering on the horizon, the sun slipping toward the wooded hills. 'Look, what are you doing here?'

'Well, I did come round for a quiet chat.'

'But I don't see how else I can help you.'

Lasser spat a flake of tobacco from his lip. 'Come on let's take a walk.'

STRANGERS IN THE NIGHT

The temperature beneath the trees was falling rapidly, the heat of the day being absorbed back into the earth dragging the cooler air down with it. Already the light was beginning to fade; Cathy Harper could see a technician in a white paper suit moving around in the gloom setting up the portable arc lights. This place made her feel uneasy; she knew in part it was because of what had been discovered in the tower, though this was not the sole reason. She never felt comfortable in the countryside, give her a badly lit street on some rough estate and she was OK but all these trees and the shadows in between filled her with apprehension.

As soon as the body had been removed, encased in a black body bag the reporters had begun to dash away, all competing to get the news out as quickly as possible. Shortly after her colleagues had slowly left the scene, Hopkins had said he wanted them all back at first light to continue a fingertip search of the area.

She could feel the weight of the tower behind her, a chill emanating from the stones.

'Harper!'

She looked over her shoulder; Hopkins was standing in the doorway, his coat hanging over one arm a frown on his arrogant face. 'Yes, sir?'

'What time are you due off shift?'

'I should have been finished half an hour ago, sir.'

'Right well I need you to stay here for a while, make sure none of the reporters double back and try to get inside.'

'No problem, sir.'

'I'll get Spenner to come over and give you a lift.'

Harper nodded, Hopkins slid his arms into the jacket and began to walk away.

'Excuse me, sir, but what time will PC Spenner actually get here?'

Hopkins looked at her with more than a hint of disdain. 'Why, are you afraid of the dark, because I can always get someone else to do the job?'

Cathy felt the blush creep across her cheeks. 'No, sir, I was just wondering.'

'Yes well don't, he'll get here when I've finished with him.'

'Yes, sir.'

He spun away and began the long climb up the hill.

Just great, she looked around, the trees were already beginning to lose their definition blurring into a single dark mass. Not for the first time she began to wonder why she'd ever wanted to become a police officer. Both her parents had been against it, in fact, her mother had scoured the papers on a daily basis hand picking the most gruesome cases in an effort to dissuade her daughter. The trouble was her mother's constant doom and gloom had only made her more determined to go ahead with her plans. Now for the first time she was beginning to think that maybe her parents had been right all along, standing alone amongst the trees, she suddenly felt vulnerable, she felt scared.

Then the area was flooded with stark white light, like a miniature super nova in bloom. Cathy turned away blinded by the onslaught, she could hear the rumble of the generator, smell the acrid scent of diesel fumes in the air. Blinking, she rubbed at her eyes, when she opened them the tower was lit by the glaring light; the edges silhouetted against the trees. She could see into the building, the bottom edge of the stairs curling around to the right leading up to... she blanked out the image and pulled her short coat tight around her, the artificial lights causing huge shadows to rear out of the dark. She didn't want to imagine what it must have been like to stand in that narrow space with the corpse hanging above.

Shielding her eyes she looked toward the light, there was no sign of the technician though she knew he had to be out there somewhere but it was impossible to see beyond the blinding arc.

'Right...'

She spun around, heart rearing, her right hand scrabbling for the baton, the image of some axe-wielding maniac bringing the blade down toward her head snapped into her mind.

'Jesus, Colin, what the hell do you think you're doing?'

The technician grinned. 'Sorry I didn't think.'

'Yeah, well next time you'll find yourself with this baton around your head.'

Colin held up his hands. 'Understood, anyway you're not on duty on your own are you?'

'I am until Spenner gets here.'

'Let me guess, Hopkins reaffirming his authority. I mean, rumour is Simms gave him a right bollocking yesterday.'

Cathy could feel her heart thundering, suddenly she felt hot and clammy her hand shook as she slid the baton away. 'Why, what happened?'

'Apparently he grassed Lasser up for being here when he should have been looking into Radfield's suicide, thing is it backfired big time.'

She smiled; any image that included Hopkins in the shit was a welcome respite from the fear of standing alone in the middle of ancient woodland as the dark crept in like an oil slick.

'It couldn't have happened to a nicer guy,' she said.

Colin nodded in agreement. 'I've yet to come across anyone who actually likes the man.'

'Meadows seems to get along with him.'

'Ah, that's because Meadows is an idiot, plus I think he has some sort of man crush on Hopkins.'

'For God's sake, Col, I have to stand out here on my own till God knows what time, I don't want an image like that wandering around my head.'

'Listen, I could always hang around until Spenner shows up?'

It was a tempting offer but she didn't want it getting around the station that she'd felt uneasy being on her own. Colin seemed like a genuine guy but she didn't know him well enough to trust him not to blab.

'That's OK, I'll be fine.'

'Are you sure?'

'Positive, besides with a bit of luck I might get a bit of shut eye.'

'Well, make sure Hopkins doesn't find you, I mean, I wouldn't put it past that bastard to turn up unannounced.'

The thought of her boss sneaking around in the dark did nothing to ease her mind.

'OK then, the generator's full so the lights will stay on all night.'

'I'm hoping to be in bed by eleven.'

Colin looked unconvinced. 'See you tomorrow.'

She watched as he wandered up the hillside, as soon as he reached the limit of the light he vanished as if he'd never existed.

The tall ferns appeared unnaturally vibrant in the artificial light, some had begun to curl as cool air seeped through the trees. Pulling her baton free she walked slowly toward the tower. When she was six feet from the door, Cathy stopped, her shadow stretched out in front, the dark shape splashed onto the granite flags.

She sniffed convinced that she could smell something fetid coming from the building, something corrupt, the stench of a corpse. A faint mist seeped from the soil, the strong lights giving it the appearance of ethereal smoke.

She cursed Hopkins, surely he should have closed the door behind him as he left, the bastard had probably left it open on purpose just to try to scare her. Taking a deep breath she moved forward her shoes brushing through the undergrowth, she tried not to think of what was shuffling about beneath her feet. She remembered a documentary from years ago, the presenter stating that we are never more than six feet away from some kind of rodent.

She grabbed the handle of the door and pulled it closed, feeling a sense of relief as it clanged shut. Hitching up her belt, she dragged out the baton and began to make her way around the tower.

Jesus Christ, she wished Spenner would get a move on, though she wouldn't put it past Hopkins to leave her alone for the whole night, just to make some kind of point.

Maybe he had a problem with female officers, though Hopkins seemed to treat everyone with equal disdain so it was impossible to tell. She continued to follow the path around the tower, when she reached the starting point, Cathy slipped the baton back into its sleeve and thrust her hands into the pockets of her jacket, early evening stars glittered between the branches of the trees.

She thought about Lasser, if he'd been in charge of the investigation she was sure he wouldn't have left her alone at the crime scene. She knew one or two of her female colleagues fancied the broad-speaking DI and she had to admit that there was something about him that she herself found appealing.

Her last boyfriend had worked for the local council in the planning office. Six months into the relationship and she'd started to put her name down for the night shift, just so she would have an excuse not see him. A few weeks after the split she'd bumped into him at the local Tesco, she remembered glancing in his trolley, the fact that he had a load of meals for one made her feel a little guilty. When she noticed they'd all been the healthy options variety she decided it had been a lucky escape. Lasser didn't look like a healthy options type of guy. In fact, he smoked too much and he always looked dishevelled and in need of a shave but there was something about him that appealed to her. Maybe it was the fact that he hated Hopkins so much. Jesus was she that shallow, the enemy of my enemy is therefore my friend? She looked over her shoulder, the smile slipped from her lips. The thought of any dalliance with Lasser was chased from her mind by the sight of the open door.

PUZZLED

Sprawled on the sofa, bare feet resting on the coffee table, Lasser had the television on with the sound turned down. The conversation with Fossey had raised more questions than answers.

'Look, Lasser, it's not an exact science.'

'Nobody's saying it is but you spent time in the house and you were the one who led us to the tank. So, you must have been running things over in your head; I mean, it's your job for Christ's sake.'

'Not anymore.'

'Don't give me that, you might write books for a living but you're still a shrink.'

Fossey sighed. 'OK, I've given it some thought but to be honest I haven't come up with anything new.'

'Look, we have Ashley Radfield in custody; believe it or not we found a cufflink with Radfield's initials on it. It was on the floor of the tower directly beneath the body of Billy Jones.'

'It was trapped underneath the body?'

'Not as such, the body was hanging from a crossbeam.'

Fossey grimaced, he could picture the scene, it was no wonder Lasser hadn't wanted to go into detail in front of Michael.

'So, it proves that at least one of the Radfields had been inside the building.' Fossey said.

'Well, that's where I begin to get a little nervous.'

'I don't follow.'

Lasser laid it all out, finding the cufflink, searching the house and finding its twin.

'I mean, come on, Fossey, why run the risk of moving the body from the old house to a tower that has links to his family going back generations. And then be so idiotic as to leave a calling card behind.'

'You think someone is trying to set him up?' Fossey had asked.

‘I know it sounds far-fetched but as far as I can see Ashley Radfield has no motive for wanting to kill anyone, especially not someone like Billy Jones, I mean, what would he gain?’

‘Well, the Radfield family would have made enemies over the years but it’s a big leap from feeling aggrieved about something that happened in the past to slaughtering a fourteen-year-old boy and then trying to lay the blame on your enemy.’

‘Agreed, but it is possible.’ Lasser said.

‘Anything’s possible.’

‘Right, so let’s work on that assumption. If someone was trying to drop Ashley Radfield in deep shit, then, it would presumably be someone who’s had dealings with him in the past.’

‘That sounds plausible.’

‘It also means that whoever did this has been inside the house.’

‘The cufflink?’

‘Precisely, though as far as I’m aware there’s been no break-in...’

‘Maybe you should double check.’

‘Don’t worry I intend too.’

‘So, you could be looking for someone who’s known to the family, someone who has access to the place.’

‘Mm, the trouble is Ashley Radfield only came down from Scotland early on Monday afternoon and according to him it was a rare visit.’

‘And Malcolm Radfield’s dead.’

‘Yeah and how convenient is that, let’s face it the killer could have been hobnobbing with his Lordship and his son wouldn’t have a bloody clue.’

‘And you’re sure Radfield committed suicide?’

‘On the face of it, though let’s say I'll be having a word with the pathologist just to be on the safe side.’

‘So, what do you want me to do?’

Lasser shrugged. ‘Look, maybe I was wrong to come here but believe it or not finding someone you can talk to about this stuff isn’t as simple as you’d imagine.’

‘You could always try Hopkins?’

Lasser looked affronted at the mere mention of his counterpart. ‘I wouldn’t talk to that prick if he was the last man on the planet.’

‘Listen, I’ll go over the stuff that Jenna sent me, see if I can find out if the family had any obvious enemies.’

‘Much appreciated,’ he paused, ‘what about Michael, you know he’s going to give you the third degree?’

‘He’s trying to come to terms with what happened to his brother, in part he feels responsible.’

‘Yeah well, compared to the rest of the family he’s a good kid.’

‘Perhaps you should have tried telling him that.’

Lasser tilted his head to one side. ‘Look, I feel for him but my only concern is catching this maniac. I mean, if all this has been done to frame Ashley Radfield, what happens when we have to let his Lordship go, when the killer sees all his hard work going to pot, do you think he’ll just shrug his shoulders and say ‘hey ho, some you win some you lose?’

Fossey looked out over the fields, he could see what Lasser was aiming at. ‘So, you think he might lose the plot.’

‘I think he lost the plot when he disembowel Billy Jones, don’t you?’

Reaching for the remote, he flicked the television off before pushing himself up from the sofa. On his way home he’d called into the station, Simms had already left for home, so he checked with the desk sergeant, Radfield was being held until morning.

He made his usual stop to pick up booze and fags then grabbed a takeaway from a curry house now housed inside an old church. Standing at what used to be the alter waiting for his beef madras; he wondered what God would make of it all.

Gathering the empty curry trays, he was halfway to the kitchen when his mobile began to vibrate in his shirt pocket.

'Shit,' he dashed down the hall and dumped the rubbish into the pedal bin, two tin foil trays fell to the floor a half-eaten onion bhaji rolled toward the fridge, Lasser scrabbled for his phone, 'Hello.'

'Is that you, sir?'

Lasser frowned, 'Harper?'

'I'm sorry to bother you...'

'That's OK what can I do for you?' The phone went quiet, he picked up the rogue bhaji and dropped it into the bin. 'Harper, are you still there?'

'Sorry, sir.'

Lasser instincts flared, something isn't right here. 'Where are you?'

'I'm at the tower.'

'What's happened?'

'That's just it, I'm not sure.'

He could hear a tremor in her voice. 'Hang on, you're not up there on your own are you?'

'I am at the moment, PC Spenner was meant to be joining me but...'

Lasser interrupted. 'Spenner's been on duty since five this morning; he should be at home in the land of nod.'

He could hear her breath down the phone, it sounded ragged as if she had been running. *'I'm sorry, I didn't realise.'*

'Who told you he was on his way?'

'Sergeant Hopkins, he said he would...'

'So, you're at a major crime scene in the middle of nowhere on your tod?'

'Yes, but it's not that. You see when Sergeant Hopkins left earlier he left the door to the tower open...'

Lasser rubbed a hand through is hair. *'You are fucking kidding me?'*

'No, so I decided to close it.'

'Thank God for that.'

'The problem is I did a circuit of the perimeter just to check that everything was OK, but when I got back the door was open.'

Lasser thought for a moment. 'Have you tried to contact the station?'

He could hear rustling coming down the phone as if she were walking through tall grass. *'No, not yet.'*

'Right, I'll be there in twenty minutes.'

'Should I go into the tower?'

Lasser grabbed his coat from the back of the chair. 'No, you don't go near the bloody thing is that understood?'

'Yes, sir,' he could hear the relief in her voice, sense the tension easing a little.

'Now listen, as soon as I put the phone down you get onto the station and tell them you require assistance,' another long pause, he pulled on his shoes and grabbed the car keys from the dresser. 'You still there, Cathy?'

'Yes, sir, it's just ...'

'Look, being left up there on your own is breaking so many rules I don't even know where to start. But don't worry, I won't mention the fact you called me, I know what some of the tossers at the station can be like.'

Cathy heaved a sigh of relief. *'Thank you.'*

'Right I'm on my way,' he ended the call and hurried out to the car, his anger as hot as the madras he had eaten earlier.

DON'T GET AROUND MUCH ANYMORE

Ronnie couldn't remember the last time he'd driven through Hindley; it was a place he tended to avoid. Though he was surprised by how little the town centre had changed; he could see the old Palace Cinema on the left, he had done most of his courting in the dark of that cinema. It was a sobering thought when he realised that it had been over fifty years since he had set foot in the place.

The building was boarded up, big sheets of plywood sprayed with random graffiti and peeling flyers covered the doors and windows.

After dropping Michael and Tina off, Fossey had made his way back through the town centre. The pavements full of Friday night revellers. Twice he'd slammed on the brakes to avoid running one of them over as they staggered into the road. Ronnie looked in the mirror; Jenna was sitting on the back seat, her eyes closed as if she couldn't bear to open them. When Michael had discovered the house where his brother had died belonged to them, he had looked at them both as if this fact somehow implicated them in the murder. He hadn't actually come out and said anything; then again, he hadn't needed to. When they'd climbed from the car Tina had thanked Fossey for the lift home, she had even given Jenna a quick hug. Michael had just walked away without uttering a word.

'Are you OK, Jenna?' Fossey asked.

When she opened her eyes, she could see Patrick looking at her in the rear view mirror.

'I'm fine,' she didn't think she would ever be able to forget the way Michael had looked at her and the way he had found out had been awful. While Patrick had been out talking with the disgusting Lasser, Tina had woken up and put on the television. When Jenna had entered the lounge, they had been watching the news; it was like witnessing some horrible montage. First, an image of

Billy had appeared on the screen, he was like a miniature version of Michael, the same thin features the same pale blue eyes. Then the picture had flicked to the tower, she had glanced at Michael his eyes glued to the screen, she could see the muscles in his jaw clenched tight.

'What is that place?'

'That's the needle house, lad.' Ronnie's voice was low, no more than a rumble.

Jenna had wanted to dash over and turn the thing off but her legs had felt incapable of moving her forward.

'Do you know where it is?'

Jenna had never seen her grandad look more uncomfortable, when she looked back at the television the backdrop was the old house.

A woman moved into the picture. *'It's believed that William Jones died in this derelict house.'* The camera zoomed in on the windows; the boards ripped off, though no light seemed to penetrate the place. *'The building is owned by the Fotheringays, a local farming family who have declined to make any comment on the situation.'* She watched as the frown formed on Michael's face, when he turned to look at her, she couldn't meet his eyes.

He had turned back to the television and Jenna had felt her face freeze in disbelief, the screen showed her mother pulling out of the bottom of the drive in the Land Rover, she appeared to look directly at the camera, before pulling onto the lane.

'Though it's now believed that the body was at some point removed from the house and taken to the tower known locally as 'the needle house.' The building was originally built by the Radfield family and is now owned by the local water authority.'

Michael had turned and left the room without looking back.

Tina had moved quickly to the television and turned it off, her face burning with embarrassment.

'I'm sorry, Jenna, I had no idea...'

'Don't worry, lass, you weren't to know.' Ronnie sighed and pushed his flat cap back onto his head.

Jenna didn't know what to do, part of her wanted to follow Michael to try and explain how sorry she was for what had happened, another part wanted to run and hide.

'Jenna, you have nothing to feel guilty about.' Fossey was waiting for the traffic lights to turn green; he turned in his seat a concerned look on his face.

'I just feel so...' she struggled for the right word, her head heavy her brain disengaged.

'I'm sure when he's had time to think rationally, Michael will realise that you and your family had nothing to do with any of this. '

She didn't see how that was possible, it was as if they had been withholding information from him, she felt disgusted with herself, she was no better than Lasser.

When the lights changed to green, Fossey moved forward and then slammed on the brakes as a blue Audi bulleted from the left missing the front of the Range Rover by inches. Jenna screamed and Ronnie lunged forward, the seatbelt saving him from hitting the windscreen. Fossey saw Lasser hunched over the wheel of the Audi before it screamed across the junction and vanished from sight.

'That was him!' Jenna sounded out of breath, her voice quivering in anger and shock.

Fossey checked his mirrors then made his way across the junction. 'Are you two alright?'

'That man is an idiot!' she could feel her heart racing, the blood thundering in her ears.

Ronnie adjusted his cap. 'Well, the bugger was definitely in a hurry.'

'Probably off to harass some twelve-year-old for not having lights on their bike' Jenna snarled.

Fossey smiled. 'Believe it or not, Jenna, Lasser's one of the good guys.'

Jenna locked her gaze on the mirror. ‘You’re joking, right?’

He indicated and pulled the car over to the curb. ‘Listen, I know you think he was hard on Michael but he wants the best for the boy.'

‘He’s got a funny way of showing it; I mean, he hit him...’

‘No,’ Fossey shook his head, his face serious. ‘He defended himself; Michael was the one doing the hitting.’

‘But that’s only because he wouldn’t tell him anything.’

Fossey thought for a moment. ‘Believe me, Jenna; he was doing Michael a favour.’

‘I don’t see how you can say...’ she stopped, as Fossey’s words sunk in, Jenna closed her eyes. Lasser hadn’t said anything because it was too gruesome, too horrific. She could feel the sting of tears; feel a sense of despair smothering her, her familiar world fragmenting around her.

MIXED BLESSING

Driving along the pitted lane in broad daylight had been bad enough but at night even with the headlights on it was proving cataclysmically bad for the suspension. Lasser gave full vent to his frustration as the front wheels slammed down another yawning pothole.

'Son of a fucking bitch!' he flicked on the main beam, just in time to see a fox disappearing into the hedgerow. After two more minutes of torturous bump and grind, he pulled up; the darkness beyond the windscreen was a solid block.

Leaning over he fumbled in the glove compartment and pulled out a torch before climbing from the car. He could feel a chill in the air, a thin breeze whispering down from the moors bringing with it the scent of heather. Finding a collapsed section of the wall, he clambered over and headed off between the trees.

Under normal circumstances, a place like this could mess with your head but when you took into account that some maniac could have been walking along this very path with the butchered corpse of Billy Jones slung over his shoulder, then he could see why Harper had sounded so nervous.

He had to bend to avoid the low branches of a huge oak, the torchlight picking up the thick trunk of the tree. This was a place of shadows and threats, anyone could be hiding yards away, and you wouldn't have a clue. When he saw the arc of light in the distance, it was with a genuine sense of relief. He made his way down the hillside, a couple of times slipping on the leaf-littered floor, his feet leaving a black scarring in the earth.

'Harper, where the hell are you?'

'I'm over here, sir!' she shouted in reply.

Lasser moved to the right, and then, from nowhere it began to rain, for a moment he looked up confused, the drizzle on his face feeling like a new sensation.

She was standing in the centre of the circle of light, the rain falling around her like a fine silver mist.

He trudged over. 'You OK?'

She looked relieved to see him, a nervous half smile on her face. 'I'm not too bad, sir; I see you brought the weather with you.'

'Black clouds seem to follow me everywhere; now did you get in touch with the station?'

'Yes, sir...'

'Listen drop the *'sir'* I don't like it, never have.'

She looked at him in surprise. 'Oh right, well Meadows said he'd get help up here when someone became available.'

'That means never,' he looked toward the tower. 'So, you're sure about closing the door?' When he saw the frown on her face, he held up his hands. 'I know it's a stupid question but I just need to be sure.'

'I'm positive.'

'Right we'd better take a look,' he walked toward the tower, Harper falling in at his side.

'Do you want me to come in with you?'

He pushed the door open. 'No, you stay here, I won't be a minute, besides there's hardly enough room to swing a cat around up there,' he shone the torch toward the narrow stone staircase.

'OK, sir,' she blushed when Lasser looked at her with a raised eyebrow. 'Sorry, force of habit.'

'No problem.' Four strides took him to the bottom of the steps, the torch illuminating a multitude of cobwebs clinging to the rough sandstone walls. He began to climb, counting the steps, giving up when he reached sixty-seven. By the time, he got to the top his calves were throbbing. Poking his head through the trapdoor, he shone the beam around the narrow stone room, his face at floor level.

He could see the bloodstain on the wooden floor, a dark tinge that would probably remain for eternity or at least until the tower was demolished. Apart from the fact that all the boards had been removed from the narrow slots, there was no evidence that the forensic team had even been there.

'Sir!' Harper's voice sounded muffled, the stones absorbing the sound.

'What is it?'

'The lights have gone out!'

He turned on the steps; the darkness appeared to swirl toward him.

'Sir,' he could hear the tremor in her voice, sense the urgency.

'I'm on my way.' Despite the panic in her voice, he took his time, the last thing he wanted was to slip on the steps, he could imagine himself arriving at the bottom in a tangled heap, limbs twisted and broken. When he reached the exit, Cathy had her Maglite on, the beam sweeping back and forth between the trees. 'The tech guy said he'd filled the generator with enough fuel to last until morning,' she said in a tight voice.

'Yeah and Hopkins said he was sending someone out to partner you.'

She threw him a sour look. 'You think this was done deliberately, just to spook me?'

'There's only one way to find out, come on,' they headed out toward the generator, Harper's light picking up the bulky shape in the darkness. When they reached it, he shone his torch over the casing until he came across the clear plastic fuel gauge; he tapped the glass with his finger. 'According to this it's showing three quarters full.'

'So, why would it just stop running?'

He crouched down, the beam flickering on the metal body of the generator, when he came to the power cut-off button he frowned.

Harper moved behind him, peering over his shoulder. 'What's the matter?'

Standing up, he made a sweep of the area, the light slithering out between the trees, shadows rising and falling like huge black waves crashing against the face of a cliff.

'Someone's pulled the cut-off switch.'

'What do you mean, *pulled?*'

'Don't worry; we should be able to fire it up again,' he pushed the button back in until it clicked, then flicked the ignition switch, the engine rumbled but refused to start, he tried it again, a frown on his face, a bead of sweat trickling down his forehead. Moving around the back of the machine he suddenly stopped, two of the heater plugs were gone.

He looked toward Harper; she was sweeping the beam back and forth slowly, a section at a time. Somewhere close by an owl screeched, Lasser pulled out his mobile, scrolled through the numbers then pressed connect.

'Meadows, is that you?' he turned and flashed Cathy a smile. 'Right, I'm up at the tower; I want you to get bodies up here ASAP.'

Harper could hear a mumbled response, though she was unable to make out what the desk sergeant was saying.

'What do you mean everyone's busy?' He paused to listen *'I don't care if Wigan are playing at home, it doesn't take the whole squad to police a game of football, now...'*

Harper made another sweep with the light.

'I don't give a *flying fuck* what Hopkins said, I'm telling you what I need, now get on with it. I'll ring back in five and you'd better have good news for me, do you understand?' he thrust the phone back into his pocket.

'Problem?'

'Someone's removed one of the heater plugs,' he saw her eyes spring open in panic. 'Come on, we'll wait over by the door.'

When they reached the tower, Lasser pulled the metal door closed and slipped the padlock through the hasp.

'I'm glad you're here,' she said.

'Yeah well, I don't know what Hopkins was playing at but he's fucked it this time,' he paused, 'you'd better turn your light off, it's no use running down both sets of batteries.'

A second later, her light vanished. 'Who do you think took the plug?'

'I don't have a clue and to tell you the truth I'm in no hurry to find out.'

'But they've got Radfield in custody.'

Lasser looked at her, there was no doubt she was a good looking woman, her features delicate, eyes a deep brown, problem was she was only twenty-six maybe twenty-seven and he was the wrong side of thirty. 'Thing is, I don't think Radfield had anything to do with this.'

Cathy looked at him in surprise. 'But I thought they found evidence that tied him to the murder.'

'Oh, we have the evidence alright; the trouble is I think it was planted.'

Harper slid her hand onto the handle of the baton. 'Jesus, so you mean the killer's still out there?'

Lasser grunted. 'It might be a good idea if you got your nightstick out, Cathy.'

He heard a familiar sound of a baton sliding from its sheath.

'I don't mind admitting this place scares me witless,' she said.

He didn't reply, instead he pulled out his phone and hit the redial button. 'Meadows, you'd better have good news or so help me...' he listened for a few seconds; his eyes scanning the trees, everything about this place made him feel uneasy. 'Right good, and don't think you've heard the last of this as far as I'm concerned you're a bloody idiot. An officer contacted you for assistance and you fucking well ignored it,' he paused as Meadows tried to explain. 'Not good enough, dropping a bollock is one thing but failing to do your duty is entirely different,' he ended the call. 'Let the bastard stew on that for a bit.'

'Is he sending someone?'

'They should be here in the next thirty minutes,' he paused and pulled his phone back out. 'In fact I'm going to ring Hopkins while I'm in the mood,' he slapped the phone to his ear and waited. Harper held her breath, concerned about what Lasser was going to say, if he mentioned her then Hopkins would make her life a complete misery.

'Bastard's not answering,' he paused, 'come on, I can't see the point in hanging around here we might as well wait in the car.'

Cathy didn't need telling twice, she clicked her light back on, a thin mist curled around the base of the trees, where the ground dipped it was thick and impenetrable. The rain intensified. Lasser could hear it on the leaves above, feel it landing heavy on his face.

Halfway up the incline, Cathy lost her footing, her feet skidding from under her; Lasser hooked an arm around her waist and lifted her upright.

'Thanks,' she straightened her jacket, Lasser caught sight of milk white skin before she pulled it down, then she turned to look at him. 'You're stronger than you look.'

'Are you saying I look like a weakling?'

She felt her face burning in the dark. 'I didn't mean it like that.'

'Come on, let's keep moving.'

She kept hold of his sleeve, prepared to let go if he so much as looked at her. He kept the torchlight trained in front; Cathy swept hers from side to side. When her light hit the ruined face, she screamed, the sound muffled by the damp air, the torch jerked from her hand as if suddenly charged with a blast of electricity.

Lasser tried to grab her as she spun away retching, the baton slipping from her left hand; she landed on her hands and knees and began to scuttle away through the wet leaves.

'Cathy, what's the matter?' he strode toward her and knelt by her side, resting a hand on her heaving back. When she lifted her head, he could see shock etched onto her face her eyes wide and frantic.

'Over there,' she pointed a quivering finger to the left; Lasser aimed the beam into the darkness the body was slumped against the thick trunk of the huge oak.

'Stay here,' the rain was soaking through his jacket, setting up a chill against his skin. Lasser kept the beam moving, the light lancing out, trying to see everywhere at once. He kept getting glimpses of the body, the shoes, the dark suit jacket, shirt, tie, all seen through the strobe effect of the jittering beam. When he was six feet away, he raised the light.

Lasser ran a shaking hand over his scalp, the head was resting on the left shoulder, face tilted skyward. Both eyes open, the yawning mouth gathering rainwater, locked in a silent scream. He flicked the light away, it was little wonder she'd thrown up. Taking a deep breath, he pointed the torch back toward the corpse; the throat had been slashed wide, dark blood oozing from the wound. He glanced over his shoulder; Cathy was still kneeling amongst the leaves, her face tilted toward the sky, as if hoping the torrential rain would wash the image from her mind. Pulling out his phone, he scrolled through the menu and pressed the call button, a few seconds later the muffled sound of Beethoven's fifth symphony came from the body.

Ending the call, he turned and moved quickly back down the hill, his feet slithering on the wet grass, arms wind milling for balance. By the time he reached Cathy, she'd managed to haul herself to her feet.

'Come on, back to the car.'

'Is he dead?' she whispered.

Without answering, he grabbed the sleeve of her jacket and began to pull her away, giving the body a wide berth.

'Is he dead?' she repeated, her breathing ragged.

'You could say that.'

'Do you know...?'

'No more questions, let's just concentrate on getting out of these fucking woods.'

He tried to keep the torch steady, his hand still grasping her sleeve, twice she slipped and he dragged her unceremoniously to her feet, pushing her up the hillside, rainwater mingling with the sweat that coated his face.

When they reached the wall, Lasser shone the light back down the hillside as if he expected some shadow shape to come screaming out from beneath the trees, brandishing a cutthroat razor, lathered in blood. Cathy scrambled over the wall; he leapt after her and beeped the alarm. Once inside, he jammed the key into the ignition, started the engine and flicked the heater on full, before finally switching on the headlights.

The windows began to steam up, Cathy, swiped a sleeve down the glass and peered out into the night. 'You're sure he was dead?'

'Positive.'

'I mean, who the hell would be wandering around here at this time of night?'

Lasser glanced sideways at her. 'You didn't recognise him?'

She turned towards him. 'What do you mean?'

'Cathy,' he paused, 'it was Hopkins.'

She wiped at her mouth with a trembling hand. *'Are you sure?'*

'I'm sure.'

'Can I have a cigarette?'

He pulled one out, lit it and handed it over. 'I didn't know you smoked?'

‘I packed it in about six months ago,’ she took a pull and then coughed as the smoke hit her lungs, ‘God, that’s good.’

Lasser raised an eyebrow. ‘It sounds it.’

She looked at him, even managing a weak smile, then he saw a change in her eyes ‘If you hadn’t turned up, it would have been me next.’

Lasser blew out through pursed lips. ‘Don’t even go there; you should never have been left on your own in a place like this.’

‘Christ, he must have been killed as soon as he left me.’

‘And I must have walked straight past him, so what does that say about my detective skills?’

She puffed at the cigarette, as if the rush of nicotine somehow allowed her to think more clearly.

‘What about Colin?’ she asked.

‘Who's Colin?’

‘The guy who set the lights up.’

Lasser thought for a moment. ‘There’s no sign of a van, so I presume he must be OK.’

Harper frowned. ‘What about Hopkins's car?’

‘I didn’t pass it on the way up here.’ Slipping the car into gear, he began to move forward.

‘What are you doing?’

‘I just want to see if he parked further up the lane.’

She sighed and clicked her seatbelt into place, glad to be doing something, rather than just sitting in the car with the dark looming against the glass.

Lasser pulled out his phone and tossed it into her lap. ‘Ring Meadows, tell him we want an ambulance up here and the forensic team, in fact tell him we want the works.’

She hesitated. ‘Wouldn't it be better coming from you?’

‘I’m sick of talking to that *prick*, if he tries to give you any grief use your initiative.’

He spun the wheel to the right in an effort to avoid a large pothole; he could see a curve in the lane ahead, the headlights swept out over the moors.

'Sergeant Meadows, it's WPC Harper,' she went quiet as she listened to the desk sergeant. Lasser kept his eye on the road and his ears open.

'Yes well, a change of plan we need an ambulance ASAP and also the SOCO team out here as quick as you can.'

As the car bumped around the corner Lasser spotted the white Audi parked tight to the wall, if there had been a sliver of doubt in his mind it was dispelled by the sight of Hopkins's car.

'I realise that, but we have a body up here and we need the area securing,' she paused, 'yes, I'm with Sergeant Lasser now.'

He pulled up behind the car then looked at Cathy; she glanced at him then gave a small apologetic shrug. 'He's busy, that's why you're talking to me but I can always get him if you want, though to be honest I don't think he'd be too happy about being disturbed.'

He could hear nonsensical chatter coming down the phone; she pushed a stray strand of dark hair back behind her ear. 'Thanks, I appreciate that,' she snapped the phone shut and handed it back to Lasser.

'Did he give you any grief?'

'He tried to, though when I mentioned about putting you on the phone he suddenly became cooperative.'

Lasser snatched on the handbrake. 'I bet he did,' dragging a hand across his hair, he flicked the droplets of rainwater onto the dashboard.

'I didn't think we'd make it back to the car,' her voice was low and brittle. 'He must have been somewhere in the trees, watching me, watching us.'

He saw a flash of headlights in the distance, though from up here it was difficult to judge how far away the vehicle was.

'It seems you were right about Radfield, I mean, he's off the hook now,' she said.

'Yeah, but until we catch whoever did this I wouldn't want to be in his patent leather brogues.'

'Where do you think the killer is now?'

'If he has any sense he'll be far away from here.'

Lasser saw a flash of blue, a few seconds later, two or three more lit up the valley. 'It looks like the cavalry are on the way.'

She wiped at the knees of her trousers, trying to get rid of the mud stains, some of the morons she worked with would only make some sexist comment about her being down on her knees in front of a superior officer.

When she looked up Lasser was watching her, a slight smile turning up the corners of his mouth.

She frowned. 'Are you a bloody mind reader or what?'

Holding up his hands, his smile turned into a wide grin. 'No comment,' he opened the door and climbed out, the sound of sirens bleating in the distance gradually getting louder as the rain hammered on the roof of the car.

The next minute headlights blasted into his eyes, forcing him to look away, he squinted into the night, a white van was pulling up, the side door slid open and a dark shape climbed out a camera already on his shoulder. Lasser saw the interior light come on as the driver opened the door and jumped out.

'I don't believe this; the bloody media get here before our lot, how pathetic is that?'

She looked at him over the roof of the car. 'Do you want me to get rid of them?'

'Save your breath, these bastards never listen; you'll simply find yourself on the six o'clock news looking like a total bitch.'

Lasser pulled up the collar of his jacket in an effort to keep out the rain as the two men approached.

'God, where did all this rain come from?' The driver of the van asked, his hair slicked back; the man was wearing an old Belstaff wax jacket over a crisp white shirt and tie, a stud glinted in his left earlobe. When he was a couple of feet away he stopped, the camera operator standing slightly to his left, already filming.

Lasser pointed a finger to the sky. 'Well, I'm no expert but I think it's coming from up there somewhere.'

The man smiled, his teeth flashing in the darkness. 'My name's Mike Brewster, Orbital Television.'

The sound of the sirens grew louder, Lasser moved around to the front of the car.

'Well, Mr Brewster, I'm afraid I'm going to ask you to move your van.'

'Why, officer, is there a problem?'

'Not at the moment but there will be if you don't move it in the next thirty seconds.'

Brewster frowned and then glanced over his shoulder. 'The keys are in it, just move it will you, Bob.'

'Move it where, boss?'

'I don't care where; just get it shifted,' Brewster snapped.

Bob trudged back to the van and started the engine, as he pulled away, the line of police cars arrived. Lasser walked toward them, as he reached Brewster he stopped. 'Thanks for your cooperation, Mr Brewster.'

'No problem, Mr...?'

Lasser ignored him and moved forward, he could see car doors opening and dark shapes in luminous vests climbing out.

'Right, lads, I want a perimeter set up, no one gets over this wall is that understood?' He hooked a thumb over his shoulder.

A mumble of responses, flashlights switched on, he noticed a few stifled yawns, the faces pale blobs in the moonlight. 'Has Paul Collins arrived yet?'

'I'm here, sir.' Collins moved forward, the large German Shepherd pulled tight to the side of his leg.

'Right, half a dozen of you stay here, the rest with me,' he made for the gap in the wall, under the trees the rain was gathering on the leaves before falling in heavy drops.

'What are we looking for, sir?' Collins asked.

'Hopkins has been murdered; I want you to see if you can pick up the scent of whoever is responsible.'

He could hear the shocking news travelling down the line, furtive whispers and hissed expletives.

A multitude of torchlight swept back and forth careering off the trees, criss-crossing one another in the darkness.

'Hopkins?' Collins asked in disbelief.

'Don't make me repeat myself, Paul,' he moved to the right, ducking under a low hanging branch.

After fifty yards, Lasser held up a hand and turned. 'OK, lads, I want tape set up between these trees, twenty yard perimeter and keep your eyes open. I don't want any possible evidence trampled underfoot, Collins, you come with me.'

The men began to fan out, Lasser and the dog handler slithered further down the hill, the dog becoming agitated, nose to the ground, the panting increasing as the animal picked up a scent.

Lasser didn't know if he expected the sight of Hopkins to be any less shocking second time around, if anything it was worse. The rain had washed the blood away from the neck wound, the torchlight showing just how deep the cut had been.

'Christ, it looks as if they tried to take his bloody head.' Collins made the dog sit at his side, resting a hand on its head, almost as if he were trying to shield the horrific sight from the animal.

'Right, Paul, whoever did this must be covered in blood, so I want you to see if you can pick up the scent.'

'OK, sir,' he moved forward keeping a tight grip on the leash; Lasser could smell the wet earth, he had no idea whether the rain would help or hinder the animal.

'Sir, the SOCO team have arrived,' he looked over his shoulder; Cathy was walking toward him her eyes locked onto his.

'OK, what about the reporter?'

'He's making a nuisance of himself but I think he's got the message about keeping the right side of the wall.'

When she reached his side, he saw her glance toward the body then quickly look away.

'Are you OK?'

She looked up at him, squared her shoulders and nodded.

He could see the paper-suited forensic team moving down the hill, as they came closer he recognised Carl carrying a small metal briefcase in his right hand.

'Carl, over here, mate!'

Carl looked up and raised a hand, then slithered his way over.

'Alright, boss, I thought you'd have been tucked up in bed by now?'

'Remind me, what does a bed actually look like?' he nodded toward the body; Carl's eyes widened in shocked when he saw the figure slumped against the tree.

'Jesus, is that who I think it is?'

'There are no flies on you, are there, mate.' Lasser replied.

'Well, the shit's going to hit the fan, that's for sure.'

'That's why I don't want any fuck ups, I...'

'Sir, he's onto something.'

Lasser turned, the dog was going berserk hind legs digging into the soft earth as he tried to drag himself forward.

'OK, Paul, let's see where he takes us. I can leave you in charge, Carl?'

The SOCO man nodded, snapping a paper mask over his nose and mouth. 'No problem, boss.'

'Are you coming, Cathy?'

She paused for a moment then nodded; Collins let the leash reel out, the dog-bulleted forward, the extending lead unravelled with a high-pitch screech.

Lasser cursed his choice of footwear, he could feel the water soaking through his socks, his feet beginning to go numb.

Collins was ten yards ahead and pulling away, everything was seen through a jumble of torchlight making it difficult to judge distance.

When he looked up Collins had stopped and was looking back toward them. 'He's definitely onto something, sir.'

Lasser flapped his hands. 'OK, Paul, I believe you, just *get going.*'

Dog and handler set off again, further down the hillside they came across a huge fallen beech tree, its roots and branches snapped and tangled, Collins and the dog scrambled over. Lasser placed a hand on the wood, the surface slick with rain, taking a step back he tried to vault over, when he was in mid-air his right hand slipped and he slammed down hard onto the trunk before slithering into the wet mud on the other side.

Cathy shone her light over the tree, he was scrambling to his feet, the left side of his jacket and trousers saturated and slicked with mud.

'Are you OK?'

He grinned up at her. 'I'm a fucking idiot.'

She slithered over; her feet splashing in a puddle of muddy water.

The dog began to bark, Lasser shone the torch through the trees, he could see Collins high viz vest in the distance.

'Bastard weather men never said anything about this,' Lasser snarled as they set off again, though running beneath the trees was proving difficult, every time they tried to increase their speed, one of them would slip or stumble.

Gradually the larger trees began to thin out, laurel and rhododendron bushes taking over. Thin moonlight washed down onto the forest floor. When the trees suddenly ended, it came as a shock, like walking out into an alien landscape. Collins was standing at the water's edge, the reservoir stretched out before them. The dog sweeping left and right sniffing at the ground, the rain hissing into the black water.

'What's the matter, Paul?'

'It looks like he went into the water, sir.'

'Shit,' Lasser looked across the vast expanse; in the distance, he could see the pale yellow lights of the dual carriageway curving away to the right, overhead, the heavy rumble of a plane, its undercarriage lights blinking.

Collins reined the dog in and gave it a sharp order to sit. 'Which way do you want me to go?'

Lasser kicked at a loose stone. 'It doesn't matter, he's long gone.'

'I'll try left, sir.'

He shrugged, the killer would have stayed in the water washing as much blood off as possible before heading back to dry land. He looked at his watch, it was half past one, he'd raised the alarm at midnight, so the killer had well over an hour to make good his escape.

Cathy was wandering along to the right, shining the torch along the edge of the water.

When his phone began vibrate, he fished it from his pocket before slapping it to his ear.

'Go ahead, Carl,' a drop of rain slid down his nose and dripped off.

'OK, boss, I'm just letting you know Simms is on his way.'

'Thanks, what about the body have you turned up anything useful?'

'As far as I can tell he died from a single wound...'

'Jesus, Carl...'

'I'll know more when we get him back to the lab, I mean, I'm working virtually blind here.'

'What about the search parties?'

'Well, there have been no shouts of eureka, so I don't think they've found anything.'

'OK, let me know if they do.'

'Straight away, boss.'

He snapped the phone shut, when he looked up Cathy was trudging back toward him.

'I can't find any trace.'

Lasser shivered. 'It's hardly surprising, if Scooby Doo's lost the scent then what chance do we have?'

Grabbing her ponytail, Cathy rang the water out as if ringing a dishcloth. 'I'm absolutely bloody freezing,' she shivered.

Lasser looked down at her. 'What time did you come on duty?'

'Eight o'clock,' she paused, 'Yesterday morning.'

'Right that's it, we're going home.'

'But what about all this?' she spread her arms; the water was a black slab behind her, the moon a sliver of silver.

'Listen, we've done all we can for one night besides there are enough bodies on scene to do the donkey work, plus I don't know about you but I feel shagged.'

She looked out across the water. 'I could do with a hot bath.'

'And I could do with a couple of beers, you want to join me?'

LOOK BEFORE YOU LEAP

The first thing he did when he arrived home was strip off the blood-soaked clothing. Opening the door to the wood burner he shoved the bundle inside then lit a couple of firelighters and tossed them in before opening the air vent; the flickering flames suddenly began to rage as air was drawn through, feeding the fire.

A couple of minutes later he stood in the shower, the fine spray of water needling his face, the burning anger gradually subsiding as he tried to come to terms with what he had done.

He'd been crouched in the undergrowth as the copper walked past, concealed, invisible. So, why had he broken cover, what had possessed him to move forward in a crouch and draw the blade across the man's throat? He had died without a sound; he tried to remember what he had been feeling, as the man's legs buckled, but his mind seemed to skip forward as if feelings were inconsequential. He had dragged the body to the base of the huge oak and slammed him against the trunk, though he had no idea why.

The man scrubbed at his face in an effort to clear his thoughts; as soon as he drew the blade across the paper thin skin, he had ruined everything. The plan to make Ashley Radfield pay for the sins of his family was now meaningless. As soon as the media discovered a senior police officer murdered then the death of the boy diminished. So, why didn't he feel distraught, why wasn't he raging at his own stupidity? Reaching forward he turned the dial on the shower the cascade gradually turning to ice. He struggled to think of a word that summed up how he was feeling, after a few moments it came to him, invigorated, he felt invigorated.

Climbing from the shower, he sat naked on the narrow sofa, watching as the flames consumed the clothing. He had spent so long planning, it seemed as if his whole life in one way or another had been absorbed with the

Radfields. He smiled, Radfield had pleaded for his life as he led him to the greenhouse, in much the same way an adult would lead a child. All the bluff and bravado vanished as he promised to give him money, power, anything, his voice weak and pitiful, his breath coming in short sharp gasps.

In fact, he was sure the old bastard's heart had given out as he forced him to sit on the dry earth among the plant pots and weeds. His watery eyes had glazed over, any notion of escape had evaporated, and Lord Malcolm Radfield had started to cry. It was no more than he'd expected, after all the family were good at making promises and even better at breaking them. Now he wished he hadn't taken the time to make it look like suicide, he should have gutted his Lordship, cut off his head and stuck it on the railings of the huge gates, made the killing as horrific as possible. That would have made Ashley Radfield really suffer, rather than this pointless charade. The image of Malcolm Radfield hacked and gutted made his mind jolt with a sudden surge of pleasure.

Murdering the boy had been the first link in the chain, the sole aim to bring retribution upon a family that had schemed, lied and eventually committed murder. Prospering whilst others had suffered. Over the years, his mind had fashioned a plan that gave him the right to kill within a rigid framework, when in reality the urge to take life, any life, had been there all along. The realisation was like suddenly gaining freedom after years of incarceration, the reason he had killed the police officer was simple he had done it because it gave him a sense of joy. He felt the shackles of the plan fall away, everything now seen with a clarity that astounded him, at last, he was in a place where he could admit his true nature.

He would kill Radfield next, then an image of the young girl with long blonde hair swept into his head and the man smiled in anticipation.

DRIVING WITH THE BRAKES ON

Cathy sat on the sofa, legs curled beneath her, the towelling robe felt warm and cosy. As soon as they'd arrived at Lasser's home, he had cranked the heating on full and poured them both a drink.

'Are you hungry?'

She had stood in the lounge a small puddle of water gradually forming around her feet.

'Starving,' she shivered.

'Right I'll make us some food, the bathrooms at the top of the stairs, why don't you go and grab a shower.'

'Are you sure?'

'Positive, there's a bath robe hanging on the back of the door.'

Twenty minutes later, she had come back into the room, her wet clothes rolled into a bundle.

'Here give me those I'll stick them in the washer.'

She closed her eyes for a moment; while she had been in the shower he had made them both a cheese omelette, now she was beginning to feel sleepy, the effect of the food, drink and heat making her yawn; she shook her head a little and sat up straight.

DCI Simms had arrived as they trudged back to the murder scene; wearing a pair of Hunter wellies with a heavy wax jacket covering his uniform. His face set in a deep frown.

'Get a bloody move on with that generator; I want lights down here now!' he bellowed.

Lasser looked up the hill; he could see a couple of uniforms dragging the small generator down the steep decline, the wheels getting bogged down as the ground turned to mush.

'Right, Lasser, I want to know what the bloody hell has happened here?'

Fifteen minutes later, he and Cathy were climbing back to the car, the rain coming down heavier than ever, Lasser didn't think he had ever been so cold and wet. Now with the central heating blasting away, the drenching was becoming a distant memory.

Cathy took a sip of wine. 'Simms didn't look happy.'

Lasser stuck his bare feet onto the coffee table.

'It's hardly surprising, he's only got a couple of years to go before he retires and this is probably the last thing he needs.'

She placed the glass on the table. 'Do you think they'll find anything?'

'Not in this weather. I mean, this guy's a maniac but he's no fool.'

'Still, you never know he might have got careless.'

'Well, we should know more in the morning but I'm not holding my breath.'

She looked around the room; it was tidy but lived in. The empty vase that should have had flowers in it, the thin film of dust on top of the television all pointing to the fact here was a man who lived alone.

'What I can't get my head around is why he should kill Hopkins in the first place?'

Lasser stifled a yawn. 'I've been wondering about that,' he paused, 'it was dark when Hopkins left you, right?

Cathy shivered. 'Very.'

'So, the killer could have remained hidden, I mean, that place is perfect for it.'

'I suppose so.'

'Right, so if this man has gone to so much trouble to convince us that it was Radfield who killed Jones, then why would he suddenly decide to break cover and kill Hopkins?'

'Maybe he wasn't trying to frame him after all.'

'Look, I admit coincidence plays a part in what we do. But this guy took the time to move Jones to a place that has direct links with the Radfield family. If you take into account the cufflink we found at the tower, then it all points to a setup.'

'Maybe the killer just wanted to scare him.'

He sat up; he could almost feel the light bulb going off above his head. 'I think you could be right, whoever did this isn't really interested in framing Ashley Radfield. This is,' he paused, 'or rather was, all about revenge.'

'But revenge for what?'

'Who knows but ultimately that's no longer important.'

'Because of Hopkins?'

Lasser nodded and drained the glass. 'The man kills Billy Jones, apparently a random act of violence. If he'd left the body intact then we'd have concentrated our efforts around the old house. But he takes the effort to drag the poor little sod three miles across country to leave him hanging from a crossbeam, complete with a piece of incriminating evidence. Old Man Radfield tops himself...'

'But did he really?' Cathy asked, she could feel a strange kind of excitement beginning to build in the room.

'Don't worry, I intend to find out, and, in between, Kitts dies of so-called natural causes that we now know was a load of bollocks. So, at that point the killer was still intent on pointing the finger at Ashley otherwise he wouldn't have been so careful with Kitts.'

Cathy slid her hands through her damp hair. 'So, why kill Hopkins?'

'Because, he can't help himself.'

'I don't follow.'

'Look, maybe this whole thing started off with the killer feeling he had a legitimate reason for wanting revenge on the Radfield family. Nevertheless, killing Hopkins reeks of someone who has lost the plot; let's face it the man has to be seriously unhinged. Molder said that whoever killed Billy had to have had a level of skill and control but who has the mind-set where they can slice open a fourteen-year-old boy and pull his organs out?'

Cathy shivered as she remembered the sight of the grey mass slithering from the plastic feed sack. 'God, don't remind me.'

'So, in reality, this fucker has never been in control of anything. All the effort with Billy was done to give him a twisted sense of legitimacy. It's the same with Kitts an old guy who just happened to be in the wrong place at the wrong time.'

'What about Malcolm Radfield?'

'It might be difficult to prove, but it would hardly be surprising if the killer were responsible. So, that leaves our esteemed colleague.'

'But why would the killer come back to the tower in the first place, I mean, why take the risk?'

'This guy knows the area that much is obvious, he could have been watching the place for hours just waiting in the undergrowth...'

'I get that, but why bother. I mean, I know some people who murder will return to the scene of the crime but that's usually after a level of time has passed. To do it when the place is crawling with coppers is madness.'

'Maybe Hopkins wasn't just a random victim.'

She drained her glass and placed it on the table. 'You mean he was waiting for Hopkins to show?'

'Well, it's a possibility; we both know he took every opportunity to get himself in front of the cameras. When the body was first found and I came up here, Charlie was already holding an impromptu press conference; in fact Simms gave him a right bollocking for it.'

'What's your point?'

Lasser thought for a moment. 'If you were the killer and you wanted to bask in the glory of your handiwork then how would you keep tabs on the situation?'

'You'd watch the media output.'

'Correct and who would you see when you flicked on your television or opened your daily rag?'

'Hopkins!'

Lasser grinned and lit another cigarette. 'Precisely.'

'I still don't understand why he would want to kill him though?'

Lasser pulled out a cigarette and rolled it between his fingers. 'It's like I said before, where this nutter is concerned we have to think laterally. I could be wrong about the whole thing or maybe the killer didn't like the things that Hopkins was saying or didn't like the shirt he was wearing. It could be any number of reasons but he had to have been out at the tower for a reason and let's face it, Cathy, he cut the lights and we both know that he could probably have killed us both, yet he didn't.'

'So, why cut the lights in the first place, why didn't he just give the tower a wide birth and scarper?'

Lasser looked at her across the coffee table, unsure of how to proceed. Before he could think of what to say he saw her eyes widen in shock. *'He thought I was alone?'*

Lasser smiled grimly. 'If you remember when he sabotaged the generator I was already inside the tower.'

'And he had no idea you were there, so he killed the light to make it easier to get to me?'

He saw her swallow and reach for the wine bottle. 'As soon as the generator stopped you shouted up to me.'

'Jesus, if I hadn't, he could have slaughtered me like Hopkins!'

'Yes well, he didn't.'

'But...'

'Listen, Cathy, its all ifs and buts, we could be way off the mark. Besides you can't afford to think like that.'

She filled her glass and took a large gulp.

Lasser glanced at his watch. 'Jesus, look at the time.'

'I should get going.'

'Sleep in the spare room, it seems stupid dragging yourself back into the rain, besides your clothes won't be dry yet.'

'Are you sure, I mean, I could get a taxi?'

'Come on, it's been a shit day, just try and get some rest.'

She nodded and slipped to her feet. 'Thanks, serg.'

'No need to thank me, it's only a bed.'

'No, I mean, thanks for everything.'

Lasser raised his glass in acknowledgment.

BIG NEWS

'I can't believe you haven't heard.' Ronnie had his tin out, today he had swapped his old jacket for a raincoat, though during the night the clouds had drifted away, leaving the sky clear once more. The rain had left everything looking brighter; it was as if the fields and trees had been given a lick of vibrant paint.

They were standing in front of the house, waiting for Jenna to put in an appearance.

'I was listening to a CD so I've not had the news on. Why, what's happened?' Fossey asked.

'What's happened?' Ronnie looked at him in disbelief. 'They only found a copper in the woods, stone bloody dead, that's what.'

'Are you sure?' he had a sudden image of Lasser sprawled on the wet earth, the rain washing away the blood.

The old farmer threw him a withering look. 'It's been bedlam, cop cars coming and going all night. I tell you it's a good job it's not lambing season otherwise the place would be littered with dead lambs.'

A moment later, Jenna came out of the front door the air around her agitated.

'It's him!' her face was flushed with anxiety. 'I've just heard it on the news, I can't believe it, he was...'

Ronnie took a step back from his granddaughter, as if he didn't recognise this force of nature. 'Calm down, Jenna, I don't have a bloody clue what you're talking about.'

Jenna ignored him and stood in front of Fossey.

'It's Hopkins!'

Ronnie looked at her wide-eyed. 'The bugger that gave us the third degree?'

'According to the news he died after a frenzied knife attack, so its job done, Grandad,' her voice was thick with disdain, her eyes flashing anger.

'Hey, lass, I hope you're not saying I'm glad about any of this.'

Fossey took a step forward and took hold of her arms. 'What else did they say, Jenna?'

She looked at him in confusion; it was as if she had voices in her head all clambering to be heard. However, when she opened her mouth she found the words locked in. Her eyes filled with tears and then she fell forward into his arms, the sobs breaking free, her body shaking.

Ronnie looked dumbfounded. 'Hey come on, love, everything will sort itself out,' he shuffled his feet. He'd never been any good with emotions, he could never think of the right things to say and when he did open his mouth he usually put his foot in it.

Fossey eased her back until he could look into her eyes. 'Listen, Jenna, none of this is your fault...'

'Of course it's not her fault, she knows that it's bugger all to do with us!' Ronnie's voice rose in anger.

Fossey ignored him. 'Whoever did these things is sick and needs help...'

'They need a twelve bore shoving...'

Jenna spun toward him. *'Shut up, Grandad! You just don't get it, do you?'* she screamed the words, each one louder than the last. Didn't he realise that everything was falling apart that their lives would somehow be changed forever. Their name would be linked with the murders and no amount of time would change that fact. People would point in the street; college would become a living nightmare.

Ronnie looked as if he had been pole-axed and then he spun on his heels and strode away.

Susan appeared at the door. 'What are you two shouting about?'

Jenna looked at the ground, the sobs lifting her shoulders, tears falling to the ground. Ronnie carried on walking, without looking back; he disappeared around the side of the house.

GOOD MORNING SUNSHINE

'I'd say the man you're looking for is at least six-three.' Molder was standing by the coffee machine feeding it with small silver. 'Are you sure you don't want one?'

Lasser shook his head, the sight of Hopkins body grey and lifeless on the slab had left him feeling nauseated.

'And there are no other wounds?'

Molder pulled the cup from the slot. 'With a cut like that there wouldn't need to be.'

'So, no struggle?'

'Absolutely not, he was attacked from behind, the killer simply reached over the shoulder and the rest is self-explanatory.'

'Anything else?'

'Apart from the fact that the killer is right-handed, no.'

'Well, that's not much to go on. I mean, come on I thought you guys were meant to be experts?' he tried to sound light-hearted.

Molder looked at him over the top of the plastic cup, his eyes cold. 'I'm not in the habit of fabricating evidence, Sergeant, whoever did this knew exactly what they were doing. He's big and strong and if you ask me this individual has no moral compass, he's...'

'Jesus, Molder tell me something I don't know.'

The pathologist shrugged. 'Sorry, I can't be more helpful.'

'Right well, if you do happen to find anything else...'

'It seems highly unlikely.'

Lasser closed his eyes for a few seconds. 'Fair enough, but if you do, then you have my number.'

Dropping the cup into the bin, Molder patted the pockets of his lab coat as if he were looking for something. 'Well, don't hold your breath.'

'And what about William Jones?'

Molder pulled out a pack of mints and popped one into his mouth. 'I'd say that both the boy and Sergeant Hopkins were killed using the same weapon.'

'You mean killed by the same guy?'

'I said weapon, Sergeant, finding out if it was the same man is your responsibility, not mine.'

'You lot are all the same...'

'If you mean we're cautious then we have a right to be, I've seen too many of my colleagues badgered into making educated guesses that have ended their careers. So, if you're looking for a scapegoat then I suggest you look somewhere else, because you won't find any here.'

'I presume it's pointless asking you about Thomas Kitts?'

'Kitts was smothered, not stabbed.' Molder replied, a slight smile on his commandant like face.

'And Malcolm Radfield?'

'What about him?'

'Can you be sure it was suicide?'

Molder sighed, as if he was becoming bored with the conversation. 'Look, Lasser, as far as anyone can tell, Malcolm Radfield took his own life.'

'But it's possible that he could have been murdered?'

'Good God, man, you're turning into a conspiracy theorist.'

Lasser could hear the derision coming through loud and clear. 'It's called doing your job, Molder, you should try it sometime.'

He turned and began to stride down the long monotonous corridor, what was the point in having an expert when they were unwilling to give an opinion. It was like paying for a prostitute only to discover that she didn't give blowjobs. His shoes squeaked as he walked. Simms had rung him at the crack of dawn and told him to get out to the lab and find out everything he could about the demise of Detective Sergeant Charles Hopkins. He barrelled his way down the corridor until he came to the door of the hospital canteen.

He spotted Cathy sitting at a corner table, a large coffee cup clamped between her hands. As he pulled the chair out she looked up.

'Any luck?'

'Molder loves to point out the obvious but as soon as you get to the serious stuff, you can forget it.'

'So what do we do now?'

He stifled a yawn, he felt like going home, grabbing a beer from the fridge and then crashing out for a few hours. 'Look, I know I said that finding out why the killer wants to frame the Radfields was fruitless but that family is the only connection we have to any of this.'

Cathy dropped a sugar lump into the cup and stirred it with a plastic spoon. 'Well, I'd imagine they've made enemies over the years but where would we start. If Ashley Radfield can't point the finger then what chance do we have?'

'Maybe he knows and isn't saying?'

Cathy looked unconvinced. 'If someone were trying to frame me for murder and I could point the finger then I wouldn't hesitate.'

A couple of nurses sat down at the table next to theirs, both plates heaped with sticky buns and biscuits.

Lasser felt his stomach rumble. 'Perhaps we should have another chat with his Lordship, maybe we can pick his brains about the family history.'

'But you said Ashley only came down from Scotland when he absolutely had to.'

'What's your point?'

'Well, if that's true then it seems unlikely that the killer would bear a grudge against someone who doesn't even live in the area, surely it seems more likely to be the father he had the problem with and he's dead.'

'Fair point.'

'I mean, maybe Radfield did end his own life, perhaps he realised that someone had some sort of vendetta against him or knew of something that would ruin the family.'

Lasser mulled it over. 'The killer must have known that we wouldn't be looking seriously at Malcolm for the murder of Billy Jones. I've read the autopsy report, the old guy was on his last legs, there's no way he would have been able to tackle a kid like Billy.'

Cathy sighed. 'We're just going around in circles.'

'Yeah, though if you take into account all of this coincided with Ashley coming down from Scotland then it suggest the killer knew of his visit,' he saw her eyes widen.

'It's almost as if the killer was waiting until Ashley arrived before he started to kill.'

Lasser nodded. 'So, if we can find out who knew about his visit then it could at least throw up some suspects.' he said. 'As far as I can see it's the only option we have.'

She drained the coffee cup. 'I'm ready whenever you are.'

'OK, I'll just get a coffee and you can drive while I get my caffeine fix.' Lasser slid the car keys across the table and then headed to the counter.

FIVE BAR GATE

'It's not bloody right.' Ronnie rested his arms on the top of the gate, looking out onto a view that had changed very little in his lifetime. He could remember sitting on top of the gate when he was a child, his father pointing out the boundaries of the land they owned.

Swallows flitted back and forth, feeding on the wing. 'It's not that she blames herself...' Fossey said.

'Well, it sounds like it to me.'

Susan had taken Jenna back into the house an arm around the shoulder of her sobbing daughter. 'She's frightened, Ronnie.'

'But she knows we'd never let anything happen to her,' he pulled out his cigarette tin and fumbled a stump out.

'This has nothing to do with fear for herself; she's scared of the changes. Jenna thinks this will impact on all of you, not just her.'

'Look you don't get to my age without having a thick skin.'

'I understand that but you have to see this from her perspective. I mean, can you imagine what it'll be like for her when she goes back to college? The finger pointing, the sly comments. She has to go, Ronnie, she doesn't have the luxury of simply staying on the farm.'

Ronnie glared through a cloud of pale grey smoke and then his shoulders sagged. Fossey was right; his life consisted of mooching around the farm and the occasional game of dominoes in the pub. He had no commitments, he could avoid the outside world but Jenna had a life to build and now she had this hanging over her head, a stigma that could follow her for years.

'Listen, when we went up to the needle house I got the impression that you perhaps knew more about the Radfield family than you were...'

Ronnie's face hardened. 'Is that all you're bothered about, your damn book?'

'This has nothing to do with the book; it's about trying to help your granddaughter.'

'Oh aye and how will idle gossip help her, eh?' Ronnie spat.

Fossey sighed. 'I'm not saying it will but I know William Jones died so the killer could try and pin the blame on the Radfields....'

'How the hell do you know that?' Ronnie's eyes sprang wide in surprise.

'When they found his body in the tower, the police also discovered a piece of evidence that pointed to the Radfields.'

Ronnie could feel the blood drain from his face, the smoke suddenly making him feel light headed.

'But Malcolm was an owd man, I mean, the last time I saw him he was hobbling around with a bloody stick.'

'That might be true but someone hates that family enough to try and frame them for murder.'

'Ah, but what about Hopkins, this twisted bugger can't frame them for that, can he?'

'You're right but initially laying the blame on the Radfields was all the killer was concerned about. Now I know you say idle gossip won't help but a family like the Radfields must have made plenty of enemies over the years, so who would hate them enough to commit murder just to point the finger?'

Ronnie looked flustered. 'How should I know?'

Fossey rested his arms on top of the gate and looked at the old farmer. 'You've lived your whole life on this farm, according to Jenna's research your family's links go back at least three generations...'

'Four.'

'And you're trying to tell me that there've been no rumours about the Radfield family, no skeletons in the cupboard, no grudges?'

'There are always rumours, lad.'

'Right, so who would bear a grudge?'

‘Bugger me, you don’t get to own half the bloody county by treating folk with respect.’

‘But that's just it, Ronnie, they don’t own half the county do they? You said yourself the family have been selling off huge chunks of land for years.’

‘Aye well...’

‘So, it sounds to me as if maybe the coffers are not as full as they could be.’

‘It’s hard times for everyone.’ Ronnie mumbled.

Fossey sighed.

NEW

Lasser stopped the car and slid down the window, the huge wrought iron gates blocking the drive to Radfield Manor.

'Now then, who have you managed to upset?'

Spenner peered in through the window, when he saw Cathy he frowned.

'DCI Simms asked me to keep an eye on the place, sir,' somehow the young constable made it sound as if he were the only man for the job. 'Just in case the media decide to return,' he explained.

Lasser nodded, keeping his face serious. 'I can't think of anyone more suited for the job, now is his Lordship in?'

Spenner straightened his shoulders, pulled out his notebook and flicked through the pages, Mr Officious. 'He arrived home at nine twenty-seven, sir.'

'Right, could you open the gates we need a word?'

'Oh right.' Spenner looked confused as if he had failed to understand the request.

Lasser drummed his fingers on the steering wheel. 'Is there a problem?'

'Well, sir, I thought WPC Harper was here to replace me?'

'Why have you somewhere you need to be?'

'Er...'

'WPC Harper is here to assist me, now, of course if you foresee a problem with that..?'

Spenner blushed. 'No, sir, no problem.'

'Glad to hear it, now if you don't mind will you please open the sodding gates.'

Spenner strode around the front of the car and swung the gates open, as he drove through Lasser gave a small wave.

'You don't like him much do you?' Cathy asked.

Lasser looked at her in surprise. 'Spenner's OK, he just needs to realise that this job isn't about sliding over the bonnet of your car and chasing the bad guys over the rooftops, it's about standing around for hours on end with your thumb up your arse.'

He pulled up in front of the sprawling house; Ashley Radfield was striding toward them; even from twenty yards away Lasser could see the scowl on his narrow face.

Cathy looked uneasy. 'He doesn't look happy.'

'Fuck him,' Lasser said evenly as he opened the door and climbed out.

'What the hell do you want, Lasser?'

He didn't bother with a reply until his Lordship was standing in front of him. It was obvious that spending twenty-four hours in police custody had been an ordeal for the man. He had dark circles under his eyes and a five o'clock shadow across his chin, even his hair looked in disarray.

'I wonder if I could have a word?'

'Get off my property,' Radfield pointed a quivering finger towards the gate.

'Five minutes of your time, that's all.'

Radfield laughed aloud, a brittle, mocking sound. 'You've got a nerve, you accuse me of murder and then you lock me up for over twenty-four hours and now you have the audacity to turn up here. Yes well, I have nothing to say to you, so you had better make yourself scarce before I contact your superior and put in a formal complaint.'

'You've already tried that, remember?'

'Go. Now.' Ashley headed toward the front door, his feet crunching on the gravel.

Lasser followed. 'Listen, I can understand you feeling miffed but we're trying to catch a multiple murderer, who obviously despises you or your family.'

Ashley stopped and turned. 'And you think I might have an idea who that someone could be?'

'Not necessarily,' he paused, 'but perhaps your father did?'

Radfield narrowed his eyes. 'Just what are you implying, Sergeant?'

Cathy climbed from the car, even in bright sunlight, the house looked drab.

'I'm not implying anything.' Lasser patted his pocket. 'I just can't fathom why you're being so defensive.'

'Considering the night I've had, I cannot fathom how you can be so dense.'

Lasser smiled and shrugged his shoulders. 'Fair enough but I was only doing my job.'

'Look, don't you think that if I had the slightest suspicion about who was responsible for any of this I would tell you?'

'I'm sure you would, that's what makes me wonder about your father.'

'I've already told you about the sort of man he was.'

'But you said yourself that contact between you both was virtually non-existent and it seems obvious to me that whoever did this believes that either you or your father have done something to warrant all this.'

'Well, they're obviously deranged.'

'Tell me, who knew you were coming down here?'

'Excuse me?'

'Did you mention your plans to anyone?'

'Not that I'm aware of.'

'So, your father had no idea you were paying him a visit?'

Radfield smiled, to Lasser he looked like a grinning fox. 'I wanted it to be a surprise.'

'Was there any particular reason for that?'

Radfield looked toward the sky and then checked his watch. 'You had better come in,' he said with a sigh before spinning on his patent leather brogues and for the door. Lasser looked over his shoulder and gave Cathy the thumbs up.

Even if she had a major win on the lottery, Cathy could never live in a place like this, it was dark and gloomy, redolent with age and decay. The room Radfield led them to was huge and full of furniture that belonged to a bygone age. He motioned them to a large Chesterfield before sitting in a chair that resembled a large wooden commode.

'Right, Sergeant, as I said yesterday, I came down from Scotland to discuss business with my father...'

'Just out of curiosity,' Lasser interrupted, 'what business are you actually in?'

Radfield cocked his head to one side and smiled. 'I would imagine you see me as nothing more than some sort of parasite. A privileged life spent shooting grouse and hunting foxes, with no idea how the rest of society lives.'

'I bet you can't tell me how much a pint of milk costs?'

Radfield ignored the question. 'Look around you, you see the large house and the extensive gardens...'

'Yeah, but the grass could do with mowing.'

'Precisely and the windows need replacing and the roof in the north wing leaks. The whole place needs rewiring and the plumbing is antiquated. So, believe me, Sergeant, when I say that paying someone to mow the lawn isn't really at the top of my *'things to do'* list.'

Lasser could see the head of a deer mounted on the wall, cobwebs stretched between the antlers. 'You still haven't said what you do for a living?'

'I'm coming to that. I just wanted you to be aware that I don't live the privileged life that you undoubtedly expected.'

If his Lordship was waiting for him to pull out the violin, then he was in for a long wait. 'Well, if times are rough you can always sell off some land can't you?'

Radfield peered at him coldly. 'There's been far too much of that done already.'

'Do you mind if I smoke?'

Radfield waved a languid hand. 'Go ahead.'

Lasser lit up then offered the pack to Cathy.

'No thanks, sir. If you don't mind me asking, how much land do you actually own?' she asked.

Radfield uncrossed his legs, and leaned forward in the chair. 'Just short of ten thousand acres.'

'Well, it's been a while since I read the Farmers Guardian but it still sounds like a lot to me.' Lasser said.

'Yes, I suppose it does, yet if you go back to nineteen sixty the estate covered over eighty thousand acres.'

Lasser had failed his A level maths but even he could see the point Radfield was making. 'And when did your father inherit the title?'

'I would imagine you could hazard a guess.'

'And how does that make you feel?'

Radfield looked at him in amusement. 'Forgive me but you're beginning to sound like a therapist, rather than a police officer.'

Lasser smiled. 'So, over the years your old man got rid of over seventy thousand acres?'

'Correct.'

Lasser looked closely at Radfield, in a strange kind of way he did feel sorry for the man. However, ultimately, he could always sell up and live the rest of his days in some sort of luxury, no one forced him to stay in this draughty mausoleum. 'Tell me; were you aware of just how much land your father had sold?'

In a darkened corner of the room, a grandfather clock chimed the hour. 'I was aware that land had been sold, of course I was. However, if you're asking to what extent, then the answer would be no.'

'When did you find out?'

Radfield paused before answering. 'The day I arrived I went to see the family solicitor, he informed me of the gravity of the situation.'

'I bet you were upset when you found out what he'd been up to?'

'Not the vernacular I would use but its close enough.'

'And how did your father react when you confronted him with the news?'

Radfield picked up the decanter then topped up his glass before answering. 'He didn't, Sergeant, because when I arrived back from Manchester, he was nowhere to be found, as you are well aware.'

'What about the house in Scotland?'

'What would you like to know?'

'Well, is it as big as this place?' Lasser spread his arms.

'The estate in Perth is worth a considerable sum of money, however…'

'It's up for sale, is that what you're saying?'

For the first time Radfield looked uncomfortable. 'Unfortunately it's unavoidable.'

'It's your intention to sell the house in Scotland and move back down here?'

Radfield sighed, a sound full of regret. 'Yes.'

'So over the years your father sold off vast areas of land and yet at the end of the day he had nothing to show for it?'

'You're very astute.'

Lasser couldn't tell if he was being sarcastic or not. 'I mean, you seem to have spent your life trying to avoid any contact with the man, so it must have been galling to find yourself in a position where you would be living under the same roof again?'

'At the end of the day he was still my father,' it was said without a hint of compassion, no more than a stock reply.

'I can understand that but the chances of your father living a long life were minimal. The autopsy report stated that he was suffering from a heart condition and approaching liver failure due to his consumption of alcohol.'

'What's your point?' Radfield snapped.

'Tell me, does this house actually mean anything to you, I mean, is it a place full of good memories?'

'I fail to see what that has to do with anything, Sergeant.' Radfield was beginning to sound annoyed, it was obvious he didn't like answering questions about his family history.

'What I can't understand is why you don't sell this place and live in Scotland?'

Radfield shrugged. 'You're quite right, in an ideal world I would sell this place and what little land remains and live in Perth. Unfortunately, any revenue raised from the sale would be swallowed up by the house in Scotland and I would soon find myself in a similar position to the one I'm in now.'

'So, this is the lesser of two evils.'

'Yes,' Radfield paused, 'I was left with no alternative.'

'In your opinion would any of this have led to your father contemplating ending his life?'

Radfield smiled. 'Although, I avoided contact with the man, Sergeant, I can safely say that he was not the type to concern himself with the realities of any given situation.'

'So, you're saying basically he didn't give a toss about the dwindling pot?'

'Once again, your use of language is somewhat basic, though you're right, my father was the kind of man who lived for today and bugger the consequences.'

'It almost sounds as if you hated him?'

Radfield looked at him over the top of his glass. 'I despised him for more reasons than I intend to discuss with you.'

Lasser nodded. 'I can appreciate your position, nobody likes to have their secrets dragged kicking and screaming into the light but nonetheless we can't lose sight of the fact that someone tried to frame either you or your father for the murder of William Jones.'

Radfield blinked twice and then placed the glass onto the table. Lasser continued. 'Whoever did this was obviously aware that you would be down here, which leads me to believe that it was you he wanted to pin the blame on rather than your old man. Now I ask you again, have you any idea who would want to go to such extreme lengths?'

'How many times do I have to say it, Sergeant?'

Lasser sighed. 'Fair enough, I'm going to need access to all business transactions conducted by either yourself or your father over the last...'

'I hardly see the relevance...'

'Maybe not but if you're unable to assist us then we need to look in more detail at your business dealings.'

Radfield looked annoyed. 'I can assure you the books will make for very boring reading.'

'And why would that be?'

'I've already stated that my father was only interested in spending money, now I came down here to put a stop to all that, because for the past thirty years this family has had no income. Do you understand that, Sergeant, I have spent the last five years in Scotland, trying to persuade people to spend their holidays in a stately home that is crumbling to the ground. So, it will come as no surprise when I tell you that as a business venture it is no longer viable. Having to contemplate moving back down here has been a nightmare for me and then I discover that my bastard father has virtually wasted what little money is left.'

Lasser watched as his Lordship's anger bloomed into outright hatred for the position his father had left him in.

'So, why not sell both houses, I mean, you'd have money in the bank and you could forget all this.'

'Because, unlike my father, I care about what happens to the family name, I take my responsibilities seriously.'

'So, how do you intend doing that? I mean, forgive me for saying this but I can't see the public wanting to pay good money to look around this house.'

'I'm under no illusions, Sergeant, but I have certain business opportunities that I intend to pursue.'

'Such as?'

'That's *my* business,' his face became impassive, his eyes guarded.

'Look, I don't really care what you have to do to get a new roof on this place, as long as it's not illegal.' Lasser let the sentence hang in the air. 'But I do want to catch the killer before he decides to come after you.'

It was almost comical to see Radfield's face, first he frowned, and then his features slid into a weird amalgamation of disbelief and scorn, eventually settling on undiluted fear. Though to give the man credit it didn't last for long, he sat up ramrod straight, squaring his shoulders.

'Look, Sergeant, I have no idea who this lunatic is and why he would want to try and include me in his twisted plans. But rest assured I am more that capable of taking care of myself...'

'You wouldn't be saying that if you'd seen what this killer is capable of and I would suggest that until we catch this guy it might be a good idea to make use of the house up north.'

Radfield snapped his head from side to side. 'Out of the question, I have things to take care of here, my father's funeral for one. Then of course I have to try and sort out the mess he left behind.'

Cathy leaned forward. 'He didn't owe money to anyone, did he?'

Lasser gave a flicker of a smile.

'Not that I'm aware of.'

'But you can't be sure?'

'Look, I have always known that my father was a wastrel, though I will admit the scale of his deceit has been a surprise even to me. Now, at the moment I can't gain access to his personal papers...'

'No, but we can.' Lasser said.

Radfield looked at them both, his eyes sliding from one to the other. 'Go ahead, if you think it might help catch this man.'

It was strange how cooperative he had become since discovering his own life might be in danger, there was nothing like the fear of violent death to focus the mind.

Lasser fiddled with the lighter in his pocket but resisted the urge to pull out the pack of cigarettes. 'Can you give us some idea how your family made their money in the first place?'

'You want a history lesson, is that it?'

'The unabridged version if you don't mind.'

Ashley Radfield pointed to a portrait hanging on the wall. 'William Radfield made the family fortune. You'll probably think I sound like a pompous fool but he was a great man, a visionary, who...'

Lasser held up a hand. 'Like I said the unabridged version, if that's OK?'

Radfield glared and then shrugged. 'He made the family fortune through the quarrying of local stone, the reservoirs were being built and he provided all the aggregate. Then of course there was the dry stone walling and the roads and the building projects, it was a time of great expansion.'

'He made a killing?'

Radfield spoke as if he was addressing an idiot. 'He built an empire, Sergeant, and his philanthropic endeavours are well documented.'

'Very commendable,' Lasser paused, 'so where did it all go wrong?'

'It's not a new story, when William died he had two sons, each had their own ideas about how best to take the company forward. Unfortunately, rather like my own father they were both idiots. They spent their time trying to gain full control and while they were fighting, the business suffered.'

'So, you're saying that things have been on the skids for how long exactly?'

'Over eighty years.'

Lasser didn't know if Radfield was taking the piss or not but the idea that a family could have been losing money for that length of time seemed ridiculous. 'Of course, there have been certain members of the family who managed to stop the rot for a short time, though unfortunately there have been an equal number like my own father who have been remiss in their duties.'

'And you intend trying to turn things around?'

'I shall do my best.'

Lasser stood up. 'Right well, just to be on the safe side I'll make sure you have a man on the gates until all this is sorted out.'

Radfield tilted his head. 'Thank you, Sergeant, and I shall contact my solicitor to make sure you have full access to the family papers.'

'No problem and if you do think of anything that might be of help then don't forget to get in touch.'

Cathy stood and followed Lasser toward the door.

'The policeman who died, was he a friend of yours?' Radfield asked.

Lasser turned. 'I'm afraid I'm a bit like you, Mr Radfield, I don't have many friends.'

Radfield raised his glass, a thin smile on his lips.

WORRIED

'Well at least nineteen, probably more over the years, it were a tough life back then.' Ronnie chewed on a stalk of grass. They had wandered through the gate and into the field. Fossey could see the woods in the distance, a dark green mass on the steep hillside, giving way to endless miles of open moorland. 'I know for a fact that eight died in a week when they were building the top reservoir.'

'How did it happen?' Fossey asked.

'They finished building it in eighteen ninety-five. Radfield made a fortune from the sale of the land and then he supplied all the stone that lined the basin, a canny man, William. Any road it took three weeks to fill it, apparently it's always a risky time, a gang of navvies were working at the bottom of the embankment, I know shoring it up, when the pressure of the water blew a hole in the side.'

'Drowned?'

'Aye, I suppose so. I mean, can you imagine being stood in front of the bloody thing when it went, the force of the water would have taken your head off.'

'I don't suppose Health and Safety was as strict as it is now.' Fossey said with a hint of irony.

Ronnie raised a wiry eyebrow. 'No such thing back then.'

'So, did these men work directly for the Radfield family?'

'Not a clue, I mean, the reservoirs are built on land that they used to own but they could have been working for some other bugger, you know just contracted out type of thing.'

'What about the others?'

'Aye well, they were quarry workers, so they did work for his lordship.'

'Local men?' Fossey glanced sideways, Ronnie spat out the grass and reached for his cigarette tin.

'Some of them were.'
'When was this exactly?'
Ronnie pulled his cap back down, shielding his pale blue eyes. 'Nineteen twenty-six, eleven killed.'
'Do you know what happened?'
Ronnie shrugged. 'Just rumours really. I mean, back then these things happened but when your employer is a titled gent...'
'You're saying things were covered up?'
'Nowt new about that, lad, if you're a big knob folks turn a blind eye, always have, always will.'
'So, how did the men die?'
'Some sort of explosion, according to rumours they only found three of the bodies.'
'And what about since then, have there been any more accidents?'
Ronnie shook his head. 'Not at the quarry, in fact after the men were killed the quarries were closed down.'
'Because of what happened?'
'Nah lad, if there was still money to be made they would have carried on as if nowt had happened. Truth is people stopped using as much sandstone, after all it don't wear well.
'What about elsewhere?'
Ronnie peered at him, a frown on his crinkly face. 'You're a persistent bugger, aren't you?'
'Come on, Ronnie, I know Jenna's provided me with background information but you know as well as I do, it's the rumours that tell the whole story about a family.'
T reappeared from the tall grass, his tongue lolling grass seeds trapped in his fur.
'Two died in the early sixties, they were working up on Winter Hill in one of the old tin mines.'
Fossey remembered reading a brief section on Jenna's disk about the mines, though he hadn't realised that they had still been working them into the sixties.
'So, they owned mines as well as the quarries?'

'Aye, but the mines never made any money; it was only ever small scale.'

'For local use?' Fossey asked.

'Mainly, of course the family were hoping to find a decent seam but there have been mines on the moors for hundreds of years and it's never been more than a cottage industry.'

'What happened exactly?'

'Well, unlike the others this one was well documented; they got caught underground in a heavy downpour and drowned.'

Fossey looked up at the moors, the whole area acted as a huge sponge absorbing the rain and feeding it into the reservoirs.

'I tell you, if it pisses it down for ten minutes and you're underground then you've had it.' Ronnie said with a sniff.

'Anything stick to the family?'

'Not so you'd notice. I mean, it were nearly seventy years since the disaster at the quarry. That's the problem, a family like the Radfields have been around for so long that memories fade between disasters, if that makes sense?'

It made perfect sense, the passage of time changed people's perspectives, facts became myths.

'To tell you the truth the Radfields have been struggling for years. I mean, have you ever been up to the house?'

Fossey shook his head. 'No.'

'Well, the state of the place tells you all you need to know.'

'So what do the locals think of the family now?'

Ronnie pulled a match from his pocket and began to chew the end. 'Folk around here don't really bother with the Radfields anymore.'

'Come off it, Ronnie, I know how these things work. You have a pub in the village named after them and I dare say they had a hand in keeping the church and school open?'

'It's different now, when I were younger you would see Malcolm now and again, half the village worked up at the manor, either in the gardens or in the house. I spent a few years as a beater, when he had his mates up for the grouse shooting but them day are long gone now.'

Fossey pulled out his mints, flicked one to the dog before popping one into his mouth, chewing while he thought about what Ronnie had said.

'The men who died in the mine?'

'What about 'em?'

'Did you know them?'

Ronnie sighed and looked up at the sky, his Adam's apple bobbed up and down as he swallowed. 'Aye, lad, I did.'

'Grandad!'

As Ronnie turned away, Fossey saw the relief plastered on the old man's face.

'Coming, love!' he shouted and then began to hurry toward his granddaughter, his wellies swishing in the tall grass.

Saved by the bell.

DID YOU BELIEVE HIM?

Lasser stuffed a handful of fries into his mouth, his stomach rumbling, crumbs dropping into his lap.

Cathy nibbled on a chicken nugget. 'Do you think he was telling the truth?'

'I don't think he has a clue about any of this, though that doesn't mean he hasn't rubbed some nutter up the wrong way.'

Cathy dipped the remainder of her nugget into the little pot of barbeque sauce. 'Maybe when we get hold of the family records it might throw up some clues.'

'Well, if he is telling the truth about the lack of money, then it seems unlikely this has anything to do with dodgy business dealings.'

'But what about all the cash from the land his father sold, I mean, it's obvious he wasn't spending any on the house?'

'According to Molder the old man liked his whisky but I can't see him spending the proceeds from the sale of a seventy thousand acres of land on booze alone, though it'll be interesting to see who he actually sold the land to.'

He glanced out of the side window, a bus rumbled to a halt on the High Street, it took him a couple of seconds to recognise the kid running along the pavement, a rucksack on his shoulders, dodging in and out of the road to avoid colliding with other passers-by.

'Now, why is Michael Jones in such a hurry?'

Cathy raised her head; a nugget halfway to her mouth. As the bus began to pull away Michael caught up and began to hammer on the door, the driver stopped and the doors hissed open.

Lasser frowned as the boy disappeared inside, a moment later it joined the steady stream of afternoon traffic.

'Now that's something I don't like.'

'It's not a crime to catch a bus.'

'Did you notice the destination?'

'Sorry, I was feeding my face.'

'Horwich, now why would Michael be heading out that way?'

Cathy swivelled in her seat. 'Maybe he's not going all the way, I mean, that bus goes all around the estates before it heads out of town.'

'Right, let's see shall we?' he clamped the burger between his teeth and started the car.

A few seconds later, he pulled into the traffic; the bus was a hundred yards ahead pulling up at another stop.

A blob of mayonnaise dropped from the burger and plopped into his lap.

'For fucks sake!' he tossed the remains of the Big Mac back into the box and grabbed a napkin from the dashboard before mopping up, while trying to keep his eyes on the road. When he glanced at Cathy, she had a hand to her mouth, a second later she burst into laughter.

'Something funny, WPC Harper?' he asked with mock severity.

He scanned the pavement, not that he expected to see Michael, after all, you didn't run for a bus just to get off at the next stop.

Cathy dabbed at her eyes with the napkin before gathering up the rubbish and dropping it into the brown paper bag at her feet. Outside, she could see the buildings slipping by, many of the shops were boarded up.

'Do you like working around here?' she asked.

'Is that a trick question?'

She smiled. 'No, I'm serious. I mean, some coppers prefer working in the city, others...'

'I don't think geography comes into it, you either love the job, or you don't. I happen to fall into the category that doesn't.'

Cathy looked at him in surprise. 'Oh come on, you wouldn't do the job if you didn't enjoy it.'

He eased off the accelerator, letting a car out from a side street. 'Ten years ago I was probably as keen as Spenner, but not anymore.'

'What happened to change your mind?'

'Let's just say they lied to me in the job description.'

She took a sip from the carton of Cola. 'So, why not do something else?'

Lasser watched as the bus took a right turn at the traffic lights, by the time he reached them they had flicked to red. 'Believe me I've thought about it often enough but the truth is I haven't a clue what I would do. I mean, I can't see myself getting any further up the ladder....'

'You don't really strike me as the type who would be happy sitting behind a desk.'

'You're probably right, not that I'll ever get the opportunity to try it out.'

As soon as the lights changed, he turned right; there was no sign of the bus.

'Bloody great.'

'Don't worry; take a left at the island that bus goes around the Lancaster Road estate.'

'Takes in all the local beauty spots, does it?' he asked, his voice heavy with sarcasm.

REVELATIONS

Ronnie remembered a time when making a noise in a library was like farting in church, it was frowned upon. However, the library in Horwich was buzzing with sound. He couldn't remember the last time he'd been in the building but it had to be at least thirty years ago and he hardly recognised the place. Two walls were lined with computers, every chair had someone sitting in it, either surfing the net or playing on some game. At the far side of the room, a group of small children were sitting on the floor in a semicircle while a young woman read them a story, every few seconds they would laugh with delight.

'Are you OK, Grandad?'

Ronnie looked up at her and gave her a half smile. 'I was just thinking how much this place has changed.'

'It's just that you seemed quiet on the way here, I mean, you hardly said a word in the car.'

'Where's Fossey?

'He's in the reference section.'

'Right well, I'm going outside for a fag.'

She watched him walk toward the door and decided to follow, something wasn't right here. Ever since they'd climbed into the car, her grandad had looked on edge. On route to the library he'd smoked two full cigarettes, one after the other, something she had never seen him do before.

She found him sitting on a bench under the shade of a large hanging basket, the colourful blooms spilled over the sides. He had yet another cigarette clasped between his lips, elbows on knees, his eyes fixed firmly on his old work boots.

She slid in beside him. 'Grandad, what's the matter?'

He glanced at her then looked back at the ground. 'Oh, it's nowt, love.'

'Come on, who are you kidding, you look like you're waiting for something bad to happen.'

He dropped the cigarette onto the floor and ground it under his heel. 'Just leave it, Jenna.'

'So there is something?'

'How long's he going to be in there?'

'Has Patrick said something to upset you?'

'Not yet.'

She frowned. 'What sort of answer is that?'

He slid the cap from his head and began to ring it between his hands. 'Look, love, when he turned up I thought he'd just be here for a few hours and if you were lucky he might put a page or two in his next book about the gardens or maybe the needle house.'

'Well yeah, that's what I thought as well.'

'But it's not working out like that is it?'

'You make it sound like he's been here for months.'

'Bloody feels like it.'

She frowned and then reminded herself to act like an adult; shouting and bawling would get her nowhere. 'It's only been a week.'

'So what's he doing in there?' he hooked a thumb over his shoulder, 'Raking up old bloody gossip and sticking his nose into other people's business!'

'What are you talking about?'

When he turned to her, she thought for one horrifying second he was going to cry, she placed her hand on the top of his. 'Look, just tell me what this is all about, I mean, what does it matter if he's trying to find stuff about the Radfields, most of it will be on the disk that I gave him anyway.'

'Aye, but not all of it.'

She shrugged her narrow shoulders. 'He might find something new, but I doubt it. I mean, I've been through all the old papers, you know I have.'

'I know, love, but I've got a feeling he's looking for summat specific.'

'Such as?'

For a moment, she didn't think he was going to bother with a reply, then he sighed. 'The farm.'

'What, our farm?'
'Aye.'
'But why would Patrick be interested in where we live?'
'It's probably because we got it on the cheap.'
'Hang on, Grandad, the Radfields were selling off loads of land back then.'
Ronnie nodded. 'I know that, love,' he paused, 'but you see we paid a lot less than most.'
Jenna felt she should be able to work out what he was hinting at but this past week had left her feeling numb, her brain disengaged. 'I'm not following you?'
When he looked up, Fossey was standing a few feet away, a thin blue file clasped in his right hand. 'Why don't you ask him, from the look on his face I think he would be able to tell you better than I could.'
Jenna looked at Fossey. 'Have you got any idea what he's talking about?'
'I think I might but let's go to my place, we've still got apples to pick and it's quieter there.'
Ronnie rose to his feet. 'Aye, lad, apples never fall far from the tree, do they?'
Jenna looked from one to the other, completely baffled.
'Bad ones don't, Ronnie.' Fossey replied

DISAPPEARING ACT

'There he is,' she pointed through the side window of the car. Lasser caught sight of a rucksack disappearing into the busy crowd of afternoon shoppers.

The traffic on the High Street began to move forward again, he swung the car down a narrow side street and parked up on double yellow lines.

'Do you want me to try and find him?'

'Don't bother, Cathy; we know where he's heading.'

'So, what do you want to do?'

'I'll get in touch with Simms; put the ball in his court for a change.'

'You don't think he'll go up to the tower?'

'No way, he knows we had Radfield in for questioning, so why would he waste time going to the woods. Besides chasing Michael Jones gets us nowhere nearer to catching the bad guy does it?' he paused for a moment. 'I suppose we could chase up Radfield's solicitor, get our hands on the paperwork and see if that leads us anywhere.'

Cathy checked her watch. 'It's half three now.'

'Right, we can sort that out first thing in the morning,' he pulled out his mobile. 'I'll ring Simms tell him what's going on.'

'We passed a coffee shop on the High Street, do you want one?'

'Yeah please, white, three sugars.'

'Three!'

'So, I've got a sweet tooth.'

She shook her head and pulled on the door handle.

'Hello, sir, it's Lasser...'

Closing the car door quietly she headed around the corner, it was surprising, Horwich was only twenty minutes away from Hindley but the shops were all open and busy. People were milling about in the afternoon sunshine, carrying shopping bags with the stores names stencilled onto the side, H and M, Monsoon, River

Island, it made a change from Bargain Booze and Cash Converters.

She entered the coffee shop and joined the queue, unlike Hindley nobody glared at her uniform, in fact, one or two people even smiled at her. What a difference a few miles could make. Five minutes later she headed back to the car armed with two coffees and a pack of chocolate biscuits. When she rounded the corner, she could see Lasser talking to a traffic warden.

'Look, pal, this is police business.'

The warden looked at Cathy as she approached the car and raised an eyebrow. 'Yes it looks like it.'

'And here's my colleague with the evidence.'

The man adjusted his cap and walked away with a sour frown on his face.

A moment later, Lasser was ripping open the biscuits. 'Simms said he would put a couple more men up at the Manor House, just to be on the safe side.'

'What did he say about Michael Jones?'

'Not much, I mean, the lad's done nothing wrong but I told him it wouldn't surprise me if he turns up to have a quiet word with his Lordship.'

'So what's next?'

'He didn't say and I didn't ask.'

'Did he mention how the search was going?'

'Not good, they think they might have a partial shoe print from the edge of the reservoir but of course it could belong to anyone and the dogs haven't picked up anything else. But he did say they're going to carry on as long as daylight lasts.'

'So what do you want to do?'

'I fancy having another word with Fossey.'

'The guy who found the body?' she looked surprised.

He spent the next five minutes telling her about his meetings with Fossey, ending with his confrontation with Michael at the writer's house.

'You know, maybe we should look more closely at this guy?'

'Forget it, he's clean.'

'So why do you want to see him?'

'Because the alternative is going to the woods and I don't fancy another soaking.'

He started the car, placed his cup in the plastic holder, and then clicked the seatbelt into place.

'Can I ask you something?' she asked.

'Sure.'

'Why are you doing this?'

He slipped the car into gear. 'Doing what?'

She looked out of the window, suddenly unsure of how to continue. 'Well, I mean, you don't have to keep dragging me around with you.'

'Dragging you around?'

'I'm sorry, that came out wrong, what I meant to say is that I don't want you to think that because of what happened I can't do my job.'

Lasser pulled away from the curb. 'I'm not following you, if you're saying you'd sooner be up at the woods then I can drop you there, it's not a problem'

'No, it's not that...'

'So, what is it?'

'Oh come on, you know what this jobs like. Before you know it people will start to question why you're singling me out for favouritism.'

'You mean, they'll say we're shagging one another?'

She felt the heat in her face go up a couple of notches. 'Jesus, can't you be more subtle?'

Lasser shrugged. 'And that bothers you does it?'

'Of course it bothers me, I want to get 'on' in this job on merit not because people think I sleep with my superior officer!'

She was right of course, coppers were like everyone else, susceptible to petty jealousy and rumour and once you were labelled it never went away.

'Listen, if you feel in any way compromised by assisting me with this inquiry then I suggest you start looking for another job.'

'Another job!' her embarrassment was rapidly turning to anger, was he threatening her in some way.

'Listen, it's admirable that you want to build a career but in order to do that you'll have to get used to working with all sorts of people.'

'I get along with people just fine, thank you.'

'And if you concern yourself with what other colleagues think then you can forget about climbing the greasy pole. Now have I given you any cause to think that our relationship is anything other than totally professional?'

'No of course not.'

At the junction, he paused to get his bearings before turning right. 'If I make you feel uncomfortable then I'll take you up to Radfield's place and you can take over from 'James Bond' on gate duty.'

Cathy squirmed in her seat. 'I'm sorry, OK.'

'I don't want your apologies, I asked for you because I think you can do the job, you keep your eyes and ears open and your mouth shut. If I wanted someone who'd spend their time kissing my arse then I'd have brought Spenner.'

She suddenly felt ridiculous, he was right; she needed to grow a thicker skin.

'I'm being stupid, aren't I?'

'Forget it; if I thought for one minute that you were going to be a hindrance then I wouldn't even entertain you.'

'Thanks very much,' she paused, 'I suppose because of the way I acted in the woods, I thought perhaps you were feeling sorry for me.'

'Something you should know about me, Cathy. I very rarely feel sorry for anyone.'

She looked at him, unsure if he was joking but his face was stern, his eyes serious.

'You're kidding, right?'

He turned and smiled, the corner of his lips curled but the humour didn't reach his eyes.

THE DEVILS FRUIT.

Ronnie dropped his cap onto the table and took a long gulp from the cold can that Fossey had provided. The bench was tucked away in a corner of the garden, shaded by a bank of tall conifers.

Jenna was sitting on the short grass, chewing vigorously on a fingernail. 'So, we got the farm because my great-grandfather was blackmailing the Radfield family?'

'Hang on, love, I never actually said that.'

She shook her head in disbelief; it was as if they had slipped into some parallel universe. 'I don't understand any of this.'

Ronnie lowered his head and flicked the cigarette ash onto the grass, he could hear the anguish in her voice and it made him heart sore 'Believe me, Jenna, I didn't have a clue about any of it. I only found out after my old man had been dead about five years.'

Fossey took a sip of his drink; the small dog lay in his lap fast asleep. 'How did you find out?'

Ronnie sighed, he couldn't look at Jenna he felt like some sort of low-life criminal as if knowing about something meant guilt by association. Maybe he did bear some of the responsibility, after all he'd known about it for over forty years and said nowt. 'My old man left a kind of diary, I found it when I was clearing out his stuff.'

Jenna felt like a fool, she was supposedly an expert on the family history and here she was suddenly finding that she knew sod all.

'How come I've never seen this diary?' she asked.

'I don't know, Jenna, I...'

'You mean you've kept it hidden.'

'Oh come on, I didn't know if it was all bollocks, I mean, my old man was always keen on keeping everything in order, he had receipts for bloody everything going back donkey's years. They were all kept in this old binder, bills paid, cheques he'd written to buy animal feed, he even kept the receipt for my mother's wedding ring, absolutely everything, except what he'd paid for the farm. That's why I went to see owd Malcolm, I mean, I looked everywhere but I couldn't find any legal papers about what we paid for the place.'

Jenna knew this to be the truth, she'd spent enough time rummaging through the old family papers, so why had it never occurred to her that something like that was missing, her research had been laughable.

'What did he say when you asked him?' Fossey queried.

'He wouldn't say owt at first but I stuck at him, it was kind of eating away at me. In the end he said the farm had been gifted to my father, though that's all the old sod would admit to.'

Jenna frowned. *'Gifted?'*

'Aye, love, my old man paid bugger all for the place.'

'But why would Radfield do something like that?'

Ronnie looked at her but he couldn't hold her gaze. 'I honestly don't know, I mean, I never thought there would have been owt shady going on...'

'But what did he know about the Radfields that would make them hand over *five hundred acres of land and a house!'* Jenna snapped.

'Did it have anything to do with the men who died in the mine?' Fossey asked.

Jenna looked back and forth between the two men, confused.

Ronnie cleared his throat, his eyes suddenly guarded. 'What makes you think that?'

'It's just that when we were talking earlier, you couldn't get away fast enough when I asked you if you knew the men who died.'

'You mean the mine that flooded?' Jenna asked.

Ronnie suddenly felt as if the conifers were closing in on all sides, the air felt rarefied his head weighed heavy on his shoulders. 'You know about that, do you?'

'Of course I know, Grandad, but what has it got to do with us?'

The silence seemed to stretch out, the sun blasting down on Ronnie's head like an accusation.

Fossey leaned forward, the dog jumped down and went to Jenna. 'Listen, Ronnie, whatever happened was not of your doing, you already said that you only found out after your father died.'

'I know, lad, I just wish I'd never been up to see Radfield. I should have just forgotten about the whole thing, kept my bloody big nose out and got on with life.'

Jenna hugged the small dog to her chest. 'Come on, just tell us, like Patrick said it can't be anything you've done.'

Ronnie sat up and squared his shoulders. 'I said I knew the men who drowned, one of them was George Woodman...'

'Jim Woodman's dad?' she asked.

'No, love, it was Jim's grandad.'

'I never knew that.'

'The other bloke was Brian Denney, he used to work for the Radfields as a stable hand.' Ronnie swallowed before wiping a shaking hand across his forehead. 'The trouble is, according to the diary there were three men died in the mine, not two.'

Fossey took a sip from the can. 'Do you have any idea about the third man?'

'He was a traveller.'

Jenna twisted her legs and sat up on her knees. 'You mean a gypsy?'

'Not as such, he lived on a narrow boat, back then it were a kind of annual thing, when it was time for gathering the crops you'd get em turning up. They'd moor themselves up at the top lock and come down looking for work; of course a fair few worked for the Radfields.'

'You mean they'd exploit them?' Jenna said, imagining countless unfortunates, bent double as they toiled away for next to no pay, while the Radfields played cricket and sipped champagne.

'Boat folk always lived cheap, love, I can remember times when the canal banks were lined with barges for at least half a mile,' he paused, 'in fact we used to have a few families who would work on the farm, all through July and August...'

'I never knew that,' she couldn't believe this hidden history that she knew nothing about.

'Aye, they'd work during the day and then head off back to the barge at night. It was a good setup and they worked bloody hard too.'

Fossey watched Jenna's face closely, he saw the frown form, the realisation that maybe her family had exploited the barge people in the same way the Radfields had. She glanced at him and then quickly looked away.

'So what happened?' Fossey asked.

For a few seconds he looked confused. 'Oh aye, sorry I was getting carried away.'

'His name, Grandad, what was his name?'

'Sam Wickham.'

Jenna looked disappointed, she felt like the name should have meant something to her, like some great mystery would have been revealed.

'How come he was working on the moors, I mean, did he have any knowledge of working the mines?' Fossey asked.

Ronnie snatched his cap from the table. 'How the hell should I know, it was the Radfields he worked for not us,' his grizzled face was suddenly florid with anger. 'Besides I don't know why I'm even telling you this, I mean, this is just some bloody gossip you can stick in your next book ain't it.'

'Grandad, for God's sake, calm down!'

When Ronnie opened his mouth it was with the intention of apologising, it was as much a surprise to him when he began to rant. 'No, Jenna, it's alright for him, writing his bloody daft books, not giving a toss about what he says. But it affects us, I mean, you'll just move on to your next victim, with a clear conscience, won't you?'

Jenna felt mortified. 'Grandad, he's only trying to help.'

'Oh aye and how's he doing that?'

Fossey sat back in the chair and crossed his legs. 'Look, I'm sorry if I've offended you in some way.'

'You don't have to apologise, Patrick,' she spun around in anger. 'Grandad, you're being ridiculous....'

'Well, let's see if you feel the same way when he's writing about us, telling the world and his wife about how we only got the farm because we had some dirt on the Radfields.'

For the first time Jenna looked unsure, she glanced at Fossey, a hint of caution in her eyes.

'Look, if you'd sooner forget the whole thing, then I understand completely.'

'Aye well, maybe we do.' Ronnie snarled.

Jenna rubbed the palms of her hands down the front of her jeans; it was something she would do as a child, when she felt agitated. 'Hang on, this is stupid...'

He stabbed a finger at Fossey. 'Nay, lass, I know what these buggers are like.'

'Look, maybe it would be best if I ran you both home?'

'What!'

'Listen, Jenna, I'm not interested in how your family came to own the farm, it has nothing to do with me.'

Ronnie stood up and slapped the cap onto his head. 'Come on, Jenna, I'll give your mother a ring, she can pick us up.'

Her head was in turmoil, she could feel another crack open up in the foundations of her life. 'No way, I'm going nowhere, Grandad, not until you start making sense!'

When he grabbed her arm, she nearly cried out in shock, his fingers digging deep. 'Never mind *"no way"* you heard what he said....'

She snatched her arm free. 'You're right, I did and he said he wasn't interested in the farm.'

'If that's true, then why is he asking all these bloody questions, eh, you answer me that?'

Fossey hadn't moved from the bench, now he stood up and looked at the old man, white spittle had formed in the corner of Ronnie's mouth, sweat coated his forehead. 'It might be best if you explain things to us, Ronnie.'

'Oh aye and why would that be?'

'Because the police will be looking into the Radfield's background and they might not be as sympathetic.'

Ronnie swallowed, a dry click in his throat. 'You're bloody lying, why would they be interested in summat that happened over forty year ago?'

'Because, while you're concerned with skeletons in the cupboard, they're more interested in finding a multiple killer. Now, one of the first places they'll look is into the family's business dealings.'

Jenna could see the colour draining from her grandad's face. *'But they can't...'*

She took hold of his sleeve, giving it a slight tug. 'Come on, Grandad, sooner or later they'll come knocking on our door wanting to know why Radfield handed over the farm for free. You won't be able to tell them to *'bugger off'* will you?'

He licked his lips, this whole thing was turning into his worst nightmare. He could envision people in the village talking about his family behind their lace curtains. An image flitted through his mind, walking into the Radfield Arms and seeing the faces he knew so well all regarding him with contempt. Christ alone knew, over the years he had done more than his fair share of slagging off the Radfield family, it was all part of village life and now everyone would know that he was a bloody liar and a fraud, taking his fifty pieces of silver, like some kind of Judas.

'Listen, Ronnie, why don't we go inside and you can tell us what this is all about, then if we think the police need to know anything I'll give Lasser a ring and take it from there.'

Jenna nodded. 'It sounds fair, Grandad.'

He looked from one to the other and then he squared his shoulders, a sudden look of determination in his eyes. 'Alright then have it your way but don't say I didn't warn you.'

He stormed toward the house.

Jenna looked bemused.

'Come on, Jenna, before he has a change of heart.'

'You wouldn't say anything bad about us would you, Patrick?'

He stopped and turned, she looked suddenly younger than her years. 'I promise, I won't write anything until you've given it the go ahead.'

She smiled, though the shock was still evident in her eyes. 'It'll probably turn out to be nothing; I mean, my grandad's prone to exaggeration.' Despite her best efforts, her voice was shaking.

Fossey nodded; as they walked to the house she found her legs felt heavy, like a condemned soul walking to the electric chair.

Sitting on the huge sofa, Ronnie looked somehow diminished, as if talking about what had happened was drawing the life from him.

It was cool in the lounge but he looked sickly, his forehead beaded with sweat, the huge picture window awash with late afternoon sunlight.

'According to the diary, it was my old man who found the men,' he ran a hand across his bald head. 'Back in the early sixties we used to keep sheep up on the moors, it was lambing time and you know how busy we get, Jenna. You're out all hours trying to make sure the ewes are OK,' he looked at her, his eyes pleading.

'I know, Grandad,' she smiled, encouraging him to go on.

'Well, apparently my father was out doing the rounds, checking if any lambs had got caught in the downpour, I mean, sheep will give birth in small gullies to get out of the wind and if they flood, then...' his voice trailed off.

'How did your father find the men, if they were underground?' Fossey asked.

Ronnie sighed and slapped his big hands onto his knees. 'My father went to Radfield, to see if there had been anyone working down the mine that day. I mean, some days depending on the weather they would work on top, you know checking the machinery, doing odd jobs.'

'So, what happened?' Jenna asked.

'Well, Radfield and my old man must have gone to have a look, because when they arrived they found the two bodies floating at the mine entrance.

'Woodman and Denney?' Fossey asked.

'Aye.'

Jenna looked confused. 'So, what's the problem, it's terrible what happened but if your father raised the alarm then surely he did the right thing?'

'Oh, he raised the alarm alright, of course it took a good couple of hours to get the police up there, in fact it was my father who ran down to the village to get them. He says that when they eventually made it back, Radfield had somehow managed to drag the men free.'

'So, it was an accident?' Fossey asked, keeping his voice neutral.

'No doubt about it, of course nowadays it would never happen but back then you could work on your own if you wanted to, so two men working down a mine was seen as more than adequate.'

'Look, Grandad, I might be missing the point here but you haven't said anything that would lead to blackmail.'

'I know that, love,' he paused, 'as far as I can gather, that came later.'

'But...'

'Just carry on, Ronnie, in your own time.'

Jenna blushed. 'Sorry.'

'Look, I know you think I have all the answers but the truth is I don't, a lot of this is just guesswork on my part.'

'So, what else does it say in the diary?' she asked.

Ronnie looked toward the window; the bright light was beginning to subside, the sky splashed with crimson. 'He wrote summat about a woman turning up at the farm.'

'She was looking for Sam Wickham?' Fossey asked.

Ronnie looked shocked. 'Aye, apparently it was his wife, she'd read in the paper that it was my old man who'd found the bodies.'

'But why would she think your father knew anything about her husband?' Jenna asked.

Ronnie shrugged. 'It doesn't say, it just mentions he'd been missing for three weeks and she was trying to find him. Then it all turns a bit bloody strange, my old man offered to take her up to see Radfield but according to the diary she went berserk when he suggested it.'

'Does it mention if Wickham had worked for the Radfields in the past?'

'Not that I can remember but it wouldn't have been a surprise if he had, like I said they used plenty of casual labour back then.'

'Why, does it matter?' Jenna asked.

'Well, if what your great-grandfather wrote is true, then it seems an overreaction, I mean, going *'berserk'* suggests that she'd dealings with Radfield in the past and didn't want a repeat. Are you sure he didn't mention why she was so reluctant?'

'Positive.'

Fossey sunk back into the sofa and waited for Ronnie to continue.

'So, did she ever find out what happened to her husband?' Jenna asked.

Ronnie's face went blank, Fossey resisted the urge to lean forward in his chair, it was a tortuous process, though it felt as if they were reaching the point that Ronnie found difficult to talk about.

'No, love, the authorities never found him.'

'But your father did?' Fossey said.

The old farmer looked away, Jenna felt something slip in her mind, a terror of the unknown being made real. 'Is it true, did he find out what had happened to Sam Wickham?'

When he looked at her, she was horrified to see the tears sliding down his cheeks. 'It says he found Wickham at the mine...'

'But you said...'

'I don't know how he knew, Jenna, I swear on my bloody life. He just talks about returning to the mine a week later and finding a body, he says he'd been shot in the head and the body had been pushed back into the mine as far as it would go.'

'I can't believe what I'm hearing.'

'What did Radfield actually say when you went to see him?' Fossey enquired.

Ronnie's smile was full of heartache and irony. 'Oh, he wasn't shocked, it was almost as if he had been expecting me to call.'

'When was this?'

'My old man died in sixty-five, so it must have been nineteen seventy.'

'And what did he say about the body?'

'Nothing.'

Jenna's head snapped up. 'He must have said something. I mean, you turn up and accuse him of God knows what and he says nothing!' her voice dripped contempt, her eyes were lit with a slow burning anger.

Ronnie climbed unsteadily to his feet. 'I'm telling you what happened, now if you think I'm talking rubbish then that's up to you....'

'What do you expect me to think, I mean, do you have any idea how ridiculous you sound?'

'I...'

Jenna swiped a hand to one side cutting him off. 'Just forget it, I mean, it's obvious your father didn't go to the police when he found Sam Wickham did he? All he was concerned with was trying to blackmail Radfield.'

'But that had nowt to do with me, love.' Ronnie pleaded.

'Don't give me that, you've known about this for over forty years and kept it to yourself.'

Ronnie fumbled the tobacco tin from his pocket, his fingers ripping at the lid, a second later the tin fell to the floor spilling dark brown tobacco over the polished oak boards. Ronnie kicked it across the floor. *'So, go on, love, eh, you tell me what I should have done?'*

'What about his wife, don't you think she deserved to find out what happened to her husband?'

Ronnie's face was completely devoid of colour, his chest heaving. 'Of course I do, but...'

'But you put the farm first didn't you, just like your father?'

Ronnie glared at her and then he turned and stormed from the room, snatching the cap from his pocket as he went. Jenna watched him leave; it was like watching a stranger.

OLD NEWS.

According to the brass plaque on the wall, the barn was built by William Radfield in eighteen seventy-six, as a meeting place for the village. However, in the early eighties it had been turned into a gift shop-come-cafe, selling homemade cakes and scones. Michael Jones stood out like a hoodie at a garden party. The barn was busy with people queuing to get a slice of carrot cake, a large blackboard stating that the soup of the day was lentil hung behind the long counter. He could feel people giving him a wide berth as he flicked through the brochures on the revolving wire rack, after a few minutes he came across one that had a small map and a description of Radfield Manor; slipping it into his pocket, he made his way outside.

The car park was crowded with motorcycles of all shapes and sizes, people milling about looking at and in some cases taking photographs of the machines. Couples lay on the grass enjoying the last of the afternoon sun; a burger van was doing a roaring trade.

A copper wandered past, he looked at Michael his eyes taking in the tracksuit and trainers, the baseball cap perched on his head. He turned away and hoisted the bag onto his shoulders before making his way across the grass that led back to the road. After a few hundred yards, he pulled the map out, then took a turn to the left, following a path that led up through the trees, according to the guide it was the shortest route to Radfield Manor.

TIME GENTLEMEN PLEASE.

Ronnie strode down the driveway, the flat cap screwed up in his shaking hands, the image of Jenna's accusing eyes seared onto his brain. She would never forgive him for this; the way she had looked at him had made that quite clear. Disappointment he could live with but her eyes had sparkled with something that went way beyond that particular emotion.

He cursed his creaking knees, the way his lungs wheezed like old factor bellows, he wanted to run, like a dying animal trying to escape the pain but his ancient legs wouldn't oblige.

She was right, he should have gone straight to the authorities, but over the years, the whole thing had faded in his mind until he'd convinced himself that nothing would be served by dragging up the past. Ronnie swiped a shaking hand across his forehead, then spat a sour taste from his mouth, his work boots slapped on the tarmac as he trudged down the narrow lane. Everything was falling apart, the police would find out what had happened and the onus would fall on him to try to explain. He could hear the blood thundering in his ears, from nowhere an image of his father came to mind; Ronnie had been about fifteen when they took delivery of the new tractor. He remembered standing in front of the house as his old man drove it around the yard, a wide grin splitting his weather beaten face. Ronnie could recall the feeling of pride; the Fotheringays were a family who looked to the future, who weren't afraid to spend money. He could see himself at the young farmers meetings; people would treat him with respect; he came from a family who were making a success of themselves. Christ, he used to strut around as if he owned the bloody place, dishing out advice to anyone who wanted it. When the reality was they only had money because they never had to pay the Radfields any rent, his old man had seen to that.

He felt the dull watery thud of his heart and pressed on regardless, quickening his pace, if a man had the ability to choose the time of his own death then he would have chosen right now.

Everything ached, the throb in his temple intensified, Ronnie stumbled, and his legs became entangled. It was bizarre to see the ground rushing up to meet him, he tried to lift his arms to cushion the fall, but a savage pain flared in his chest obliterating everything else. He hit the ground with a sickening thud, somewhere close by he could hear the sound of a skylark blasting out a trembling song. He tried to move and found both arms trapped beneath his body, the sun blasted across his head and shoulders. Occasionally, he would feel his legs jerk as if they were still striding down the road. Slowly his vision began to clear, a purple-black beetle scuttled across the tarmac a few inches from his sweating face. He swivelled his eyes in an effort to track its movements but the effort made him feel nauseous. Everything felt heavy; the air, like syrup pressing down on his back, he could feel blood slick on the side of his face. The sound of bees droning in the hedgerow seemed to fill the air, maybe he was dying after all. He wished that Jenna were here, despite his anguish at recent events, he didn't want to die alone.

'Get on the blower, Cathy, we need an ambulance.' Lasser pulled the car across the road and slapped on the main beam and hazard lights before leaping out.

He recognised the figure in the road immediately, Ronnie the cider maker. He knelt down and rolled him gently onto his back, for a couple of seconds his right eye fluttered open and he tried to speak but all that came out was a wet gurgle. The left side of his face was badly grazed, Lasser could see grit from the road mashed into the broken skin his left eye swollen shut.

'It's OK, Ronnie, you take it easy, mate, the ambulance is on its way,' he just hoped he was speaking the truth, because the old man looked like death, his features were devoid of colour, apart from the blue thread veins that ran across his cheeks. Lasser eased him onto his side and then quickly slid his right leg up to support the body.

'They're on their way.'

He glanced up; Cathy was standing on the curb.

'ETA?'

'Fifteen, maybe twenty minutes, is there anything I can do?'

'Well, he's breathing, so that's something.'

He pulled out his mobile and scrolled through the names until he came to Fossey's, he pressed call and slapped the phone to his ear. 'Might as well call the cavalry.'

Cathy looked at him in confusion.

Fossey tried to keep up with Jenna, though by the time he reached the end of the drive she was already bolting down the road. He could see the blue Audi parked across the narrow lane, the hazard lights flashing intermittently.

She skidded to a halt and fell to her knees. *'Oh God, tell me he's not dead!'*

'He's still breathing and the ambulance should be here any minute.' Lasser explained.

She glanced at him, her eyes swimming with tears. *'Come on, Grandad, wake up,'* she reached down with one hand and gave his shoulder a shake. *'Please, you've got to wake up.'*

Ronnie remained motionless, Lasser bent in close, his breathing sounded worse, the gaps becoming longer.

Fossey stood looking down, hands on hips, his face red with exertion. 'Is he OK?'

'He's dying.' Jenna wailed, her hands fluttering over the body.

Lasser eased Ronnie onto his back and began giving CPR, it had been over two years since he'd been on the refresher course but the instructor had said it was like riding a bike, when you needed it you'd know what to do. Though he wasn't so sure, the ribcage beneath his interlocked hands felt spongy and fragile and he wondered if he doing more harm than good.

Jenna plucked at the sleeve of his shirt. *'Please don't let him die.'*

When she felt the hand on her shoulder, she spun around ripping a hole in the knees of her jeans.

'Why don't you come over here, sweetheart, give him room to work.'

'But...'

'I know but we don't want to get in the way.' Cathy smiled and Jenna stood up, letting herself be led to the side of the road.

Behind her, she could hear Lasser counting and grunting as he tried to keep her grandad's heart working.

'He can't die,' she whispered.

Cathy placed an arm around her shoulder. 'Is there anyone you want me to ring?'

'Ring?'

'Your mother or father, perhaps you should let them know what's happened.'

Jenna looked over her shoulder, Lasser was hunched over her grandad, arms locked, hands thrusting down on his chest.

'Jenna?' She turned back to the police officer. 'Try not to worry; Lasser knows what he's doing.'

They all heard the siren at the same time, apart from Lasser they all turned; the ambulance appeared out of the shimmering heat. Jenna began to leap up and down waving her arms as if the rescuers might go flying by.

A minute later and the paramedics were taking over, Lasser moved back, dragging his tie loose, and reaching for his cigarettes. Fossey walked toward Jenna, the next thing she was in his arms, the sobs racking through her chest.

'I've killed him, it's all my fault.'

'Jenna, try and keep calm, they're doing all they can.'

Lasser propped himself up against the wall and took a long pull on the cigarette, watching as the paramedics slipped an oxygen mask over Ronnie's face.

Something wasn't right here, what had the old man been doing, half a mile from Fossey's house and from the way he'd been lying it looked like he had been heading away from the place.

The paramedics loaded Ronnie onto the stretcher and hurried toward the van.

'Tell me he's going to be alright.' Jenna stood back as they slid him into the ambulance. One of them climbed into the back while the other closed the doors. 'I want to go with him?' she asked, the tears sliding down her cheeks.

The paramedic shook his head. 'I'm afraid not, love.'

'But...'

The man disappeared down the side of the van, a few seconds later she heard the engine start up, when she felt a hand on her arm she turned.

Lasser smiled at her. 'Better stand over here, love; they'll need room to turn around.'

'Why won't they let me go?'

'Listen, Jenna is it?'

She nodded.

'Why don't you get into the car we can follow them to the hospital.'

'You don't mind?'

'Not at all.'

Jenna climbed into the back of the Audi. 'Patrick, you're coming aren't you?'

'Of course I am,' he slid in beside her.

Cathy jumped in and fumbled with the seatbelt as Lasser turned in the road. Seconds later, he was accelerating down the narrow country lane his face set with grim determination.

THEY'LL SAY ANYTHING

By the time they arrived at the hospital, Ronnie had been spirited away, first to A & E and then off to the bowels of the building. Cathy had gone to get them all coffees, Jenna sat slumped in one of plastic chairs, head in hands, long blonde hair hanging down.

Fossey had tried to find out what was going on but all the doctor would say was that they were *'doing all they could.'* Lasser recognised the stock reply; after all, he'd used it himself on more than one occasion.

While he was outside smoking a cigarette, he spotted Fossey talking to a blonde haired woman and a big bloke in a check shirt. They had to be Jenna's parents; the woman had the same bone structure, the same blue eyes. Her father looked like your typical farmer, all brawn, and curly dark hair, like some Heathcliff clone. The woman had looked at him through the window and smiled half-heartedly.

When Fossey had pushed his way through the glass doors, Lasser had been waiting, now they sat in the Audi, all the windows were up and the air con was on full.

'So, let me get this straight, Ronnie's old man got the farm and the land for nothing?'

Fossey sighed. 'That's what he said.'

'Because of a body his father found over forty years ago?'

'Yes, but Ronnie didn't know about any of this until after his father's death.'

'It still doesn't explain why he was lying in the middle of the road, half a mile from your place?'

Fossey rested an arm on the door. 'He became agitated...'

'I gathered that, but why exactly?'

A car pulled up beside them, a young nurse climbed out, she smiled at Fossey then beeped the alarm and headed toward the hospital entrance.

'Look, Lasser, he was ashamed, Jenna had no idea about any of this...'

'Any of what, come on, Fossey, I'm all for a tall tale but you're dragging it out, mate.'

Fossey gave him a sharp look and then sighed. 'Although he never came out and said it, it seems that his father must have been able to link the death of Sam Wickham directly to Malcolm Radfield.'

Lasser sat up straight as the penny dropped. 'So, Ronnie's old man was doing a bit of the old blackmail?'

'I think that's what he was implying but Jenna started to get angry and I don't think Ronnie could actually bring himself to say it.'

'That's when he went walkabout?'

'Unfortunately, yes.'

'And that's why she blames herself for him being in intensive care?'

'Which is, of course, nonsense.'

'Not as far as she's concerned.'

'Don't even go there.' Fossey warned.

Lasser nodded and pulled out his cigarettes. 'So, you say Ronnie only found out about this, when his old man was dead and buried?'

'Before you ask, it was in his diary.'

'And where is it now?'

'I don't have a clue.'

'Let me get this straight, you said Wickham's wife turned up looking for her hubby?'

'That's right, she somehow found out that it was Ronnie's father who'd found the two bodies that drowned in the mine.'

'And she flipped when he tried to get her to go to Radfield's house?'

'So he says.'

Lasser lit the cigarette, before sliding the window down a fraction. 'But why would this woman think that Radfield would know anything about her husband?'

'I asked him about that and he had no idea.'

Lasser thought for a moment. 'So, she'd had dealings with Radfield in the past, otherwise why would she have become upset.'

'I agree.'

Lasser looked toward the hospital entrance; he could see an old man in a wheelchair, dressed in a pair of pyjamas, smoking a cigarette. 'I presume if Ronnie hadn't had a heart attack, you would still have given me a ring.'

He waited for a few seconds, when Fossey didn't reply he turned his head.

'I don't honestly know, I mean, all this happened over forty years ago...'

'That's the wrong answer and you know it.'

'Look, a lot of this is only what Ronnie believed might have happened...'

'But if his father did get the farm for nothing, something must have happened between Radfield and his old man. I mean, people like his Lordship weren't in the habit of handing over land for nothing,' Lasser paused. 'What we need to find out is if any of this is tied into the murders.'

'Right well, if it's OK with you I'm going to go back in there and see if Ronnie's still alive.'

Lasser frowned. 'Listen, he seems like a decent old guy and I hope he pulls through...'

'What, just so you can question him?'

Lasser could feel his temper begin to build. 'I've still got a job to do, Fossey.'

'Yeah, but you don't need to look so pleased about it.'

A moment later, he was striding away from the car.

The refectory was surprisingly quiet, the air filled with the scent of spaghetti bolognaise. Lasser spotted the blonde haired woman sitting alone at a corner table, a plastic cup held between her hands, grabbing a coffee from the machine he made his way over.

'Mrs Fotheringay?' She looked up, her eyes full of confusion. 'I'm Detective Sergeant Lasser.'

'Oh, I'm sorry I was miles away.'

He slid into the seat opposite. 'Is there any news?'

'Not yet, I keep trying to get some answers but nobody seems willing to commit to anything,' she paused. 'Look, I want to thank you for what you did, the paramedics said that if my father hadn't received CPR at the scene then his chances of survival would have been next to none.'

'I just hope he'll be OK...'

'They also said he'd been found collapsed in the middle of the road?' she sounded perplexed, as if the notion was too bizarre to contemplate.

'That's true.'

'So, what was he doing wandering around in the middle of nowhere?'

Lasser took a sip from the plastic cup. 'I'm afraid I can't help you there.'

'But you were going to Patrick Fossey's house?'

Lasser smiled to himself, it was obvious she'd been turning thing's over in her mind, trying to make sense of it all. Now she had someone in front of her she was firing the questions thick and fast, maybe she was wasted as a farmer's wife, the way she was going she would have made a good copper.

'Look, Mrs Fotheringay...'

'Please, call me Susan.'

'I was on my way to see Fossey but obviously when we came across your father things changed very quickly.'

'But why were you going there, I mean, has it anything to do with the murders?'

'I'm afraid I'm going to sound like a doctor now but I'm not really at liberty to say.'

She smiled sadly. 'I understand but you can see how confusing it all is, I mean, they go to spend the day picking apples and he ends up having a heart attack half a mile from the house,' she pushed her hair back from her eyes. 'I tried to ask Jenna about it but she said now wasn't the time.'

Lasser gave a slight shrug. 'Maybe she's right.'

As if on cue, Jenna came in through the revolving doors a tray laden with plastic coffee cups held in her hands, she looked toward Lasser and her mother then hesitated for a few seconds, before making her way over.

'Mr Lasser, I thought you'd gone, I mean, I didn't get you a coffee...'

'That's OK, I've already got one.' Lasser lifted the cup as proof. 'I just called in to see if there was any news about your grandad.'

'Oh right.'

Susan took the tray and placed it on the table. 'Where's your father?'

Jenna glanced at her mother and then quickly looked away. 'He's with Patrick.'

Susan picked a coffee from the tray. 'Sit down, Jenna.'

'Well, I thought I might go and find them.'

'They'll be fine.'

Jenna hesitated and then sat down, keeping her eyes on the table top, as if she already knew what was coming.

'Now, I want to know why your grandad was found lying in the middle of the road and don't even think of telling me that *'this isn't the time.'*

Jenna had her hands folded in her lap like a school kid caught telling a nasty little lie, Lasser felt sorry for the girl but kept his mouth shut and waited.

'Look, Mum, I know you think I'm stalling but I really think it's best if we talk about this when we get home...'

'Well, I don't.'

When Jenna spoke, her voice was little more than a whisper. 'It's all my fault, I lost my temper and Grandad got upset and...'

'You had an argument?' Susan looked at her daughter in disbelief.

Jenna squirmed. 'It wasn't really an argument...'

'For God's sake, either you did or you didn't.'

Jenna looked around the room as if she were praying for some kind of divine intervention. 'Look, Mum, it was nothing really, we were just talking about...'

'Nothing really,' Susan pointed toward the door. 'Your grandad is in intensive care and you tell me it's *"nothing".'*

'I didn't know that was going to happen,' Jenna lowered her head, the tears sliding down her cheeks.

'Yes well, it has and you are going to tell me why.' Susan's face was a mixture of frustration and anger.

'I can't, Mum.'

'Oh you can, young lady...'

'Look, maybe I can help.' Lasser leaned forward, placing his elbows on the table.

'You?' Jenna lifted her head and dabbed at her eyes with the sleeve of her sweatshirt.

'Look, Susan, I was talking to Patrick and he filled me in on what happened.'

Susan glanced at her daughter and then turned her attention back to Lasser. 'Go on, I'm listening.'

'It seems that Jenna became upset when Ronnie was discussing the farm....'

Susan looked confused. 'The farm, what has the farm got to do with anything?'

Lasser pursed his lips. 'Well, I don't know if you're aware but according to your father the farm was gifted to your family rather than sold.'

'I'm sorry but I don't have a clue what you are talking about.'

'Grandad said his father got the farm for nothing, Mum,' Jenna felt the words rushing from her mouth.

'You're trying to tell me that my own grandfather somehow *'tricked'* Radfield into giving us the house and land?'

'He didn't trick him; your father said Radfield was blackmailed into handing the farm over.' Lasser dropped the bomb and waited.

'Blackmailed!'

Jenna looked down at her hands clasped in her lap, she couldn't bring herself to lift her head, couldn't stand to see the look she knew would be on her mother's face.

Lasser picked up a sachet of sugar and began to roll it between his fingers. 'Apparently it had something to do with an accident in the early sixties...'

Susan stood up the chair legs squealing as she pushed it back. *'This is ridiculous...'*

'It's true, Mum, there was this man, Sam Wickham and...'

'Wickham!'

Lasser frowned. 'You've heard the name before?'

Jenna had never see her mother looked so shocked, so anxious, the colour bled from her face. She took a hesitant step back nearly stumbling as her legs hit the chair.

'Mum, are you alright.' Jenna reached out a hand.

'I don't have to listen to this,' Susan thrust the chair away, sending it skittering across the floor, a moment later she was heading for the door.

'Mum, where're you going?' Jenna took a couple of hesitant steps forward.

Susan didn't turn around, didn't hesitate, she slammed through the door and vanished.

SNEAKING.

As soon as Michael spotted the police car parked on the lane, he cut to the left and made his way into the dense cover of the trees. The light was rapidly fading, the shadows lengthening as he scrambled up the hillside, nearing the top; he angled right and made his way toward the house. As it came into view he stopped, amazed by the sheer size of the place, it was no wonder the pigs had let Radfield go, this tosser probably had access to the best solicitors, the best everything. He fumed at the injustice, left to the coppers Billy's murder would be dismissed, and Radfield would carry on living in his big fuck-off house.

Slipping the bag from his shoulder, he rummaged inside until he felt the handle of the knife, when he pulled it free the blade glittered in the last of the fading light. He moved forward in a crouch, easing under the low-hanging branches of the trees. When he heard voices, Michael stopped and slid onto his stomach before snaking his way to the lip of the hill. Two coppers were standing in front of a pair of huge iron gates; one of them was smoking a cigarette, the grey smoke curling into the air.

'Have you ever thought of packing in?'

Michael was close enough to hear the other copper sigh. 'Give it a rest, Spenner, what else is there to do out here?'

'Well...'

'I mean, I can't see Simms turning up out of the blue can you, not with Hopkins's killer still on the loose, besides I don't even know what were meant to be doing up here.'

'We're here in case the media turn up.'

Brittle laughter floated up the hillside. 'The media aren't interested in Radfield...

Michael backed away until the voices were mere mumbles, back beneath the trees, he stood up and looked down the hillside. The house was all lines and shadows, the windows opaque, a large red brick wall encircled the property. At the bottom, he could see a huge oak overhanging the wall alongside a crumbling greenhouse. Shrugging the backpack onto his shoulders, he started down the steep embankment, his trainers fighting for grip. He slid the last six feet, a trail of dead leaves and displaced soil slithering down behind him, sounding startlingly loud in the gloom.

When he reached the wall, he followed it away from the gates until he came across the gnarly bough of a huge oak. Michael scrambled up the trunk until he came to the branch that cleared the wall, he slithered along and then dropped to the ground with practised ease. He remained hunkered down in the long grass while he studied the house. The last time he'd broken into a place it had been one of the boarded-up council houses on the estate, somewhere to get pissed and keep out of the rain, there had been two windows at ground level, one kitchen, one dining room, no problem. Eventually, the council had found out and covered the windows with metal sheets. He counted the windows in front of him, ten that he could gain access to, the size of the place seemed to mock him, making him feel small, inadequate. He moved to the edge of the greenhouse and then sprinted across the lawn aiming for the left hand corner of the house. Skidding to a halt, he flattened his back against the wall. It was cold in the shadow of the building though he could feel the sweat sliding down between his shoulder blades. He peered in through the windows; the kitchen was in darkness, though he could still make out the dull shine of the sink and worktops. Lifting his left arm, he slammed it back, the glass cascading into the room, sliding the bag from his shoulders he swiped it along the window ledge to remove any shards of glass, before climbing through and disappearing into the dark.

SEEN BETTER DAYS.

Ronnie looked dead; his face was the same hue as the pillow beneath his head, grey and washed out. Susan was sitting at his bedside, arms on the mattress, hands clasped together, as if praying. Instead of taking him to a ward, they'd moved him to a private room, which in Lasser's opinion was never a good sign. He was standing in the corridor looking into the small room, the dividing window had stickers on, smiley faces and daffodils, it even had an acrylic painting of Mickey Mouse plastered across the glass, the bright cheerful colours at odds with the old man on the bed. A couple of minutes after Susan had stormed out of the refectory, Jenna's father had walked into the room and she had dashed towards him tears streaming down her face. When Lasser left, she had been trying to explain what had happened but the sobs and hiccups were making it hard.

He looked up and down the long corridor and then tapped on the glass, Susan turned and frowned, and for a few seconds he thought she was simply going to ignore him. Then she stood and made her way to the door.

'How is he?'

She pushed her hair back, although her cheeks were stained with tears, she looked at Lasser with more than a hint of disapproval. 'Look, Sergeant, I've already said I appreciate what you did for my father and at the moment he's stable...'

'Good, I'm glad.'

'But that's not why you're really here is it?'

'I don't want to hassle you but I do need to know why you reacted so strongly when Jenna mentioned the name...'

'Wickham.'

Lasser nodded. 'After what your father admitted to Jenna, then you can understand I have to look into it.'

She moved into the corridor, quietly pulling the door closed. 'You mean the blackmail?'

'Do you know anything about it?'

'No I don't.'

'But you believe him?'

'My father isn't in the habit of telling lies, Sergeant, though he does get confused at times.'

'It's just that you don't seem overly surprised.'

'What are you saying, that I knew about it and kept my mouth shut?'

Overhead one of the strip lights flickered. 'I'm not saying that at all,' he paused, 'but you know something about Sam Wickham.'

Susan looked over her shoulder; Ronnie remained motionless, every few seconds the heart monitor flashed, a tiny red light.

She sighed. 'The last time I heard that name I was fifteen years old.'

'It must have made quite an impression?'

'One thing you have to understand about my parents is that they never argued. I know it sounds like a cliché but they really did have the perfect marriage.'

She was right there, as far as he was concerned it sounded like total bollocks. 'Not many of those about,' he replied.

'I had a very happy childhood, I could not have asked for better parents.'

Lasser could hear the *'but'* coming from a mile off. 'Go on.'

'The sound of raised voices was alien to me, that's why at first I thought it was the radio on too loud,' she paused and swallowed, as if the recollection was painful. 'Then I realised it was my mother shouting.'

'What were they arguing about?'

Susan straightened her shoulders and looked Lasser in the eye. 'She kept asking him if it was true that he'd had a child with Emma Wickham,' she pulled a sour face as if speaking the woman's name left a bitter taste in her mouth.

Whatever Lasser had been expecting, it certainly wasn't this. 'She was accusing your father of having an affair?' he glanced through the glass, trying to imagine Ronnie as some kind of ladies man was nigh on impossible.

'No, he would never have cheated on my mother, he loved her too much.'

'I'm sorry I don't follow.'

'My parents only got married when they were in their mid-thirties, this was meant to have happened before he even met my mother.'

'I see.' Well, Ronnie was a farmer; sowing wild oats was all part of the job. 'So what happened?'

The light above their head pinged and then went out. 'I don't know, I couldn't stand to hear them shouting so I left the house and went for a walk.'

For the first time Lasser looked at her and thought, I don't believe you. 'So, you have no idea if it was true or not?'

'Look, my mother died when I was eighteen and my father was devastated, he never knew that I'd heard them arguing and I wasn't going to drag it all up.'

'Tell me, before they argued had you ever heard either of them mention the name before?'

'Definitely not, that's why I was so shocked when Jenna said it.'

Deep in his mind, Lasser could hear the clanging of alarm bells. 'And you've never been curious to find out the truth?'

When she looked at him her eyes had hardened, it was hard to think that a couple of minutes earlier she had been close to tears.

'I can understand to some people it might be important but I already have my family, Sergeant, and they mean the world to me...'

'I don't doubt it,' he paused, 'but you could have a half-sister or brother out there and surely they deserve to know?'

Susan shrugged. 'Maybe he already does, I haven't a clue.'

'So, you presume the child was a boy?'

She looked at him in confusion and then blanched. 'What do you mean?'

'You said you heard your parents arguing about a *'child'* and you left because you couldn't stand to hear them shouting, so why would you refer to the child as a he?'

'It's just a term of phrase, that's all,' she turned again to check on her father, though this time he was convinced it was to break eye contact, when she didn't turn around he moved forward to stand beside her.

'Look, I need you to help me here...'

'I'm afraid I can't, now if you'll excuse me I'm going to spend some time with my father.'

She was through the door in an instant; he watched as she pulled out the chair and sat down at the side of the bed. Lasser's hand automatically went to his pocket to pull out his cigarettes, then he remembered where he was. Going into a room where an old man was clinging to life, to question his daughter, you needed to be some kind of bastard.

He mulled it over for a few seconds then placed his hand on the door handle.

NOT IF YOU PAID ME.

Everything creaked, every floorboard, every door. Michael winced as he crept from one cavernous room to the next. The place reeked of damp, like old books left out in the rain. Beneath his feet, the carpets were threadbare; the furniture like something you would chuck on a bonfire. If he hadn't seen the coppers standing at the gates he would have thought he'd made a mistake and broken into the wrong house. After checking the last of the downstairs rooms, he found himself standing at the foot of a huge staircase. Michael adjusted the backpack and began to climb, the knife gripped in his right hand the handle slick with sweat. Every step seemed to draw the darkness toward him; shadows melded together forming a seemingly solid block of black. When he reached the top he swiped an arm across his forehead and then turned left before moving slowly down the landing. Opening the first door he came to moonlight flooded in through the window, pooling at his feet. He hesitated in the doorway, letting his eyes adjust to the pale half-light. In one corner he could see the skeleton shape of a four-poster bed, the pelmet in tatters, a huge wardrobe stood opposite, apart from that the room appeared empty. He left the door open and moved to the next, his hand curled around the handle. Like the rest of the house the air in the narrow passage was fetid, yet here there was another underlying scent, something that he could almost taste. He spat onto the carpet, then twisted the handle and pushed, the rancid odour swept out and slammed into him, Michael took a backward step, his arm lifted to cover his nose and mouth.

Unlike the other bedroom, this one had curtains up at the window, thick drapes that blocked out the moonlight. He licked his lips and strode across the threshold, heading quickly toward the window; he grabbed hold of the material and yanked the curtain back. The room was almost identical to the previous one, the same wardrobe, the same four-poster bed, the only difference being that this bed was occupied. He lifted the knife his heart hammering and strode forward, time for some answers. When moonlight splashed onto the body, Michael crashed to his knees, the knife fell from his jittering fingers, and skittered away beneath the bed, the raw meat smell engulfed him. When his hand hit the floor, he gasped and snatched it away, blood coated his fingers, slick and cold.

The head, where was the fucking head? He sprang to his feet, eyes riveted to the sight spread out before him, he could see the dark stain spreading out from the shoulders, saturating the mattress, could see the bone white hand of the corpse gripping the sheet. All thoughts of his brother vanished; any notion of revenge swept away on a tidal wave of fear. Dragging his eyes away from the ruined body the shadows seemed to crowd in around him pushing and jostling. Michael hesitated for a second and then bolted for the door, as he dashed onto the landing he felt his left foot slide on something wet, he slammed against the opposite wall, the breath firing from his lungs, part gasp, part scream. Scrambling to his feet, Michael careered down the landing taking the stairs two and three at a time. He hit the floor hard and then arrowed straight toward the kitchen, all the time convinced that he was being watched, being stalked. When he reached the broken window, he dragged the pack from his shoulders and threw into the garden, then slithered through, landing in the flowerbed, a tangle of arms and legs. Grunting, he gained his feet and sprinted across the lawn toward the huge oak. Michael leapt for the overhanging branch and swung himself up, when he reached the top of the wall, he risked a glance over his shoulder, convinced that he would see a black shape crawling toward him. The looming bulk of the house stood stark against the slate grey sky, a monstrous silhouette. Turning away, he dropped over the wall and then began to scramble up the hillside, his trainers slipped on the wet grass, his breath rattled in his ears.

'Stop right there!'

He snapped his head to the left, the terror that the killer was giving chase almost made him weep, when he saw the two coppers blundering up the hill, he actually cried out in relief. Digging the toes of his trainers into the soft earth, he made it to the top before they were halfway up. He stood for a moment looking down at them, then turned, and set off running through the trees.

FLAT OUT.

Cathy watched the speedometer creeping above eighty and gave the seatbelt a yank to make sure it was secure. The siren was a high whine in her ears, Lasser jabbed the brakes as a silver grey BMW pulled out in front of him.

'Prick!' he bellowed.

As soon as the car swerved back to the left, he slammed his foot down on the accelerator, the big Audi bulleted forward.

Just as he'd been about to enter the room to have another crack at Susan Fotheringay, the door at the end of the corridor had slammed open and Cathy had come dashing toward him, dark ponytail bobbing on her shoulders.

'Hang on!' her cheeks flushed with colour, her eyes alight with a kind of fervour. 'You've got to come now, sir.'

'I thought I told you to drop the 'Sir.'

She shook her head dismissively. 'Simms has been trying to get in touch with you, he's going ballistic.'

Lasser let his hand slip off the handle. 'Why, what's the problem?'

'Ashley Radfield's been murdered!'

Now they were barrelling down the dual carriageway all guns blazing.

'It's the next exit.'

'I know the way,' he checked the mirror and then shot across the two lanes of traffic and down the slip road. Cathy had both hands on the dashboard, her feet digging into the car mat as Lasser screeched around the roundabout. If she thought, he was going to slow down when he hit the B roads she was wrong. He only eased slightly for the bends, any straight sections of road he treated like an empty motorway. The stone wall to her left flashed by in a blur, she closed her eyes in an effort to dispel the image of the car smashing through the stonework, she could envision them slamming end over end and then igniting in a ball of fire and twisted metal. When he reached the lane that led to the house he slowed and flicked off the siren, though he left the blue light flashing, the driveway was lined with assorted police cars. Uniformed officers stood in small groups as if waiting to be told what to do. The manor was lit up from the inside, light spilled out onto the gravel driveway, illuminating small pieces of quartz, sparkling like tossed-away diamonds. He parked and headed for the front door with Cathy scurrying to keep up; Spenner was standing guard, his hands locked behind his back, like a cardboard cut-out.

'I see you're in the thick of it as usual, Spenner.'

'Yes, sir,' he replied without a hint of irony.

'So what's happened?'

'It was the kid, sir; we saw him on top of the wall and gave chase...'

'The kid?'

'Yes, sir, DCI Simms told us to be extra vigilant, he said that Michael Jones had been seen in the area and he might try and gain access to the house but I'm telling you, sir, that little sod can run, he...'

'Are you sure it was him?'

Spenner looked confused by the question. 'Well, who else could it have been?'

Lasser nodded, thank Christ he had told Simms about following Michael, at least none of this could be laid on his doorstep. 'Where's the chief now?'

'Top of the stairs, turn left, second door on the right but I have to warn you, sir, it's bloody horrific in there.'

'Thanks for the warning,' he crossed the hallway and made his way up the stairs, even with all the lights on the house still felt gloomy. When he reached the top, he saw the bright flash of a camera bulb to his left, illuminating the hallway.

Lasser stood in the doorway, Cathy at his elbow. As he stepped over the threshold, he saw Simms standing at the foot of a huge four poster bed, Monty's camera flashed again, drawing his gaze to the bed. It took him a couple of seconds to realise that the head was missing. Monty looked at Lasser and grimaced.

'Normally I'd say smile for the camera but in this case it would be a pointless exercise.'

Simms looked over his shoulder. 'Ah, Detective Sergeant, glad you could make it.'

'Evening, sir.'

'It seems our killer has tired of playing games,' his voice was matter of fact, always a dangerous sign.

'It seems that way, sir.'

'I tell you one thing, I can't wait for the day I retire,' he looked toward the ornate ceiling, probably trying to imagine what it would be like when all he had to worry about was getting his golf handicap down.

'We found this under the bed,' Carl appeared from the shadows, holding a kitchen knife by the tip.

Lasser peered closely at the blade. 'No bloodstains.'

'No, boss.'

Simms grunted. 'Could it have been used to decapitate the body and then cleaned?'

'I doubt it the blades too short.'

Simms sighed and gave a dismissive wave of his hand. 'Bag it and get it down to the lab.'

'Right, sir.' Carl moved away, his white paper suit rustling as he walked.

'I take it you saw Spenner on the door?' Simms asked.

'Yes, sir, he told me about the boy running from the house.'

'I've got half the force out looking for him, with a bit of luck we should pick him up by morning.'

Lasser looked down at the body; he could see the expensive brogues, the crisp white shirt the collar ragged and saturated with blood, bone white hands grasping the sheet. 'Are we sure he actually gained entry to the house?'

'Positive, the kitchen window has been smashed and there are bloody footprints leading from this room down toward the kitchen, he even left a rucksack under the kitchen window.'

Lasser sighed. 'Right.'

'What we don't know is if it was Michael Jones who actually did the killing.'

Lasser looked at his boss with admiration, the likes of the late Sergeant Hopkins would have had the armed response team camped at the Jones's house with an order to shoot on sight.

Simms sniffed and then checked his watch. 'You've met the lad, do you think he's capable of something like this?'

Lasser looked back at the bed; he thought back to when Michael had come at him with all guns blazing, though it was a massive leap from a fistfight to decapitation. 'To be honest, I don't think so'

'Explain.'

'Well, if it was Michael Jones, I would have expected the attack to be more frenzied.'

'And the removal of a man's head doesn't strike you as *'frenzied'* is that what you are saying?'

Lasser glanced at Monty, who raised an eyebrow.

'I just think there would have been multiple stab wounds to the body.' Lasser explained.

Simms looked at the bed and nodded. 'Of course without the rest of him we can't say what level of violence was actually used, can we?'

'That's true.'

The flashbulb went off again, Simms rocked back and forward on his heels. 'So, what do you think happened here?'

'If I had to hazard a guess, I'd say that by the time Michael arrived, Radfield was already dead.'

'So the boy panics and does a runner?'

'Well, wouldn't you, if you came to give someone a good hiding and you find the man you're after in that state?'

'You could very well be right, Sergeant, what I can't fathom is why the killer would take the head?'

Lasser tried to think of a reply but in the end he gave up, all this went way beyond rational thought.

'By the way, how come it took us so long to get hold of you?'

Lasser could hear the subtle change of tone in Simms voice, he looked toward Monty, if he was going to get a bollocking then he preferred it done in private. 'Maybe it would be better if we talked about that outside, sir.'

Simms rubbed his hands together. 'Ah, a tall tale, lead the way, Sergeant.'

'So, you're saying there is a definite link between this Fotheringay family and the Radfields?'

They were sitting in the Audi, after the site of the decapitated Ashley Radfield Lasser was gagging for a cigarette.

'It seems that way, I did question Susan Fotheringay, but to be honest she didn't seem to know anything about the blackmail.'

'And you say she had no idea if her father had a child with this Emma Wickham?'

'She admitted to hearing her parents arguing about the possibility but she says she doesn't know for sure.'

Simms raised a wiry eyebrow. 'And you believe her?'

'Not entirely.'

'So how does this tie in with what's happened here?'

Lasser thought for a moment, unsure of how to continue.

'I'm waiting, Sergeant.'

'It just doesn't feel right.' Lasser closed his eyes waiting for the tirade of abuse.

'Considering the current situation, you're being more than a little vague.'

'Say Ronnie did have a son, then why has he kept it to himself all these years?'

'Come on, Lasser, people keep secrets all the time, for a multitude of reasons.'

Simms moved in his seat, until he was facing Lasser. 'I can understand he would be angry with this Ronnie fella but what would he have against the Radfields?'

Lasser was desperately trying to join the dots, to make links. 'Well, apparently after Wickham went missing, it was suggested to his wife that maybe Malcolm Radfield might be able to help find him.'

'And?'

'She wouldn't hear of it, apparently she went ballistic at the mere suggestion.'

Simms sighed. 'It's all 'ifs and buts,' Sergeant.'

'I realise that.'

'And you say all this happened over forty years ago?'

'Yes, sir.'

'Right, look into it.'

Lasser looked at his boss in amazement.

Simms smiled, though there was no humour behind it. 'Let's face it, we have nothing else to go on, so you try and find out if this 'bastard offspring' really exists and if he does I want to know everything about him.'

'Very good, sir.'

A tap on the window, Simms slid down the glass. 'What is it, Spenner?'

'The press are here, sir.'

'How wonderful, the vultures have arrived,' as he climbed from the car, he looked over his shoulder. 'Keep me informed, Sergeant.'

Lasser nodded and started the engine; flashing the headlights until Harper turned around, a few seconds later she climbed in and they headed down the driveway.

Once clear of the commotion, Lasser pulled into a lay-by, slid the window down, and lit a cigarette, before offering the pack to Cathy.

'No thanks, I don't want to get back into bad habits.'

'I don't blame you,' he fished the mobile from his pocket.

'Who are you ringing?'

'Fossey,' he scrolled through the numbers and slapped the phone to his ear. 'Ah hello, mate, are you still at the hospital?'

He frowned, pressed a button and Fossey's voice came through on loudspeaker.

'No, I got a taxi home.'

'Any news?'

'They said he was comfortable, though that could mean anything. Anyway, have you any idea what time it is?'

Lasser frowned and checked his watch. 'Sorry, pal, I didn't realise it was so late, I was wondering if I could nip round to see you?'

Cathy tightened the rubber band in her hair, the smell of smoke making her crave a cigarette.

Fossey sighed. *'Look, I don't know what else I can do to help.'*

'Well, I wouldn't normally bother but I've just left Radfield's gaff.'

'And what did he have to say?'

'Not much. Then again it's hard to hold a conversation with someone who no longer possesses a head.'

'What?'

'His Lordship is dead and according to a couple of eye witnesses they saw Michael Jones running away from the scene of the crime.'

'I don't believe it.'

'Afraid it's true, now what I want to know is if you have any idea who the girl was?'

'Which girl?'

'The one with the false tan and dodgy hair extensions?'

'Her name's Tina.'

'Is she Michael's girlfriend?'

'I'm not sure, they didn't act like they were but then again he was upset at the time.'

The reproach in Fossey's voice came through loud and clear, Lasser ignored it.

'Do you have any idea where she lives?'

'Look are you sure it was Michael? I mean, he doesn't strike me as the type who would do something like that.'

'We're certain he was in the house but you're right I'm not convinced he was the one who did the dirty deed.'

'So, you think Radfield was already dead when he got there?'

'It seems that way to me but obviously we need to catch up with him to find out if he saw anything that could help.'

'I dropped him off last night, I think the name of the road was Sussex Close but I don't know the number of the house.'

Lasser looked at Cathy, who nodded.

'One more thing before I let you go.'

'Go on.' Fossey sounded guarded.

'When Ronnie was giving you a family history lesson, he didn't happen to mention if he had any other children, did he?'

'No. Why do you ask?'

Lasser thought for a moment before replying. 'When I was talking to the mother, she mentioned there was a possibility that Ronnie could have had a child with Emma Wickham.'

'What do you mean by 'possibility?'

'Well, she said she'd heard her parents arguing and...'

'Did she actually say that Ronnie had any other children?'

'No, that's why I'm asking you.'

'Look, I know you have a job to do but these are good people going through a very difficult time and I don't think harassing...'

'Harassing!'

Cathy winced when she saw the look of anger flare on Lasser's face.

'I spoke to Susan before I left the hospital and she mentioned you'd been asking questions about how they came to own the farm.'

'That's right and to be honest if Radfield hadn't turned up dead, I'd still be up at the hospital trying to get to the bottom of this.' he yanked out another cigarette and slid it behind his ear.

'Just because you don't have any clues about the killer, it doesn't give you the right to question a woman when she is at the bedside of her seriously ill father.'

'Are you trying to tell me how to do my job?'

Fossey's voice remained calm, as if he were giving a lecture. *'I agree, this man needs catching but I don't think the answer lies with the Fotheringays. Now I suggest you concentrate your efforts by looking into whoever had dealings with Malcolm Radfield rather than grasping at straws.'*

Lasser looked at Cathy and raised an eyebrow in disbelief. 'So, you don't think we're already doing that? Come on, you know how these things work, it isn't just me bumbling around in the countryside trying to find this maniac.'

The line went quiet for a few seconds. *'Look, if you think it will do any good, I'll be at home in the morning.'*

'Fine,' Lasser paused, 'and if Michael turns up at your place, do the right thing will you?'

Silence, Fossey had hung up.

HE AIN'T HEAVY.

As soon as Michael saw the headlights in the distance, he vaulted over the stone wall and crouched down in the long grass. As the blue lights streaked into the field, he pressed back into the cold stone, watching as the lights spiralled off into the distance. When he was sure the cop car had gone he leapt back onto the narrow pavement. The flight through the woods had been the stuff of nightmares; convinced that behind every tree the killer was lying in wait, a machete in one hand severed head in the other, dripping blood and gore onto the leaf-littered floor.

Michael started to run, keeping his eyes fixed on the road ahead; throwing frequent glances over his shoulder, the only thing he could think of was getting back to town, back to jaundiced street lights and drunken revellers, away from these empty murderous fields.

The thing that concerned him most was where he was going to stay when he reached the town. He had no doubt the filth would be waiting for him at home but that was the last place on earth he would go. In the end he knew the only person he could trust was Tina, she would let him stay there until he figured out what he was going to do. She wouldn't question him, wouldn't grass him up and Christ alone knew he needed time to think.

The only sound was the rhythmic slap of his trainers on the asphalt, his breathing coming out in ragged bursts, the moon hung in the sky like a freshly minted coin.

When he reached the junction, he stopped to grab his breath. By now the police would have found the knife, they would have discovered the backpack under the kitchen window. Both of these items would prove that he had been in the house.

Lasser had been right, after this, he would never be able to live a normal life. The irony didn't escape him, in the end, he had done nothing wrong but would probably spend the next few years locked up, pissing in a bucket and smoking roll ups.

Michael started to run again, trying to leave the pain and anguish behind; it felt as if he was carrying the dead weight of his brother on his shoulders, a constant reminder of all his failings.

ANOTHER EMPTY CORRIDOR.

Jenna sprawled in the horrible hospital chair, feigning sleep; she could see her mother through half-closed eyes, sitting by the bed, her face etched with worry.

She had no idea of the time, though it felt like she had been in this sterile room for days. The only sound was the regular beep of the heart monitor, occasionally she would hear the squeak of rubber shoes on the tiles as someone walked down the corridor.

For a while, she had sat at the opposite side of the bed just looking at her grandad's face, praying that he would open his eyes and give her a lopsided grin. Occasionally she would catch her mother looking at her and look away, afraid that she would see blame in her eyes.

She moved slightly to ease the creak in her back and then she lay still again.

'Jenna, are you awake?'

She allowed her eyes to flutter open, her mother smiled, though she looked anything but happy.

Jenna yawned and stretched. 'What time is it?'

'Twenty to two, why don't we get a coffee?'

'What about Grandad?'

'We won't be long and I need to stretch my legs,' she stood and slid her bag over her shoulder. 'Come on, you never know the cafe might still be open.'

'I'm not really hungry.'

Susan frowned. 'But you've had nothing to eat for hours, so, come on my treat.'

Jenna rubbed her eyes and grabbed her fleece from the back of the chair before following her mother through the door. The lights in the corridor had been dimmed, though as far as Jenna was concerned it just made the place feel gloomier, more oppressive. The lift doors were open and they stepped inside, Susan jabbed at the button and they slid closed.

'Do you think he'll be alright, Mum?'

Susan slid an arm around her shoulder. 'I hope so, love, I had a word with the doctor while you were asleep and he said the longer he goes without having another attack the better his chances of making a good recovery.'

'Really?'

'Absolutely, he said that if your grandad was going to have another attack then he would have probably had it by now, so you see that's some good news.'

When the lift door opened they stood back to let out a porter who was pushing an empty wheel chair. Susan pressed the ground floor button and the doors slid shut.

'I shouldn't have had a go at him...'

'Listen, I don't know what your grandad was thinking but none of this is your fault.'

'But what if it's all true, Mum?'

'If there is any truth in what he said then it has nothing to do with us.'

Jenna felt her stomach rise and fall as the lift stopped. 'But of course it does.' The doors opened onto another empty corridor.

Susan turned and took hold of Jenna's shoulders. 'Listen, sweetheart, your grandad is basing all this on some diary that none of us have ever seen. Now, I'm not saying that it doesn't exist...'

'Well, it sounds like you are.'

Susan gave a brusque shake of her head. 'OK, let's say for arguments sake that you're right but all this happened years before you were born. I mean, I don't even remember my grandfather, so how can we be held responsible for something that was beyond our control?'

The lift doors hissed closed. 'I know what you're saying, Mum, but I don't think other people will see it the same way.'

'I don't care what other people think, we've worked hard to make the farm a success....'

'I know you have but if the police...'

'What have the police got to do with anything? You're just letting your imagination run riot and you need to stop it.'

'But...'

'No 'buts,' this family sticks together; we carry on as we've always done. Now if the police decide to look into our affairs then we have nothing to hide, nothing to be ashamed of. I mean, how do you think families like the Radfields came to have all that wealth, do you think it was because they were honest in all their business dealings.'

'No, of course not, but…'

'All we have to concern ourselves with is getting your grandad back on his feet and maybe then when he's feeling better we can all sit down and try to get to the truth of all this.'

It made sense but she couldn't shake the feeling that her mother was somehow fobbing her off, trying to get her to tow the line. When they reached the cafe they found the doors locked and the place in darkness, though further down the corridor there was a food and drinks machine humming away quietly in the half light.

'Now, what do you want, Kit Kat, Mars bar?'

'Just a hot chocolate, please.'

Susan rooted in her purse pulling out some loose change. 'I saw Patrick before he left, he said he'd visit your grandad in the morning.'

It was strange but she hadn't thought of Patrick in hours, in fact, now that her mother had mentioned him the only thing she could think of was how he had just stood there while Lasser had been busy saving Grandad's life.

'What about Lasser?'

Susan waited for the chocolate bar to drop into the slot before bending to fish it from the tray.

'I don't know, sweetheart, I spoke with him earlier, you know thanked him for what he'd done...'

'Grandad would have died if he hadn't helped him, wouldn't he?'

'It's best not to think about that, like I said we have to take each day as it comes and stay strong.'

'Can I ask you something?'

'That depends, because to be honest I don't want to talk anymore about what your grandad was meant to have said...'

'It's just that when I mentioned the name...'

'Enough, Jenna.'

'But...'

'But nothing, I've asked you nicely to stop going on about it, now I'm telling you. I have more important things to worry about. Now if you can't do what I ask, then you might as well get a taxi home.'

Jenna looked at her mum in astonishment but her mother didn't look away, didn't flinch, her eyes deadly serious.

'You want me to go?'

'I want you to respect my wishes.'

'But you can't just expect me to forget about what I've heard. I can't pretend it didn't happen.'

'You're going to have to, because I can't give you any answers.'

'But why did you dash off when I mentioned the name Wickham.'

Susan leant forward, her face inches away from her daughters. *'Let-it-drop,'* each word was clipped, a kind of smothered fury behind every syllable.

Jenna swallowed, for the first time in her life she realised that the people she loved were capable of keeping secrets from her. This was just another example of how little they trusted her, this wasn't about protecting her from the big bad world it was about concealing it was about lying.

'OK, Mum, I understand.'

Susan looked at her closely and then smiled. 'Come on, let's get back.'

As they moved back down the corridor, her mother took hold of her hand and gave it a squeeze, inside, Jenna cringed and resisted the urge to pull away, bitch.

DISTANCE.

After dropping Cathy at her apartment, Lasser had made his way home, grabbed a quick microwave meal that tasted like shit and now he was sitting on the sofa, turning recent events over in his head. For the first time in months he didn't have a beer clasped in his hand, didn't even feel like cracking open a can. Problem was he was beginning to think he did his best work when he was half crocked. Maybe this whole thing with Farmer Ronnie was irrelevant; the truth was if you looked hard enough then all families were fuck ups. However, one of the things he couldn't fathom was why Ronnie had decided to come clean after all these years. Lasser reached for his cigarettes, it didn't make sense, unless he had somehow become convinced that it was all going to come out anyway. He lit up and blew smoke toward the ceiling. You keep a secret for nearly forty years and then suddenly decide to blurt it out to your granddaughter and a virtual stranger and then do a runner, having a heart attack in the process. He pursed his lips, Ronnie had told Fossey and Jenna about the blackmail but nothing about his possible relationship with Sam Wickham's widow. Perhaps that's why he'd stormed out, admitting to the blackmail had been bad enough but coming clean about the affair had been one step too far.

Lasser flicked his ash, it was plausible, Ronnie could distance himself from the sins of his father, after all his old man had been solely responsible for that little business venture. Though he couldn't blame his father for shagging the widow, he smiled, that was more like it. It was obvious that Jenna was close to the old man, after all, it was rare these days to find a young girl who actually enjoyed spending time with her grandfather, a relationship built on respect and trust. Yeah well, all that had been blown out of the water, Ronnie was in intensive care and Jenna's image of him had obviously been damaged.

He needed to get his hands on the diary, because he was convinced that Ronnie had been selective with the facts, cherry picking only the parts that he thought would cause him the least damage, it was human nature, deep down everyone had their own agenda.

Picking up the empty plastic tray, he headed for the kitchen and dropped it into the bin, then opened the fridge and eyed the cans of lager lined up with military precision. He could feel the cool air wafting out to meet him, could see the beads of moisture coating the metal tins. Slamming the door, he went to the sink to pour a glass of tepid tap water, grimacing as he took a long gulp. It was frustrating to be standing around doing nothing, he should be out there, but the truth was he didn't know what to do. He had a sneaking feeling that Fossey wouldn't be able to help him, in fact it was obvious that he blamed Lasser for hassling the family. He poured the rest of the water down the sink and wandered back into the lounge. Maybe Michael would turn up at Fossey's house, though even if he did Lasser wasn't convinced the writer would let him know.

Plumping up a cushion, he lay down on the sofa. The important thing was to establish if what Susan had heard all those years ago had been true. Pulling out his mobile, he set the alarm for half six before turning on his side. Ten minutes later he was in the land of nod.

FOR A FEW HOURS.

According to the doctor, waiting for Grandad to wake up was a pointless exercise; he said he could remain unconscious for hours, even days. However, given the circumstances, he was comfortable and his vital signs were good, so he suggested they both go home and get some rest. As far as Jenna was concerned, he was talking rubbish, besides he looked like an impostor. One of those weirdoes who sneak into a hospital pretending to be a doctor when really they were escapees from some mental health institution. She chewed another fingernail as she listened, when her mum agreed she nearly choked. What was she thinking; patients died while you were at home trying to get a few hours sleep, loved ones just gave up, thinking they had been abandoned.

As soon as the charlatan had left the room, Susan had pulled out her mobile.

'What are you doing?'

'I'm sure I have the number for a taxi company in here somewhere.'

'You're not seriously thinking of going home are you?'

'You heard what the doctor said, he'll be fine for a few hours, and besides we have a farm to run, Jenna.'

'But earlier you said Grandad was your one and only concern.'

Susan slapped the phone to her ear, her eyes narrowing. 'Don't start, Jenna.'

'Well, I'm not going.'

'Look, all we're doing is going home to get a few hours' sleep and pick up some things for your grandad.'

'Things, what things?'

'He'll need fresh pyjamas and clothes for when he's moving about, slippers, toiletries...'

'You go, I think one of us needs to be here in case anything happens.'

'Oh hello, could I order a taxi please.'

Jenna turned away and looked out through the huge glass fronted window. She could see a couple of people standing under the small Perspex smoking shelter, they probably had lung cancer and emphysema yet the craving to inhale smoke still had a hold on them. In the end people were weak and selfish, only ever thinking of themselves.

'They'll be here in ten minutes.'

'I'm staying here.'

'No, you're coming home with me, you need to rest.'

'I can sleep in the chair; I mean, he needs to know that one of us is here.'

'You heard what the doctor said, if we're going to be any use then we have to plan for the long term and that doesn't mean sitting by his bedside twenty-four seven.'

'But...'

'Just a few hours at home and then we can come straight back.'

'Why don't you go and then when Dad drops you off later I can go back with him.'

'But your dad won't be bringing me back, you know he has to get the rapeseed in and we only have the combine for four days, so he won't be able to spare the time to keep going back and forth.'

Jenna couldn't believe what she was hearing, it was as if no one gave a shit about Grandad. 'But I thought you said Jim Woodman was going to help?'

'He is but it's still a two-man job. Now, I promise we'll be back here by teatime. Besides you know your grandad wouldn't want us making a fuss.'

'You make it sound like he's in bed with the flu.'

Her mother pushed her hair behind her ears, a sure sign that she was beginning to lose her patience. 'Why do you insist on making things harder, Jenna?'

'I'm not, I...

'I'm just asking for your cooperation. I need you to act your age and stop all this nonsense.'

'Nonsense!'

'Now get your coat, we'll wait at the front for the taxi.'

'But...'

'Now, Jenna!' Susan snatched up her purse from the bedside table and left the room without a backward glance. Jenna looked down at her grandad and then bent down brushing her lips across his grizzled cheek.

'I won't be long, I promise,' she stalked from the room, her fury bubbling away just below the surface.

The journey home was completed in virtual silence, both sitting on the back seat of the taxi, an empty gap between them like an invisible force field. Occasionally Jenna would see the driver glance at her in the mirror, twice he tried a winning smile, Jenna scowled back at him, pervert. As soon as they pulled up at the house, she climbed out and headed for the door leaving her mum to pay the fare. The way she was feeling she just wanted to get inside then she could lock herself in her room and brood. When she opened the front door it felt like she was entering a house that was no longer a home and the realisation came to her of what it would be like if her grandad didn't make it out of the hospital. She could see his old tobacco pouch on the small table, standing alongside the reading glasses that he hated to wear because he said they made him look like an old codger. His favourite chair with yesterday's paper folded neatly on the arm, slippers by the side of the fire. Everywhere she looked, there was a little piece of him, it felt as if he was already dead, she heard her mother come in and close the door behind her.

'Do you want a cup of tea, Jen?'

She looked over her shoulder in surprise, she couldn't remember the last time her mother had called her that, it was a name from her childhood used to comfort when knees were grazed, or she was laid in bed with chickenpox. A peace offering, a way to try and mend broken fences. Jenna could see the tears shining in her eyes, all of a sudden she felt appalled for the way she had behaved. Mum was right, the last thing he would have wanted was for them to sit around moping and bickering at one another.

'Jenna?'

'Sorry, Mum,' she whispered the apology and then looked down at her feet, why was everything going wrong, the murders had been bad enough but this was somehow worse, which only made her feel more guilty, more repelled at her own selfishness.

Susan tossed her bag onto the sofa. 'It's OK, love, if you'd sooner just go to your room I understand.'

'I've been a complete bitch, haven't I?'

Susan smiled weakly. 'Of course not, we're all upset but I just need to try to keep things as normal as possible.'

'I just want him home,' the tears slid from her eyes. When she looked up, she could see her mother standing in front of her through a blur of tears. Susan reached out and she fell forward into her waiting arms.

EARLY RISER.

By six thirty, Lasser was heading out of the door, showered and shaved. He'd given Cathy a ring, told her to be ready for seven; they were going to pay Tina Sheldon an early morning visit. Cathy had sounded half asleep, mumbling her responses, still smothered in the fog of slumber. The sun was low in the sky, slowly building for another day of blistering heat. When he arrived at the apartments, she was already standing on the curb, she climbed in looking bleary eyed.

'Morning,' she yawned.

'Did you manage to sleep?'

'Put it this way, if you hadn't rung I would still have been in bed at dinnertime.'

'Sussex Close?'

'Just get to Lancaster Road, I'll direct you from there.'

Apart from the council worker picking up litter, the town centre appeared deserted, the high street festooned with empty pizza boxes and tin cans.

'Do you think Jones will have headed back to Sheldon's?'

'Hard to tell, I mean, I can't see him going home to his mother's place, not unless he intends taking her head as well.'

'You think he killed Radfield?'

Lasser slowed down as a mongrel dog ambled in front of the car. 'Nah, but the way the lad feels about this mother, then the murder of Radfield might have given him ideas.'

'Take the next left.'

Sussex close was a street made up of prefabs, tin houses, built just after the war, unbearable in weather like this.

'Did Fossey give you the house number?' she asked

Pulling tight to the curb, he switched off the engine. 'No, we'll give it five minutes and then knock on a few doors.'

Cathy waited for him to pull out the cigarettes and light up but his hands remained on the wheel, every few seconds he checked in the rear view mirror. After a couple of minutes, she saw him smile as he swung the door open and climbed out. She swivelled in her seat, she could see him talking to an elderly man who had a newspaper clasped under his left arm. After a moment, he patted the old man on the shoulder and made his way back to the car.

'Number twenty-six.'

'How did you know someone would come along?'

'The paper shop at the end of the road, don't tell me you didn't see old father time going in as we turned.'

Cathy raised an eyebrow; she hadn't even noticed the shop let alone the customer. 'You're rather good at this aren't you?'

'Just a nosey bastard that's all.'

Lasser was surprised to find the garden of number twenty-six looked trim and tidy, the grass short, four large pots full of colourful flowers arranged under the front window.

Halfway down the drive, he stopped and looked at the front of the house; both the upstairs and living room windows had the blinds drawn. 'Do me a favour, Cathy, ring the doorbell?'

She moved past him and pressed her finger on the button, holding it there for about five seconds, Lasser kept his eye on the windows. 'Same again.'

Cathy did as he asked.

'Someone's coming,' she could see movement through the frosted glass of the door. A couple of seconds later the door opened a fraction, Lasser zeroed in.

'Who is it?'

'Mrs Sheldon?'

'Do you know what time it is?'

'My name's Detective Sergeant Lasser, I wonder if we could have a word.'

They heard the rattle of a chain being dragged back then the door opened about eight inches.

She was about forty with dyed blonde hair frizzing around a thin face. 'What do you want?'

'Is Tina in?'

'What do you want Tina for? She hasn't done anything.'

'We realise that Mrs Sheldon, we just want a quiet word.'

'You call this quiet, leaning on my door bell at half past seven in the morning?' she pulled the housecoat tight around her waist. 'Besides she's in bed.'

'Do you mind just giving her a shout?'

'Have you got a warrant?'

'We don't want to search the premises; we just want a few words with your daughter. Now if you insist on refusing this simple request, then I'll be forced into thinking you have something to hide.'

'Oh yes, you lot are good at that aren't you, forcing your way into a house and planting evidence.'

'OK, have it your way, Harper could you contact the station, tell them we need a van down here ASAP.'

'Right, serg.'

She backed away pressing the two way strapped to her shoulder.

'You would an' all, you'd get a gang of thugs down here just to be bloody minded.'

'I'm just doing my job.' Lasser smiled.

'Wait there.'

'Not a problem.'

She left the door open then turned and headed off up the stairs. 'Tina, are you awake, love, the police are here to see you.' Lasser heard the slamming of a door and then Tina Sheldon's mother was suddenly bawling like an old fishwife. *'Who the bloody hell are you?'*

Lasser looked up at the front of the house and then went dashing down the narrow passage that ran down the side of the property. He hit the gate hard, slamming through into the back garden. Michael Jones was halfway across the lawn, limping his way toward a six foot panel fence that separated them from next doors.

'Michael, wait!'

The kid threw a glance look over shoulder; face twisted in pain, his eyes laced with blind panic.

'Leave him alone, he hasn't done anything!'

Lasser looked up; Tina was leaning out through the bedroom window, her hair tied up in a tight bun, face florid with anger.

Lasser stopped and held up his hands. 'It's OK, Michael, I know you're not responsible for what happened at the house.'

Jones stopped and turned, his chest heaving.

'He didn't have a head,' a trail of snot slid from the end of his nose and he swiped it away with the back of a shaking hand.

'I know, son,' he moved closer, when he was about six feet away he stopped. Under normal circumstances, Michael would have been over the fence and away and there was no way Lasser would have been able to stop him, but the jump from the bedroom window had damaged his ankle.

'I didn't touch him; he was just lying there and there was fucking blood everywhere!'

'Michael, I need you to calm down and tell me if you saw anything while you were in the house?'

The boy sniffed and tried to place some weight on his left leg, a second later, he was sprawled on the grass, rubbing at his ankle a grimace of pain on his face.

Moving forward Lasser crouched down at his side. 'Just try and think, did you see anyone else, either when you were in the house or maybe you saw someone when you were making your way to the property?'

'I didn't see anyone, apart from the coppers who chased me.'

'And you definitely got in through the kitchen window?'

Michael eased his leg straight, wincing with the effort. 'Yeah, at first I thought the house was empty.'

'It must have been a shock finding him like that.'

Michael shuddered at the memory. 'I wanted to kill the bastard, I... I thought he was the one who did Billy but he wasn't, was he?'

'No, lad, it wasn't him,' he could see Cathy from the corner of his eye standing guard by the side gate.

Michael looked up at the sky. 'When I saw the state of him, I realised I could never do anything like that.' His voice shook with emotion; his eyes seemed unable to focus, as if he were trapped in some terrible loop were the only thing he could see was the headless corpse sprawled on the big red bed.

'Did you take a knife with you, Michael?'

He nodded in response. 'Yeah, but I dropped it when I saw...' he shook his head, like a dog trying to shake an annoying tick.

Lasser sighed, breaking into the house carrying a knife showed intent and that would be enough to get the lad banged up at least until all this was sorted.

'Think carefully, when you were on your way to the house did you see anyone in the woods, anyone at all?'

'Look, I went to the barn late in the afternoon and when I came out the place was crawling with bikers and I spotted this copper hanging about, so I decided to go before he started asking questions.'

'So, what did you do next?'

He took a deep breath his cheeks ballooning. 'I waited in the woods until it started to go dark.'

'And you didn't see anyone acting suspiciously?'

Lasser watched as a frown of concentration formed on the boy's face.

'There was a bloke,' he gave a small shrug. 'But he was only walking his dog.'

'What did he look like?'

Michael ran his hands through his hair, his face twisted in the parody of a smile. 'He was a big fucker I know that much and he was wearing this backpack.'

'Like an Adidas, or Nike?'

Michael shook his head. 'No way, it was the type you see soldiers carrying, you know the kind that can hold a tent and all that shit,' he paused, 'I remember there was something weird about his keys.'

'What do you mean?'

'He had them clipped to the bag,' he paused, 'but they had these two weird ball things hanging off 'em.'

Lasser looked at a sky criss-crossed with vapour trails, perhaps the night's terrors had scrambled the kid's brains.

'They were about the size of a couple of pool balls but they looked like they were made of cork or something light. I remember they were bouncing as he walked past.'

'So, he didn't see you?'

'Nah, I was hiding in the tall grass, I didn't want anyone seeing me and he strode right past.'

'And he was heading away from the house?'

'Well yeah I suppose so but, I mean, he could have come from anywhere, those woods are full of small paths.'

Lasser thought for a moment. 'When you last saw him, which direction was he heading?'

'He went up the hill toward the canal.'

'Anything else you can remember?'

Michael shrugged. 'Not really.'

'What about his age?'

'I don't know, about forty, something like that, he was wearing black combat pants and a black T-shirt.'

'What about his hair, was it long or short?'

Michael looked at him. 'Longer than yours but his was like a dirty blonde colour.'

Lasser was beginning to get a picture of the man in his head. 'You said he had a dog with him?'

'Yeah it was a black German Shepherd.'

'Suppose you were lucky the dog didn't sniff you out, it would have looked odd you hiding out like that.'

'No way, that dog stuck to his leg like bloody glue.'

'So, it was well-trained?'

'Fuck me yeah. I mean, I had a Shepherd when I was a kid and it used to run around like a mad bastard but not this one.'

Lasser pulled out his cigarettes and offered one to Michael, just as Tina tried to push her way into the garden.

'Get out of my way,' she spat at Cathy.

Lasser waved a hand. 'It's OK Cathy, we're almost done here.'

Tina glared at her as she strode onto the lawn. 'He was with me all night.'

Lasser raised an eyebrow, why was it always the first instinct for people around here to lie through their teeth?

Michael looked up, shielding his eyes from the sun. 'It's alright, Tina, I've told him everything.'

She ignored him and carried on. 'It's not right; you should be out there catching this monster, not harassing my boyfriend.'

Michael looked at her in surprise.

'Breaking and entering is still a crime, love.' Lasser said.

'But he only went there because you lot can't do your job.'

It was hard to take insults from a girl when she was wearing slippers with pink kitten's heads sowed on the top and a little miss bump T-shirt covering her bump.

'What's going to happen to me?' Michael asked.

'You'll have to go to the station to make a statement.'

'He can't do that; they might think he did it.' Tina said wide eyed.

Lasser ignored her. 'Listen, why don't I take you?'

Tina crouched down behind Michael and laced her hands around his neck. 'No way, as soon as you get him down there, you'll lay into him until he admits to doing it.'

Michael patted her hand. 'Leave it, Tina.'

'But...'

'He's right; I need to get this sorted.'

'But you can't trust them you know what they're like; they say one thing and do another.'

'Look, I'm trying to do him a favour here. I could have brought a van with me and dragged him off kicking and screaming but I didn't. Now I've already said I believe Michael didn't commit any murder, though he admits he broke into the property and he has to answer for that.'

'Will I get banged up?'

'You'll be held for questioning. House breaking is a criminal offence but you haven't been in trouble with us for a few years, so that shouldn't be a problem. And if you come with me voluntarily then it's another tick in your favour.'

Michael nodded his head and Tina shredded a fingernail. 'OK.'

'Good lad.'

He struggled to his feet an arm thrown across Tina's shoulders. 'Can I come with you?'

'You're going nowhere, Tina,' her mother was standing by the side gate; arms folded a scowl spread across her narrow face.

'Give it a rest, Mum, you can't tell me what to do.'

'I can, as long as you live under my roof.'

Tina laughed a sound full of mocking disbelief. 'It shows how much you take notice; you didn't even know Michael was here, did you?'

Her mother moved to one side as Michael hobbled past. 'Yes well, you're just like your bloody father aren't you, he was always one for his little secrets.'

'Do us a favour, Cathy, bring the car to the front will you.' Lasser asked, handing her the keys, she spun on her heels and hurried down the path to the front gate.

Tina scrubbed a hand through her hair. ‘Mum, I’m not in the mood.’

‘Oh her ladyships not in the mood, well forgive me for breathing!’ she turned and stormed into the house.

Michael sighed. ‘Are you going to be OK?’

‘Don’t worry about me she’ll be glued to the telly by now.’

They reached the kerb just as Cathy pulled up; Tina threw her hands around Michael’s neck and gave him a kiss on the mouth. ‘Let me know as soon as they let you out?’

‘I will.’

Lasser opened the back door and Michael struggled his way in.

‘Don’t worry, love, he’ll be fine.’ Lasser said as he climbed into the passenger seat.

Tina looked at him with a frown of disbelief.

Cathy pulled away, Lasser could see Tina in the wing mirror, looking like an orphan standing at the roadside in her fluffy pink slippers.

LANDSLIDE

For the first few seconds Jenna thought she was still asleep in the hospital chair, her back ached, she felt hot and sticky, and her T-shirt was twisted around her body like a tourniquet. When her eyes focused, she saw familiar objects swim into view. She remembered falling asleep on the sofa, had a vague recollection of her mum covering her with a travel rug.

When the facts of the night before came crashing down like a landslide of emotion, Jenna leapt from the sofa and headed to the kitchen on legs that felt as if they belonged to someone else. Her mother looked up and smiled, she was on her hands and knees scrubbing at the parquet flooring, mop bucket at her side, her hands full of bubbles the cloying smell of bleach filled the room.

'You're awake then?'

Jenna rubbed at her eyes. 'What time is it?'

'Half past seven.'

'It can't be!'

Susan dropped the brush into the bucket and stood up. 'I've already spoken to the hospital; your grandad had a comfortable night.'

Jenna heaved a shuddering sigh of relief. She remembered waking with a terrible certainty that he had died while they had been away, gone forever, while she and her mum had been sipping wine and cherry picking fond memories of what he meant to both of them.

'When are we going back?'

Susan rinsed her hands under the tap. 'I thought we could go this afternoon, I have a few deliveries to make this morning, but I should be done for two o'clock.'

Jenna would sooner have gone this instant but she bit her tongue determined to be a help rather than be a hindrance. All the stuff about the farm she was prepared to put on the back burner, at least for a while.

'OK, is there anything you want me to do while you're gone?'

'You can run the Dyson over the living room, if you like?'

'What about Dad, do you want me to take him some sandwiches for his dinner?'

'No!' Susan snapped, a look of fear flitting across her face. 'I mean, he took them with him when he left and he has a flask, so he'll be fine.'

It took her a few seconds to work out why her mum had looked so shocked, in all the commotion Jenna had forgot that there was still a killer out there.

'I was listening to the radio before you woke up,' Susan slid out a chair from the table and sat down, 'I'm afraid it's more bad news.'

Jenna was confused, at the sudden change of direction. 'What do you mean?'

Susan looked up at the gleaming copper-bottomed pans hanging from rack attached to the ancient oak beams. 'They found Ashley Radfield late last night, he's been murdered.'

Jenna felt the shrug slide from her shoulders, 'Oh no, not again.'

'I'm afraid it's true, love.'

'That must be why Sergeant Lasser left in a hurry.'

Susan shrugged. 'Perhaps.'

'So what else did they say?'

'I don't know, I turned it off.'

Jenna looked at her mother in confusion, 'But why?'

'Because I couldn't stand to listen to it anymore. These last few days it's like we've been living in a nightmare and when I heard what happened, I'd just had enough.'

Jenna could understand where she was coming from it was emotion overload. 'OK, Mum, I won't leave the house.'

'You could come with me if you like?'

'No it's OK, I'll do the cleaning and then I might send an email to Patrick just to let him know what's happened.'

'That's fine,' she stood up. 'Now, I've got my mobile and it's fully charged...'

'That makes a change.'

'OK, madam, no need for sarcasm.' They both knew they were playing at normality, trying to inject a sense of the familiar, the first step in trying to rebuild their relationship.

Susan dragged her coat from the back of the chair.

'And your dad said he'd call back in a couple of hours.'

Jenna raised an eyebrow, though she kept her lips firmly closed.

'I don't care if you feel I'm being paranoid, I'll just feel better knowing you're OK. '

'It's alright, Mum, I understand. Now would you like me to pack some stuff for Grandad?'

'It's OK, Jen, I sorted it earlier. In fact, it's in a holdall in the living room, remind me to pick it up when I get back.'

'I will.'

'Right, I'm off.'

Jenna watched her drive away, before closing the back door; she turned and eyed the Dyson standing in the corner. Walking straight past it she went through the lounge and headed quickly upstairs to her grandad's room, time for some answers.

DON'T GO THERE.

Fossey rolled up the sleeves of his shirt and rubbed gingerly at the sunburn on his forearm. 'You know Michael's not responsible for his actions.'

Lasser took a gulp from the can of cold lager; they were sitting on the bench in Fossey's garden shaded by the large conifers. Lasser squinted up at the pale yellow orb, he was sick of this heat, it gave the illusion of making time itself slow down, made it hard to concentrate. He rubbed at his temple the dull throb of a headache building slowly.

'He still broke the law.'

'Given the circumstances it's hardly surprising.'

'I'm not here to argue over why Michael took it upon himself to break into a house armed with a kitchen knife.'

'Why are you here?'

'The Fotheringays.'

Fossey sighed. 'We've been over this before.'

'I know, but bear with me. I need to know if this diary that Ronnie spoke of actually exists.'

Fossey looked perplexed. 'Why would he make up something like that?'

Lasser flicked the ring pull on the can, making little 'tinging' noises. 'Have you any idea why he suddenly decided to come clean about the farm?'

Fossey crossed his legs, moving into shrink mode. 'It's difficult to tell, I mean, perhaps he'd been wanting to say something for years and decided that now was the time to bring it out into the open.'

Lasser drained the can and smiled. 'And that's what you believe is it?' he didn't bother trying to hide his disdain.

'I thought I'd make it clear that I don't for one second think the Fotheringays have anything to do with the murders.'

'I'm not saying they do but we've already established that Ronnie kept one secret for over forty years. Now I want to know what other little nuggets he's been keeping to himself.'

'You mean did he really have a child with Emma Wickham?'

'Bingo!'

Fossey ran a hand across the back of his neck. 'I think he's the only one who can answer that, don't you?

'Well, did he say anything specific about the woman?'

'Not much, he certainly never said anything about having a relationship with her.'

'But he did refer to her?'

Fossey thought carefully before answering. 'Only in the context of her husband, he mentioned the fact that before he vanished, the Wickhams lived on a canal barge...'

'A barge?'

'Mm.' Fossey flicked a mint to the dog. 'According to Ronnie, families used to moor up on the Leeds and Liverpool canal and come down to the farms looking for work in the summer months, it was something of a local tradition.'

Lasser felt something slipping by, a link he felt he should be able to make yet couldn't.

He listened as Fossey told him about the body of Wickham turning up in the old tin mine, the more Lasser heard the angrier he became. When Fossey had finished, he took a few moments to fathom it all out.

'And you thought it best to keep all this to yourself?'

'Like I said as far as I'm concerned none of this has any bearing on...'

'You can't make that judgement, it's…'

'Ancient history.'

'Don't give me that...'

'You're making assumptions based on next to nothing. Someone obviously hates, or should I say hated the Radfield family but you've no grounds to link the

Fotheringays to any of this. Even if they did come to own the farm by breaking the law, then it still doesn't explain why you're so determined to give them grief?'

'I get paid to make assumptions.'

'But you don't get paid to fabricate evidence.'

Lasser dropped the empty can onto the table before holding up a finger. 'One, Ronnie's old man was bent; I didn't fabricate that did I? Two, Susan heard them arguing about a child that Ronnie was meant to have fathered with this Emma Wickham and three, if it's true then it isn't beyond the realms of possibility that this man would have a bone to pick with Ronnie...'

'But it's the Radfields who've been targeted, not the Fotheringays.'

Lasser grimaced. 'I'm telling you there has to be a link....'

'Come on, Lasser, you don't even know for sure that there was a child. I mean, you can't simply make stuff up just to suit your own,' he paused, 'misguided theories.'

Lasser chewed the inside of his cheek in anger. 'It was Susan who told me about the possibility of a child, I didn't just pluck it out of thin air.'

'Yes, but she said it was just a rumour, you told me she couldn't tell you definitively if it was true or not.'

'OK, so you don't think it's worth checking it out, is that what you're saying?'

Fossey shrugged. 'That's up to you, but if you want my opinion then it seems more likely that the Radfields had dealings with the wrong people....'

'Bollocks! If that was the case then why murder Billy Jones, what the fuck did he have to do with all this.' Lasser knew he was losing the plot, could feel the red mist descending.

Fossey didn't move, he looked at Lasser as if the outburst was confirmation of some serious flaw in his character, the knowing look on Fossey's face only infuriated him more. 'We have people looking into the family background and they've come up with nothing. In fact, the Radfields were skint. They didn't mix with gangsters and drug dealers, they lived in a house that had grass growing out of the gutters and rising damp in the walls and over the years Malcolm had sold off almost all the land, just so he could keep his crystal decanters topped up with malt whisky.'

'That still doesn't mean the Fotheringays have...'

'Listen, I don't know them the way you do and I'll admit that they seem like a nice normal family...'

'That's because they are, a nice normal family.'

'Fine, and like you said earlier, all families have things that they keep hidden from the outside world.'

Fossey picked up his can but didn't take a drink. 'Go on.'

'Now I'm not saying that they've *knowingly* done anything wrong and to be frank I don't really care how they came to own the farm,' he paused. 'I do care about catching this maniac. Now, I could be 'misguided' in wanting to find out if Ronnie had a child. I might end up looking like a complete dickhead but believe me at this precise moment I couldn't give a toss.'

Fossey drummed his fingers on the arm of the bench. 'I just don't want this family dragged through the mill, they don't deserve it and I've seen it happen before.'

'Yeah and Billy Jones didn't deserve to be gutted and left to hang from the rafters. I didn't have much time for Hopkins but some animal opened his throat and left him to die. Now, I admire your loyalty but come on, pal, you're taking it too far.'

A silence fell between them, broken only by the screech of a magpie as it strutted across the lawn. Lasser thought about his own rabbit hutch home, with its back garden that looked drab, the lawn covered with anaemic grass, the tiny border a hotbed of weeds.

'What do you want me to do?' Fossey asked.

'Have a word with Susan or maybe Jenna, they might be willing to talk to you...'

'I don't think Jenna knows anything, when Ronnie was talking about the farm she was distraught, it was obvious that she couldn't believe what she was hearing.'

'Is that why he did a runner, because of her reaction?'

Fossey took another sip from the can. 'When Ronnie tried to justify what had happened she became very angry and felt he was somehow holding out on her.'

'And was that how you saw it?'

'Well, wouldn't you, I mean, he did his best to explain that for years he knew nothing about any of this.'

'But she didn't believe him?'

'She believes that once he'd discovered what had happened, he should have gone to the police.'

'So, because he kept his mouth shut, she thinks he was guilty by association.'

Fossey pursed his lips and nodded. 'She couldn't get past the fact that Sam Wickham's wife had come to them for help and that they'd somehow used that fact to profit. It didn't matter to her that Ronnie only found out after the event, she still thinks he should have tried to set matters straight.'

It was starting to make sense. 'And if it was true about Ronnie having a child with this woman, then coming clean would be the last thing he would want to do.'

Fossey's face slid back into impassive mode. 'Possibly.'

'Poor sod.'

'Look, we still don't know if any of its true...'

'Fair enough but it's obvious Ronnie was devastated when Jenna blew up at him. If he had intended telling her more, then her reaction to the blackmail would have convinced him to keep his mouth shut about any other secrets he was keeping to himself.' Lasser licked his lips, wishing he had another can to get stuck into. 'Look just try and have a word with Susan, maybe she might feel like unburdening herself.'

'I won't badger the woman, especially not at a time like this.'

‘I don’t expect you to, she might have been telling the truth, maybe she knows nothing about her father and Emma Wickham.’

‘But you don’t believe that do you?’

He pictured Susan at the hospital, the way she had tried to avoid giving him a straight answer. ‘To be honest, no,’ he checked his watch. ‘Look, I'd better get going, I’ll give you a ring tonight if that’s OK?’

He stood up and stretched, wincing at the sharp pain in his back, maybe falling asleep on the sofa hadn’t been such a good idea, then he headed off across the immaculate lawn.

‘Don’t expect a miracle, Lasser.’ Fossey shouted at his disappearing back, Lasser waved a hand in the air and kept on walking.

CAUGHT IN THE ACT.

The battered old suitcase was the colour of a weathered house brick, Jenna found it tucked away beneath the bed. At first she thought it was full of nothing but ancient copies of the Farmers Guardian, dating back to the mid-sixties. It felt strange but she hardly ever went into her grandad's bedroom. Then again she never really had reason to, he was never one for lying in bed, he was always up by six and never ill. She felt the sting of tears, he should be home where they could fuss over him, where he could have the window open to let in the warm summer air, not lying in some sterile room where he was just a name scrawled on a whiteboard. She found the photographs tucked away at the bottom, lifting out the envelopes she hesitated for a moment before pulling open the flap and sliding them out. Jenna rifled through the first pack, black and white stills showing herds of cows and farm implements, one showed a collie in mid flow, tongue lolling. Pushing them back into the sleeve she reached for another, the first one had her grandad leaning on the five-bar gate that led to the top field. It must have been taken in the summer months, because he was dressed in a check work shirt, the sleeves rolled up past his elbows. She flicked through a few more and then stopped; frowning down at the image, a woman with long dark hair was standing by the same gate. This time he was sitting on the top gate, his wellies dangling, arms draped around her neck, a wide grin splitting his face. She flicked the photo over but the back was blank, so she turned back to the image. Grandad looked to be in his late twenties, it felt weird seeing him as a younger man, back then he sported a full head of dark hair, slicked back and wavy. The woman looked to be about the same age, though unlike Ronnie she had a frown on her face as if she wasn't enjoying the experience of having her photograph taken. She placed it on the bed and carried on shuffling through the photos. The last one showed the woman again, but this time she was on her own, sitting in a meadow that Jenna didn't recognise, her legs stretched out in front of her, leaning back on her arms. Jenna could see the pastel blur of wild flowers surrounding her. Unlike the last image, this showed her laughing, head tilted, highlighting the long slender curve of her neck, black hair spilling across her shoulders and down to her breasts. Jenna could see the shadow of the picture taker patterned on the grass. This time when she looked on the back she could a faint scribbling. *'Emma. Nineteen sixty-eight,'* she picked up the photograph from the bed and held them together, looking at each in turn, a nervous feeling prickling at her senses. The woman had to be Emma Wickham but if that was the case then why was her grandad draped all over her? She looked again at the picture of them together, concentrating solely on his smile. After a few seconds, she dropped it onto the bed; it was like looking at a stranger, someone capable of keeping secrets, telling lies. She tried to push the thought from her mind and found that it had lodged there. When he'd been talking about Emma Wickham, there had been no hint that he had actually known the woman. It had all been about what his father had done a blatant attempt to force the blame onto someone else. Jenna stood up, feeling agitated, aggrieved at the deceit. Her mind pulsated with images of her grandad collapsed on the hot tarmac, the anguish she'd felt when she thought he was dead had been unbearable, all her anger toward him had vanished. She would have forgiven him anything just so long as he didn't die. Now she felt the anger flare, a heady concoction threaded through with guilt. Crouching, she closed the suitcase and pushed it back under the bed.

When she turned, she froze, there was a man standing in the doorway, her heart reared her eyes flicked toward him and then away, taking in nothing, her mind splintered with fear. She gasped and took a hurried backward step her legs hit the bed and she stumbled, throwing out a hand to stop her from falling on the mattress. When she looked up he was moving across the room, two strides and he was nearly upon her. Jenna sprinted to the left, her eyes fixed on the doorway, if she could just... Savage pain exploded inside her head, sending her sideways into the dresser, the corner slamming into her ribs forcing the air from her lungs. She tried to scream but the air was locked in her throat, her vision twisted, the room reared and tilted around her. Her right arm flayed out sending the photo frames on top of the dresser crashing to the floor. She felt a hand close over her wrist and looked up just as the fist slammed into the side of her face. She slumped to the carpet, her legs jerked. Jenna felt her bladder empty before the darkness swallowed her.

RUNNING LATE AGAIN

By the time Susan made her last delivery she was running an hour late. Old George Crabtree had grilled her for over twenty minutes. Asking her what had happened to her dad, how was he, what hospital he was in?

As soon as she said her goodbyes, she knew George would leap into his electric wheelchair and head straight down to the post office to spread the gossip. In a few hours, all outlying farms would know what had happened.

On the way out of the village, she found herself stuck behind a caravan that crawled along at a snail's pace. She could imagine Jenna sitting at home becoming more agitated as the clock ticked by. She knew her daughter was trying hard to remain calm, though Susan knew her well enough to recognise the signs; it was all bubbling away beneath the surface, the anger, and frustration.

When the caravan turned into Jim Woodman's field, Susan breathed a sigh of relief and got her foot down. Ten minutes later, she pulled onto the long lane that led to the house. Parking in the shade of the barn, she climbed out and headed to the back of the house. The first thing she did when she entered the kitchen was flick on the kettle before making her way into the lounge.

'Jenna!' When there was no reply, she frowned; perhaps she'd fallen asleep again. 'Jenna love, are you awake!'

Starting to feel uneasy, she moved quickly up the stairs and tapped lightly on her bedroom door, after a few seconds she opened it and poked her head inside, the room was empty the bed neat and tidy. A shimmer of anxiety crawled along her spine, turning, she went back to the top of the stairs unsure of what she should do next. When she looked down the long landing and saw the door to her father's bedroom standing open, she felt the panic bloom and dashed toward the open door.

'Oh Jesus, no!' she looked around the room, the photo frames that Dad always kept on the dresser were scattered on the carpet, a chair had been overturned, the bedside lamp yanked from the wall and thrown into the corner of the room, the flex curled on the floor like a question mark.

'Jenna?' she whispered her name before taking three unsteady steps to the bed. The photograph lay crumpled on the duvet. It was as if time ground to a halt, she watched as her hand reached out and picked it up. When she saw the image of her father his arms draped around the neck of the dark haired woman her hand made a fist. She must have been searching the bedroom, Susan felt a sudden burst of anger, that was why she'd declined to come with her, she'd wanted her out of the house so she come up here and ransack the room like a common thief. Jenna had found the photograph and then trashed the room, Susan spun on her heels, seething with anger and outrage.

When her eyes fell on the stain she simply stopped and stared, her mind suddenly full of confusion, then she saw another a few inches to the left, then another, small droplets leading to the door. Susan crossed the room and onto the landing, following the trail. The word, 'Blood' erupted in her mind. She ran down the stairs her frantic eyes scanning the floor, the drops diminishing as they led to the front door. When she saw it hanging open, the wood casing splintered, she started to scream.

CATCH UP.

Lasser was in the process of ordering a Big Mac meal when his phone began to chime, handing over a tenner he scrambled in the pocket of his jacket.

'What drink would you like with that?' The girl smiled at him through the tiny window.

'Strawberry milk shake, please.'

'And would you like...'

'No thanks, love,' he pulled the mobile free. 'Patrick my man, what can I do for you?'

Thirty seconds later he slammed the car into gear and screeched off the car park, the young girl stood perplexed with the brown paper bag in hand. He shot out in front of a white transit and slapped on the siren before hurtling past a line of queuing traffic. Fossey had said he was on his way to the Fotheringays. Apparently, Susan had been unable to get in touch with her husband, according to her, he was out on the combine and not answering his phone. Lasser edged his way through the traffic lights and then crashed through the gears, the car bulleting forward.

Once clear of the town centre he opened the taps, surging over the Canal Bridge and heading out into the countryside.

Three cigarettes later, he pulled up in front of the farmhouse. Fossey must have made good time; his dust covered Range Rover parked at an angle. The front wheels had slid onto the lawn, the driver's door hanging open. He climbed out just as Susan came around the corner of the house, Fossey had his arm around her shoulder. As soon as she spotted Lasser she broke free and ran toward him.

'You have to find her, please God, you have to look for her,' her eyes were frantic, her face twisted in anguish.

He glanced at Fossey who looked back at him with a bleak expression.

'Try and stay calm, Susan, and tell me what happened.'

'Just look at the door,' she pointed a shaking finger at the splintered woodwork.

Lasser bent down for a closer look, he could see where the wood had been pushed back, whoever had gained entry had used a narrow jemmy to force the door.

'You're sure she isn't with her father?' It always paid to get the stupid questions out of the way.

'She isn't there, I've just spoken to David,' her voice trembled with emotion. 'I found blood in the bedroom and some on the stairs. I was only gone a couple of hours,' she started to cry, twisting the crumpled paper in her hands, her breathing irregular, laboured.

Lasser moved through the open door and into the lounge. Inside, the room was cool, a haven from the blistering sun. He weaved his way around the furniture and started to climb the stairs, halfway up he spotted the first small bloodstain. He strode over the step and continued to climb. When he reached the landing, he turned right and followed the irregular pattern, small droplets no bigger than a five pence piece trailed into the bedroom. Standing in the doorway he looked around the room, the shattered photo frames on the floor, the lamp in the corner, over near the dresser the stain was much bigger, yet somehow paler than the others. Lasser crouched to his knees, the blood had seeped into the weave and spread, dipping his head he sniffed at the wet patch, the copper smell of blood mingled with the tart scent of urine. He pulled the phone from his pocket and rang the station, the cavalry would be there within the hour but with the way things were panning out, the cavalry might consist of nothing more than a couple of constables on mountain bikes.

Walking over to the window he looked out, it must be nice to wake up every morning and look out onto an ever-changing landscape that somehow never changed at all. It appeared the lies told four decades earlier were finally coming home to roost. Turning, he spotted the crumpled photograph at the side of the bed.

He remembered thinking it had been hard to picture Ronnie as a *'jack the lad'* after all he was an old man lying in a hospital bed, his face devoid of colour, the flesh hanging from his skinny frame like an ill-fitting suit. However, the man in the photo belied that image; here was Ronnie in the prime of life, a wide carefree smile splitting his suntanned face, hair black and glossy. He had his arms draped around the woman's neck, the left hand brushing her breast. When he looked up Susan was standing in the doorway, Fossey behind her, his hands resting on her shoulders.

'He's got her hasn't he?'

Lasser walked around the bed and held out the photograph. 'Is this your mother, Susan?'

She didn't look at the image, her eyes staring away into a world filled with pain.

'Susan?' Lasser prompted.

Her eyes refocused. 'No, it's not my mother but you need to be out there looking for my daughter, not standing here trying to dig up dirt.'

'I understand how you feel but...'

Anger flared in her eyes, sweeping away all other emotion. *'You can't understand how I feel, how dare you stand there and tell me that!'*

Fossey rested his hand on her arm. 'Take it easy, Susan, he's trying to help.'

She spun around, her hair whipping over her shoulder. 'He isn't interested in Jenna, he doesn't care about what happens to her. All he's bothered about is some bloody old photograph, how is that helping my daughter?'

'So, you don't know who she is?'

She turned slowly. 'It's Emma Wickham, so how does that help you, what difference does that scrap of knowledge make to all this?' she spat the words at him. 'You're no different to those bastard reporters. All you're interested in is trying to twist things, so you can make ludicrous links that don't exist.'

'I'm sorry you feel that way but believe me I do care, I...'

'Don't lie to me!' she screamed. 'As far as you're concerned this is just another piece of evidence, she's not a human being to you, she's just another piece in the puzzle.'

Lasser looked down at his shoes, trying to keep his own anger in check. 'Just tell me one thing; do you have any idea why someone would want to target your daughter?'

Her eyes sprang wide. *'Target?'*

Fossey moved into the doorway. 'You don't know that for sure.'

Lasser ignored him. 'When we were at the hospital I asked you if you knew about Emma Wickham and you said no.'

'What are you talking about, what has any of this got to do with anything?' she looked at Lasser as if she couldn't comprehend the stupidity of the man standing before her.

'It has to do with this woman,' he held up the photo. 'And your father.'

'Get out,' her voice was clipped, dripping venom.

'Why would someone target this house, Susan, I mean, they haven't taken anything...'

'My daughter's been taken, you bloody fool!'

'Losing your rag solves nothing.' Lasser said.

'Losing my rag,' her voice was incredulous. 'You think I'm throwing a little tantrum, over-reacting like a hysterical woman who can't control her emotions!'

'Susan!' They heard thundering steps on the stairs, the next instant she spun away and fell into the waiting arms of her husband.

'It looks like they used a jemmy, boss.'

Lasser was standing at the front of the house looking out over fields. 'Yeah, Carl, I figured as much.'

'Do you think it's the same guy?'

'No doubt about it.'

Carl scratched at his chin. 'Jesus, he's running rings around us.'

Lasser watched as a buzzard swept across the field, wings outstretched, riding the warm air, the blue sky segmented by hulking black clouds. 'How are things panning out at Radfield's place?'

'Well, we got a partial boot print, in fact it matches the one we found down by the side of the lake.'

Lasser pulled out his cigarettes. 'That's something I suppose.'

'In fact when they got the dog in, he followed the scent up through the woods.'

Lasser turned, the cigarette hanging from his mouth the lighter held in his right hand. 'And?'

Carl shrugged. 'Dogs are fucked when they come to water, boss, you know that.'

'Water?'

'Yeah, the canal runs along the top edge of the woods, Colin reckons he must have tossed the head into the water.'

'What did Simms make of it all?'

'They've got frogmen up there now but sooner them than me. I mean, can you imagine swimming around in that shitty water looking for a head.'

Suddenly, he thought back to what Michael had said, a big fucker with these weird ball things hanging from his keys. *'Fuck me,'* he muttered.

Carl frowned. 'You OK, boss?'

'He has them in case he drops the keys into the water.'

'I'm sorry, you've lost me?'

Lasser looked at him, the flicker of a grin on his face. 'Michael Jones said he saw someone walking through the woods while he was waiting to pay Radfield a visit. He reckons he had a bunch of keys attached to his rucksack and there were a couple of rubber or cork balls hanging from them.'

Carl looked at Lasser as if he'd finally lost the plot.

'The fucker lives on a canal barge, if he drops the keys into the water then the cork stops them from sinking.'

Carl raised an eyebrow. 'But what makes you think this man's the killer?'

'You said yourself the dog lost the scent when he reached the water.'

'Well, yeah but loads of people go walking in the woods; he could have been going anywhere.'

'Don't be so negative. I mean, Jones was hiding in the woods waiting for it to go dark and this guy was the only person he saw, he was heading away from the house and toward the canal, carrying a rucksack.'

'So, what are you going to do?'

'Get up there and take a look around.'

Carl pulled out a pair of latex gloves from his pocket. 'And what about me?'

'Find out if the blood belongs to Jenna Fotheringay, you never know we might get lucky, perhaps she managed to draw blood before he took her.'

'What do you reckon her chances are?'

Lasser thought for a few moments. 'I think she's still alive but for how long is anyone's guess, if anything turns up you can get me on my mobile.'

Carl nodded. 'Straight away, boss.'

MEETINGS IN STRANGE PLACES

When the first smattering of rain hit the windscreen the man smiled and started the engine before flicking on the wipers, the blade smearing grey dust and grime across the glass. He glanced into the back of the van. The girl was looking up at him, her eyes huge in the gloom, long blonde hair hanging loose. Turning away, he watched as the summer downpour intensified. In the distance, he could see the blurred grey green smudge of the forest, the conical roof of the needle house jutting out from the centre of the trees. He knew Radfield Manor was hidden away in the distance, the local news had been full of the fact that Ashley Radfield had been murdered, he just wished he could have been there watching the police as they stood around scratching their heads. However, he'd had more important things to do. Before he had died Ashley Radfield had begged, pleaded, squirmed like a dog, and boy had he talked, couldn't shut the fucker up. Yet threaded within the garbled nonsense, the man had picked out some startling revelations. He smiled as he conjured up the memory of Radfield trying to twist his head away, his eyes screwed tight in fear had sprung open as he felt the cold sliver of steel against his throat. Then the man had seen it in his eyes, the realisation that he was going to die and the body had gone limp as if suddenly resigned to his fate. Fucking weakling, giving up life so easily, so readily, it made you wonder how the Radfields had ever managed to get on in life. When he was dead, he had taken the time to look around the house, the peeling silk wallpaper, the mothballed rooms, he had even thought of torching the place. He patted the dog that lay stretched out on the passenger seat, truth was Radfield had led him to the Fotheringays which was good, in fact it was more than good, it was life affirming. After all what was the point of having a vendetta if there was no one left to hunt? He could hear muffled groans coming from the girl, sounding like a mantra. Ignoring her, he pulled out the binoculars and trained them on the woods, making a slight adjustment he swept them to the right, he could see the canal running along the embankment then vanishing from view as it threaded its way between the valley. Sliding down the side window, he twisted his head and raised the glasses again, the canal reappeared for about two hundred yards. He could see the red strip of the narrow boat moored to the bank. A figure was walking along the towpath, a small black dog dashing off in front and then someone in a yellow high visibility vest came into view, closely followed by two more. He frowned and zoomed in on the small group, his hand shaking slightly causing the people to jitter, the blue strip on the back of the jackets had the word ‘police’ stencilled in silver. He lowered the glasses, for the first time a realisation dawned on him that the police might not be as stupid as he imagined.

For a few seconds he felt a flicker of panic bloom like some wild animal slamming against the bars of a cage, frantic to break out and flee. The man glanced over his shoulder, the girl had balled herself into the corner of the small space, the sight of her had a calming effect, she wasn’t an impulse she was family.

'Right, Spenner, I want you to find out who owns this boat.'

'How do I do that, sir?'

'There's a licence in the window, see if there's a phone number and if there is, then ring the bloody thing.'

Spenner blushed and headed over to the boat pulling out a small note pad as he went.

The narrow towpath was clogged with police officers, milling around trying to look as if they had some purpose in being there. The last thing any of them wanted was to be singled out by Simms; his face was florid with frustration all he needed was a spark to send him into the stratosphere. Lasser was crouched by the side of the boat, trying to find a gap in the curtains so he could peer inside.

'Lasser!'

'Yes, sir,' he stood up just as Spenner began to jot down the phone and serial number. Simms gave a twitch of his head and began to walk away down the path, avoiding the puddles that had quickly formed after the downpour. When they were about twenty feet from the boat, he stopped and turned.

'Are you sure about this?' he nodded toward the barge. 'I mean, Michael Jones could hardly be classed as a reliable witness, especially considering the fact that at present we have him banged up.'

Lasser looked down at his mud-spattered shoes. 'He only described the man, he has no idea about the connection...'

'To be honest, Sergeant, neither do I.'

Simms listened as Lasser explained everything, occasionally his wiry eyebrow would flick upwards in surprise, apart from that he showed no emotion. When Lasser finished, Simms looked out at the water, a couple of ducks bobbed on the choppy surface. 'So, you think that this Ronnie Fotheringay has a son and he's the one responsible for this?'

Lasser nodded. 'I think that's why he's taken the girl.'

'Explain?'

Lasser took a moment to get things straight in his mind. 'Now the Radfields are dead, I think he's turning his attention to the Fotheringays.'

'You think he's aware of what went on between his mother and Ronnie?'

'Some of this is still guesswork, but it seems strange that a few hours after Ashley Radfield is murdered the killer turns up and takes the girl.'

'So Radfield spilled the beans?' Simms grunted.

'Well, I know I would if some maniac was holding a bloody big knife to my throat, I'd try and say anything to keep myself alive.'

Simms nodded. 'It sounds plausible, but...'

'Sir!' Spenner came striding toward them.

'What have you got?'

'I've just been onto British Waterways, I spoke to the department that deals...'

'Stop wittering, Spenner, and tell me what they said.' Simms snarled.

Spenner cleared his throat. 'The boat is registered to a Mr James Wickham.'

Lasser thrust his hands into his pockets, to keep them from punching the air.

Simms gave a curt snap of his head, as if this latest news was no surprise. 'Right, Sergeant, I want access to that boat. Now.'

Lasser resisted the urge to run but only just, he climbed onto the back, the small twin doors were locked a padlock threaded through the clasp 'Anyone got a crowbar?' Blank faces peered back at him. 'For God's sake, will one of you go and grab one from the van?'

You had to give Spenner his dues, as soon as he heard the request; he was off down the towpath, his long legs catapulting him along at a furious pace. Lasser noticed one or two of his colleagues smirking.

'Something funny, Watson?' he asked.

Watson looked about the same age as Spenner but there was something of the schoolyard bully about him, he had the same mean eyes and slab like forehead that Donald Fletcher sported.

'What do you mean, sir?' he asked, an innocent frown on his face, his eyes full of insolence.

'Don't fuck me about, sunshine. I want tape set up, twenty yards in either direction, see to it,' he snapped.

The men began to disperse; Watson glared and stalked off, leaving Simms standing alone on the bank. 'It looks as if you were right, Sergeant.'

'Well, until we actually get our hands on the bastard, I'm taking nothing for granted.'

'Wise man,' he looked at Lasser and smiled, his face full of weariness. 'Now we need to find out if he lives here permanently or if he has a house somewhere. And the bugger must have a car or a van.'

'Yes, sir.'

'Black, come here.'

A thickset officer walked over, hair shaved short, fat face sweating. 'I want to know everything about James Wickham, where he lives, what car he drives, where he works, absolutely bloody everything and I want it ASAP, understood?'

'Sir' Black turned away and pulled the two way up to his mouth, head tilted, turning his two chins into three.

Spenner appeared from the undergrowth and began to sprint toward them brandishing the crow bar as he ran. 'There you go, sir.'

'Thanks, Spenner,' placing the bar behind the clasp Lasser yanked down, two, three, four times and the lock clattered to the floor. He pulled open the doors and climbed down the three narrow steps that led to the tiny engine room, a faint smell of diesel laced the stale air. Moving along the narrow passageway, Lasser passed a small bunk on the left, a sleeping bag rolled up neatly on top of a thin mattress. Yanking open the curtains, he peered down the length of the boat.

'Anyone home, Sergeant?' Simms voice sounded loud in the narrow confines of the boat.

He slid open a small door, showing a portable toilet and shower space. 'No luck!'

The boat swayed slightly as Simms climbed on board, a few seconds later his boss appeared.

'It looks like our friend likes to keep things neat and tidy,' he said.

Lasser pulled open a couple of cupboard doors, one had a solitary tin of beans on the shelf the other was empty. 'There's no way he's living here, at least not on a permanent basis.'

Simms crouched down and opened the door of the small wood burning stove, the grate was spotless. 'I get the feeling our friend is very meticulous.'

Lasser looked out of the window, it was surprising how high the water level was, the two ducks reappeared and paddled past. He resisted the urge to pull out his cigarettes and spark up, when he had been snapping off the lock he had imagined finding Jenna alive and well, the hero of the hour, discovering evidence that would lead them straight to the killer. Now, as he looked around the narrow space he realised that Simms was right, this bastard wasn't one for leaving clues.

'Right, we'll get forensics in here, see if they can find anything, if he has been spending time here then he must have left traces.' Simms said.

Lasser loosened his tie. 'I wonder if it's worth hanging fire before we get them in.'

Simms pulled the cap from his head and gave his scalp a quick scratch. 'You think he might show up?'

'It's a possibility; I mean, he must have left the boat moored here for a reason.'

Simms slid open a small overhead draw and peered inside and then closed it with a sigh. 'From the look of this place he either doesn't come here often or he makes sure he cleans the place every time he leaves,' he checked his watch. 'Right, we'll give it a few hours; if he doesn't show we get them in.'

'Right, sir.'

'We need to clear the area and get a couple of teams in place, before it gets dark.'

'I'll see to it,' he made his way outside, the wind had picked up, sending the black clouds scuttling across the sky.

Five minutes later, the tape had been removed from the towpath and Lasser was looking for the best place for concealment, it was going to be a long night.

They were crawling over the boat, invading his space, fucking with him; the copper with the dark hair had smashed his way onto the boat and then disappeared inside as if he had a right to be there, Cunt! He twisted in the seat, she was lying still, her back turned to him, the pale yellow T-shirt had ridden up showing the curve of her hip, they were all cunts every last one of them. The filth in the yellow jackets were walking along the towpath one of them picked up the police sign as he passed, they were so obvious it was laughable. They would hide in the grass, skulk amongst the trees, waiting to ambush him, weaklings, ineffectual boys trying to do a man's job. Yes well, let them waste their time, while they were spending the night getting cold and wet, he would be busy elsewhere.

Everything was in place, there were ten officers concealed at the bottom of the embankment, spread out over a distance of fifty yards, another fifteen hidden in the woods. Lasser had managed to salvage a waterproof jacket from the back of one of the vans before it had been driven away from the immediate area. The sky overhead was squally with rain clouds; he flicked up the collar and leaned against the trunk of a huge oak. Just one break, just one piece of good luck and they would have him, he heard a rustling sound to his left, Simms emerged out of the gloom, a tartan scarf had materialised around his neck, matching the flat cap.

'James Wickham owns a house in Southport,' his voice sounded triumphant, his eyes suddenly sparking in the half-light.

'So what are we doing about it?'

Simms checked his watch. 'Merseyside CID should just about be kicking his door in as we speak.'

Bloody typical, you spend all this time busting a gut and some scouser comes along and steals your thunder. 'What else do we know about him?'

'He's thirty-nine, spent his younger years in the army...'

'That's why he keeps everything clean and tidy.'

'Since leaving the forces he's moved around a lot, he settled in Southport seven months ago.'

'Wife and kids?'

'Apparently not.'

'So what do we do now?'

Simms tucked the scarf into his jacket, adjusted his cap. 'Stay here until we hear from the Liverpool boys. In an ideal world they'll find him at home, and the girl will be alive.'

Lasser fished out his cigarettes and then remembered who was standing a couple of feet away.

Simms waved a hand. 'It's OK, have your cigarette, you've earned it.'

Lasser didn't need telling twice. 'Do we know what he does for a living?'

'His last job was a fitness instructor, he worked in the Lake District, you know the type of thing, bonding weekends for companies that have more money than sense.'

It was no wonder he had proved so hard to track down, in places like this he would be in his element, sneaking around in the undergrowth pretending he was on manoeuvres, Hopkins hadn't stood a chance.

Simms yawned and rubbed at his eyes. 'Right, I'm going to head over to Radfields, I've had portable incident room set up in the grounds, as soon as I find out how it's gone you'll be the first to know.'

'Thanks.'

As he walked past, he patted Lasser on the shoulder. 'Well done again, Lasser, good work.'

With that, he wandered off between the trees, after a few seconds he was lost from site.

Lasser smoked the cigarette down to the stump before dragging his phone from his pocket, he scrolled through the menu until Fossey's number appeared in the window; his finger hovered over the call button. Sod it, he pressed the green phone sign and waited.

DARK NIGHT OF THE SOUL

David Fotheringay stalked the room, occasionally he would cross to the window and look out as if he expected to see his daughter come strolling up the drive. Susan sat rooted to the sofa, her eyes fixed on the blackened grate of the fire. When Fossey's phone began to chime, she looked up confused, as if she had never heard the sound before.

He checked the number and headed toward the front door; he didn't answer the call until he was striding away from the house. 'Any news?'

'His name is James Wickham.'

It was said without a hint of 'I told you so.' a statement of fact, nothing more.

'What about Jenna?'

'We don't know yet.'

Fossey walked away from the house his feet crunching on the gravel. 'So, what's happening now?'

'At the moment I'm up in the woods waiting for my boss to get in touch, apparently Wickham has a house in Southport and let's just say we're hoping to find him at home.'

'Right,' somewhere in the darkness a curlew screeched.

'How are they bearing up?' Lasser asked.

'Same as anyone in their position, they want to be out there looking, yet they know it's pointless.'

'What about Ronnie?'

'David rang the hospital earlier; they said there was no change.' When he turned he saw Susan standing in the doorway, staring out at him, he raised a hand, but she didn't respond. 'Listen, Lasser, is there anything else you can tell me?'

'Come on, pal, by rights I shouldn't even be ringing you....'

'I know and don't think it isn't appreciated but when I tell them they're going to want to know everything.'

Fossey heard the sigh down the line.

'He has a boat on the canal but he's not there, we broke in earlier to check it out. But just in case they have no luck at the house we thought it best to hang around...'

'In case he shows up?'

'Yeah, but to be honest I'm not sure he will, it's registered to Wickham but it doesn't look like he uses it on a regular basis.'

'Perhaps he's just used it as a base while he scouted out the area.' Fossey offered.

'I don't doubt it.'

Susan walked slowly down the steps, moving slowly toward him, a shadow in the darkness.

'He took a risk though; I mean, you can hardly class a canal barge as an appropriate getaway vehicle.' Fossey said.

'As far as he's concerned there is no risk, I mean, if Ronnie had kept quiet about the blackmail then we'd be no nearer to catching this guy, there would have been no way to link him to Radfield.'

'Listen, Susan's on her way...'

'No problem, as soon as I hear anything I'll let you know.'

'Thanks,' the line went dead.

'Who were you talking to?'

She looked shattered, dark circles smudged beneath her eyes, a woman whose life was unravelling into oblivion.

'It was Lasser,' he paused, 'they think they know the name of the man who took Jenna.'

It was like watching a spent candle suddenly splutter back to life. *'What! I mean, who... who is he?'*

'James Wickham.'

She took a step backward, her features melding with the shadows. *'Wickham!'*

'They know where he lives, in fact the police are on their way there now, so...'

'Tell me,' her eyes only moments before listless and devoid of any hope suddenly appeared energised.

'I don't know the specifics...'

'Well, get back on the phone and tell him that I have to know,' her anger bloomed; all the fear and frustration swept away leaving only an acute sense of fury. She reached out and snatched the sleeve of his jacket. *'You make him tell me!'*

'Susan, I can't; besides I don't think Lasser has an actual address.

'Ring him now!'

'What's going on?' David appeared out of the gloom.

Susan turned. 'Tell him, David.'

'Tell him what?'

'They know who's taken her and he won't tell me where he lives.'

When Fossey saw the look on his face, any hope he had of David being the voice of reason was blasted away. 'You know who he is?'

Fossey held up his hands. 'Lasser gave me a name but that's all.'

'What about an address?'

'I was just trying to explain to Susan, I don't know.'

'Where's Lasser now?' David asked, he kept clenching his fists, his chest heaving as if he had just staggered through the red tape after a gruelling marathon.

'Look, David, he only rang because he thought you deserved to know. By rights he shouldn't have even done that, if his superiors find out... '

'I don't give a shit about his superiors, where is he?'

'I can't...'

Fossey felt himself propelled backwards. *'Tell me or I'll beat it out of you!'*

'David, let him go!' Susan snatched at her husband's shoulder; he shrugged her off and carried on pushing until Fossey slammed up against the fence.

'Where is he?' each word was clipped with fury.

Fossey resisted the urge to defend himself, keeping his hands by his sides, the last thing he wanted to do was infuriate the man further.

'I don't know where he lives.'

'That isn't what I asked; I want you to tell me where Lasser is!'

'No.'

'What do you mean no!' he gave Fossey a shake, his head bounced off the wooden fence.

Fossey could see Susan from the corner of his eye, hands held up to her mouth, her face a mask of fear and hope.

He tried to ease away but David slammed him back.

'OK, David, let's say I tell you, what will you do then?'

'I'll find him and make him tell me where she is,' it was said with utter certainty, his eyes blazed with murderous intent.

'Listen to me, if you do that then you could be putting your daughter's life in further danger.'

Susan pushed at her husband until he took a backward step. 'What do you mean?'

'Wickham has a house...'

'Who's Wickham?' David asked.

'They think he's the one responsible for all this.' Fossey watched David closely; it was obvious from his response that the name meant nothing to him.

'He has a house, where?' Susan slipped in between the two men, turning her back on her husband.

'Southport,' Fossey paused, 'though apparently he has a narrow boat up on the canal, that's where Lasser is now.'

'Right,' David spun on his heels.

'David, wait!' Fossey eased Susan to one side. 'If the police don't find him at home, they're hoping he might return to the boat. If you go up there then it might alert him to the fact that the police are waiting.'

He stopped and turned, his face in turmoil, a father desperate to protect his only child.

'David, we can't risk it.' Susan whispered.

'But I have to do something,' his shoulders were dragged down, all the anger seemed to evaporate, leaving a man who looked damaged, broken.

She reached out and took hold of his hand. 'I know, love, but he's right, we have to let the police handle this,' she paused, 'for Jenna's sake.'

RARE FIND

When the van lurched to one side, Jenna groaned in pain. Every part of her ached, the right side of her face felt as if someone had stamped on it, she tentatively slid out her tongue and touched it against her swollen lip, wincing at the raw sting.

Rolling slowly onto her back she twisted her neck until she could see the back of his head, dirty blonde hair brushing the collar of a dark camouflage jacket, the wipers swiping back and forth across the glass. She tried to clear her mind of the fear but it seemed to fill every part of her like a virus running rampant through her system. When the dog suddenly draped its head over the passenger seat, she nearly screamed in shock.

'You're awake then?' he asked, without turning. She held her breath; the dog looked at her and whimpered, before licking its lips.

She shuffled her way across the metal floor, until her back hit the tailgate; the sour tang of her own urine mixed with the scent of wet dog filled the small space.

Suddenly the van stopped, she heard the ratchet sound of the handbrake, and then the man turned in his seat, peering into the back, his face wreathed in shadow.

'Do you know who I am?'

'No,' the word came out as a hoarse whisper, her throat parchment dry, she shifted slightly, the cord binding her wrist tightened.

'Are you sure?' he flicked on the interior light. 'Go on, take a good look.'

Jenna screwed up her eyes at the sudden onslaught.

'Take your time.'

She blinked, once, twice, until her eyes gradually became accustomed to the light. She was sure she had never seen his face before, his eyes were pale blue, his skin looked tanned as if he had spent a lot of time in the outdoors. His blonde hair was unruly, as if he never considered running a comb through it.

His face split into a wide grin. 'So, what do you think, do I look familiar?'

She shook her head and then wished she hadn't, for a few seconds her vision blurred, pain rattled around behind her eyes.

The smile vanished; he frowned as if disappointed by her response. 'No family resemblance?'

'Look, I don't know who you are...'

'Quite right, you don't.'

He was insane, she was being held captive by a maniac and whatever she said, he would twist to suit his own purpose. There would be no pleading with him, no rationalising; the realisation that he would kill her slammed home, her heart juddered as she gasped for breath. Jenna gripped her legs together tightly, trying to keep control of her bladder. This was the man who had killed Michael's brother; he was the one who had murdered the police officer and Ashley Radfield. Human remains, those were the words Hopkins had used, it seemed a lifetime since he'd stood in their kitchen full of his own self-importance. Now he was dead and when they found her body that was how reporters would refer to her, nothing more than, *'human remains.'*

'Please...' she whispered, inside she felt a flicker of disgust at the whining tone of her voice.

The man tilted his head and looked at her quizzically. 'Please, what?'

'I don't know what I'm meant to have done but if you let me...'

'Go?' he paused as if pondering some great problem. 'You promise to keep all this secret, is that what you're telling me? You'll simply return home and explain to your parents that you decided to go out for a stroll and lost track of time, and they'll say 'it doesn't matter, there's a killer out there, but hey ho you're back now.'

'I...'

He laughed. 'Come on, Jenna, think how that sounds.'

She felt the colour drain from her face. ‘How do you know my name?’

He reached across the seat and stroked the dogs head. ‘All this has been something of a shock to me to, Jenna.’

She cringed as he spoke her name again; somehow, it made her feel even more vulnerable. Suddenly she thought of her grandad, he could be dead or maybe he was awake and asking where she was. What would happen when he was told that she had been taken, she screwed up her eyes and tried to breath, tried to think. If he wanted her dead then surely he would have done it by now, it sounded rational though in reality she knew it was a flawed premise. He was in control, any idea of escape was farcical, she gritted her teeth, felt the pain in her jaw and relished it, stay calm, keep focused and you might get a chance.

‘What are you talking about?’ she asked, trying to inject some confidence into her voice, if she sounded like a victim chances are he would treat her like one.

The man smiled. ‘I mean, it’s not every day you find out you have a family that you knew nothing about.’

Inside her head something twisted, seized gears suddenly straining to move. *‘Family?’*

‘Mm, I don’t have it all worked out yet but I’m fairly sure I’m your uncle.’

Jenna felt her legs twitch, she tried to comprehend the words but it felt surreal, the van closed in around her everything intensified, she could hear the rain bouncing off the roof, could smell her own stale sweat, his smile grew until it appeared like a red slash across his face.

‘That’s not true!’

‘Well, the woman in the photograph is my mother and I presume the ‘Farmer Joe’ draped all over her is your grandfather, which ultimately makes him my dear old dad.’ His voice was conversational, just two long lost relatives catching up on the family gossip. ‘Tell me, Jenna, is the old cunt still alive?’

At first, she thought she'd misheard him, his smile was bright and cheery but the look in his eyes made her push herself back into the cold metal of the tailgate, she tried to break contact and found it impossible. He regarded her with eyes that lacked any shred of compassion, she felt like a lab rat pinned to the dissecting board.

'Well, is he?'

'Leave me alone,' she whimpered.

'Come on, there's no need to be like that, blood's thicker than water, you should know that.'

'He's not your father,' she spat, for a fraction of a second all thought of her own safety was obliterated by blind fury.

'You love him don't you?'

'I would have known, he would have told me.'

'You think so?'

'Yes!' she hissed.

'So, he told you he was fucking my mother, did he?' his smile widened when he saw the look of shock on her face. 'I see he didn't, that's the problem; you can never tell when someone is telling you the truth. In fact, my own mother was a lying cold-hearted bitch.'

'I don't know what you're talking about.'

'Course you don't, but you will.'

Jenna riddled into a sitting position. 'I want to go home.'

His face shifted, he looked like a spoiled child, just before they stamp their foot in temper. 'My mother died late last year; she spent the last few weeks in a hospice. I tell you, Jenna, you wouldn't have recognised her. You saw the picture, you saw how beautiful she was...'

'I don't care, she...'

'Shut the fuck up,' the terrible darkness in his eyes slid down like the blade of a black guillotine.

She swallowed the panic and drew her legs up in fear, don't talk, don't provoke.

When he began to speak again, it was as if nothing had happened. 'I don't think you could ever say we were close, I mean, when you're brought up on a narrow boat you tend to get under one another's feet, not enough room.' He smiled again; the anger gone like a grass fire that had temporarily died down. 'Back then nobody bothered about us, if you lived on a barge you might as well have been invisible. I never went to school, never learned to read and write properly; of course, when you're a kid you can't imagine a world where something like that will be important. As for my dear mother, let's just say the bottle took precedent over any motherly instinct she might have once possessed. She'd disappear for days on end, didn't leave me any food let alone money to buy any.'

Jenna shivered as she watched his lips mouthing the words.

'I used to snare rabbits and catch fish from the canal; otherwise I'd have starved to death,' he tilted his head. 'Do you believe me, Jenna?'

'I don't know.'

'Very wise, you see you're getting the hang of it but it's the truth. I mean, you know what it's like living out here, isolated, the nearest shop miles away. It's hard to make friends, you feel cut off from the rest of the world. Imagine it back then, we didn't own a car, I couldn't jump on the nearest bus and go into town,' he turned and flicked off the wipers. 'So, I used to wait until dark and then go to the nearest farm and nick a few eggs, grab some milk but I wasn't stupid, I only took what I needed that way I didn't draw attention to myself, can you understand that?'

She nodded, despite her terror she found herself engrossed in what he was saying; besides the longer he talked the longer she stayed alive.

'One winter I nearly died; I didn't see my mother for three months. You have no idea how cold it gets on the water, especially when you have no wood to burn. I couldn't catch any fish because the canal was frozen and the thought of going out at night to try and steal food became a nightmare. I had visions of dying out there in the snow, I used to dream of foxes closing in while I lay welded to the ground. Not nice, Jenna, not nice at all.'

She began to imagine the life he'd been forced to lead, a sliver of sympathy fluttered in her mind and she crushed it before it had chance to grow.

'I was fifteen when I left, of course the booze had a grip on her by then, and it was obvious that she didn't give a fuck about me. So, I set fire to the barge, just to spite her.' he smiled at the memory; Jenna thought she saw the flicker of remembered flames in his eyes; he waved a hand in the air. 'You can imagine the rest, a bright girl like you; I got in trouble with the police, blah, blah, blah. Joined the army, which was the making of me. I see from the look in your eye that you'd dispute that, Jenna, but that's not really important.'

'What's all this got to do with my family?'

'I like that, straight to the point, no fucking about, you remind me of', he paused and smiled 'me.' The dog panted, it looked as if it was laughing at the quip. 'I didn't see my mother for over twenty years; in fact I thought she might have even been on the boat when I torched it. Either way it didn't matter, I had a new family; the army, I needed nothing else,' he leaned forward over the seat. 'Can you imagine, Jenna, a kid like me with no mother to speak of and a father who had run out on me?' He stopped and pulled out a cigarette, when he struck the match she noticed his hand shaking as he touched it to the paper. 'You see that's what she'd always told me, so I knew no different. But the army,' he paused a look of genuine pleasure on his face, 'they took me in, made me believe in myself, gave me a set of skills that have served me well.'

Jenna cringed, a set of skills that had left him with no moral compass, it sounded like the army was just one huge dysfunctional family taking broken and damaged individuals and turning them into psychopaths.

'When I was a kid I used to hate to leave the boat, twenty years later I'd been all over the world, mind-blowing, that's the only way to describe how my life changed,' he slid down the window to let out the smoke. 'Trouble is nothing lasts forever,' his voice was heavy with regret, he sniffed and carried on. 'So, after twenty years I was out, and for the first time in two decades I thought about my mother. I'd like to be able to tell you that I forgave her but all this is about honesty, Jenna. The first time in the hospice I walked straight past her, you see I was looking for a beautiful woman with black hair. Instead I found a woman who already looked dead, cancer does that to you, it shows you your own death.'

'I'm sorry,' the words slipped from her lips, though it was as if someone else had spoken them.

He looked at her, a frown creasing his forehead, then he relaxed and nodded. 'Don't misunderstand me, I'm not after sympathy, I'm not built that way. Besides at first she didn't recognise me either, the last time she'd seen me I'd been fifteen but eventually I got through to her.'

'Did she apologise for what had happened?'

'Actually, she did but then again people will say anything when they're close to death.'

Another rusty gear clanged in her head, he winked at her as if he could see exactly what she was thinking.

'No, Jenna, I didn't kill her, I could have done, I won't lie to you I wanted to but there was no need the cancer was seeing to that.'

'You make it sound as if you were glad she was dying.'

'I was glad to find her alive; it gave her the chance to unburden herself.'

'About what?'

'Lift up your arms.'

'What?'

'Your arms, Jenna, hold them up.'

'Why?' she could see his face ripple and change, his eyes began to cloud, his lips compressed into a thin line.

'I won't hurt you.'

It felt as if she had heavy weights attached to the end of her arms, when they were outstretched she could feel the vibration in her shoulders, she could see her hands shaking. A second later, he stretched over the seat and grabbed her wrist, when his right hand came into view and she saw the blade she tried frantically to pull her hand away and found that she couldn't, his grip tightened. She screwed her eyes closed, before she could open her mouth to scream she felt the pressure around her wrist vanish. When she looked, he was back in his seat there was no sign of the knife, the dog slid across the seat and licked his hand.

'Better?'

She looked at the red marks on her wrist, could feel the tingle in her fingers. 'Thank you.'

'Now where was I... ah yes, Mother. You see after a while she started to talk about my old man, something she had hardly ever done before. However, some of the things she said didn't add up, when I was a child she had always insisted that he had been the one who ran out on us but now she started to change her story. I'd always thought he had been a labourer now she said he was a landowner, all very confusing.'

'Maybe she was the one who was confused, I mean, if she was ill...'

'She started to talk about Sam Wickham, the man I had always presumed was my father, it turns out he hadn't simply done a runner he'd gone missing,' he moved in his seat and lit another smoke. 'Of course I didn't just take her word for it, I spent a day at the library, going through the files, believe it or not she was telling the truth.'

'What else did she say?'

He looked at her and smiled. 'Interested now, aren't you?'

'I still don't see what any of this has to do with my family,' she lied.

'Come on, Jenna, I think you know bits and pieces...'

'I don't know anything.'

He pulled hard on the cigarette, peering at her through a cloud of smoke. 'Bear in mind if you choose to lie then I have no further use for you.'

She swallowed and rubbed her hands together, desperately trying to get some feeling back into her fingers. 'I...

'Then she started to talk about the Radfields. I didn't have a clue who they were, after all why would I? By this time the cancer was really starting to take hold, sometimes I would visit and she wouldn't have a clue who I was, other times she would see me as a child. Although, there were the odd occasion when she was lucid and everything was clear in her mind. People get like that when they're being eaten alive. I can remember when I was in the forces we had a padre, he served with us in Bosnia, offered spiritual guidance,' he pulled hard on the cigarette. 'It takes a special kind of person to listen to a soldier talk about how he shot a ten-year-old girl by mistake and then offer solace and compassion. The only vice he had was smoking, it must have been all the stress but he had one after another, you never saw him without a cigarette in his hand. I suppose it was inevitable, in the end he got lung cancer. I went to see him a couple of days before he died, he was busy calling all the other residents *'cunts'* called the nurses *'whores.'* I could see the disgust on their faces but you see they didn't know the real man, they only saw what the cancer had done to him, extremes, see?'

She nodded, she understood and hated herself for it, how was this happening, this man had broken into her home, smashed her in the side of the head and trussed her hands before bungling her into the back of the van. He was responsible for the violent death of three people and yet she was beginning to sympathise with him, understand him, Jenna dug her nails into her forearms in an effort to bring her back to reality.

'One day she told me that Wickham wasn't my father,' he clicked his fingers to emphasise the point. 'Just like that, I didn't believe her at first, she kept talking about Malcolm Radfield, calling him all the names under the sun,' he paused and licked his lips, 'she claimed he raped her.'

She looked up; he had flicked the wipers back on, the view through the window was nothing but blackness.

'I can never remember my mother crying about anything, but she did then.'

'I'm sorry,' she said automatically.

He looked at her in surprise his eyes narrowed for a moment and then he nodded. 'I appreciate that, Jenna, I really do. According to her when she told Sam what had happened he stormed off.'

'And disappeared?'

'You're either very perceptive,' he paused, 'or you've heard this tale before?'

'I haven't, I promise,' she replied hurriedly, afraid to say the wrong thing in case his eyes flared in the darkness.

He blew more smoke out through the window. 'Of course I can't be sure where he went, but I know where I would have gone.'

'So, Malcolm Radfield was your father?' she grasped at the words and pushed them to the front of her mind.

'The day after she told me all this she died, so you see my mother never actually said 'Radfield is your father,' but what conclusion would you have reached?'

'I would have believed her, I mean, if Radfield raped her...'

'It's not an easy thing to come to terms with, finding out you're the product of rape. Of course it would explain why my mother had never really shown me any affection; after all I would have been a constant reminder of what had been done to her.'

She tried to block it out but his words seeped into her brain, she could see him as a young child having to fend for himself, wondering why his mother would disappear for days and weeks on end. Living alone on a canal barge, no food or wood for the burner, no neighbours to call in and check that he was OK. Sitting alone in the dark, as the water around you froze to a ghost white sheet.

'You can understand how angry, it made me?'

His voice brought her out of the stupor. *Ye...yes.'*

'He had to be made to pay.'

'You killed Malcolm Radfield?' her voice cracked as the enormity of her position reasserted itself. She could sympathise all she wanted but when the time came, he would slaughter her without compunction.

He ran a hand across his stubble. 'We had quite the conversation, me and his Lordship.'

She shifted in an effort to ease the ache in her legs. 'Did he admit to what he'd done?'

'Are you cold?'

'A little,' she admitted.

He tossed a heavy tartan throw into the back; Jenna snatched it up and wrapped it around her shoulders, for a few seconds she shook uncontrollably, her arms and legs vibrating beneath the cover as her body tried to generate heat.

'He denied it, I...'

'But he would, I mean, if people had found out it would have ruined him.'

He smiled at her and shook his head. 'Don't be naive, Jenna, people like Radfield don't concern themselves with trivialities like that.'

'But...'

'He tried to say it was consensual, said it was she who made the first move,' he turned the key and the engine rumbled into life then he flicked the heater on before turning back to her. 'You know something, when you're in the army, in a war zone, you soon learn that people lie, it's the default mode of the human race and the only way to get to the truth is by threatening violence.'

She pulled the blanket even tighter around her, dreading what he was going to say next.

'Eventually I persuaded him that clearing his conscience would be beneficial, in the end he admitted the sex part, which was cathartic for him. But you see the really interesting thing was, he still denied being my father...'

'Well, he would...'

He held up a hand and Jenna snapped her mouth closed. 'It's one thing to deny something when you don't feel threatened, to stick to your story when someone is forcing the twin barrels of a twelve bore into your mouth, well that's another thing entirely.'

'You...'

'When I asked him if Sam Wickham had been to see him, he spilled it all out without further prompting from me,' she found herself drawn into the rhythm of his speech. It was bizarre, one minute he sounded as if he were giving evidence in a courtroom, choosing his words carefully to avoid any confusion, the next she could hear the latent hatred in his voice. 'He said when Wickham turned up he was drunk, banging on the door at midnight, demanding to know what had happened. Even as Radfield was telling me, you could see the disbelief in his eyes, hear it in his voice. What right did this low-life scum have to turn up and demand an explanation from a peer of the realm? You see it's ingrained in people like him, they get used to not having to explain their actions, especially to someone like Wickham. He was a commoner who lived on a tatty old barge, with no money, no voice, a piece of shit,' he dragged a hand through his unruly hair, a savage swipe that left it sticking up in all directions.

'So, what did he say had happened?'

'He tried to say that he'd thrown Wickham off his property but I could tell he was lying. Sam Wickham spent his life getting work wherever he could, doing all the donkey work for people like Radfield, building stone walls, working out in the fields in all weathers, hard graft, Jenna.'

'I know.'

He smiled, a wolf's grin. 'I suppose you do. I knew that Radfield wouldn't have been able to 'throw' him from his land, the only heavy lifting his lordship did, was picking up his glass of whisky and his Cuban cigars.'

'So what happened?'

'Malcolm Radfield shot him, he said Wickham had him by the throat and I could see the remembered terror in his eyes, he was a weak, spineless bastard. Wickham said he was going to the police, as he was walking down the drive Radfield shot him in the back of the head.'

'Oh Jesus.'

'He said he put the body in the old workings of a tin mine, you see there'd been an accident a couple of weeks earlier...

'Two men died.'

He paused a vague look of satisfaction in his eyes. 'See, Jenna, you do know things.'

'I...'

'It's alright; none of this is your doing.'

'I remembered reading about it,' she explained hurriedly.

He tossed the cigarette out of the window. 'I'm sure you did.'

He doesn't believe me, he's picking my brains trying to find out how much I know but eventually she knew that the big knife would reappear and this time it wouldn't be to help her. 'It's the truth, I was doing some research into my family history, and I remembered seeing it on one of the micro fiche files that they have in the library.'

He carried on as if he hadn't heard a word she'd said. 'Radfield knew that he was going to have the mine capped, so it was the ideal place to hide the body,' he paused, 'the trouble is somebody saw him.'

Jenna clamped her mouth closed.

'Bear in mind, Jenna, all this information came from a man who knew I wasn't fucking about. I told him about living on the barge, how hard it had been for me but he wasn't interested,' he paused, 'but he listened when I told him how I gutted the boy.'

Jenna felt the bile rise in her throat; she gripped the blanket and pulled it up to her mouth.

'He listened when I told him of the others I'd killed, the girl in Bosnia, the ones I gunned down on active duty.'

'Please, I don't want to hear this.'

He leaned over the back of the seat. 'I know all about how you got the farm, Jenna, I know about the blackmail. Radfield said six months after he killed Sam, he started to see Emma Wickham in the village and guess who she was with?

'Please don't,' she begged, her world splintering around her, the rusty gears were oiled and in full motion, her mind full of images that rattled through her brain like a freight train. She joined the dots; at last, she could see the bigger picture. When she vomited it spilled from her screaming mouth, splattering on the floor of the van, human remains.

THE WAITING GAME

Lasser was hunched at the base of the oak; collar turned up, hair wet through, trying his best to avoid the heavy drizzle that fell from the blackened sky. He could just make out the shape of the barge about twenty feet away, in the distance he could see the flashing red lights of the television mast that stood on top of the moors.

When his phone began to flash, he flipped it open. 'Sir.'

Simms sounded, tired, deflated. *'No luck, Sergeant, the house in Southport was empty.'*

'Shit.'

'Precisely.'

'So, they didn't find anything?'

'I've just come off the phone to the man who led the raid; he said the house was spotless, according to him it didn't look lived in.'

'Then where is he?' Lasser fumbled for his cigarettes, two left, he pushed the pack back into his pocket.

'We have people checking out the camp in Cumbria but to be honest I'm not hopeful.'

Lasser shivered as the rain began to soak through his so-called waterproof jacket. 'It's as if he was expecting this, he knew sooner or later we'd find out who he is and...'

'Regarding that, he's served all over the world, if there was a shit-hole hotspot then he's been there, fighting the good fight.'

'What about a car?'

'A dark blue Land Rover but he could have ditched that by now. We've got road blocks set up on the three main routes that lead out of the area but to be honest, Sergeant, if he wanted to he could probably have gone via another route.'

'I don't think he's interested in leaving the area.'

'It would be the sensible thing to do.' Simms said.

'I realize that but I think the link the Fotheringay family will keep him close.'

'But he has the girl, if he wants to make them suffer then its mission accomplished.'

Lasser shivered as the rain intensified. 'I think he's taken her to find out how much she knows about what went on between the Radfields and her family.'

'Guesswork, we have to have more to go on than bloody guesswork.'

Sod it, Lasser pulled out the penultimate cigarette and lit it, drawing the smoke deep before blowing it out with a sigh, might as well throw the ball back into his court. 'So, what do you want me to do?'

'Do you think he'll put in an appearance at the boat?'

'No, I think he knows we're onto him...'

'How do you come to that conclusion?'

Lasser thought for a couple of seconds before answering. 'I think he's been watching us all along, in my opinion that's why he killed Kitts, he was keeping tabs on the farmhouse when the old guy showed up. It's the same with Hopkins he could have killed Cathy Harper but he didn't, he singled Hopkins out. By rights he should have been miles away from the needle house, he knew we would be crawling all over those woods but he knows he can avoid being seen, after all it's what he's been trained to do.'

'So, you're saying he knows we've been on the boat?'

'I think he does, he's moored it in the only stretch of water that isn't lined with trees, and it's in a gap between the valleys with easy access from the road...'

'That way he can keep an eye on it from a distance.' Simms voice began to come back to life.

'I think he takes the time to check before he does anything.'

'A cautious man.'

Lasser cupped the cigarette trying to keep it away from the persistent downpour. 'Unfortunately, yes.'

'Right, Sergeant, we know he has the girl and we can only presume that when she tells him what she knows, which could be absolutely nothing, then he'll kill her.'

'I agree.'

'Question is what will he do then?'

'He'll probably want to pay the rest of the family a visit, especially Ronnie...'

'You still think he could be the father?'

'Jenna won't be able to help him on that score, but to be honest I don't think it matters.'

'Why do you say that?'

Lasser heard his phone bleep; someone had sent him a message. 'Well, we don't know if Malcolm Radfield actually topped himself...'

'The pathologist said he did, and don't you think we have enough on our plate without conjuring up another victim?'

'Well, either Ashley or his father must have pointed him toward the Fotheringay family, I can't see of any other way he could have made the link.'

Another heavy sigh floated down the phone. *'Right, get over to the Fotheringays, if they're holding anything back I want to know what it is.'*

'I've already tried...'

'Well, try again!'

Lasser winced and moved the phone away from his ear, the bastard nearly perforated his eardrum. 'OK, no problem.'

'Tell them that if they don't cooperate, I'll drag them in for questioning.'

'But...'

'Don't argue with me, you said yourself you thought the mother knew more than she was letting on.'

'That was before her daughter went missing...'

'I don't care, if they're holding out then I want to know why.'

Lasser grimaced, he could see where Simms was coming from but the only one who could clear any of this up was Ronnie, he was the one with the answers the one with the key, the one at deaths door.

'OK, I'll get straight over there.'

The phone went dead, Lasser shivered and pushed himself away from the tree, the mobile beeped again, he pulled out the phone; it was from Fossey, two words, *'Ronnie's awake.'*

CHEWED FINGERNAILS

Fossey had gone back into the house to find Susan standing in the corner, peering through the window into the blackness beyond. David was perched on the sofa, head in hands the sense of despair buoyant in the air between them. 'Look, Sue, you go, I'll wait here.'

She turned away from the window, when she saw Fossey standing in the doorway; she blinked as if she couldn't remember his name. 'My father's awake,' she sounded flat, as if the news was of no real importance.

Fossey breathed a heavy sigh of relief. 'That's good news, Susan.'

'He's asking where we are.' David said, 'I've told her she should go and see him.'

'I can't, I need to be here, besides how can I stand there and tell him what's happened.'

'He has to know, love.'

'He's just had a heart attack, what do you think will happen when he finds out about Jenna?'

'That's why you have to go and explain it to him,' David pleaded.

'I...'

'David's right, it's better coming from you rather than hearing it from another source.'

David glanced across the room and gave a brusque nod. 'If anything happens I'll ring you straight away.'

Susan shook her head, her face set with determination. 'I've told you I'm going nowhere...'

'But...'

'Just leave it will you,' she spat the words at her husband, her eyes charged with anger, 'I'll ring the hospital later and see if I can speak to him.'

'You can't do it over the phone, Sue. I mean, it's your father for God's sake.'

'Would it help if I went in your place?' Fossey asked, trying to diffuse the situation.

'You?'

'Look, I understand completely why you want to stay here, if I were in your place I'd probably feel the same way.'

'What do you think, Sue? David asked.

She looked at Fossey, a cautious look in her eyes, it was as if she were trying to fathom if he had some ulterior motive. 'I don't know.'

'Once he knows the situation, I'm sure he'll understand why you couldn't come.' Fossey said.

It was a full thirty seconds before she replied. 'You'll ring me as soon as you get there?'

Fossey slipped his hand into his pocket and pulled out his car keys. 'Of course I will.'

By the time he made it back through the woods, Lasser was shivering, dumping the waterproof into the boot, he climbed into the car and slapped the heater on full blast.

His stomach rumbled, reminding him that he hadn't eaten anything since the burger that morning. Sodding job, four hours standing in the rain for nothing and now he had to go and grill the grief stricken Fotheringays again. He thought about ringing Fossey then decided against it, after all, Ronnie wasn't going anywhere. Pulling the car out from beneath the dripping trees he drove slowly along the narrow lane; the windscreen began to steam up, so he slid the window down letting in the cool night air. The killer had to be around here somewhere, trouble was there were a thousand places he could be hiding, flicking on the main beam he fished out his last cigarette. If Jenna was still alive it meant that the killer would be burdened to some extent, alone he could probably disappear but with the girl in tow, well at least it would slow him down. He pulled hard on the cigarette, grimacing at the foul taste in his mouth, twenty cigarettes and no food, had left him light headed. In a moment of madness he flicked the cigarette through the window and then immediately regretted it.

As he reached the junction, his mobile began to ring.

'Hello.'

'Hi, serg, it's me.'

He screwed up the empty packet and threw it into the passenger foot well. 'Alright, Cathy, where are you?'

'Just on my way to Fotheringay farm....'

'What for?'

'Simms is sending a fire arms detail to keep an eye on the place and I get to tag along.'

Made sense, if the killer couldn't get the information he wanted from Jenna he might well decide to pay Susan a visit. 'Listen, Cathy, where are you now?'

'Just coming through Hindley.'

'Good, would you call at the Tesco and pick up twenty cigs for me?'

'Sure.'

'Oh and grab me something cheap off the 'whoopsie' shelf will you.'

'What do you like?'

'Just a pie or a sandwich, as long as it's not egg, I don't want to be farting while I'm interrogating the family.'

'You're going to the house,' she sounded surprised. *'I thought you were stuck up in the woods?'*

'Change of plan, Simms wants know if they've been holding out on us.'

'It seems unlikely; I mean, he's got their daughter...'

'True enough but if it gets me out of the *'forest of doom'* then I don't really care.'

'Right I'm just pulling onto Tesco now.'

'OK, I'll meet you at the entrance to the property, about half an hour.'

'No problem,' she paused, *'do you want something to drink as well?'*

Lasser thought for a moment. 'Get us a Red Bull will you.'

He pushed the last piece of the steak slice into his mouth, brushing the crumbs from his pants as he chewed. Cathy watched him as he swallowed before reaching for the chocolate muffin that sat on the dashboard.

'This is above and beyond, Cathy,' he said as he peeled back the wrapper.

On the back seat was a four pack of Red Bull. His damp shirt had been screwed into a ball and tossed into the foot well, Lasser was now resplendent in a new sweatshirt, dark blue with a hood.

'I'll pay you for the shirt and stuff when we get back to civilisation.'

'No worries, I wasn't sure what size you wear, so I got large to be on the safe side.'

'Are you calling me a fat bastard?' he grinned at her and then took a huge chunk out of the cake.

'So you don't think Wickham will go back to the boat?'

'I doubt it, besides we have the intrepid Spenner hiding in the bushes so we can all relax.'

She took out a pack of chewing gum. 'What I can't understand is why he took the girl in the first place?'

They were parked at the end of the lane the car hidden in dark shadows cast by the huge trees. 'Deep waters, Cathy, we know Wickham hated the Radfields and we have a good idea why, and it seems that while he was busy having fun with Ashley, he found out some things about the Fotheringays that he found interesting.'

'Do you think he'll kill her?'

Reaching over onto the back seat, he grabbed one of the cans. 'At first I would have said yes, without doubt, now I'm not so sure.'

'What makes you think that?'

'Think about it, if he thought that Sam Wickham was his father and he somehow knew that Malcolm Radfield had been responsible for his death, then you have the perfect motive. But what if he found out that Wickham wasn't his father after all.'

'Ronnie?'

Lasser nodded. 'That's why he's taken the girl, now if it turns out to be the truth then Christ alone knows how he'll react.'

'What a mess.'

'Precisely,' he snapped the ring pull back and took a long gulp from the can. 'One piece of good news, the old man is awake.'

'Is he able to talk?'

'I don't know yet, I just got a message from Fossey, he didn't go into detail.'

Two more swallows and the drink was gone.

'Right then, let's go and see what they have to say for themselves.'

I'M FINE

As soon as Fossey had finished explaining what had happened, Ronnie tried to climb out of bed, his eyes frantic, he got as far as sitting upright before collapsing back, the heart monitor began to chatter as he gasped for breath.

'Take it easy, Ronnie, try and relax.' Fossey covered the frail hand with his own.

A young doctor moved swiftly into the room, frowning at Fossey as he adjusted the drip. 'This isn't a good idea,' his voice was heavy with disapproval. 'Listen to me, Mr Fotheringay, you need to rest, I'm...'

'I want out of here, now!' Ronnie's voice was surprisingly loud, belying his frail body.

The doctor shook his head. 'Not possible.'

Ronnie swivelled his eyes, looking at Fossey with tears sliding down his gaunt face. *'Patrick.'*

'The police think they know who he is, Ronnie, and they're out there looking for him.

'It's him isn't it?'

The young doctor moved over to the machine, bending to read the monitor.

Fossey leaned over the bed. 'Who are you talking about, Ronnie?'

'I should have known he'd turn up one day,' Ronnie swallowed. 'Now he's got my Jenna and I don't know what to do,' he drew a quivering liver spotted hand across his cycs.

'Ronnie, if you know anything...'

'I don't even know his bloody *name,*' he replied, eyes screwed up tight, a vein in his temple throbbed like an aching tooth.

The doctor appeared at the foot of the bed. 'Just try and keep calm, Mr Fotheringay, I can't stress enough how important these next few hours are.'

'Bugger off.'

The doctor sighed. ‘I can always ask your visitor to leave, if I believe his being here is having a detrimental effect on your health.’

‘Don’t try and threaten me, you...’

‘He’s right, Ronnie, you’re no use to anyone if you have another attack.’ Fossey interjected.

The old man glared at them both.

‘I’ll be back to check on you in twenty minutes and then I must insist you try to get some rest,’ he left the room without a backward glance.

‘Who is he, Ronnie?’ Fossey asked.

For a few fleeting seconds, he could see the battle being fought behind the old man’s eyes, then he blinked and stared straight at Fossey. ‘He’s my son.’

Inwardly Fossey sighed; Lasser had been right.

‘You need to speak to Sergeant Lasser, anything you can tell him...’

‘I can’t really tell him anything,’ Ronnie’s voice was filled with anguish, an old man suddenly realising that he was helpless as a new-born baby.

‘Try to think, Ronnie, anything, anything at all.’

‘I’ve never laid eyes on him. My own son and I could pass him in the street and I wouldn’t have a clue.’

‘So Emma left before the child was born?’

Ronnie pulled the sheet up to his chin. ‘Emma Wickham was a beauty, she was a couple of years older than me,’ he cleared his throat, his Adam’s apple bobbed up and down. ‘I tell you, lad, I’d never seen anything like her.’

‘So, how did you two end up together?’

‘Christ knows.’

Fossey could feel the dismay starting to build. ‘Ronnie, let me ring Lasser.’

‘It won’t make any difference, he’s got her and he’s never going to let her go, is he?’ his face seemed to age on the pillow. His skin appeared to draw back from the bone, a man close to death who felt he should have had all the answers and discovered he had none.

Fossey reached for his phone.

David was a mass of seething rage, chest heaving; nostrils flared, like some bull getting ready to charge and flatten anything that stood in his way.

Susan stood at his side, her eyes red rimmed; she rested a hand on her husband's arm.

'Calm down, David,' she looked downtrodden as if internally she was working through the grieving process, coming to terms with the possibility that she might never see her daughter alive again.

'I want to know what they're doing about finding our *daughter!'* he stabbed a sausage-like finger towards Lasser.

'Everything we can,' he answered.

Cathy stood behind him, her hand hovering near the handle of the quick release stick.

'You expect me to believe that do you?' he spat. 'I mean, why aren't you out there? When that copper got killed you couldn't get down the lane for cop cars, the place was crawling with the likes of you...'

'Dave!' Susan glared at her husband.

He snapped his head around. 'Oh come on, Sue, you know it's true...'

'We have men up at the woods, Mr Fotheringay, our colleagues on Merseyside have just gained access to a property owned by the suspect...'

Susan clasped her hands to her chest. 'Did they find anything?'

'Unfortunately not, but please be assured we're out there in force,' he glanced pointedly at David. 'We take every case seriously.'

'Patrick said he has a boat on the canal?' Susan looked at him hopefully.

'We have the area under surveillance in case he decides to return,' he felt the phone vibrate in his pocket, a couple of seconds it began to chime; Susan looked up at him her eyes panicked.

'Excuse me a minute,' he headed out of the front door and strode out into the garden. 'Alright, Patrick, how is he?'

'Well, he's awake and he's talking,' he paused, *'he admits to having a son with Emma Wickham.'*

'Decided it's time to spill the beans, has he?'

'He says he's never met the man.'

Lasser headed over to his car and beeped it open. 'Do you believe him?'

'He has no reason to lie, not now.'

Sliding into the driver's seat, he grabbed a cigarette, after the pie and cake he was gasping for a smoke. 'So, does Ronnie think his long lost son is responsible for all this?'

'Come on, Lasser, he's beating himself up about it, I mean, he's devastated.'

'It's just a pity he didn't decide to come clean before it got to this stage.'

'And how was he meant to have known...'

More excuses, more tiptoeing around the bloody obvious. 'Is he up to having a visitor?'

A long pause, he pushed the cigarette lighter in and waited, counting down the seconds.

'The doctor thinks he should be resting.'

'And what does Ronnie think?' The lighter popped out.

'Obviously, he wants to help but to be honest I don't think he can offer anything...'

'I'll be the judge of that, he had a relationship with Emma Wickham, he knew the woman...'

'But he knows nothing about the son.' Lasser could hear the underlying annoyance in Fossey's voice.

'I'll be up there shortly,' he ended the call and pushed the phone back into his pocket. When he saw the shape moving out of the dark towards him, he climbed from the car.

'Who was on the phone?' Susan's voice was tentative as if she dreaded his response.

'It was Fossey, he says your father has admitted to having a child with Emma Wickham.'

She stopped, her face hidden in shadow. 'Has he?'

'Come on, Susan, it can't be that much of a shock.'

'Is he the one who took Jenna?' Her voice was flat, emotionless, as if she were beyond feeling any more pain.

'We can't say for sure...'

'But you think it is?'

Lasser thought for a moment before answering, tiptoe or hobnail boot time. 'Yes I do.'

He heard her feet moving on the gravel, a sigh unravelled in the darkness. 'I suppose you think I should have said something sooner.'

'I thought you didn't know about the child, you said...'

'I know what I said!' she snapped. 'But you didn't believe me, did you, you thought I was trying to hide something?'

A fifteen-year-old girl listening at the door, turning her back just as it became juicy, too right, he hadn't believed her.

'Listen, Susan, I'm going to go to the hospital to see if your father can remember anything that might be useful,' he flicked the ash from his cigarette. 'Is there anything you want me to tell him?'

She stepped forward out of the gloom, her face blank in the moonlight, her eyes baleful. 'Yes, Sergeant, tell him I'll never forgive him, tell him I blame him for what's happened,' she must have seen the shock on Lasser's face, she smiled, a bitter parody of humour. 'Tell him I won't be visiting, not now, not ever.'

Lasser stuck the cigarette in his mouth and took a long drag. 'I'll tell him you said, hi.'

FAMILIAR PLACES

As soon as the back doors opened, she could smell the familiar scent of moorland heather. It brushed through her senses, a vivid reminder of everything that was important to her, the fragility of life.

'Are you coming?'

She wriggled to the tailgate and slid out, her legs felt unsteady, pins and needles thrummed along her calves. She recognised the place immediately, they were parked in front of the old crofter's cottage. Whenever she looked out across the moors, it had always been a small dot on the horizon, on a clear day she could even see it from her bedroom window.

Just keep calm, she told herself, her home was less than three miles away; she had dreaded getting out of the van and finding an alien landscape. To her right she could see the familiar shape of the mast on Winter Hill; she could make out the dark bulk of the Chinese Gardens, all familiar places that somehow strengthened her resolve. She was still alive, this one simple fact made her feel light headed; she could sense the blood thundering through her veins, the muscles in her legs quivered like a race horse ready for the 'off.'

'I know what you're thinking but believe me you wouldn't make it,' his voice was light and full of self-assurance. She was a seventeen-year-old kid and he was ex-army, trained to live and function in places like this, she felt the fleeting confidence begin to ebb away.

'What are we doing here?'

'I own the cottage, it belongs to me.'

She looked at him uncertainly; her world had suddenly turned into a place where she could no longer trust her instincts. All the things she had known to be true had turned out to be a nonsensical pack of lies.

'Did you think I lived my life under canvas?'

'I don't know what I thought.'

The building was squat, hunched down into the ground, built low to keep out of the wind and rain, a structure that had fought a two-hundred-year war against the elements, ding, ding, round two.

'Come on, I'll show you around,' he set off across the uneven grass without a backward glance.

Jenna scanned the immediate area around her feet, hoping to find a chunk of rock that she could hurl at him before making a break for it.

He stopped, a silhouette against the patchwork sky, shades of greys and blacks. 'If you run, family or not, I'll kill you and feed you to the dog,' the words drifted towards her, promises, carried along by the ever-present breeze that raked the high moors.

She closed her eyes for a moment, her stomach rolled and lurched and then reluctantly she moved forward.

At one time there must have been a low wall surrounding the house, though over the decades it had fallen into disrepair, the grass was littered with chunks of stone, all too heavy for her to lift.

When he reached the door, he removed a large key from the pocket of his camouflage jacket and slipped it into the lock.

'I'm sorry the place is a bit sparse but then again I never imagined I'd be entertaining family,' his teeth flashed in the dark then he moved inside and the darkness swallowed him. 'I've never really been one for home comforts, Jenna,' she could hear him moving around, looking over her shoulder the track that led from the property was visible, weaving its way down the hillside until it vanished into the night.

'Come in, don't be shy,' he emerged from the shadows with paraffin lamp in hand.

She hadn't known what to expect, the room was tiny the stone flags swept clean. In one corner she could see a solitary chair, a pile of cut logs stacked against the open fire. The roof space was open; revealing the slate grey tiles above, interlaced with thick oak beams, the faint scent of pine disinfectant wafted on the air. A camp bed occupied one wall, a rolled-up sleeping bag placed neatly at the foot, the inglenook fireplace looked a black doorway leading straight to hell.

It reminded her of the gingerbread house in the fairy tale, had he brought her here to fatten her up and then kill her, she shuddered and pushed the image from her mind.

'I did my basic training at Preston barracks, we came up here on manoeuvres, and that's when I first saw this place. I was only a kid so the prospect of buying somewhere was out of the question, especially on a squaddies wage,' he smiled at the memory. 'Besides I wanted to see the world, I didn't give this place a second thought, not until ten years ago. By then I had some cash, so I decided to buy it,' he looked around the small room. 'The estate agent couldn't believe his luck, he looked at me as if I'd gone off my fucking rocker. The description said *"quaint, in need of modernisation, ideal as a second home."* He nearly snatched my hand off when I offered him the full asking price.'

'So, you don't live here, permanently?' This was good, act nonchalant, chat shit; it didn't matter as long as it kept his eyes from clouding over, from changing.

'Take a seat,' he perched on the end of the camp bed; she reluctantly moved over to the chair and sat down. 'Recently I've been living on the boat,' when he saw the look on her face he lifted up a hand. 'I know, you'd have thought I'd had my fill of living on the canal especially after the way things went with my mother,' he leaned forward, resting elbows on knees. Jenna eased herself back into the chair, a reflex action; he looked at her knowingly, missing nothing.

'But, believe it or not, I missed the sense of impermanence that living on the water offers. I had money in the bank and as you can imagine I'm very self-sufficient. Of course, I can't go back there now which is a pity,' he pursed his lips, a sad frown settled on his face. 'By now, the police will know my name and I'd imagine they're slowly becoming aware of my links with your family.'

'Why are you doing this?' she asked, a sudden burning need to understand ate away at her in the same way a rat nibbles its way through a live electric cable.

He pulled out a pouch of tobacco and quickly rolled a cigarette, a moment later, he lit up and blew the smoke upwards watching as it curled its way through the rafters. 'Well, the first part you already know about,' she found herself nodding in response. 'As for the rest, let's just say I'm thinking on my feet. I mean, by now I should be well away from here that was the way I originally planned it. Malcolm or Ashley Radfield was to have been blamed for the murder of the boy; you see I left clues that pointed toward them.' For the first time a look of confusion flittered across his face. 'The trouble was, the thought of them being ruined by scandal began to lose its initial appeal. After all the Radfields were fucked years ago, they had no money, no self-esteem; people had lost any sort of respect for the likes of them.' Reaching under the bed, he pulled out a small tobacco tin and flicked his ash inside.

Jenna swallowed. 'So, you decided to kill them instead?'

'I thought the punishment should fit the crime, Radfield had killed the man I thought was my father, so why should he spend his remaining days on the hospital ward of some open prison where he could tend the roses and sit in his own private room listening to the Archers.'

Jenna frowned, she had no idea what the *'Archers'* were and she didn't think Radfield would have been allowed to grow roses, though she decided any form of contradiction would be like signing her own death warrant.

She tried to think of something else to say, something that would keep him talking. 'So, what are you going to do with me?' It was as if someone had slipped into her body and usurped her will, a dumb puppet with some sadistic marionette tugging on the strings.

He looked straight through her as if he were alone in the small room, then his eyes refocused, the madness flickering, the bush fire ready to leap into life again and go on the rampage, she pushed herself back in the chair, the fear clicking up another notch.

'Tell me something, Jenna,' he paused, 'what would you do in my situation?'

'I don't understand?' Although she did, she understood him completely.

'You see, I always blamed two people for the way my life turned out. My mother who it later transpires was supposedly raped by Radfield and my father who I thought had run out on us.'

Jenna could feel her heart racing, the cloying smell of paraffin seemed to suddenly fill the air, she knew where this was going, could almost see the words writ large in the smoky air.

'I've gone from having a father who I thought had simply abandoned me, to thinking I was a child who came into life through the act of rape, none of which turns out to be true,' he gave a slight shake of his head as if he found the whole thing ludicrous.

'I...'

'I've already told you that I wanted to kill my mother, I had every intention of doing it, but cancer causes more pain than I could ever inflict.'

'My grandad didn't know, I swear it,' she could feel the tears running down her cheeks. Everything was rapidly building to some horrific climax, the hatred this man had for her family was shining from his eyes. No amount of calm talk and wolfish smiles could disguise the fact, he wouldn't be satisfied until they were all dead, stamped out, wiped from the face of the earth.

'And how can you be sure of that, Jenna?'

'Because he'd have told me, we're close we tell each other everything,' she was aware that she was pleading but the time for bravado was rapidly slipping away.

'I'm touched by your belief but save your breath. Malcolm told me some of what happened and just before I cut off Ashley's head from his shoulders he confirmed it.'

The walls seemed to pulsate with a viscous life all their own; closing in around her like some filthy glove, her breath caught in her throat and lodged there, a rancid ball of fear that couldn't be denied.

'It's like I said before, people will lie to you, Jenna, especially the ones you think you can trust, the ones closest to you,' he whispered as if he were confiding some great universal truth to her.

'No!' she gasped, unsure if it was a denial or a response to the horror sitting on the camp bed; he appeared calm and composed like the grim reaper dressed for an activity weekend in the countryside.

'Just think if your grandfather had been honest then maybe I wouldn't have had to kill the boy or the old man in the woods...'

'Shut up!' she screamed, clamping her hands over her ears, anything to blot out his voice, suddenly she yanked them away terrified by her own thoughts. The small voice inside her head that said he was telling the truth, in some unfathomable way it was all true.

'So, what would you have me do?' he repeated.

'Please.'

'Should I walk away, give myself up to the police, leave you in peace?'

'We didn't know,' she sobbed, the last of her defences were crumbling like the remains of the wall outside, scattered and obsolete.

'Why would he do it, Jenna, why would this man you obviously love so much, deny my existence for all these years?'

'I don't know!' she was fully aware that she was shouting but the thick walls soaked it up and then threw it back in her face.

'When we were in the van, I asked you if he was still alive and you didn't give me answer.'

'He's dead,' she snapped instantly.

'Jenna,' his voice was full of reproach, like an adult chastising a small child, giving her the opportunity to tell the truth before he slapped her legs.

'He had a heart attack two days ago, we got him to the hospital, but he died during the night.' She could feel the cold sweat drying on her skin, she held her breath and blinked back the sting of tears. In that fraction of a second the knife appeared in his hand, the blade looked oily in the flickering light, dull and lifeless, a harmless piece of metal. When he turned the blade it caught the lamplight and flashed, tiny rays of light lancing from its surface.

He stood up. 'Remember what I said, violence is the great leveller, it drags the truth out of people kicking and screaming. It loosens the tongue, so while you've still got one I suggest you start being honest.'

She started to scream.

BLOOM

Fossey had said that Ronnie was drained; he hadn't said he looked like Old Father Time, on his last legs.

When he opened his eyes and saw Lasser sitting at the side of the bed, he reached out a skeletal hand and grasped the sleeve of his jacket.

'Have you found her?' his voice was little more than a wheeze.

'Not yet,' he saw the despair in the old man's eyes, the agony of not knowing. 'Listen, Ronnie, we need to know everything we can about James Wickham.'

He released Lasser's sleeve, his fingers plucking at the bed sheet in agitation. 'I don't know what I can tell you...'

'You've got to think, anything you can remember could help us find your granddaughter.'

Lasser was aware he was piling on the pressure, pushing Ronnie further down heart attack avenue, the cul-de-sac of no return, but if the girl turned up dead then what sort of life was left for the old man?

'I've never even seen the boy,' his chest heaved and fell.

Lasser patted his hand. 'OK, Ronnie,' he paused, 'tell me about Emma?'

He turned his watery eyes toward Lasser and swallowed. 'I loved her you know.'

'I'm sure you did but what was she like, how did you two get together?'

Ronnie licked his lips. 'The Wickham's worked on the farm, they helped us when we were gathering the corn and barley. Oh there were one or two other families but I always remembered Emma.' His eyes drifted away as he thought back over the years. 'I suppose you'd say I had a crush on her, she had this mass of jet black hair and her eyes...' he fell silent for a few seconds and then sniffed. 'I'd never seen owt like her...'

In any other situation, it would have brought a smile to Lasser's face, an old man reminiscing about the love of his life, touching stuff. 'She was a bonny lass?' he asked.

Ronnie sighed, a sound full of regret. 'Aye, lad, you could say that.'

'And did they ever do any work for the Radfields?'

He managed a slight nod, the pillow making a scrunching sound as he rested his head. 'As soon as his lordship set eyes on her he wanted her.'

Lasser sat further forward in the chair. 'What do you mean?'

'Back then Radfield still owned plenty of land...'

'Including your own farm?'

'Aye we were just tenant farmers, so of course we had no say in the matter.'

'I'm sorry, Ronnie, you've lost me?'

'Malcolm wanted her up at the house, he offered them a few bob extra. Of course he had Emma working in the house and he stuck her husband out in the bloody field all day.'

Lasser was starting to get the picture a titled knob chasing Emma around the pantry while her old man worked his bollocks off. It sounded like a Dickensian novel or a pants-down farce.

'I only found out what happened a year after we started seeing one another, she told me the bastard had raped her,' he wiped a quivering hand across his eyes.

'I take it she didn't go to the police?'

'And say what, I mean, back then folks that lived on the boats were treated no better than thieving scum. It's not like today when you see a barge floating by with some retired doctor steering it with his little sailors cap on. They were second class citizens and he was Lord bloody Radfield, justice of the peace, head of the local hunt, what chance would she have had?'

Lasser could see the colour rising in Ronnie's cheeks, his breathing quickened, sweat coated his gaunt face. 'I get the picture, Ronnie, just try and keep calm.'

'When her husband went missing she came to us for help, the police spent half a day poking around the woods and then they gave up.' he paused and swallowed. 'Half a bloody day, she was desperate so we started looking proper, me and my old man and a few others who knew Sam and liked him.'

Lasser unzipped the sweatshirt; the heat in the small room was stifling. 'This diary, Ronnie?'

For the first time the old man looked cagey. 'What about it?'

'Well, if it's OK with you, I'd like to take a look at it.'

Ronnie turned his face away the seconds ticked into infinity, Lasser kept his mouth closed; sometimes it paid to let the silence turn the screw.

'I can't remember where I put it,' Ronnie mumbled.

Lasser yanked the fleece shirt off and placed over the back of the chair. 'There is no diary, is there?'

'I...'

'Come on, you don't seriously expect me to believe that your father wrote all this down?'

When he twisted his head around he was crying, an old man whose life had been turned into wreckage in a matter of hours. Ronnie the cider maker, a man who loved his family without question. Tethered to the memory of a woman he was once besotted with and trying to come to terms with the fact that he had a multiple murderer for a son and a granddaughter he would probably never see again.

'My father told me what had happened,' he swallowed, his throat made a dry clicking sound.

'When?'

'I'd been with Emma for about eight months.'

Lasser fiddled with the keys in his pocket. 'How did he feel about you and Emma being together?'

Ronnie tried to push himself up on the bed and then gave up. ‘We didn’t tell him, at first.’

‘Why not, was it because Emma was still classed as a married woman or because she lived on a boat, a bit of a gypsy?’

Ronnie glared at him.

‘Come on, Ronnie, I don’t have all night, why did you keep your relationship a secret from your old man?’

‘Because he was a bloody *snob,* OK, is that what you want...?’

‘I want the truth, so we can catch the man who has your granddaughter.’

Ronnie grabbed the sheet, wringing it as if he had his hands around the killer’s throat. ‘He didn’t blackmail Radfield, my old man was close to Malcolm, he thought the old bastard walked on water!’

Suddenly the bigger picture sprang up in Lasser’s mind, links forming, merging from the fog. ‘Your father helped Radfield didn’t he, he didn’t simply find out what had happened, Radfield told him what he’d done and your old man helped dispose of the body?’

Ronnie squared his narrow shoulders and nodded. *‘Aye.’*

Bingo!

‘And Radfield gave him the farm for services rendered?’

‘Yes,’ Ronnie whispered his voice thick with shame and resentment.

Bloody hell, it all made sense, the Fotheringays didn’t have one skeleton rattling in the cupboard they had a graveyard full of the buggers.

‘When he found out you and Emma were having a relationship it would have been the last thing he would have wanted. Jesus Christ, Ronnie, he helped you look for Sam Wickham knowing he was already dead and knowing where the body was hidden!'

‘I knew nothing about any of that,’ he gasped.

Lasser saw the young doctor through the window; he smiled and nodded, receiving a sour frown in return.
'So how did your father find out about you and Emma?'
'I bloody well told him,' a spark of defiance lit up Ronnie's eyes, a second later it vanished. 'Emma begged me not to say owt, she thought it was all too soon. Back then people could be cruel and nobody knew that more than she did.'
'Why didn't you listen to her?'
'Because I was stubborn and young and thought I knew best,' he snorted. 'I thought I was my own man, biggest mistake I ever made.'
Lasser could picture the scene, for a while the thrill of illicit love must have been a powerful emotion, a woman grieving for the loss of her husband. Young Ronnie sniffing around, playing the night in shining armour while all the time secretly wanting more. Emma feeling weak and vulnerable suddenly finding herself in a relationship and maybe realising it was a mistake, heady times.
'And what did he say when you told him?'
Ronnie snorted. 'My old man was a hard bastard, he told me to *'get shut'* as if she was some sort of bloody whore. I can remember standing there, struck dumb, I couldn't believe what I was hearing.'
'Did you try and tell him how you felt towards her?'
Ronnie snorted. 'Course I did but he wouldn't listen, he went berserk, told me straight that if I didn't end it then I could fuck off, I was no son of his, that kind of thing.' Ronnie shook his head. 'I should have packed my stuff there and then.'
'But you didn't?'
Ronnie laid his arms by his sides as if he was being measured for a pine box. 'I wanted to but Emma wouldn't hear of it. We talked about it for hours; I tried to persuade her that we would manage but she bloody knew. I had no cash of my own, all I could do was work

the land, it would have been hard,' he sounded as if he was trying to convince himself that he'd made the right decision, however his eyes told a different story.

'So, she left?'

'Mm, I went up to the boat one day and she'd moved on. You see I was a coward, I convinced myself that it was for the best, I towed the line but up here,' he tapped a bony finger to the side of his head, 'I always planned to go looking for her.'

'So why didn't you?'

'Four years after she went, my old man got lung cancer. I tell you, son, I couldn't wait for the old sod to die. The only thing I could think of was trying to find Emma,' he paused, 'trouble was he knew it.' Ronnie fell silent; the memories were falling through his mind thick and fast, like filthy black rain.

Another piece of the puzzle slotted into place. 'That's when he told you about his part in Sam's disappearance?'

Ronnie wiped a tear from his eye. 'Aye, he knew it would stop me from trying to find her, after all how could I look her in the face knowing it was my father who had a hand in killing her husband, knowing where he was buried?'

'Jesus.'

'So now you know.'

'And you didn't see her again?'

Ronnie flicked his eyes towards Lasser and grimaced. 'Once, about eight years later. I was in town, one of these young farmers piss ups. Of course, by then the farm was making plenty of cash, I'd married Susan's mother. You should have seen me, strutting around as if I owned the bloody place, a young farmer running a successful business; I thought I was really somebody,' he shook his head in disgust at the memory. 'I spotted her coming out of one of the boozers in town, she was with this bloke. I can see her now laughing, her head thrown back and all that dark hair falling down her shoulders.'

'You didn't go over to her?'

'I couldn't, you see by then she was a dark secret, I knew what had happened. I knew the only reason I was strutting around was because my old man had helped to commit a murder and been recompensed by Radfield. If that hadn't been the case we would still have been like all the other tenant farmers in the area, scratching around trying to make a living and paying all the profits to Radfield, instead we had the new tractors and all the latest gear.'

'You weren't to know, Ronnie. It was your father that did the deal.'

Ronnie shook his head. 'I appreciate that, son, but I should have done the right thing, not for me or Emma, I should have done it for Sam Wickham and I didn't and it's haunted me ever since.'

Lasser thought for a millisecond before dropping the bombshell. 'When I spoke to Susan a couple of days ago she told me she'd overheard you and her mother arguing about the child.'

Ronnie's eyes shot open as if spring loaded. *'What!'*

'She remembers it well, she was fifteen and according to her you were both in the kitchen and her mother was going ballistic.'

'I...'

'You told me that after you split you only saw her once and you didn't speak to her. So why were you and your wife arguing about a child you said you knew nothing about?'

Ronnie looked around the room in desperation, Lasser felt sure that if he were fit enough then he would have leaped out of bed and dashed for the door. 'How did you find out about James?' Another turn of the screw. 'Either you heard it from someone or Emma told you?'

'It was Emma, OK, are you bloody satisfied!' he spat.

Lasser felt his own anger flare. 'What are you talking about, this isn't about me you're the one with all the secrets. It was your old man who helped to cover up a murder and you can try and justify it but you kept your mouth shut because it suited you.'

'Shut up!' Ronnie's face began to turn puce, his breathing rattled.

'Then tell me, your granddaughter's out there somewhere,' he stabbed a finger toward the window. 'And you're more bothered about coming across as the injured party....'

'You bastard, I love my Jenna do you think I wanted any of this to happen?'

The machine in the corner began to beep loudly; Ronnie slumped back onto the pillow, closing his eyes his bottom lip trembling.

'Then help me, be honest and let's see where it takes us.'

Ronnie took a huge shuddering breath; the machine began to return to normal. 'The night I saw her in town, I followed her, when she reached the taxi rank the bloke she was with got into a cab.'

'She didn't go with him?'

'No, she started to walk along King Street, you know heading toward the train station.'

Lasser nodded. 'Go on.'

'I caught up with her,' he smiled sadly at the memory. 'She hadn't changed a bit.'

'What did she say?'

'She just threw her arms around me, can you imagine that, this woman who I'd never stopped thinking about, seemed happy to see me.'

'Well that's good, isn't it?'

'Oh aye, lad, it was the best moment of my life. Just for a few seconds I forgot all about Sam and my bloody father, it was just the two of us.'

'So, what happened?'

'We sat on the steps of Saint Mary's church and talked.'

'It must have felt good seeing her after all those years.'

Ronnie looked at him his expression full of regret. 'Thing was, I was married by then.'

'Life can be a bitch at times, Ronnie.' Lasser mused.

'Aye, lad, it can.' Ronnie nodded, he either refused to hear the sarcasm or he was so lost in the memory that it went straight over his head.

'And what did you talk about?'

'I told her about my old man dying.'

'Did you tell her you were married?'

Ronnie shook his head. 'I'm not proud of the way I behaved.'

Lasser sighed, he could see how tempting it would have been to keep the truth from her, here was the first woman he had ever loved suddenly turning up unexpectedly. Ronnie must have been devastated at the thought of losing her again.

'So you tried to make out you were still single.'

'Pathetic isn't it, I mean, all I knew was that I couldn't stand to see her walk away from me, not again.'

'And where was she living?'

'She said she'd been staying at an old crofter's cottage up on Banks moor.'

'Is that local?'

Ronnie smiled sadly. 'It's about three miles from the farm.'

'And you never knew.'

'Ironic isn't it, I always thought she'd moved miles away and yet here she was virtually on my doorstep.'

'You started seeing her again?' Lasser asked although he already knew the answer.

'Aye, she still had the boat, kept it at top lock so a couple of days after we met I went up there. I tell you, lad, I knew it was wrong, I had a wife at home, a good woman but you see it should have always been me and

Emma. I should have looked for her as soon as my old man died, no excuses, I should have done it.'

'So, what went wrong?'

'At first nothing, I'd tell my wife I was going to the village for a pint then I'd go up to the boat.' Ronnie looked shamefaced at the admission.

'And how long did you carry on seeing one another?'

'About six months and then one day I went up and the boat was gone.'

'Gone?'

'Aye, lad, I didn't know what to do.'

'Had you had an argument?'

'No, we loved one another, we didn't argue....'

'But something must have happened?'

He ignored the question. 'I used to go up to the canal at least twice a week; you know just to see if she'd come back.'

'And did she?'

Ronnie looked up at the ceiling. 'Aye, lad, she did, twelve months later. I went up there almost every day, it was like a habit I couldn't break. When I saw the boat, I thought I was bloody dreaming. She was standing on the towpath as if she'd been expecting me, she was holding a baby and I knew straight away...'

'Your son?'

'No doubt about it.'

'That must have been a shock?'

'You could say that but you see the thing was she was completely different.'

'In what way?'

'It was as if everything had been an act, she told me straight out the lad was mine. Then she said to take a good look because I'd never see him again. She actually spat at my feet, I mean, I couldn't understand it, I tried to ask her what was going on and she just laughed in my face.'

'Maybe it's because you'd let the grass grow beneath your feet, instead of going to look for her.'

'Oh aye it was that all right but there was more,' he paused and swallowed. 'She said she knew all about my family and what we'd done.' Ronnie's voice dropped to a whisper. 'I just stood there; I didn't know what to do, she knew bloody everything, about my old man, my marriage...'

'How did she find out?'

Ronnie looked up at the ceiling. 'Radfield told her.'

Lasser stopped his mouth from falling open in surprise. 'Why would he have done something like that?'

'He told her everything but with his own little twist on the truth. He admitted that Sam had come up to the house and that her husband had attacked him because of what had happened to her. But he said it was my old man who pulled the trigger...'

'Hang on, Ronnie, what was she doing even discussing all this with him. I mean, he raped her for God's sake!'

Ronnie's face bloomed with shame. 'Aye, lad, that's what I thought.'

The heart monitor continued to beep, the overhead light flickered.

Lasser felt another piece slot into place. 'It wasn't rape it was consensual and Sam found out what'd been going on between them and confronted Radfield.'

'That's what she took great delight in telling me.'

'So, when you were out looking for him she already knew he was dead?'

'No, she didn't, she only found out later but you see Radfield laid a lot of the guilt over what had happened on her shoulders. After all, she'd known what she was doing, so she had to share some of the blame. Plus Sam Wickham hadn't been the perfect husband, according to her he used to get drunk and then take his frustrations out on her.'

'What a bloody mess.' Lasser paused, 'and she wanted to get you up there just so she could tell you all this?'

'She hated me with a vengeance because I hadn't had the guts to be honest with her.'

To a certain extent, he could see where she was coming from, married to a man who knocked her about, then having Radfield fucking her simply because he could. Then young Ronnie, swearing his undying love and finding out he was married with a kid on the way and to ice the cake nicely, finding out that Ronnie knew all about the murder and had profited from it, while she was left to fend for herself with a young baby in tow. It was little wonder she was pissed off with the male species.

'It was as if she blamed me for everything. I tried to explain about Radfield but she wouldn't listen, she said he was *'sorry'* for what had happened. She told me he'd signed over the crofter's cottage to her as a peace offering, he...'

'Wait, you're saying he bought her silence by giving her the cottage.'

'Well, I suppose so but she'd never have gone to the authorities because they wouldn't have believed her, you see to a certain extent she was implicated, she knew what had happened to Sam and said nowt.'

Lasser stood up and grabbed his fleece from the floor. 'This cottage, Ronnie, could you tell me exactly how to get there.'

Ronnie frowned. 'Aye but no buggers lived in it for donkey's years.'

'How far away from the canal is this place?'

He could see the old man thinking about the question. 'About three quarters of a mile.'

Lasser wanted to get out of there, he could see himself already in the car hammering his way back toward the moors, the killer had a boat on the canal just as his mother had done, so maybe he was using the old house as a base, it made sense, it felt right.

'So, you'd be able to see the canal from the house?'

'Well aye, at least parts of it.'

Lasser pulled out his pad and pen. ‘Directions, Ronnie, quick as you can.’

MOVE ON

Fossey sat in the passenger seat, listening as Lasser explained the situation to DCI Simms.

'And you say the road that leads to the cottage is only fit for four wheel drives?' His voice sounded thin through the small in-car speaker.

'According to Ronnie Fotheringay,' he paused. 'Besides I think under the circumstances we should try and approach the area as quietly as possible.'

'I'm not an idiot, Lasser.' This time Simms voice boomed out of the hands free, the annoyance coming through loud and clear.

'Of course not, sir.'

'Right well, get your arse up to the woods, we can leave from there.'

'I'm setting off now.'

'And don't be all night about it.'

The call ended abruptly, Lasser lit a cigarette and blew the smoke out through his nose before starting the engine.

'Are you sure you want me to come?' Fossey asked.

'Positive,' he pulled off the car park and headed toward the ring road, at this time of night the roads were deserted apart from the odd milk float and bread wagon starting their early morning rounds.

'So, Ronnie opened up about Emma Wickham?'

'Eventually.'

Fossey watched as the speedometer climbed up to eighty. 'You can understand his reluctance.'

Lasser glanced sideways, the car twitched. 'It just seems a pity it took the abduction of his granddaughter before he decided to come clean.'

'That's harsh; he spent forty years keeping this secret, basically to protect his family.'

The lights on the ring road had been turned off, the council's way of trying to save money.

‘I’m not a complete bastard, I do realise it was hard for the old guy but don’t try to tell me he did it just to avoid hurting ...’

‘But imagine what this will do to his family.’ Fossey interrupted. ‘I hope to God we find Jenna, but what happens when all this is over?’

‘I’m sorry but that isn’t my problem,’ he pointed the car down the slip road and then headed into Hindley. ‘That’s your area of expertise.’

‘So, you haven’t simply brought me along for the ride?’

‘You know the people involved...’

‘Come on, I only met them a week ago.’

‘Fair enough but it hasn’t been your average week; I can guarantee that any friends of the Fotheringays will know less about the family than you do.’

‘OK, I can see where you’re coming from, and...’

‘Good that’s settled then.’

Once clear of the town centre he put his foot down and Fossey decided it best to keep his mouth shut so Lasser could concentrate on the driving. When the car reached ninety he began to get nervous.

Lasser flipped on the wipers when the first smattering of rain hit the windscreen.

‘You do realise that Susan blames Ronnie for what’s happened?’ Fossey said.

‘I can see it from all sides, I totally get why Ronnie kept his mouth shut and I’d probably have done the same myself. But all Susan sees is her daughter in the hands of a nutter who happens to be her half-brother, it’s no wonder she’s lost the plot.’

Fossey gripped the armrest as Lasser rocketed around a long left hand bend.

‘Do you mind slowing down?’

He eased off the gas and looked at Fossey with a quizzical expression. ‘Why, what’s the problem?’

'Well, I'm sure your boss would rather you get there in one piece rather than having to arrange a tow truck to pull us out from the middle of the field.'

Lasser grinned. 'Come on where's your sense of adventure?'

'I think one maniac on the loose is more than enough, don't you?'

Lasser laughed and shook his head.

'So, what do you think Simms will want to do when or should I say if we get there?'

'If he has any sense he'll make sure we have a tactical back-up squad to cover our arse and then just try and get to the place without making it too obvious.'

'And does he have any sense?'

'Yeah, he's one of the good guys, he won't take any unnecessary risks and he's too close to his pension to be gung-ho.'

They sped under a tunnel of overhanging trees, Lasser flicked on the main beam, he could see the driving rain illuminated by the headlights, a few seconds later he slowed down and took a narrow cut off to the right.

'And what do you want me to do?'

'Let's just play it by ear, either Simms will give me a pat on the back for using my initiative, or he'll call me all the names under the sun and make you sit in the car like a naughty schoolboy.'

The road straightened out dissecting a huge reservoir. In the pale moonlight, the water appeared placid and black as pitch. As the road dipped the water vanished, hidden by the high stonewalls that ran down either side of the road, once they'd crossed the stretch of water the road turned tightly to the left and began to weave its way up the side of the hill. Trees overhung the right hand side of the road, a black impenetrable mass that loomed over the ribbon of tarmac. To Fossey, it felt as if they were trying to force them toward the water. He could imagine the car rolling down the steep embankment bursting into a fiery ball of twisted metal before hitting the water and sinking to the bottom, trapped and screaming in the mangled wreckage.

After half a mile of climbing, the ground suddenly opened up, to the left Fossey could make out the lights of Liverpool and beyond, like jaundiced diamonds flickering in the rain. To the right the moors seemed to sweep upward toward a sky angry with bloated rainclouds. Lasser took another right turn, the road curling around the top edge of the woodland, after fifty yards he caught sight of the assorted police vans and cars parked on the right. Flicking off the main beam, he looked for somewhere to park.

Fossey could make out a group of about ten officers, standing in a rough semicircle around a tall man with short steel grey hair.

They climbed out and headed over, Simms voice was loud, his tone forthright. 'Nobody does anything without my say so and if anyone thinks this is just me spouting my mouth off, making idle threats then think again, gentlemen. Because I will personally see to it that anyone who decides to be the hero will be fucked.' Simms took his time, looking at each man in turn.

Lasser smiled, he could see the look of shock on a few of the faces in the group, Spenner looked as if was about to burst into tears.

Over to the right, Fossey could make out a group of four men standing by the side of a dark blue van, dressed completely in black, each held a short-nosed machine pistol across their chests, the guns pointing at the ground.

When Simms turned, he spotted Lasser standing behind him.

'Who's this?' he asked, nodding toward Fossey.

'This is Patrick Fossey, sir.'

Simms pursed his lips. 'I see.'

'He's offered to assist us should we need it.' Lasser kept his face straight and his fingers crossed; a gust of wind hurled a spattering of rain into his face.

Simms turned to Fossey. 'You know the Fotheringays?'

'Of a fashion.'

'Well, I appreciate your help,' he thrust out his hand and Fossey grasped it.

Lasser blew out a sigh of relief, the sound dragged away on the wind.

'Right, Sergeant, I've left five men down by the canal in case our man decides to put in an appearance.'

'What about the farm?' Lasser asked.

'WPC Harper is still there and I've left one of the armed response team on site just for peace of mind.'

'Right, sir,' it appeared the old man had thought of everything but in situations like this covering all the angles was never going to be an exact science.

Simms clapped his hands together, rubbing them vigorously as if he was trying to generate some heat. 'So, come on, Lasser, I take it Mr Fotheringay has furnished you with the directions we require.'

'He says there's a path about a quarter of a mile from here that should lead us directly toward the property.'

'Right then, lead the way.'

Ten minutes later, they stood at the bottom of a rutted track; the cover of the trees had gone leaving them exposed to the howling wind, the driving rain slanted in from right to left.

Simms grunted and turned his face into the onslaught as if relishing the sensation of the elements whipping into his grizzled face. When he turned to Lasser his eyes where alight with a kind of fervour. 'How far is it to this place?'

Lasser did a rough calculation. 'About three quarters of a mile.'

'Right, you lot, listen up, I want all lights off, if our man is up here somewhere then we don't want the place lit up like the illuminations.'

One by one, the torchlights vanished, the darkness closed in around them.

'Break my leg at this rate,' someone tried to whisper to a colleague.

'Black, if I hear another peep out of you. I'll be the one breaking your bloody legs.'

'Sorry, sir.'

'Right, spread out and keep your eyes peeled.' Simms set off, striding across the heather, the men fanning out on either side.

The four firearms experts split into two groups and cut off left and right, moving forward in a crouch.

After a couple of hundred yards, the ground began to grow steeper making any sort of conversation difficult. Not for the first time, Lasser wished he didn't smoke as every demon weed came back to haunt him, he heard grunts to his left and right as men lost their footing on the uneven moorland grass. He flicked up the hood of the new sweatshirt in an effort to keep out the swirling rain but the wind simply ripped it back from his head. The moon put in an appearance, the open fields filled with pale light before disappearing again behind swollen rain clouds.

When they reached the crest of the hill the wind came raging across the miles of open country picking up pace and slamming into them.

'Fuck me' Lasser gasped leaning forward into the gale in an effort to stay on his feet.

Fossey yanked up the collar of his jacket and grinned. 'A bit breezy, isn't it?'

Both men battled their way across the ground, in the gloom Lasser could see that most of the others had adopted the same approach, looking as if they were burdened by some invisible weight strapped to their shoulders. The ground began to dip and undulate, in the gullies the wind would die down to a whisper, though as soon as they reached the top of the next incline it battered them into submission.

When the dark shape of the house morphed into view, Lasser stopped and peered into the darkness. 'There it is, sir.'

Simms stared out across the field, it took Lasser a couple of seconds to realise that his boss could see bugger all.

'Are you sure?'

One of the firearms officers walked over. 'How do you want to do this?'

Simms wiped a hand down his face and flicked the droplets away. 'Right, Morris, I want you and your men to get as close as you can to the house but remember, no unnecessary risks.'

'Should we gain entry if we feel it's safe to do so?'

Lasser had never seen Morris before, he was dressed like an action man his clothing seemed to consist of belts, buckles, and pockets. It was obvious; he wanted to make sure if it went tits up, then it wasn't going to be his arse on the line.

Simms yanked the tartan flat cap from his pocket and plonked it onto his head. 'Tell me, Sergeant Morris, are you trained to enter a hostile environment?'

'Yes, sir,' he replied, a slight note of hesitancy in his voice.

'So, why would I bring a dog and bark myself.' Simms sounded annoyed. 'Just do what you're trained to do.'

'Yes, sir.' Morris barked and then moved quickly away. Gathering the other three to him they spoke for a few seconds, two of them looked toward Simms though it was too dark to make out their expressions. Lasser could well imagine they were pissed off having their professionalism belittled by an old DCI in a tartan flat cap.

The four of them began to move quickly toward the cottage, crouched low. As soon as they vanished into the darkness Simms waved his hand, and they all started to follow.

Even though the wind was still howling Fossey could feel the sweat trickling down between his shoulder blades, he slid down the zip of his coat in an effort to let out some of the heat.

When the four men came back into view they were about twenty yards from the house, fanning out with a distance of fifteen feet between each of them. Simms held up his hand and the men under his command stopped and watched as the four closed in on the cottage.

Lasser raised his head slightly, he couldn't be sure but he thought it was Morris he saw flattening himself to the side of the front door, he gave a signal and his three colleagues swept in to join him.

Lasser would swear that he never heard the first shot, he saw the man by the front door suddenly snap upright his body twisting to the right and then he pitched forward, vanishing in the tall grass. If he didn't hear the first then he certainly heard the second, it screamed just above his head, forcing him down onto his face.

A second later Fossey was sprawling at his side, right arm thrown up to cover his head.

'What the bloody hell!'

Lasser glanced up, Simms was still standing, a confused expression on his face as if to say this isn't the way it's meant to be, this isn't cricket.

'Get down!' Lasser bellowed and watched as the wind lifted the tartan cap from his head and tossed it away, a second later the top of his head followed suit.

He watched as Simms legs buckled the same perplexed look on his face as he smashed to the ground. Fossey automatically rose to his knees and Lasser slammed into his back.

'For fucks sake, keep your head down!'

Then the sound of returning fire shrieked overhead, Lasser heard someone to his left scream in agony, the highly-trained firearms team were returning fire, shooting blind into the darkness.

'Stop fucking firing!' Lasser screamed, though they either didn't hear him or chose to ignore the fact that their colleagues were trapped in the crossfire. Fingers curled around triggers, spurting out red-hot chips of metal that ripped out across no man's land.

'Come on, Fossey, those daft bastards are going to kill the lot of us,' he began to belly forward, the front of his shirt and pants lathered with mud, his shoes trying to dig into the ground in an effort to push himself forward. Trouble was he couldn't stop shaking, he could feel the tremors crashing through his body his heart slammed like a warhorse on the run.

Seconds later the sound of the guns stopped, he could hear men shouting around him, but he didn't have a clue what they were saying. He was vaguely aware of Fossey crawling alongside him. Another single shot rang out, another agonised scream from the front of the house; the two remaining gunmen began to fire again, the bursts short and measured, as if they were trying to conserve ammunition, a few seconds later they stopped altogether.

'Stop shooting, you pricks!' Lasser waited for a response.

'Morris and Charnel are dead!' The voice that drifted across the field was full of terror, all shred of professionalism vanished. The years spent training, breaking down doors and bursting into rooms, shooting blanks at cardboard cut-outs, it all amounted to nothing when two of your partners were lifeless lumps of meat and you knew that any second you could be joining them.

Lasser leapt to his feet, keeping his body bent and dashed toward the house, he expected to feel the savage pain of a bullet drilling into his back but he was convinced that if they stayed out in the open he would kill them all, come daylight the field would be littered with corpses. He threw a look over his shoulder; Fossey was about three yards behind head down arms and legs pumping.

Five yards, four, the bulk of the house loomed, the sadistic bastard would wait until he reached the building and then kill him just as a spark of hope flared. He ran straight into the corner of the house his shoulder slamming into the ancient stone and then miraculously he was around the side. Lasser pressed his body tight to the wall; a couple of seconds later and Fossey joined him, his face a white smear, eyes wide in shock. Ten yards to their left the two remaining firearms officers where crouched behind the low remains of a wall, both had their guns held tight across their chests.

'Come on, Fossey,' he led the way to the back of the house; halfway along they came across the door, seated back in the thick wall, grabbing the handle he yanked hard, cursing when it didn't budge.

'For fucks sake!' Stepping back, he cocked his leg and slammed the heel of his boot into the wood, the door

rattled but held, another kick; he could envision the killer snaking his way across the field until he had a clear shot of the rear of the house. He kicked again, becoming frantic; Spenner appeared around the side of the wall, the left side of his face coated with mud, his uniform dripping with water.

'Come on, Fossey, give us a bloody lift!' Lasser shouted.

Fossey pushed him aside and started to slam his foot into the timber, five kicks, and the door bounced inwards. Patrick careered through the gap; Lasser followed him inside, Spenner pushing at his back in an effort to barge past.

Lasser let him before slamming the door closed; dragging the small Maglite from his inside pocket, he flicked it on, then twisted the end to widen the beam.

Jenna Fotheringay sat huddled in the corner, her legs pulled up tight to her chest her eyes frantic; a grey piece of gaffer tape stretched across her mouth.

Lasser moved slowly forward, his hands held up in front of him. *'It's OK, Jenna, it's OK, sweetheart'*

Reaching out he took hold of the end of the tape and snatched it back, her eyes screwed tight in pain.

Fossey knelt by her side, resting an arm on her shoulder.

'Jenna, are you alright?'

Lasser eased her away from the wall, pulling out the pocketknife he quickly sliced through the nylon twine that bound her hands. As soon as the rope parted, she lunged forward into Fossey's arms, the sobs heaving her shoulder, tears smearing the grime on her face.

Standing up, Lasser made his way toward the front window and risked a quick glance outside.

'I can't believe he killed DCI Simms.' Spenner stood in the middle of the room his eyes glassy and vacant.

The back door sprung open and three more men jostled one another inside.

When the headlights flared at the front window, Lasser dropped to his haunches, moments later the light swept away. When he looked again, he could see the unmistakable glow of taillights disappearing into the dark.

'He's going,' he yanked open the front door.

'Please you have to stop him; he said he was going to kill them all!' Jenna's voice was hoarse, as if all her emotions had been spent, she sounded as alive as the speaking clock. She scrambled to her feet, blonde hair matted, her clothes filthy, he was just amazed the nutter had let her live.

Fossey still had his arm around her shoulder. 'It's OK, Jenna, just try to take it easy.'

'Please, he's going to the house to kill my parents, he said he wanted me to know that they were as good as dead.'

Shit, Cathy was at the farm trying to keep what remained of the family together and this lunatic was only a couple of miles away. 'How long will it take him to get to your house, Jenna?' he yanked out his phone and began to flick through the menu.

'Ten, maybe fifteen minutes.'

Lasser nodded, pressed the call button and slapped the phone to his ear.

'Come on you lot get outside, he's gone and we have people out there who need help,' he listened to the ringing tone,all the time praying 'come on, Cathy, for fucks sake pick up.' 'Spenner, get onto headquarters tell them we need an air ambulance up here now, and tell them to get in touch with DCI Bannister.'

Spenner looked confused. *'Air ambulance?'*

Lasser planted himself directly in front of the young constable and pushed his face in close. 'I'm relying on you to get this sorted, if anyone tries to fob you off then fucking blast them, understood?' Lasser hissed.

Spenner snapped to attention. *'Completely, sir.'*

None of the other men had made a move, so Lasser took a deep breath and stalked out through the front door the phone still bleating in his hand. He came across the two slumped figures of the marksmen sprawled by the front of the house. Crouching by the side of the first body, the black baseball cap had been blown from his head, his short dark hair plastered with blood.

Lasser swallowed his disgust as Fossey strode past heading out to where another figure lay prone in the heather.

'Hello, boss.' Cathy's voice crackled in his ear.

Lasser twisted his head to try to escape the howling wind. 'Cathy, listen to me...'

'You there, boss?'

The phone began to make small electronic pinging sounds as the signal deteriorated.

He gave it a shake and then dashed back inside the house.

'Can you hear me, Cathy?'

'Sort of, but you keep breaking up.'

'Get out of the house, you need to get...'

'Sorry sir, you're breaking up again.'

'For fucks sake!' he could see Jenna standing in the corner, her body shaking as the onset of shock began to take hold. 'Cathy, the killer is coming straight for you; he's five, ten minutes away. You have to get the Fotheringays and get out of there!'

'Damn things, never work when you need them,' her voice was as clear as crystal. *'Sorry, sir, you must be in a dead spot, I can't hear a thing.'*

Yeah, they were in a dead spot all right, he checked the phone again the contact had been broken.

'Spenner!'

'The air ambulance is on its way, sir.'

'Good man.'

Jenna snatched at his sleeve. 'What about my parents, they won't know he's coming?'

Lasser scrubbed a hand across his face. 'You stay here with Patrick, OK?'

As he headed for the door, she shouted after him. *'Please don't let them die.'*

He didn't reply, slipping the phone into his pocket, he turned and ran out of the door.

IN THE DARK

Cathy waited for the phone to ring again when it didn't she pressed the return call button but the metallic voice informed her *'that it had not been possible to connect your call.'*

'Who was it?' Susan was sitting on the sofa, a heavy throw draped around her shoulders.

'It was Lasser,' she paused, 'but the signal's died.'

'You'll never get a decent signal up here,' her voice sounded flat, lifeless.

'Would you like me to make another coffee?' Cathy asked.

Susan stood up, wrapping the shawl tight around her. 'Don't you think you should try again?'

'It sounded as if he was on the move, I'll try again in a few minutes.'

She tried a sympathetic smile. Susan looked straight through her.

Six months earlier, Cathy had been on a course that dealt with bereavement. They taught you the right things to say, explained how to keep the victim feeling strong, though at this precise moment she felt inadequate as if she were merely an intruder on their pain, a rubber-necker at a horrific crash scene.

She could almost see the grief hovering around Susan like a black poisonous shadow.

Ten minutes earlier, David had wandered aimlessly into the kitchen and hadn't returned. Cathy didn't know whether to go and check on him, she had an image of opening the kitchen door only to find him with his head in the oven, the smell of gas filling the air.

Ever since Lasser had come to her rescue in the woods, she'd been harbouring the feeling that she wasn't up to the job, both physically and mentally, she was a burden. Perhaps she should find herself another occupation, admit that she just wasn't cut out for the job.

When her phone began to ring, she didn't even hear it, she was suddenly transported to DCI Simms office. Standing ramrod straight, her notice neatly typed and encased in a manila envelope, ready to call it a day.

'Answer the phone!'

Susan's voice snapped her out of the dark fantasy; she was standing in front of the black maw of the inglenook, a look of panic in her eyes.

Cathy scrabbled in her pocket and slapped the phone to her ear. 'I'm here, serg.'

Susan couldn't take her eyes off the woman, a feeling of dread crept up her spine. When she saw Cathy's eyes widen in shock she felt her mind begin to break free from its moorings. It was Jenna, Lasser had rung as he said he would but it was terrible news. She screwed her eyes shut and waited for the inevitable.

She tried to think of the last thing she had said to her daughter and found that she couldn't. For one terrible moment she couldn't even conjure her image, it was as if she was being erased from her memory banks, her mind attempting to distance itself from the pain of losing her only child.

'Susan!'

Her eyes fluttered open, in those few seconds the room seemed to have darkened as if the light was being absorbed by the ancient walls.

'She's dead isn't she?' The shawl slipped from her shoulders like a second skin, leaving her open and raw to the coming onslaught.

'We have to leave now.' Cathy was up on her feet. *'David!'*

'What are you doing?' Susan made a grab for her as she dashed toward the kitchen.

Cathy felt the tug on her sleeve, turning, she placed her hands on Susan's shoulder and looked directly into her eyes. *'Jenna's alive...'*

Susan heard nothing else, she could see Cathy's lips forming meaningless words but everything ceased to matter, those two words were her salvation from some kind of hell.

'Susan, we have to go, right now...'

'She's alive?' her face appeared to shift, her lifeless eyes suddenly sparked; it was like seeing someone brought back to life.

'She's fine...'

'Oh thank God!' Susan started to cry, her shoulders began to shake uncontrollably, everything swept away on a tidal wave of relief.

'Susan, you have to listen to me, the man responsible for all this is on his way here, right now!'

Her words filtered through the euphoria, yet the idea seemed preposterous 'What for?'

'He's coming to kill us, Susan,' she paused, 'all of us.'

CHASE

Lasser dropped the phone onto the passenger seat, slammed the key into the ignition and started the engine, his clothes were saturated, his breathing ragged. Frantically, he spun the wheel, executed a quick three-point turn, before slamming his foot on the accelerator the wheels of the Audi spun in the mud as they tried to gain traction. *'Come on, for fucks sake!'* he rode the clutch trying to get forward momentum.

The dash back to the car had felt like a marathon run through thick molasses, it seemed as though the swollen rain clouds above were moving faster than he was. He had fallen countless times, the last one had left him sprawled in a trough of muddy water, trying simply to breathe. Every second he lay breathless like an old wino, the killer was making his way to the farm.

Suddenly the wheels snatched at the earth and the car took off, he snapped on the main beam and swung left at the junction, huge trees loomed over the road the higher branches clattering together in the howling gale.

He just hoped Cathy was in the car, heading away from the farm with the Fotheringays safely ensconced on the back seat.

When he hit the first bend he was doing almost sixty, the car slithered to the right; he grappled with the wheel as the vehicle brushed through the tall ferns that grew at the side of the road, missing the wall by inches. As soon as the ribbon of road straightened out he slammed his foot down, the car twitched, righted itself, and surged forward.

The clock on the dash said two seventeen, for all he knew the killer could be in the house by now, making good his promise to Jenna. Slowing for the hairpin bend, he was crossing the reservoir, by the time he reached the other side of the water, he was doing a hundred and ten. When he saw the flashing blue lights ahead he eased off the gas slightly, as the two cars rammed past he felt buffeted by the turbulence. In the quarter of a mile it took to reach the crossroads, four other squad cars went hurtling past. All heading up to the moors, yet the irony was when they reached their destination there would be nothing for them to do.

He turned left, all the time hoping to see red taillights in the distance but the road was empty, no sign of a Land Rover with a maniac at the wheel. It was hopeless; every step of the way the killer had been playing them. He must have been watching as they blundered toward the house. The bastard had probably found their amateurish attempts to capture him hilarious. He was in no doubt the killer could have stayed out of sight and slaughtered them all, he thought about Simms standing in the field, a look of aggravation on his face just before the bullet sliced through his head.

Lasser slammed his hand on the wheel, he knew there would be those who blamed Simms, he hadn't been prepared for this, he was too long in the tooth. Of course, while the cameras were rolling he would be 'first rate officer, who had given his life in the pursuit of a dangerous killer.'

Yet secretly the big knobs who held the purse strings would be rubbing their hands together like some Victorian miser, thinking of the money they would save when they didn't have to pay out on his pension. The same people who put community officers on the street, because it was the cheaper option, it made him seethe, made him want to find the faceless bureaucrats and… He threw the big car into a series of S bends not even bothering to slow down, driving on intuition, his mind on the rampage.

WELL HELLO

Cathy hovered in the kitchen doorway, feeling like some kind of voyeur. It was touching to see, David and Susan clung to one another the big farmer had tears rolling down his face. Cathy wondered when he had last cried, probably not since he was a boy. He was whispering something to Susan, his voice shaking with pent emotion.

'We have to go, right now.'

Ever since Lasser had told her about the killer, time seemed to have slowed down, yet she knew it was an illusion. While they were standing in this room, the man responsible for so many deaths was closing in. 'Listen, I don't want to say this but if we don't go now then Jenna will have no parents to come home to.'

David eased himself from Susan's grasp and reached up to the top of the kitchen cupboard, when he slid the shotgun down Cathy took a backward step. 'What are you doing with that?'

'If I see anyone on my property then I'm going to kill them,' he gripped the gun between his huge hands, his face rigid with determination.

'OK fine, let's go.'

'Hang on, there's a security light comes on at the back.' David slid open a drawer and pulled out a box of shells. 'Maybe it would be better to go the front way.'

'Fine, just as long as we get a move on,' Cathy urged.

The three of them headed out of the kitchen, Susan flicked off the light as they left room.

He was standing in front of the blackened fireplace, a big man with mousey blonde hair, dressed entirely in black, somehow blending in with the stone walls, all shades and shifting shadows. Cathy gasped as David shouldered past; the barrel grasped between his hands, as he dashed forward he began to swing it back. Cathy watched the man's face as David steamed towards him; the gun reached its backward ark and began its decent.

The killer remained motionless as if oblivious to the fact that he was seconds away from having his skull caved in. At the last second he dipped down, the stock of the gun whistling inches above his head. David grunted, as his arms snapped rigid, by the time he corrected the swing; the man had bulleted upright, his right fist slamming into the underside of David's jaw with sickening force. It was like watching some huge tree being felled; he went down sideways smashing through a small glass coffee table before slamming into the hard wood floor.

Susan ran across the room, a hand clasped to her mouth.

'Leave him,' the man's voice was deep, no hint of a local accent.

Susan ignored him and knelt down by her husband's side, her hand hovering in the air above his head as if she were afraid to touch him. *'What have you done?'* she snapped her head around, her eyes blazed with anger.

The man ignored her and looked toward Cathy, a smile on his face, a smile that said you have nothing to worry about, I am a misunderstood guy. Although the eyes told a different story, they said if you run, speak, or do anything other than breathe, I'll make you scream. Cathy found herself nodding, although she was sure that he hadn't actually said a word.

'Move away from him, Susan.'

'No!' her chin jutted out in defiance.

'If you don't sit down, I'll come over there and remove your husband's head,' he gave a shrug of his shoulders. 'It's up to you.'

Cathy took a backward step, he flicked her a warning glance, his laser eyes pinning her to the spot.

'You can't threaten me...'

'Susan. Do as he says,' Cathy hissed.

She glanced at Cathy a sudden look of uncertainty in her eyes. 'I'm not having this...'

'Just do it!' Cathy snapped.

'You should listen to her, Susan, I'm not known for my patience,' from nowhere he suddenly had a knife in his hand; the blade glittered as he pointed it at David. 'Last chance.'

Susan leapt to her feet as if she was seeing the man for the first time, seeing what he was capable of. *'I'm sorry.'*

'Both of you sit there,' he flicked the knife toward the sofa.

For a couple of seconds Cathy felt incapable of movement, as soon as he began to turn toward her she started to walk or rather she staggered to the sofa and all but collapsed onto it. Susan slid in by her side and reached for her hand, taking hold and gripping it tight like two best friends on their first day at infant school.

'Do you know who I am, Susan?'

'Where's Jenna?'

'I don't want to talk about Jenna.'

Cathy felt the grip on her hand tighten.

'I want to know where she is.'

'She's up on the moors in the old crofter's cottage; the police are with her so you don't have to worry.' He looked at Cathy, his eyes a swirling mass of contradictions, a flicker of pure hate, and a hatred that would see the world burn shimmered in the depths.

She dragged her eyes away.

'You see we don't have much time, now I'll ask you again, do you know who I am?'

Susan heaved in a shuddering breath. 'James Wickham.'

'And how long have you known about my existence?'

'I didn't, not until recently.'

He took two long strides toward them; both women cringed back onto the sofa, at the last instance he veered to the left before kneeling at David's side. When Susan tried to pull away, Cathy grabbed her hand tightly and dragged her back.

'Jenna told me exactly the same thing and you see I believed her,' he tilted his head to one side. 'I'm not so sure about you though.'

'It's the truth.'

Wickham reached down and grasped David's wrist. 'We had quite the conversation, she told me certain things of which I was unaware, and I told her a few home truths about her precious grandfather.'

'Shut up!' Susan could feel the anger building, this man had terrorised her family given her the worst moments of her life, hours filled with despair and horror. 'You're sick, do you even realise that?'

Cathy tried to keep a firm grip on Susan's hand but she felt it slipping away.

'You must have thought I was going to kill, her, I bet you imagined all kinds of horrors, didn't you, Susan?'

'What do you think?' she spat the words back at him.

He smiled. 'And believe me it was my intention to make her suffer but you see I like the girl and after all she's family...'

'Family!' Susan snorted in disgust.

Wickham paused for a moment and drew a deep breath as if trying to keep his anger in check. 'So, I reconsidered, it's the same with you, part of me wants to open you up right now,' he twisted the knife, drawing it through the air as if he was practicing the cut. 'Then again what would be the point?'

'They'll catch you and when they do you'll never be let out...'

'You think I don't know that.' Wickham suddenly twisted away from them, the hand holding the knife disappeared from view. When he turned back toward them, his eyes were torrid with animalistic fury. 'Catch.'

David's severed finger landed between then, Cathy scuttled across the sofa a scream locked in her throat. Susan leapt to her feet, a hand clasped to her mouth, her eyes wide and glassy stared down at the chunk of severed flesh.

'You see, Sue, you don't mind if I call you Sue?'

She didn't look at him, couldn't drag her eyes away from the finger. Cathy was clutching the arm of the chair trying to keep the bile locked in her throat.

'I'm a man with plenty of options, I could kill you all and then sit on your front step and wait for the police to arrive. Live the rest of my days in some high security prison with three meals a day and a fully equipped gym, that doesn't sound too arduous, does it?'

Susan turned and looked directly at him. 'Why can't you just leave us alone, we haven't done anything to you?'

'Maybe you haven't but what about dear old Dad, do you think he shares the blame for how I've turned out?'

'Don't you dare say that, he's a good man...'

'Well, you obviously know him better than I do but you see I look at things differently. He abandoned me, my mother turned into a drunken slut because of what your father and the Radfields did.'

'I don't know anything about that,' she glanced at Cathy, her face suddenly flushed with colour, and then she quickly looked away.

'I was left to fend for myself, ten years old and living on a barge with nothing. While my real father lived less than two miles away,' he held up two fingers to emphasise the point. 'Do you know something, Susan, I used to sneak around here at night, grab a few eggs and whatever else I could get my hands on just to survive and yet here you were brought up in a loving, caring family,' he paused, 'now you tell me, does that seem fair to you?'

'You can't hold us responsible for what happened.'

Cathy closed her eyes, oh but I think he can, Susan.

'Just before I torched the boat, my mother had been gone for three months; I thought she must have died. Truth was she was living in the crofter's cottage; Radfield had set her up nicely, his own little whore on the moors, less than a mile away from the boat. You know something, if I had known about all this when I left, I would have come down here and killed you all,' he pointed the knife at Susan. 'What's it feel like to know I was out there going through your bins, while you were safely tucked up in bed?'

'I...'

'To know, that your precious father had been fucking around with someone like my mother?'

Susan glared at him but kept her mouth closed.

'I can see you hate me, it's in your eyes. You really don't care do you, all you see is some monster who turns up out of the blue and kidnaps your child. I could tell you everything and it wouldn't make a blind bit of difference.' He let David's wrist drop back to the floor and stood up. Cathy could see the blood pumping from the wound, spreading out across the floorboards. 'I thought about paying Father a visit, Jenna told me he's in hospital, heart attack, shame...'

'Shut up!' Susan screamed, spittle flying from her lips.

'Temper, temper,' he chided. 'Then I changed my mind, why bother killing the old man, better to let him eke out his remaining years knowing what he's done...'

'He's done *nothing;* it's all in your sick head, all of it. If my father had known about you then he would have done something about it.'

'But he did do something about it, Susan; he ignored it and now look what's happened. First the boy, then the old man in the woods and Malcolm Radfield,' he paused as if trying to recollect the victims. 'Then Ashley who was so helpful and the four unfortunate policemen on the moors who died while they were trying to rescue your daughter. I'm sure that will be a consolation to their grieving wives and children that they died doing the job they loved. '

Cathy swallowed her disgust, all those people it was unfathomable.

'You...'

'Of course when all this is over, you'll get the sympathy, being held by a maniac responsible for so much horror. But inevitably questions will be asked and the truth about who I am will surface and then what?'

'You bastard!'

'What will people say when they find out that you're my sister, when it's spread on the front of every newspaper and they put our pictures together on the TV screens.'

'People around here know us, they would never...' her voice faltered.

Wickham smiled. 'So, you see, it's much more productive from my point of view not to kill you. It's all about the stigma, Sue, the gossip, the pointing fingers. Of course, Jenna will have to give up college. I'd imagine sharing the same house with you and your father will become unbearable. She will...'

'You filthy...!' Susan leapt to her feet.

In an instant Wickham reached down and grabbed a handful of David's unruly hair, yanking the head back, exposing the throat. Cathy pushed herself up from the sofa and grabbed Susan's sleeve.

'Susan, don't!'

She tried to snatch her arm free; Cathy kept hold dragging her back.

'After all what will Jenna think when she knows her father's dead and you did nothing to stop it from happening. In fact you caused it and all because you refused to tell the truth,' he grinned, the insanity flooding from his eyes.

RUNNING OUT

As soon as the dark bulk of the house came into view, Lasser turned the headlights off and coasted to the end of the drive. Climbing from the car, he walked around to the boot; the wind buffeted him as he fumbled around in the small space. Heaving up the heavy mat, he reached in and pulled out the baseball bat. It had been lounging in there since last summer, confiscated from a kid who had been waving it about in the street, off his face on some horse tranquilizer and smashing all the headlights of the cars he came across. Two weeks later the same boy was found behind Stilettos Pole Dancing bar, minus one ear. They never found out who was responsible but as far as Lasser was concerned, he had either been peeking in through one of the windows whilst having a wank or one of the irate car owners could have sliced it off as a form of retribution. The surgeon said it had been done with a Stanley knife, which, considering about ninety percent of the male population of Hindley carried one, didn't really help at all. What made matters worse was the fact that the kid wore glasses. He remembered thinking that maybe the scrote would have to make do with a monocle; pretend it was a fashion statement.

Closing the boot he set off up the drive, the sound of his feet on the gravel lost to the howling wind, the bushes either side of him taking a battering.

When he saw Cathy's squad car parked in front of the house he stopped for a moment, his shoulders sagged at the implication. Then he was running, the fury flooding through his system like a class A drug, the red mist descending.

'James, don't do this.' Cathy pushed Susan hard sending her back against the sofa.

Wickham twisted his head and looked up at her.

'Why not?' he seemed genuinely curious.

'Because these people have suffered enough, everything you said about the truth coming out is going to happen anyway.'

'I realise that, but what's your point?'

'You said you like Jenna, you could have killed her, yet you didn't.'

Wickham pursed his lips. 'Despite the rest of her family she seems like a good kid.'

'But if you kill her father then all she will ever do is hate you. She'll never understand why you did these things because she won't be able to get past that one fact.'

He frowned, the knife eased away David's throat. 'Why should I care if she hates me, I won't be around to worry about things like that?

Cathy tried to fathom the meaning but she couldn't take her eyes from his, couldn't risk breaking the contact. 'If you leave David alive then she'll question all that's happened, it will force her to see the truth and that's what you want isn't it. You want Jenna to be aware of how you were treated; you need her to know that it wasn't your fault.'

'Don't you dare try and lay the blame on us,' Susan spat.

Cathy turned to look at her, she was perched on the edge of the sofa her hands gripping her knees a look of cold defiance in her eyes.

'Someone has to take responsibility for all this...'

'Yes and it's him,' she pointed a quivering finger. 'Nobody made him kill those people, he did that by himself, and I resent you saying otherwise.'

Cathy felt like crossing to the sofa and slapping her face until her hand went numb. *'I...'*

Wickham laughed. 'Save your breath, she's like me, she'll never listen,' he turned away, Cathy saw him draw his arm back.

Then an apparition came hurtling from the darkened kitchen, grubby clothes showering filthy water as it sprinted into the room the face black with mud, eyes wide and glaring. Wickham released the hair, David's head bounced off the floor. He snapped upright, the knife lashing out in a wicked arc. Lasser spun away to the left, for a couple of seconds he had his back turned to the killer and then he twisted and swung the bat. Wickham tried to duck beneath the blow but Lasser compensated, the wood slammed into the side of his head with a sickening crunch. Instantly, the knife clattered to the floor and he staggered to the side, one hand shot out to the floor to save him from falling. Lasser waited, resisting the urge to dash in, somehow knowing that Wickham was waiting for him to do exactly that. Instead, he reached down and picked up the knife, he saw the man's eyes narrow as if he were suddenly re-evaluating his options. Blood spewed down the side of his face, his right eye swollen shut. When he looked toward Cathy, Lasser saw the void in his good eye. Any form of revenge or justification was gone, swamped by the basic urge to kill. When he began to scramble toward her, Lasser shot forward, slamming the knife into his side the blade angled upward sliding in beneath the ribs.

Wickham snapped his head around; his hands grabbed the front of Lasser's sodden shirt, ringing it between his fists, the water making a pitter-patter sound as it fell to the floor.

Lasser tried to push him away but Wickham clung on, still peering up into his face and then all notion of *'being'* dissipated, he slammed to the floor. Lasser looked down at the slumped figure; he could hear the grandfather clock in the corner, counting off the seconds, feel his own heart clattering in his chest.

When Susan began to scream, he fell to his knees, head slumped forward as the sweat and rain fell from his face mingling with the blood.

FOUR WEEKS LATER

Jenna looked out across the fields; the corn had turned from golden to a sap dead brown, a warm breeze rippled through the crop, the sound of whispering voices, a conspiracy.

'How have you been?' Fossey asked.

They were standing on the hillside; the needle house was a dark smudge in the distance.

She shrugged; dark circles clung beneath her eyes, her skin taut and pale with strain.

Fossey unscrewed the lid from the bottle and took a sip of water. 'You want some?'

'No thank you.'

'You know, Jenna; none of this was your mother's fault.'

For the first time she looked at him, her eyes had the look of someone working through things internally as if everything else were being done automatically. 'She still won't tell me everything, even after all that's happened.'

'Maybe it's because there's nothing more to tell?'

'I can't believe anything they say,' she looked away.

'What about your grandad, is he settled now he's back home?'

She gave a slight shrug. 'He's OK I suppose.'

'Have you tried talking to him?'

'What's the point, every time I go into his room he pretends to be asleep. I mean, it's pathetic.'

Fossey slid the bottle back into his backpack. 'You know people keep secrets for all kinds of reasons....'

'I realise that but usually people don't die, do they? I mean, they didn't deserve to be killed and if he'd been honest from the start then the police would have found him sooner.'

'Not necessarily, he did what he thought was right at the time, how could he have known what was going to happen?'

'That's what *she* says.'

In the distance, Fossey could see a car snaking its way along the lane, occasionally it would vanish behind the trees only to reappear a few seconds later. 'Maybe he could have done more but you can't blame him for Wickham's actions, he was a sick man with a skewed view of the world...'

'Yes but why was he like that? He told me about being left to fend for himself,' her voice began to rise in anger. 'Can you even imagine what it must have been like for him and then finding out he had a family so close, who didn't give a shit about him?'

'Nobody's saying it was easy but lots of individuals have hard lives, Jenna.'

She shook her head and turned back to the field. 'It's like I've never really known any of them....'

'What about your father, he knew nothing about any of this?'

'I've tried to talk to him,' her voice was heavy with anguish. 'But he just seems different.'

Fossey placed his hands on top of the wooden gate. 'He's like you, Jenna, he's been through a lot and it takes time to come to terms with what's happened.'

'He doesn't speak to her about it, I heard her trying to explain, and he just walked out of the room. I mean, they don't even sleep together anymore, Dad just comes in late and goes straight up to the spare room.'

Fossey placed a hand on her shoulder; she looked towards him her eyes shining with bewilderment.

'I know this is hard but until you start talking then none of it will get any better.'

'I don't care anymore, I just want to get my results, and then I'm going to move away to university.'

Fossey could imagine her trying to escape the past, yearning for a life that had been changed forever. 'Independence is a good thing but if you leave without getting this sorted then moving away won't work. I mean, your grandad's already had one scare, do you really want to leave without building bridges?' It was a cheap shot, amounting to nothing less than emotional blackmail.

Jenna wiped a hand across her haunted eyes. ‘How can I build bridges when he won’t even talk to me, I tried, but it’s always there this thing that he can’t or won’t discuss, I mean, how can we ever get back to how we used to be?’

‘You probably can’t, but you have to reach some kind of understanding; he can’t talk about what happened because he’s too ashamed. He let you down, in his eyes he knows exactly what he should have done but how can you turn the clock back, Jenna, you just can’t do it?'

‘I know that but...’

‘He’s also carrying the guilt for what happened to the victims and that’s a terrible thing for anyone to burden themselves with.’

Just for a second her eyes lit up with a kind of hope. ‘Maybe you could talk to him, perhaps he might open up to you?’

‘I seriously doubt it, his only concern is you, he hasn’t got the energy to think about anything else. He needs to know that you understand...’

‘But that’s just it I don’t!’

‘Then start preparing the barriers.’

She frowned, over her left shoulder the sun shimmered in yet another clear blue sky interlaced with the vapour trail from a high-flying jet. ‘I don’t understand.’

‘If you can’t see a way to get past all this, then you have to get used to the idea of living a life separate from your family. In order to do that you need to distance yourself from them emotionally. You can still talk to them but avoid looking for answers because there are none. Just keep things ticking over until you manage to get to away.’ Fossey shrugged. ‘It might make things easier for you in the long run.’

She looked up at him and frowned. ‘What do you mean easier?’

'Look, Jenna, I'm not going to lie to you. Your grandad will be lucky to live another...'

'Don't say it.'

He held up a hand. 'I'm not telling you anything you don't already know. He's an old man, who's had a serious heart attack, what are the odds on him living another five years?'

'You don't know that.' she sounded distraught, a flush of anger rising in her pale cheeks.

'To ease the pain, keep them all at arm's length, you'd be surprised but it's a common defence mechanism. In fact, my own father used it when my mum was dying with cancer, you could see it happening, and he wasn't a bad man. He looked after her for as long as he could but as soon as she went into the hospice, he stopped visiting, it was as if he was trying to forget all about her. I remember he took all her clothes to the charity shop, sold her jewellery, he did everything to make the transition easier.'

'Did it work?'

'Of a fashion, he got on with his life; in fact he married again which was good.'

Jenna squinted up at him. 'But?'

'But he always regretted what he'd done, they'd been together for twenty-eight years and he fell at the last hurdle and to be honest I don't think he ever forgave himself.'

Suddenly an image leapt into her mind, she was a couple of years older ensconced in a small room on some nameless campus, taking her first steps on the way to independence, trying to blot out the family she had left behind. What would she do when the inevitable phone call came, her mother on the other end trying to explain that her grandad had passed away in his sleep? The clarity of the premonition took her breath away, the realisation that she was falling into the exact same trap that had caught him out forty years earlier. Keeping secrets that ultimately ate away at your soul and left you alone and broken.

'Could you do me a favour, Patrick?'

'Anything.'

'Could you take me home?'

Lasser walked over to the table, two packets of crisps clenched between his teeth, a glass in each hand, he opened his mouth, and the bags dropped, Cathy catching them both before they hit the table.

'They didn't have smoky bacon so I got you chicken.'

She smiled. 'That's fine.'

He placed her glass of wine onto the table and then slid onto the bench. The beer garden was quiet, apart from a family of four eating burgers and chips from the *'two for a tenner'* menu.

'So, when do you start back?' she asked.

'Next week.'

'I can't believe it's taken them so long.'

Lasser sipped his drink it tasted flat and sour. It was strange but it didn't matter what he had to drink or eat it all tasted the same. 'Yeah well, you know what it's like.'

'But suspending you, it was ridiculous.'

'Full pay so I'm not complaining,' he quipped, though his eyes looked troubled.

She looked closely at him, he looked tired as if his sleep had been broken which was hardly surprising, God alone knew she couldn't remember the last time she'd slept through without waking bathed in sweat, her arms and legs thrashing under the duvet

'I looked for you at the funeral.'

DCI Simms had been buried three weeks earlier, Lasser had every intention of attending, but in the end, he'd a run-in with a bottle of vodka that had left him bedridden for two days. He had woken on the morning of the funeral, vomited in the toilet and crawled back to bed. It was hardly the honourable thing to do, but in the end, he decided that turning up reeking of booze with a weeks' worth of stubble would hardly have gone down well.

'I decided it best if I stayed away.'

'I can understand that.'

'So, what's been happening while I've been away?' Lasser asked, trying to lighten the mood.

'Just the usual, Spenner got a black eye trying to tackle someone running from Tesco without paying for a box of Carling. I wouldn't mind but he was off duty.'

'He'll go far that lad.'

'By the way they dropped the charges against Michael Jones.'

Lasser sipped at his tepid beer. 'Good, the boy's been through enough, what about his mother?'

'You didn't see the papers?'

'To tell you the truth, Cathy, I've tried to avoid them.'

'She was front cover for a couple of days, now it's all James Wickham.'

'That's hardly surprising.'

'And what about you?'

'I'm fine,' he lied. 'I rang Fossey yesterday, he said Ronnie's home from hospital.'

'And Jenna?'

Lasser shrugged. 'She's still trying to come to terms with what happened, he said she blames her family for a lot of what went on.'

Cathy took a sip from the glass. 'I suppose its hard finding out you had a serial killer for an uncle.'

'The trouble is I keep looking for someone to blame, but I don't think it would have made any difference if Ronnie had come clean sooner. I mean, how was he to know what his son was doing?'

'We know who to blame, boss, Wickham was a madman....'

'I spoke to his commanding officer, according to him; Wickham was an honourable man with an outstanding military record....'

Cathy sipped her wine. 'Well, he's hardly going to say he was a raving madman.'

Lasser tapped his cigarette on the table, he was trying to cut down, the nicotine patch on his arm was itching, and the skin around the square plaster looked red and inflamed. 'It makes you wonder though, I mean, if half of what Fossey said was true, then James Wickham had a shit upbringing...'

'I seem to remember you telling me that lots of people have reasons to hate the world but it doesn't turn them into killers.'

Lasser smiled. 'You're right, maybe I've been spending too much time with the shrink.'

Cathy pulled a cigarette free from the pack.

'I thought you didn't want to get back into old habits.'

'I just fancy one, is that a crime?'

Lasser held up his hands. 'Listen, do you fancy grabbing a curry.'

'What now?' she looked out at the sun shimmering on the tarmac car park, the idea of tackling a Vindaloo in the middle of the afternoon seemed a daunting prospect.

'I was thinking maybe tonight?'

Cathy looked at him in surprise. 'You mean like a proper date, kind of thing?'

Lasser could feel his cheeks burning and it had very little to do with the sun. 'Well yeah, if that's OK?'

'I'd like that.'

For the first time in weeks, Lasser smiled. She looked stunning; her black hair had been let loose spilling across her shoulder in waves, her face, and arms tanned by the sun, blue eyes bright in the shade of the canopy.

'I never thanked you did I?' she looked at him through a cloud of smoke.

'That's because there was never any need.'

She rolled the glass between her hands. 'That's twice you've saved my life.'

He dragged up a grin. 'That's why they pay me the big bucks.'

She looked at him and shook her head. *'What a tosser.'*

A moment later, they were both laughing.

THE END

If you enjoyed The Needle House then please feel free to contact me at

rob-roughley@live.co.uk or visit my author page at Amazon Robin Roughley.

Many thanks for taking the time to read the novel and I hope you come back for more.

Huge thanks to Odette and Val for all her hard work in hammering the book into shape, without them it would have remained a mess.

23166707R00296

Printed in Great Britain
by Amazon